The Angel House

Kerstin Ekman

Some other books from Norvik Press

The Angel House

Kerstin Ekman

Translated from the Swedish
and with a preface by
Sarah Death

Norvik Press
2002

Originally published in Swedish under the title of *Änglahuset* (1979)
© Kerstin Ekman.

This translation © Sarah Death 2002.

The Translator asserts her moral right to be identified as the Translator of the work
in relation to all such rights as are granted by the Translator to the publisher under
the terms and conditions of their Agreement.

A catalogue record for this book is available from the British Library.
ISBN 1 870041 51 8
First published 2002

Norvik Press gratefully acknowledges the financial assistance given by
The Swedish Institute for the translation of this book.

Norvik Press was established in 1984 with financial support from the University of
East Anglia, the Danish Ministry for Cultural Affairs, the Norwegian Cultural
Department and the Swedish Institute.

Managing Editors: Janet Garton and Michael Robinson.

Printed in Great Britain by Page Bros. (Norwich) Ltd, Norwich, UK.

Translator's Preface

The Angel House, original title *Änglahuset*, is the third part of Kerstin Ekman's quartet of novels known as the Katrineholm series, published between 1974 and 1983. Still in print in Sweden today, they can with every justification be called modern classics. In charting the development of a small southern Swedish railway town over a period of about a century, they also follow the changes in Swedish society over that period, not from a conventional historians' viewpoint but from the sometimes subversive perspective of the generations of women living through those times.

Having studied and written about the works of Kerstin Ekman, and this novel in particular, for some years before coming to translate it, I offer here an unashamedly personal reading of some of its characters, narrative devices and concluding chapter. Those who wish to enjoy the novel without the distraction of others' interpretations may therefore prefer to return to this preface after reading the book.

The novel opens in the late 1920s and follows characters introduced in *Witches' Rings* and *The Spring* through to the years following the Second World War. Ingrid and Jenny are the characters in focus now, two twentieth century women whose fate is that they have the time to perceive the dull monotony of their lives all too clearly. The fiercely independent Tora who stood centre stage in the earlier books is growing old, weary and sick along with her touchingly portrayed circle of friends. Her fate is mirrored in her own home, the crumbling stone building with angels under the eaves which gives *The Angel House* its name. By the end of the novel, it has been demolished to make way for new property ventures.

Society is changing fast: the war challenges comfortable assumptions and is in some ways a liberation for the women of the town, a rediscovery of camaraderie; but automated factory work is replacing many of the old crafts and skills. Change is poignantly evident in the description in the final chapter of the new cinema and shopping complex called the Grand. The scene functions as a summary of decades of social evolution: the businesses here are all shiny modern replacements for jobs the townspeople, often women, have been doing quietly through the years: the state-of-the-art cinema is the culmination of a fashion that began with the novelty of piano-accompanied silent movie showings at the community centre and then the Casino Theatre, now long past its heyday; the restaurant will threaten the livelihood of the little cafés, like the one Tora once owned; the brightly-wrapped, manufactured confectionery in the exclusive chocolate shop is the final blow to Tora's market stall where she sells home-made sweets to customers who increasingly demand commercially produced goods. The smart trio of dress shop, milliner's and hosiery shop, in conjunction with the town's big, 1930s clothing factory where Ingrid works, will totally eclipse the old sisters at Elfvenberg's draper's and Ingrid's sister Dagmar, the seamstress whose craft is so lovingly described in *The Spring*. The hairdressing salon has the town's first male coiffeur, bound to be more sought-after than Ingrid's friend and confidante Maud, who has made a modest living from the little hairdressing business she runs at home; and the continuing story of how the town's laundry has been done, synonymous until now with Frida Eriksson's labours, first as hired washerwoman and then as an employee at the much-needed municipal laundry, ends up in hundreds of smaller laundry rooms in people's homes, from Jenny and Ingrid's dank basements to the ultra-modern facilities in the attic of the Grand.

Women are now free from the hard physical tasks of the earlier novels, but no less trapped in the grinding repetition of factory jobs and domestic chores in the isolation of their new homes. A male hierarchy still dominates the town; time is ruled by financial imperatives, council chairmen's gavels, referees' and factory whistles, and military orders. Against this, Kerstin Ekman sets women's gentler, more organic timescale, an elastic time that can be a slow evolution of female bodies or a mad rush of endless work. Women in this novel are identified more with the natural world, men with the built environment; this divide is evident from the opening page in the strained dialogue between the lime tree and the old building, and reaches a climax in the chapter where Fredrik worships the Bofors armaments factory and Jenny daydreams of the simple pots of Henscroft Woman. The nurture of informal networks of friends, the unhurried cycles of trees and the winding short-cuts through overgrown gardens are a muted but insistent counterpoint to the pompous urgency of linear male ambition and civic pride. The idea of 'a pattern within the pattern', 'a town within the town,' is central to the novel, indeed to the tetralogy as a whole. This duality, male/female or however one likes to interpret it, is raised in *The Angel House* by Konrad Eriksson, a disturbingly androgynous character in some respects, and a storyteller who, arguably not by coincidence, shares his creator's initials. (Further reading: Sarah Death, 'They Can't Do This to Time: Women's and Men's Time in Kerstin Ekman's *Änglahuset*'. *A Century of Swedish Narrative*, Norvik Press, 1994, pp. 267-80.)

It is a real treat for a translator to be commissioned to translate a novel she or he already knows and loves. But what is 'knowing' a book? The translator is thrust into a degree of intimacy with the text far greater than even the most attentive reader. 'Apart from me, only my translators read every word of my books,' said Kerstin

Ekman at a recent seminar. If the translator's magnifying-glass approach occasionally threatens to cheat her/him of relaxed enjoyment of the broader canvas, there are ample compensations in the discovery of detailed texture. In *The Angel House*, for example, the narrative is forever shifting in and out of the consciousnesses of the various characters. It is a third-person narrative, but Ekman slips constantly and seamlessly from one point of view to another, with appropriate changes in style and register to challenge the translator's versatility. With *erlebte Rede* from such a variety of sources, it is sometimes impossible even to decide whether speech marks are called for or not.

Another dimension I only became aware of while translating is the pattern in the use of colour. The town and the earth on which it is built are almost always described as grey, or shades of grey like *grågul* and *gråbrun*, literally greyish yellow and greyish-brown, but perhaps better translated as dirty yellow and sludgy brown. At one point the town is said to be so grey that even a pile of dirty yellow horse manure adds a splash of colour. The forest, gardens and courtyards are of course a host of natural shades. The wood of the ageing buildings is often called silvery grey, but the colour of the future is artificial, neon red and green. Maud has her hair salon done in brick red and green; the new block of flats nicknamed the Ice Palace, where Ingrid later lives, has pale green walls and red stair rails; and the cinema foyer of the Grand is the same pale green.

Similarly, it was only by searching for an English equivalent of *Napoleonbakelse* (Napoleon slice) that I gradually realised I should not change it or Ekman's playfulness would be lost: it is eaten, after all, in the scene where Maud's lover meets his Waterloo! If other delightful jokes of this kind have slipped by, the fault is sadly mine.

A full list of the people whose help I have enlisted in this project would be extravagantly long, pointing as ever to the breadth of Kerstin Ekman's intellectual curiosity and the thoroughness of her research. My sources have included relations, friends, academic colleagues, fellow translators, specialist librarians and museum staff in both Britain and Sweden. My thanks go in particular to Pauline Bourne, Helena Forsås-Scott, Solveig Hammarbäck, Martin Naylor and Karin Petherick. I am grateful above all to the author herself for patiently answering my questions so long after the book was written, and to Linda Schenck who has read and commented on the entire translation.

Sarah Death
February 2002

The Angel House

At the windy corner of Highway Street and Industrial Road, opposite the Co-operative Stores, stood a lime tree and a large, old wooden building. There was a newspaper kiosk too, to be strictly accurate. The lime tree and the building used to talk to one another. But there were long intervals between their words.

Big buildings have a slow chronology of their own and get on relatively well with trees. They don't, on the other hand, see much in people. The kiosk, too, was difficult to understand. It had only been built to stand for a few decades, and it panted out all it had to say breathlessly and impatiently, like a dog or a radio commentator. People were shooting themselves, falling out of the skies in machines and making sausages out of horses. It was all too much for the building, and for the lime tree. The kiosk was octagonal and hunchbacked and had a nose like a beak. It was painted green and its pointed roof was covered in rough, tarred felt. It was irritable and gossipy, poor company for a lime tree and an ornate building of the nineteenth century.

The old building did not consider itself especially sluggish, because it liked to compare itself with earthfast stones. Everyone knows how slow stones are at calling out and speaking. They must start by developing a core of concentration. Then there is a slow upheaval and finally they call, but that happens in another time. It is quite simply beyond comprehension. But call they do. Even in the foundations of the old building, where cats slunk in and out, the stones called.

A street lamp shone so deep inside the crown of the lime tree that the light fell in a speckled pattern on the kiosk roof. The spots of light moved jerkily across the black felt and the drops of tar began to glisten. Then it was still for almost an hour; no wind stirred the leaves and the pattern remained undisturbed. The old building cleared its throat and eventually it began to speak. This was on a Saturday evening. By Monday morning, after many specks of light and flower husks and curls of damp mist had danced across the kiosk roof, the sentence was complete.

Perhaps the crown of the lime tree was howling inside with impatience. But beneath the ground, her roots were wrapped around the stone foundations of the building like the roots of a powerful molar embracing a jawbone, so she had grounds for believing they would stand or fall together, preferably stand of course and for eternity. She therefore controlled herself and answered before the last cold nights of late summer came to an end.

The lime tree shook in a gust of wind and sent down a shower of pale green flowers onto the kiosk roof. The old building was frightened by the sound, mistaking it for a haemorrhage. That was something it was familiar with. Not all times were convenient for conversation. Through the depths of winter when the lime tree appeared to be resting, such important things were happening in buds and incipient flowers that the lime tree could not bring herself to reply. And the bursting of the buds was a complex labour which began with the rising of the sap in minuscule vessels as fine as hairs, making all that was waxy and dry swell and straighten. Was it painful? Not really. But it was terribly hard work and she had to concentrate as she assimilated. It was most awkward of the building to chose that very time to begin a discussion that would go on until the first week of June, when the summer breeze was ruffling big, green leaves in the crown of the lime tree.

The lime tree was living wood. The building was wooden too, and its wood was not really dead. No, you can't say wood dies that easily; it metamorphoses. The building still stretched, swelled, moaned on cold winter nights, contracted and made cracks for bedbugs and silver-fish to creep through.

Of course, the building was primarily a dwelling, or a collection of flats, dens and burrows. It housed many consciousnesses, several communities, temporary and enforced associations and deep kinships. The cats crept in and out of the stone foundations; on the landings they lapped milk so violently that the chipped saucers clattered against the floor. Apart from cats there were tree sparrows, people, house sparrows and lice, cockroaches, rats and field mice, dogs and their fleas, spiders, flies, ants, threadworms, meal beetles, spinning mites and flukes and greenfly on the balsam plants. Longhorn beetles munched away at the very flesh of the building and bats hung in long rows from the beams in the attic, hanging with their heads down and their little clawed feet tightly closed.

The lime tree only took in passing guests, for it was a foreigner on the street corner. Its visitors came as envoys bearing scents unfamiliar to Highway Street and pot-holed Industrial Road, which began at a foundry and ended at a packaging factory. The lime tree stood at a drab junction, paved, odourless, howling with dreariness in every direction. It wore a cap of cotton-wool sky and all around it grew the scenery of impenetrability, of concrete, of hewn stone

13

and chicken wire, plaster, reeds, bricks and arsenic-impregnated wood. It tried to catch the winds, but up through its branches rose a smell of refuse, sweet and sickly, and of burnt rubber tyres, of oil, musty cellars and bad breath, of old shoes and earth from the cemetery where a grave had just been dug up. But if the wind was in the right direction, it could sometimes catch the scent of reseda as well.

Morning sometimes brought with it the steam from freshly-watered dung heaps, the good, carbon-dioxide manure delivered by a capricious gust of wind for the lime tree's use and nourishment. It was brushed by bumble bees with unfamiliar powder on their round, furry bodies: pollen from sour cherries, Greve Moltke and Säfstaholm apple trees. From beneath it could be heard the stiff rustle of the only copper beech in the town and the snap as the horse chestnuts down by Highway Bridge opened their thorny spheres and dropped their damp, brown fruits, untouched and unseen. Sometimes it was shaken by a gale that had torn the petals from countless anemones.

When the building was erected it had a stately facade. It had flagpoles on the ridges of the roof and two verandahs down the long side facing onto Industrial Road, weather vanes with the year of construction, wood shavings artistically mounted like scales on the gables and ornate railings along the verandahs. It had sophisticated metalwork and lots of chimneys. At the opening ceremony they planted the lime tree and the speeches clacked like pennants in a gale.

But it was a shoddy piece of construction, with built-in pests. At the last moment they decided to use demolition timber for the fittings in some of the kitchens and cooking areas. It was cold at floor level and whistling draughts blew in at the corners because there was no proper double flooring. The insulation in the walls gradually compacted downwards and the children couldn't sleep by them, or they got earache. But this was no miserable slum, far from it. Here lived the respectable members of the joinery workforce whom the speechmakers had decorated and ornamented with the finest whitewood words of the language, including conscientious and honest and positively committed to work without class egoism. They were the apples of Petrus Wilhelmsson's eye, and teetotallers to as great an extent as he could insist. There was no shortage of food here in the landing larders. People clubbed together to buy a pig and had allotments and best rooms, those holy, touching best rooms with their scent of mothballs and shrivelled apples in a bowl, where the wax plant trailed in the cool darkness, and the candles remained unlit until summer came and they drooped in the heat. Ah yes, those best rooms were an affirmation that the core of existence is blessed, neat and clean, not full of scabs and nasty smells and bleeding wounds.

The building, which had never had a youth but been trumpeted straight out onto the street and the crossroads in all its scaly manhood, soon deteriorated. It coughed out smoke and it groaned and whined in the autumn storms. Holes were torn in the roof and the wood-store got rickets. But that was as it should be, for old Sweden was now rotting away behind its ornamented facades. Now men in bowler hats were appearing; the warped doors were slamming. It was all fresh and brash. The world would be made entirely new. It smelt not of aquavit, but of hectograph ink. The old egoism and individualism were kicked around with a smack and a thud and left lying there, a bundle in a corner (but a bundle that was moving) and the blacklegs got a thrashing.

Yet the landing larders with airholes drilled in the doors were empty of food and the children had hunger pains in their bellies. The men had to go back to work.

Then came the war, and afterwards work and housing were scarce and you had to be grateful if you had a roof over your head, said David Eriksson who moved in around then. He had been in Stockholm looking for work and there were people there reduced to living behind partitions in the police gymnasium. Their rooms were made of boards nailed together, with clocks and oil paintings on the wall and children flocking in the spaces between the cubicles. That really was something else, said David Eriksson who had been places and seen a few things. It's nothing short of idyllic here, he said, and then the doors would slam and there would be knockings in the stove telegraph between the floors.

The building was no longer Petrus Wilhelmsson's; he was dead now. It wasn't even the property of the Wilhelmsson Joinery any more, but belonged to a pious builder who claimed that all was vanity, so he carried out no repairs. What he was waiting for, however, was not Judgment Day but better times, when this plot opposite the Co-operative Stores would rise in value. Then he would have the building demolished.

The attics were now no more weatherproof than an old basket made of woven bark and it sounded like the wheezing of worn-out lungs to the women who hung their washing up there. The chimney-pots were blocked ; the owls had taken a liking to them.

But the people were different too, it was said, not like Petrus Wilhelmsson's largely sober and decent workers. There were people being dragged down, it was said; they probably tried to get TB (no one believed David Eriksson any more) and were work-shy and drank moonshine down at the Unemployment Commission huts so they'd get inflammation of the pancreas. The building closed around all these and around their conviction that they were

16

a different sort, a particularly bitter and tainted sort, which society put in its mouth and then spat out.

The building, which now spent such long periods of its premature old-age asleep that it sometimes lost several years, did not notice the changes, knew nothing of the soiled best rooms within it or of the tins of brewing mash and bags of rubbish in the attic.

Kreuger shot himself and the kiosk was all in a flap, its banging shutter blabbing on about the same news for eight weeks, but neither the lime tree nor the building seemed to hear. Yes, people were as daft and careless and prone to coughing as ever, that much was plain, and the building nodded off again.

This old wreck, along with the hunchbacked outbuildings and rickety sheds in its yard, now stood marooned right on the pavement edge between new, streamlined constructions with rough-cast walls. It still coughed out smoke, but in thin streaks because now they had to break up empty boxes for firewood. Some of its window-eyes had been put out and the sockets covered by bits of cardboard, others were dimmed by dust and cobwebs, thick and evil-smelling with cooking grease. They squinted with poor-quality glass and cataracts of grey dust, those windows with stiff curtains where a beer bottle might stand untouched alongside a glass of everlasting flowers for six months.

The lime tree whispered about the forest and it made an impression on the old building. She was conscious of the forest despite having been planted on that street corner by decree of the owner of a wholesale business. All trees possess this, imprinted in their seed. There they have not only the little picture of the whole tree fully extended between sky and earth, with its two crowns, the one that seeks the light and the carbon dioxide of air and the other which is drawn to moisture and minerals, but also the idea of an endless forest.

17

And of course it is the same for all living things. Human beings imagine that there will always be human beings, even beyond the closest stars. A bedbug wants to be a million and a tree wants to be an endless forest. The lime tree's forest was the one that came after the ice age with elm and oak and hazel, with swaying leaves, with gnawers and buzzers and the smell of honey, with gleaming eyes down in the rustle of the musky, herb-scented ground cover, with nightingale and cuckoo and a scatterbrained little butterfly fluttering silently and tipsily between moist, honeyed hideaways.

The building was not conscious of a never-ending town. It wanted to surrender itself to the forest. But that was difficult. A barn, even an old soldier's cottage can surrender itself. It can fall down and allow the logs that were felled and transported in the forest and stopped up with moss for insulation to rot away and become stumps where lingonberries thrive. There is a ticking and a grumbling in silvery old houses like that, without so much as a scrap of wallpaper left on the walls. They slowly crumble and are carried off, sinking deep into the greenery.

Here on the corner of Highway Street and Industrial Road, though, it was a fair way to the forest. This was the town with its gravelled square, its rutted streets and shafts full of rocks that have been blasted, with tin roofs steaming off the overnight dampness in the morning sun; its church with spires, its secret pools and crevices, horses, shadows and steep gables, leaning fences, signs creaking as they swung on rusty hinges; its most inaccessible, rat-reeking corners, country busses with a caked and dusty skin of mud, railway tracks, piles of planks, building sites, dustbins, long chimneys rising from foundry and sawmill, the trucks in the railway yard bashing and bumping, ah yes, those sounds of metal against metal, metal against stone and metal in wood, twisting and splintering the groaning fibres. There was no way back.

Three people made their way along Store Street one afternoon in the late winter of 1931. The sleet was freezing into ice and crunched like the coconut ice Tora Otter made. Nothing frightening revealed itself as they trudged along Store Street; no gaping wounds, no secret passage down into the earth, not even a dead animal. In the window of the Savings Bank there was nothing but a notice that read:

SOUND FINANCES ARE THE FOUNDATION OF
A HAPPY HOME

But they didn't look up as they passed. First came Tora with her son Fredrik, who was wearing galoshes and a smart overcoat that had cost nearly seventy kronor. A few steps behind came her daughter-in-law Jenny; she looked disapproving. Every so often Fredrik remembered and stopped to let her catch up. She looked quite pretty in her black coat with the fur collar and the little hat pulled well down to one side. It had a little plume, a tiny one that shivered in the sleety snow. In Tora's view her stockings were far too thin.

Tora's lower legs looked stocky in brown wool. She was not one for showing off, but you could see that business at her market stall was good, because her coat was of nice, black cloth and she had fur around her neck and on her cap. She was tired, though. Christmas was when her takings were at their peak and she always used to feel tired until a few weeks into January. This year the fatigue had not abated although it was March.

She knew virtually everyone they met and was forever saying 'Good afternoon!' and nodding. An errand boy came along on his big bicycle. It was well-nigh impossible to cycle with the roads like this but he did it all the same. He was on his way from the cheesemonger and poulterer's with his big basket heavily loaded with mature cheeses, fowl and oranges.

Tora had done some jellied pig's trotters for them to have with beetroot when they got home. She didn't envy those who ate poultry, no indeed, and you could almost tell by her back view. Jenny suddenly got even crosser, she began thinking about her own mother, Stella Lans, who was also on her own. But she had had someone to provide for her. Now she was just a lost bird left in the empty autumn fields after the flocks had migrated. Soon she would freeze to death or the hawk would get her.

It wasn't market day, or Tora wouldn't have been here. The expanse of the market square was empty, except for a few people straggling across it with the wind at their backs. But in the High Street there were quite a few people about. Afternoon, good afternoon! Jenny saw her reflection in a shop window but it wasn't quite as she had imagined. The thought flew through her head that she would prefer to be somewhere else. She would prefer to be walking where no one knew her, along wide streets where indifferent faces went streaming past like leaves in the water. She grabbed hold of Fredrik's arm as if she were afraid her prayer might be answered. This was where she had to walk; her coat collar could not conceal her face. Isn't that Fredrik Otter's wife, saddlemaker Lans of Åsen's daughter? Is her mother still alive? Yes she is, though she's had a couple of strokes. Haven't they got any children yet? No, doesn't look as if there'll be any. They're cousins, that could have something to do with it.

Their eyes were like leeches, clinging on to her and slowly

moving over her body, even into her secret compartment and its emptiness. And Fredrik went trudging on. Was he slightly pigeon-toed?

He was on his way to buy a pair of shoes. But this wasn't really his idea of how a shoe-shopping expedition should be. He would have preferred to go alone of course, sauntering into the shop nonchalantly, casually, as if it had just happened to occur to him that he could do with some new footwear. Not like this, all together, he and his mother and his wife, bundled up in wool, stamping the slush from their overshoes before they stepped inside. 'Good afternoon!' said Tora to Ölander, the proprietor, as they entered beneath the tinkling bell and he ceremoniously returned her greeting. The proprietor was quite alone in the shop and there was a distinguished smell of leather with a hint of alcohol. In the shop window stood a pair of cream-coloured ladies' shoes with little beads trimming the ends of the laces at the front. There were also ladies' slippers of imitation snakeskin and overshoes with turned-down, silk-edged tops.

WELL-FITTING SHOES ENHANCE
THE ENJOYMENT OF YOUR WALK

said a sign. Tora saw the sign and felt angry, she didn't know why. But suddenly she was angry with Ölander and it was something to do with shoes. Jenny read the sign and felt that Ölander must be able to see right through her, or rather her galoshes.

Tora glowered. She disliked signs like that with pictures of permed ladies with little red mouths and raised, surprised, eyebrows plucked into thin lines, and straight noses. She caught sight of Jenny looking at her reflection, thinking no one was watching. She was probably trying to look like Clara Bow, with frizzy hair and her little head burrowed deep into her collar of rabbit fur. Tora unbuttoned her coat and took off the scarf she had been wearing crossed over her chest. Jenny turned away. Then Tora set down her handbag on the counter, making a great show of it, Fredrik thought. It was a shiny, black, leather handbag, rather worn at the corners. She liked to keep hold of it; at times it had doubtless been the family's only security. The black handle had been re-stitched and the nickel of the metal frame had flaked off, exposing the brass underneath.

Fredrik said quickly that he was looking for a pair of shoes. But Ölander turned to Tora and asked if they wanted boots or shoes and Jenny blushed with indignation. He had to get in before his mother:

'Shoes, of course!'

'Of course!' said Tora. They should have discussed it before they went, but he was pig-headed.

'Yes, shoes.'

'But they're not much use in this weather.'

Jenny burrowed her head down into her rabbit collar and thought: if he gets boots I'll just die. Heavy boots with long straps. She felt like taking him on one side and whispering, 'If you get those I'll die.' But he stood firm, thank God. Yet the annoying thing, the awful thing, was that the proprietor still did not fetch out any shoes. Only after Tora had conceded with a snort did Ölander move from his listening position, head on one side, to go over to the stepladder, climb up and take down a box from the shelf. He took off the lid, pulled back the tissue paper and said:

'This is an excellent product, really fine workmanship.'

It was a pair of blunt, solid shoes, black and newly-polished. He pulled out the little stool with the mirror and Fredrik placed his foot on the sloping section. Then the proprietor seated himself on the stool to serve him.

Sad to say, Fredrik did not have such beautiful feet as his father had done and Tora's thoughts touched on this when he took off his shoe. Not that it mattered. They were short and broad in relation to his height. Yet she had always made sure her boys had good shoes, no one could say otherwise. His toes weren't very crooked and there were no corns on the joints of the big toe. But he had chilblains on his heels, just like Jenny. Lots of people had got chilblains on their heels during the war. Jenny had got hers in Stockholm, standing in the potato queue. She had been nurserymaid to a doctor's family in Fleming Street, but he was only a teacher at a grammar school and not a proper doctor, so he hadn't been able to help her with her chilblains.

Fredrik's heels flared up in this weather, growing red and swollen. A few degrees colder and they would give him shooting pains like abscessed teeth.

He was trying on the black pair. They were good and solid, there was no doubt about it. Shoes with which anyone could be satisfied. There was an unspoken understanding that he would try more than one pair. Ölander had already brought down several boxes and put them in a pile beside the stool. But the shoes were all more or less the same, black and blunt-toed. It was just a question of the pattern of perforations or how built up they were at the back. Was the fitting wide enough?

It was clear to all four of them, though no one said it, that Fredrik's position in the world and in the town, as a mobile fitter at Swedish Motors and not yet unemployed, was matched by these black and rather thick-soled shoes. It was Tora who asked how much they were.

'Twelve kronor fifty,' Ölander replied, and she said gruffly that they weren't exactly cheap then, not now they're on a three-day-week. Perhaps she said it to underline the fact that this was her son sitting here, one metre ninety tall and weighing eighty-four kilos, and about to pay for his own shoes. Just in case anyone had thought otherwise. Jenny went a blotchy red and felt a sudden cramp of hate in her stomach.

'How does it feel at the back? Stand up. You ought to walk round a bit. Can't do any harm here on the carpet, can it?'

The other shoe was produced and Fredrik took off his own left shoe, exposing what Tora called a toadstool. It was one of Jenny's awful darns. Miserable and embarrassed, she could see Tora had noticed it. Only the proprietor floated above it all in his superior waft of alcohol and seemed not to notice. Fredrik walked up and down the grey carpet wearing the shoes and everyone agreed that this was just the footwear for a man like him. Ölander was the only one to sense something else. He hovered around this boy of not yet thirty and seemed to be breathing in the scent of him, testing the aroma, the essence of his character. And he could indeed sense something there, a slight hint perhaps, a nuance.

He climbed to the top of his stepladder. He stood on tiptoe and reached down a box. It was light brown and when he took off the lid and moved the tissue paper aside it was thick and double.

'Here,' he said. 'Something else for you.'

He placed a shoe on the stool. It was wine-coloured and narrow, with a stitched edge but no perforations. It had very thin soles and an elegant fitting to make the foot appear slender.

'Claret, kid leather,' said Ölander. He kept his eyes on Fredrik's face.

'Well, you can't wear red with a black suit,' Tora said.

Fredrik said nothing; the shoe-shop devil said nothing. The shoe seemed in some remarkable way to belong to Fredrik already, as it stood there on the stool. It had lain in its box, growing charged with all his expectations of a life. Shoes like these could turn

24

burdensome affairs into insignificant occurrences. You got the feeling you could step out of your life, out of one stage after another like wrinkled cocoons.

'Try one,' said Ölander.

He did so. Then: up on your feet and walk the few steps across the soft carpet to the big wall mirror. One foot was humbly shod in black, rather worn and cracked. But well-polished. The other in claret kid leather. He walked stiffly.

'Put your whole foot down,' urged the proprietor. 'Get a proper feel of it. Well?'

So as not to leave too many wet marks on the light carpet he had kicked off his galoshes when he came in and now they lay there gaping at him.

Jenny felt a little nervous. She looked at all the things around her in this leather-hide-scented world. A long tortoiseshell shoe horn with a silk tassel. Good grief, it was all so elegant here. Why had they come? Oh yes, because Tora knew Ölander. She knew God and the whole human race. Soon it would be thirty years she'd been selling sweets outside here.

Why didn't she ever get old? Jenny let the tortoiseshell shoe horn dangle, holding it by the long silk tassel. Tora was nearly fifty-four and had always looked just the same, thought Jenny, who sometimes got the feeling that her marriage to Fredrik wasn't actually real. It was a sort of game children play. When they slept at Tora's they didn't dare touch each other. At any rate, Fredrik didn't dare, she could feel it.

Jenny thought there were two things they needed to do: have children and move away from town. But no one moved anywhere these days. You clung on to what you'd got, even if it was only three days a week at Swedish Motors. There were twenty million unemployed in the world, Fredrik said. That's why they stayed here and every week they had Sunday dinner at Tora's along with Jenny's mother. But on those occasions Tora was always fairly mild and amenable. She was tired after market day. On Monday and Tuesday her spirits lifted; by Friday she was herself again.

He had spent a while walking about the soft carpet in the wine-coloured shoes and now he had formed an opinion. How he expressed it was:

'This is something different altogether.'

And the proprietor concurred: this was Something Different Altogether. Then Tora asked how much they were.

'Twenty-two fifty.'

Ridiculous. She didn't say it, but you could see that was what she was thinking. She looked defiant and cross and untouchable. Jenny felt such a bag of nerves that she turned her back on them and pretended to study the width fitting gauge.

'Well,' said Tora. 'If Adam turned up in a pair of those it wouldn't surprise me. When it's four kronor a kilo for coffee and two for bacon.'

Jenny felt embarrassed but Fredrik had to smile. He thought of his brother, who had been allowed to go with Bertil Franzon to the cinema proprietors' conference in Stockholm. He had gone in his Chrysler Six. Aga-Baltic had put on the conference to demonstrate projection equipment for the talkies and Franzon had gone off with a fur-trimmed coat, pale grey spats, exclusive Borsalino hat and walking stick. Adam had been nearly as elegant.

'It's quite important to have smart shoes, you know,' said Fredrik to his mother.

She knew all right. But she said nothing. Jenny was still so nervous that she wandered aimlessly around the shop, studying the calendar, the slippers in the window and the dear little miniature shoes made of gold leather. Then suddenly some more customers came in, stamping the snow off their feet and sending good afternoons in all directions. They would have to hurry up. Mother and son looked at each other.

'Take them,' she said.

What was it? She didn't know. Maybe it was the memory of a pair of extremely beautiful feet in elegant shoes from Gothenburg? Or had she conceded defeat anyway, realised that there was simply nothing else for it, that Fredrik, a metre ninety tall and weighing eighty-four kilos, had a character of his own and a kind of sensibility she could not reach?

She knew, moreover, that a pair of shoes was a pair of shoes. They did not get eaten up like bacon. They did not become worthless like shares and debentures. She liked material assets and in that respect she resembled Bertil Franzon, who had put his house in order just in time and given up paper investments.

'Take them,' she said. 'Go on.'

They all knew he couldn't afford it. Not that Tora insulted him by offering to pay the difference while they were still in the shop. Even so, her own heavy, black bag was standing over there on the counter. It had settled onto its belly.

What should she have done? If she had said no to the purchase it would have been just as bad. The only good thing was that Fredrik was alone with the shoes in a different world with a scent of fine leather and the rustle of tissue paper.

'Wrap them up for us then; we've got to be going,' Tora said. She realised it was probably the last time she would go shopping with him.

She went ahead as they came out. Is Mum a bit lopsided? wondered Fredrik, walking behind her with Jenny's arm in his. Something about her hip? He wasn't sure. It was slippery underfoot and hard going. Maybe that was why she was walking so badly. He hadn't noticed it before.

Ingrid held a tin lid with jagged edges up to the band-saw for trimming. The narrow, wobbling blade and the whine it made as it cut scared her. At seven in the morning she also found it hard to take the noise from the presses where the cans were made. On the other side of the workshop, Maud was finishing lids against sandpaper blocks in a polishing machine. It steamed and hissed.

Life went on in three places. Here at the band-saw, of course. Here it probably felt most substantial, or should at any rate. Outside the windows was the scent of spruce needles in the rising sun, the smell of wood from the sawmill, the insects, the glitter on the leaves. It was as if she could feel the gravel road under her feet whenever a breeze wafted in from outside. Inside her head, to her embarrassment, the novel went on. 'The ball went on utterly undisturbed,' she had read with a giggle in 'Married or Single' on the back page of the paper week after week, as it continued through crises and bankruptcies. Not that she was much better herself, with her stories. Several times she had hurt herself because her mind had been wandering. She knew she ought to stop it. But it was such fun. There was no real harm in it, after all. Nobody else knew. Though Maud sometimes winked from her polishing machine as if she knew. All the dust and flying sparks made it hard to see her face most of the time. As soon as Ingrid had a tray of ten lids ready, she was supposed to take them over and then they could talk for a moment if the German didn't come along.

'*Präzision*, young lady! *Präzision!*'

Damn. He had come down the steps from the lab without her

28

noticing. Over there, Maud bowed her head, her curls tied up in a scarf, and pretended not to see a thing, but her back was quivering with laughter. He came up to Ingrid and matched a tin can against one of her lids. It was a poor fit.

'Reject,' he said. '*Präzision*! Mind on the job, young lady!'

Yes, unfortunately, life went on in three places. Inside her head, the novel went rolling on, vague and mumbling. Outside the window was real life, with the scent of spruce and freedom and Stockholm. And then there was the life here at the factory which they called the Tin Can, and she supposed they had quite a good time here. But God how good it felt when five o'clock came on a summer's afternoon and she went cycling off!

Then the air would feel cool to her face. The tool bag rattled as she rode over the potholes in the road; she could feel the point of the saddle between her legs and it was not unpleasant. Oh God yes, how fast you could get away from it all if you had a bike.

It was a nearly new Hermes with pale grey inflatable tyres and shiny black paintwork. It had a carrier and a tool bag with a pump. That seemed unnecessary, because she hadn't needed them yet. Not so much as a valve rubber had let her down. From the handlebars dangled a carrier bag with her sandwiches, comb and purse. The bike had a light, shiny chainguard and a dressguard of yellow and black crocheted wool.

The Tin Can was right at the end of Industrial Road where it petered out at the sawmill. She rode all the way along to the main road and turned off at the kiosk, and then she had to stand on the pedals until she got up to the bridge. But after the railway it was downhill almost all the way to the railway workers' houses. Home and eat, that didn't take long. Both Assar and Ingeborg had a rather resigned look whenever they saw Ingrid these days. She was busy packing things in her carrier bag again.

'So where're you off to now?'

She had spread out her best blue dress on the kitchen settle and was folding it up.

'Are you taking your dress? Are you girls going out dancing?'

'I'm going up to Maud's first. I'll iron it there.'

In went the hair grips and a few other bits and pieces she preferred Ingeborg not to see, because she would only make a fuss: mirror, cigarettes, powder.

'Bye then!'

'Well, all right,' they said. 'Goodbye. Don't be late home.'

Assar had the paper up in front of his face the whole time, but he wasn't reading. He was peering over the edge.

It was quite a way to Maud's. She lived over by the cemetery. When Ingrid was riding her bike she rarely thought about anything. She was one hundred percent in the present and so was life. It was here. In the air washing over her face and in the gravel spraying up when she braked outside the Co-operative Stores to let a big country bus come rolling by. It had been standing with the sun burning down on its roof all afternoon and was now on its return journey to Stegsjö and Vallmsta with hot people in dark clothes. She felt as if everyone in the bus was looking at her. A few years ago she wouldn't have known what to do with herself, but now it just put her in a good mood. There was even a dog sitting at a window looking at her!

At Maud's she caused a draught when she opened the front door. The white curtains flapped and their brass rings jangled on the rail as the air rushed through the big, empty house. Maud was on her own at home. Her parents were at their summer cottage, which her father had built himself. She, though, refused to go with them to spend the whole summer there. She was twenty-two and pretty fed up with them. They were nice people and didn't even know she smoked.

She had been given the kitchen in the upstairs flat as her own room, now they no longer rented it out. She had silk flowers and frilly curtains so you scarcely noticed it was a kitchen. Now that she was alone, she had dragged up the big wardrobe mirror from her parents' room. She had simply taken the wardrobe door off its hinges.

'Nothing scares you, does it?' said Ingrid

'Come in and have a coffee! The iron's hot. Have you got your dress?'

It was a blue dress Ingrid's sister Dagmar had made for her. It was well-made, but Maud found it dull.

'Hang on and I'll show you something. Undo the top button.'

She had her cigarette between her lips as she helped Ingrid pull the warm, newly-ironed dress over her head; dropping ash on the collar and then brushing it off with a laugh.

'Look, I'll show you; you want two buttons undone. Look in the mirror!'

'I can't go out it like this,' Ingrid said.

'Yes you can! This is how Margit has hers. You should see what she does with that white blouse when Mum's ironed it for her. She buttons it right up and then as soon as she's out in the hall she undoes the top two. Then she runs out to Jörgen, who's been standing waiting and waiting, you know. Behind the hedge. He's petrified of Dad.'

Maud pulled and stretched the dress fabric to make the skirt flare out more.

'God, blue really suits you, though it's a little girl's colour really. Anyway...'

Maud said this very emphatically and they both laughed, because she was mimicking Edvin Jansson at the Tin Can.

'*Anyway*, she showed me how she sits. Like this, see. Sort of put

31

one arm up. No, sit here a minute. I can't show you in this kimono.'

With quick, warm fingers she undid the top two pearl buttons on Ingrid's dress and showed her how to sit with her forearm supporting one breast so she had more of a cleavage. Then she patted her and said:

'You'll never do it, I know. But think of Margit, who's taken her school-leaving certificate and everything. She's started going out with Erik Falk.'

'From the solicitor's? Isn't he a lot older than her?'

'Certainly is. But she does whatever she pleases you know.'

Maud fluttered about the room like a big butterfly in her gaily coloured kimono. In fact, with beanpole legs as long as hers she actually looked more like a daddy-long-legs. The realisation took Ingrid aback as she watched her putting on her silk stockings. You didn't notice it when she was dressed. Maud had a special way of making things magically appear and disappear.

She had borrowed some electric curling tongs from the ladies' hairdresser's where she knew a girl and where she was keen to work herself. There was something wrong with it, that was why they let her take it. The insulation round the cord had frayed and it was very worn. Whenever it stopped working, Maud had to shake it to restore the loose contact and blue sparks shot out of where the cord went in. Ingrid cowered as Maud approached with the great, smoking tool of steel.

'Oh go on, it's quite safe,' said Maud, putting it in and making the first long wave at the back of Ingrid's neck. She said she was a born hairdresser and hoped to get a job soon. Though she was too old to be a shampoo girl. She had the skill, there in her fingers. They loved to fiddle and fuss with skin and hair, they tugged at clothes and were always busy seeing to something. She wasn't really very pretty herself. Though when she was dressed up, it didn't seem to matter. Yet she wasn't the least grudging and would willingly have helped anyone make the best of their appearance, as she put it.

They used beer to set her hair because it stayed in shape better and it only smelt while it was still wet. They had little metal clips for the flat curls across the forehead and down the cheeks. Maud did the rest of her hair in long sloping waves, managing to get them to join up so Ingrid's scalp looked like a beach of golden sand striped with long, rolling billows.

Ingrid plucked her eyebrows in front of the little mirror from the top of the chest of drawers, which Maud brought down onto the kitchen table. She didn't dare to pluck them as high as Maud said, it would be too obvious at home. And it hurt. She had lots of little, pale blonde hairs growing all over the place, not in a long, thin, surprised arch like they should.

It was quiet up here now, quiet and hot. They would really have liked to sit on the balcony with their glasses. Maud had poured them some sweet vermouth. But they were too afraid they'd be seen smoking out there, so they stayed in the kitchen among the scattered clothes, bottles and pots of cream. Ingrid liked this Saturday clutter with the smell of perfume and ironing and smoke from the flat, Turkish cigarettes. Though if she smoked too many, they sometimes made her feel sick.

Maud had taken off her kimono in the heat. It was on the sofa where her dress also lay, like petals dropped from a big, wilting poppy. She was wearing cami-knickers with narrow shoulder straps and lace at the bust. They were a delicate yellow and the lace was beige. Ingrid could scarcely take her eyes off them. There was no elastic in the knicker part, the legs were loose. Ingrid herself was just wearing a vest and knickers and didn't really think she needed anything more elaborate than that either. She said so to Maud:

33

'Those things don't matter. No one sees them, after all.'

But then Maud laughed and stroked her cheek. It was not entirely pleasant. She knew that Maud thought she was something she wasn't. Ingrid didn't tell her everything. Maud often said they ought to tell each other everything. She cupped Ingrid's cheeks in her warm hands as she said it.

She simply couldn't get enough of looking at Maud. Although she wasn't really pretty, she was stunning at this moment. Her skin was warm and rosy but matte with fine powder from the Three Flowers box. Her eyebrows had that raised, surprised look and her mouth was painted red, with a Cupid's bow. Her lips weren't that shape normally. She was smooth under the arms; she had used a paste that made the hairs frizzle up and fall out. And she was shaved smooth under her silk stockings.

It was somehow hypnotic being there with her in the stuffy room above the cemetery, where people dressed in black made their way along the gravel paths on Saturday afternoons as cautiously as if they were afraid of waking someone.

Sometimes the girls sat here on weekday evenings too. They put their sweaters on and went out onto the balcony and sat looking at the men cycling past. Not the old ones or the family men with lunchboxes on their carriers who came past at the end of the shift at Swedish Motors, nor even the younger ones if they still had their work clothes on. There was nothing more depressing than that winding, intermittent procession of bikes after the factory whistle had gone. They came in threes and then the occasional lone wolf with his saddle set high, an old man. No, they didn't go out onto the balcony until it was dark enough for the street lamps to be lit. Then they couldn't be seen. They could drink coffee and smoke, inhaling deeply under cover of the soft summer darkness. As soon as the streetlamps came on, the young men came cycling along with their hats pulled well down and with shirt collars that flashed in the dark now everything else had gone colourless and woolly.

When the cyclists grew few and far between and there were no more footsteps in the gravel they would go in, because it was no fun sitting looking out over the cemetery in the dark, hearing the sound of the wind in the tops of the big trees. On those quiet and uneventful evenings, Maud would get the cards out and tell Ingrid's fortune. She laid the cards and rearranged them and talked knowledgeably about love and money. It all seemed far more distant than 'Married or Single' in the paper. But Ingrid didn't say so to Maud because she seemed to believe in it.

When Saturday evening came and they had had some sweet vermouth, they cycled to the Park or one of the other open-air dance floors, preferably Carpenter's Hill out by the estate. Everyone knew that was the best place. No one could tell you why.

They would be sticky when they got there and would have to adjust their stockings behind a bush so the seams were straight. Powdering their noses meant rummaging through their handbags and dropping their mirrors. It was nerves. They hadn't got a hip-flask but they often felt a bit tipsy after the vermouth. Naturally they didn't smoke. It would have looked bad, right at the start of the evening.

There were other girls giggling around them as they got ready and then stepped into the light on unsteady heels. Carpenter's Hill was hard going. There were stones in the grass in front of the dance floor. You could see the lake between the oak trees and there was a scent of water-lilies and sweet, black water. They didn't miss the Park with its chocolate roulette game and electric light bulbs strung in the trees. Here, the ends of cigarettes glowed in the darkness and white shirt collars glistened. Birds were startled up from their roosting places, flying swiftly and silently off as the couples came stumbling in from the dark. A lot of silk stockings got ruined. On the Saturday evening Ingrid didn't care, but on the Sunday afternoon, which gave plenty of time for reflection, she would sit trying to mend the ladders and sometimes she regretted it and wished she had gone bare-legged.

The Roxy Band who were the most popular act at the Park never played here, of course; instead you got accordion trios and other assorted groups, sometimes quite old men. They knew hundreds of sailors' waltzes. At first the talc flew up in dusty clouds and dark trouser legs turned white.

She liked the excitement. To start with she had been terrified of being left standing on her own or of having to dance with a fellow who'd had one too many. It could mean trouble if you refused. You might got your skirt pulled up, later on. Sometimes no one would ask you to dance the whole evening. And dancing was so divine, having a body so close to yours, someone you didn't even know and whose face you might not even see. The smell of a freshly-ironed white shirt sometimes made her feel dizzy. That faint smell of white spirit, giving away an unfortunate mother who had singed the collar and tried to bleach it with white spirit. You couldn't get rid of the smell no matter how many times you rinsed it; it made that hero with his heavy-lidded Valentino eyes so human. How he must have cursed, how his mother must have wailed!

Of course everyone was depressed because of unemployment but you didn't think about it much, especially not when you were dancing. You didn't see any relief work types among the men out here. She'd heard how it was at some of the other places, but no one talked about that sort of thing here. Everyone had their problems, no doubt. If you got hold of a bottle for a Saturday night it was a relief to go dancing and talk about something else, she supposed. Lots of them had to press their trousers under their mattresses, and it showed. She realised she was starting to get fussy. That was Maud's influence.

No, out here you didn't talk about the Relief Work Commission and hopeless things like that. In town she sometimes got snide comments about having a job at the Tin Can when so many family men were out of work. But never here, you never got any snide comments here. Here you were silky-legged and warm and had just plucked your eyebrows. What they really wanted here was to take you home, so they were always extra nice. She had to jump on her bike and go if they started insisting.

She and Maud got separated after the last dance. It happened more and more often. She stood looking round for her once she'd fetched her bike. She was a bit put out and supposed she'd have to try to tag along with some other people. She'd be all right. The boy she'd danced the last dance with had squeezed her arm but there were a thousand things wrong with him. Boring and heavy and too insistent, she thought. And his collar studs stuck up over his jacket.

She never really knew what Maud got up to afterwards. She didn't want to know either. Maud would tell her who she'd been with. They were to tell each other everything, she said. But Ingrid didn't want to hear. That was another world. It was more than just a good time.

You could go quite far, anyway, before it became more than just a good time. She didn't always say no if someone wanted to cycle home with her. Once she had even gone off a bit early with a boy. They could hear the music in the distance, it was rocking in that mass of illuminated leaves in the middle of the flat countryside; voices were calling. They sat down to rest on a pile of timber put ready for making hay frames and she made his shirt collar wet with her saliva. They were still near enough to hear laughing voices and the thumping beat of the bass. When she shut her eyes, she felt as if the shimmering grey darkness were rocking her and although she was aware of rough timber against her back, she felt none of the normal standards applied. She no longer had to think what she was doing. The fact that she didn't know him was all to the good at that moment. He was nothing but cold lips and hot tongue, hard back beneath her hands. She even brushed against his cock under the rough fabric of his trousers, wondering afterwards if he'd noticed.

Strangely enough, he was the one who suggested they ride on. She didn't know why he wanted to. But she felt rather relieved.

Virginity was supposed to be like a little treasure you had, a sweet nut in a secret hiding place. Ingrid didn't have that nut any longer but she had discovered that you can get on just as well without it, as long as no one knows.

It wasn't anything like the pure and precious little bud she had imagined from Ingeborg Ek's timid descriptions. It was just a little thing you were ignorant of, a risk you hadn't taken. Afterwards you felt much the same as before. The fact was, she had only done it once.

She had met a boy who was older than her. She was only nineteen at the time. It was out here at Carpenter's Hill, one August evening. His name was Åke Ekengren. It was a handsome name and he was very good-looking. When he chose her she felt she was on her way to joining the group of girls who were pretty, or at least fairly pretty. Presumably she had Maud to thank for that. She had danced with him on several Saturday nights. Sometimes his lips had brushed her temple and she could still recall it, better than what had happened later. One evening he had been at her side when one of the organisers cleared his throat and announced:

'On behalf of the local Social Democratic Party I'd like to say a big thank-you to all of you for coming tonight and hope you can join us again next week. Now Egil's Threesome are going to play positively the last dance.'

In fact there was one more after that. The warmth and darkness were all-enveloping as they cycled home. The air was soft. She couldn't remember their having said much for the first few kilometres. Then he stopped, outside a white house behind a lilac hedge. There was an orphanage out here in the muddy fields, and this was the staff quarters. He said his sister worked at the home. She would give them coffee.

But when they went inside the creaking, ramshackle, wooden house, the sister wasn't there.

'We'll wait for her,' he said.

Ingrid thought it was exciting. She went round looking, touching the hairbrush and comb on the chest of drawers, turning things over. It felt interesting and secret, this unknown girl's life, though the things she had were very ordinary: hair grips in a box, a primus on a packing case in the corner. He pumped it.

'We'll make the coffee while we're waiting.'

And there was nothing wrong with that, after all. Only now did she see what a profile he had. And a soft shirt, terribly good quality.

They drank the coffee and he sat beside her on his sister's couch and held her tightly. They started to kiss. She realised he was very experienced. She was a bit startled but it was easy to put it out of her mind because what he was doing felt so nice. And nothing could happen, after all. But he kept on stroking and stroking her until he had two fingers inside her knicker elastic and then there was nothing for it. She wanted to get up but he wouldn't let her. You just couldn't do that. If she'd let him go that far...But his sister!

'Oh, she's not coming. You must have known that.'

She couldn't get away from him, from his experience and his hardness. She liked it too, right up to when he actually did it. Then she went all cold and scared.

He was rather cold as well, afterwards. She didn't know if he was disappointed or what. He seemed almost angry with her. When she sat on the basket-chair a big, damp patch appeared on the back of her skirt.

'For goodness sake, you can't just sit straight up like that,' he said, passing her a folded towel. Then they rode home. It was much chillier now and they still had fifteen kilometres to go. Her back was aching. She was thinking: this hasn't happened to me. It didn't happen. It didn't hurt, either. It can't have been the real thing. Surely there's usually some bleeding. You usually bleed, Maud had said so.

She was so naive that she said it out loud. Remembering that was the worst thing of all: them riding along in the cold night air, the hard, monotonous pedalling, making their calf muscles ache, and her asking him if it had been the real thing, and didn't you usually bleed a bit.

'It was the real thing, all right,' he said in a rough, thick voice. He must have been smoking too much as well.

'You'd better get home quick,' said the boy she didn't know. She looked at him from the side several times but he kept his handsome profile steadfastly in her direction. She couldn't tell what he was thinking.

She only saw him at a distance after that. He would say hello. But he didn't ask her to dance again.

Anyhow, she hadn't done it again. Almost three years had gone by since it happened. Gradually, dancing had started to be fun again. She liked the excitement. It was fun riding home in a big group, or if the worst came to the worst, on her own down the back roads and over the fields if she needed to get away from someone too insistent.

'You're a funny one,' Maud would sometimes say. 'Why bother doing your hair all nice if you don't want to go with anyone?'

But she didn't reply.

It was nighttime. The leaves rustled and whispered above her head as she rode along the avenue. Warm breezes wafted in from the fields now and then, as if a summer wind had lain curled up all day and was suddenly coming to life in the dusky night. A fox rose to his feet on a flat stone out in the field. Had he been sleeping there? She could see his silhouette. He rose in a leisurely fashion, stretched like a dog and pricked up his ears. Her cycle chain was certainly making a slight rattle. But he didn't move off.

This was a man-made landscape. Arable land, fields, avenues. Copses of deciduous trees and fenced meadows with small mounds of stones. The lakes found their way in amongst the leaves, their water spilling out to mirror the sky and the trees.

Above the road, the house where the captain lived stood quiet and sleeping. It was an austere, dark red, as if it had been painted in quite another time. In the courtyard stood an iron pot with a rose bush in it. The cats were out; the cats, the fox and Ingrid. The birds were asleep, roosting on branches in thick bushes and trees that looked black. God she was tired, tired and a bit anxious in the solitude.

This landscape, with its soft, low lines, had no horizon. It was leafy and pretty, nature tamed in the calm conviction that this was what people should surround themselves with. Luminous swans floated silently on the pond. They had tucked their heads and their long soft necks under their wings. She could see the dark yellow of the manor house beyond the trees in the park. The millrace and the iron mountings of its hatches. Water purled in the wooden channels and she imagined it was talking as she rode over the bridge.

Old stone cellars crouched under a bushy growth of fireweed and raspberries. Barns almost dissolved into the gloom, so grey was their wood. Strange birds sat in the road. It took a while for her to realise they must be nightjars. She had already startled up five or

41

six. Out in the field, the corncrake called.

Was this landscape dead or abandoned? Memory or dream? Half asleep over the handlebars, she began to feel it wasn't quite real. The fall of darkness had bleached out all its colours. Yet she caught the smells now and then, released by a puff of wind. They came rolling in, a scent of lady's bedstraw past its prime and of almost rotting jasmine from a garden behind a white fence. She rode past a cowshed. The reek of manure was stern and dark, not at all like the familiar smell of grazing cows and their fresh dung in a meadow.

Here, huge horses were standing motionless. They slept nose to tail with one another, set free from flies, set free. They slept in great, deep blue dreams with their shaggy hocks and mighty hindquarters at rest. They blew gently though their nostrils. She was glad she didn't need to cross their meadow. And were they really horses? Having passed them, she turned her head. Horses or enormous boulders?

She had to go through the forest at several points and she hated those bits. It was totally alien; in there the darkness was inhumanly raw and full of twigs. The last two kilometres into town was virtually all forest. God how she pedalled. Her chest was cold right through from the persistent headwind.

She thought of the town as a canker in this quiet, benevolent, leafy world through which she had passed, a blot and an accident, perhaps. Summer cottages stood here by a silent lake in the middle of the forest, cottages on a dark, fir-lined shore. That was not where you would find old dwellings. These newcomers clung tightly to the lake edge and behind them was the darkness. A curious way to live.

She didn't want to go into the centre of town really. She felt the same aversion to it as she did to the way the others lived, the grown ups, the settled adults.

Ingeborg Ek often told her she was grown up now. As if she wanted to remind her about it. Occasionally she felt grown up, too, but she didn't want to enter the world and their lives yet. She thought of it as heavy and enclosed. A big egg. She did not want to be part of the egg of the world.

She wasn't sure which were the dangerous actions that might take her in there. Losing her virginity was one, she'd been convinced of it. Until she did it and realised it didn't change anything. Having children, getting married - that was all part of being in there, of course. But even actions and gestures that seemed unimportant could be charged with significance and destiny. When you put on a brand-new dress or coat. You never quite knew. When you let a man light your cigarette and heard your own voice go low and serious.

Hidden significance and destiny were lying in wait everywhere and could get you before you realised. It made her think twice about the simplest act. She sat there, the curling tong forgotten in her hair, until her scalp was scorching. What am I doing?

Riding her bike wasn't dangerous. She hardly had to think about that at all. She just rode. She could move through the sleeping landscape with ease. It was all unknown, there was nowhere she wanted to go in. She had no wish to share any of these lives. Was this freedom?

'Your freedom is just a feeling,' said her brother Konrad. 'It's wanting whatever can be achieved without actually changing anything.'

'Oh right,' she said, more fiercely than she'd meant to. 'In this slave colony, you mean? In this prison?'

The annoying thing about Konrad was his way of taking sarcasm so seriously.

'Well, yes,' he said. 'Though it isn't chains keeping you trapped, it's roots, roots as fine as capillaries. If you tore away from them to stand on your own, you'd shrivel up.'

She felt trapped when he said that. A stump left by a scissor cut and bandaged tightly, that was all that was left of her wobbly little bid for freedom. It was called: a secret life.

If you couldn't live in freedom, at least you could have a secret life. A life separate from the one you had to lead squeezed and tangled inside a root system.

'Every single person has a right to their own life,' she told Konrad.

At that time he was the least secret person she knew. His life was open, accounted for in constant discussion. Agnes and he lived their lives on a platter for all to see. She wondered whether Agnes liked it. It must feel like being brought before a court every day, every hour. Once for fun she had opened Ingeborg Ek's big confirmation Bible and there was the story of a man who woke up in the middle of the night and heard someone whispering to him. He shivered and his legs started shaking and he felt as if someone were gripping his face and calling him to account. It was a phantom he could not see or name. Reading that had made her think of Konrad even though she knew her brother had had nothing to do with God since he had settled up with Him at a youth club meeting decades before.

Why should a person be obliged to stand up and be held to account all the time? Why should she be obliged to work out the whole system and all the answers for herself and feel she was taking the world forward by means of decisions that were put down on the record? Who was imposing on her this dreadful obligation to spend all her life at meetings? How much of my life really belongs to other people and how much of it belongs to me? she wondered.

She didn't know that Konrad had given her any answers. There probably weren't any answers. Everything is only something we've agreed that it should be, he would say. But when you were like her and still hadn't pecked your way into the egg of the world, you hadn't agreed anything with anybody. Surely that at least was freedom?

No, there were no answers, but she sometimes thought she could see them in the air around her, just as she could see events that seemed unimportant but were actually threatening, thick with significance. Sparks flew up from a chimney against a dark, morning sky one winter's day on the way to the Tin Can. She saw that the air was full of hope. But for what? Couldn't you ever find out what for?

She would quite often cycle over to Konrad's. To get up to his flat above the old Casino Theatre you had to go round the building. There, a rickety, wooden, outside staircase led up to the door.

Franzon didn't hire out the Casino as a theatre any longer. It was too shabby. He didn't even show films there. But an auctioneer would hold sales from the stage and he kept his goods up in the attic too. The wrestling club trained here and held their contests in the big, draughty wooden theatre. They would move aside the benches and put down padded mats of grey canvas. The wrestlers used to get changed up in the gallery and the whole place smelt of sweat, the days they were there.

The Communist Party used Konrad and Agnes's parlour as its office. You went through the kitchen to get to it. The cashbox was kept under the settee. The discussions went on in there all evening and sometimes far into the night. Ingrid loathed it: talk talk talk. The smell of tobacco and the mumble of voices came filtering from the room. Sometimes the voices were raised. They held their party meetings down in the theatre, of course, on an evening when there wasn't boxing or an auction on.

Agnes and Konrad had had a son about a year after they got married and then they had a girl. It was all a bit quick. But they managed. After all, Konrad had his caretaker's job with Franzon. Then they had twins. So that meant they already had four children and Ingrid thought Agnes was looking rather big in the belly again. It was bad luck if so. She was normally as thin as a rake, that was probably why it showed so early. She was a mild and kindly individual. Ingrid thought she was too submissive and Tora said bluntly:

'She's a sheep.'

She was busy the whole time washing the children's clothes and cooking. Ingrid had never seen her sit still for a few minutes with a cup of coffee or, unthinkable, a cigarette. The children were clingy and whiny and always wanting something. If she went to the privy they would stand outside banging on the door with their little fists. She would have to let them in. Sometimes there was an unmistakable smell of shit when Ingrid came up. She wasn't used to it like Agnes was so she would say something if it got too unbearable. When Agnes took off their pants there would be yellow stuff inside. The children had bad tummies. They didn't get their meals as regularly as they should. There was too much coming and going up here. Suddenly Agnes would have to make coffee or go down and help shift benches in the theatre. She would quickly give the children a bit of cake or a treacle sandwich.

The twins were identical. Ingrid would stare at them sometimes. They both looked exactly the same, the tops of their heads lopsided after delivery. No one could yet tell for sure whether they were backward or not.

Agnes and the children plainly didn't sleep properly either

because it was never really quiet in the flat. Late into the evening and sometimes during the night, people would be coming out of the parlour. Of course they tried to make their way quietly and carefully. There was never any alcohol at Konrad's. He was strictly teetotal.

He had started work at the bakery again. He got up at four in the morning. In the afternoons he was supposed to do his caretaking duties but Agnes had to sort out anything that happened while he wasn't there. Ingrid thought their life was one big mess. But it never changed. Time seemed to stand still, like old dishwater in a blocked sink. Here he was, preaching freedom. Because Communism was freedom he said, and she was eager to believe him. But where was the freedom? In his dreams? In the little tin box with the party funds? She loathed the mess.

Konrad and Agnes apart, she didn't think the members of his party were very different in kind from their worst enemies, the Social Democrats. It seemed to her they all wanted to get somewhere and many of them were very strong people; perhaps Konrad was too. They discussed tactics. They discussed those they suspected might side with Kilbom; they didn't let those men know where the tin cashbox was kept.

The men never looked about them as they passed through the kitchen. They walked through it all, the children, the clothes, Agnes's sticky saucepans, without seeing. They spoke their terms, their doctrines, formuli and theorems. She would have liked to deal out some pungent and bitter criticism to them but did not dare, sensing that it was just the sort of act that might be destiny.

They were split by endless quarrels. The Social Democrats were their bitterest enemies. They said the town was a nest of socialists. Ingrid just couldn't get it into her head that her Uncle Valentin who worked at the foundry could be the arch-enemy. She liked going up to see him. It was clean and quiet in his kitchen. He read his newspapers and was tired by early evening. And he coughed. She was sure his lungs were affected. The great, domed furnace in the foundry smoked. He took off his elastic-sided boots and his leggings and goggles when he went home for the evening but his foundry-worker's cough came with him. Though whenever she came he would always be joking and cheerful. A girl - that was something light and ready to laugh, a sort of playful, provoking bundle. Nothing serious. And she often acted that way for him.

She wasn't so keen on going to see Frida. She didn't feel as if she and her mother had anything to say to each other and it was deadly boring in her little flat, cleared and bare and dead. She lived on her own now. The way Ingrid remembered the one room and kitchen where they had lived when she was little, with washing lines strung across the ceiling and Konrad's books and writing paper everywhere, it had at least had a homely feel. But the memory was so faint. It was really only the knotted washing lines crossing each other up by the ceiling and Konrad's settee with the books she could recall.

She didn't very often go to Store Street to Tora's. Tora was always telling her off. She would growl on about silk stockings and powder boxes.

Sometimes Ingrid thought she hated everything she came from. Frida's contentment and Dagmar's industriousness and secret tippling. It must be Fernet Branca she liked to sip. There was a medicinal smell on her breath. David was out of work for the second time. Things weren't looking good for him. And Anna was ever so secretive about what she was up to when she arrived from Norrköping in clothes that were far too smart. She said she was a waitress at The Grape. But she had been seen at Pigswill Jon's and you didn't earn the money for clothes like that there.

Ingrid didn't want to be like any of them. How do you want to be, then? Konrad looked genuinely interested when he asked. But she sensed he was trying to lure her into some trap in his discussion. In spite of that, she answered honestly enough: she wanted a job and she wanted to have fun. Life wasn't all wretchedness and misery and politics, after all! Or doing your duty or looking after your things with dusters and polish at home with Ingeborg and Assar. Though those two had got more easy-going in their old age. They let her be. Sometimes she thought they were really kind.

But now and then in the mornings when they had just got up, it seemed to her she could see them all too clearly, so clearly she found it hard to bear. There were times when the light seemed to shine more keenly and every sound was sharper than usual.

Assar Ek was eating porridge. His lips were sucking and smacking and his nose was moving. She could see all the pores. The tip of his nose was joining in with the movements of his mouth, dipping like a fleshy beak. Could you really say he was kind?

He had finished eating and was leaning back so the milky white and blue shimmer of light filtering through the thin curtains fell on the tapering crown of his head. It was bald, with only a few soft wisps curling over his ears. He didn't really give the impression of someone who had gone bald with old age; he was bare and polished as if a fever had scorched off all his hair. His eyes lay still, baked into place above the tall, furrowed cheeks. His face with its extended top lip looked like a bracket fungus in dry weather, a stiff birch fungus growing out of wood. Can you really know anything about a person you can see so clearly? It was a torment.

Quickly she rose from her seat. Dishes in the sink. Ingeborg did the washing up later, once she was up. She asked nothing better.

Why are we so mean and nasty when we only live once? If I was a nice person, I'd praise her every day. That's all she wants, lying in there in her nightdress drenched in sweat with the headache blazing behind her browbone. And she's always got a headache. Or is she lying to us? And why? Because we deny her worth and substance?

She roams about our lives like a sweaty ghost, always busy, sighing and groaning as she wields the carpet beater and the scrubbing brush: 'See, I'm alive! Can't you hear? I'm alive. Praise me.'

As soon as Ingrid was on her bike, she put it all behind her. Nobody could obtrude on her any longer. She rode through the fresh morning air and it flushed out her nostrils and ears, flushed even her brain clean. It blew her skirt out like a bluebell behind her saddle, tickled her thighs and made the little white hairs on her forearms stand on end. When am I most alive? Now perhaps.

All too soon she'd reach the Tin Can and get changed with Maud and the other girls in the changing room which they had to clean for themselves every Saturday. There were usually about ten or fifteen of them. They had to clean the lunch room too, with its splintery table and the benches and the cupboard with rat droppings. There were only five men down here in the factory. Up in the lab there were a few more, but they never talked to them. The men made the moulds and one of them, Evert Jansson, prepared the mixture of molten metal.

She often thought she ought to ask him what was in the molten mass they made the tin cans of, but she could never quite bring herself to. She felt somehow embarrassed. Sometimes they over-filled the presses, which were like enormous waffle irons. Then the greyish white mass would bubble over and get on your clothes. But was it dangerous? It smelt like some sort of acid. The acid smell enveloped the whole factory. She didn't really know what would go in the tin cans either, had never seen them on display in a shop. But she knew she'd never eat anything from a tin can like that. They got loads of rat droppings in them when they were waiting in the stock-room. She'd packed them the first week, so she knew.

She and Maud got twenty-one kronor a week each. They hadn't been working there long. A dim boy whose job was to slide the rough cans into the drying oven was the only one who earned less than them. If he took the cans out too soon they were lethal when they got to the band-saw. They just crumpled up and then your hand could easily slip and get too close to the blade. She often used to tell him off, but he didn't seem to hear.

The one thing she would have liked to do at the Tin Can was to work the paraffin machine. But that was operated by an older woman, the only one amongst them who was married. Ingrid thought her job looked fun. She had to keep a close eye on it so it didn't get too hot. Then the paraffin spread too thinly and the cans got burnt.

Sometimes she scared herself, standing at the band-saw the way she did, making up stories. The only thing she could think of that she longed for was to be allowed to do the paraffin. And for it to be Saturday.

One afternoon, the building where Tora lived underwent a transformation.

As she made her way along the street, she thought something looked unusual. She couldn't work out what it was. But she didn't want to go back to look again. Then she noticed a chunk of stone lying on the pavement in front of her. It looked so odd she just had to pick it up. It was broken and shaped like a big, snub nose. She was suddenly afraid one of the angels had fallen off the front of the building. The angels' heads with wings on either side sat up under the eaves, splattered with pigeon droppings or wearing fluffy caps of snow. What she was holding in her hand was just a chunk of cement. She threw it aside and didn't bother going back out into the street to look at the angels. She went into the courtyard instead. After a few deep breaths, she convinced herself the building was whole and beautiful. She had lived here for so long.

She was calm as she climbed the stairs of grey wood, scoured smooth. But freezing cold. It was cold in the kitchen and the iron stove was cool. She lit the stove. There was plenty of wood in the box, wood she didn't recognise. It looked like demolition timber but it wasn't in the least rotten. She felt grateful to whoever who had chopped all this wood and brought it up, but she had no idea who it could be.

She sat in front of the stove with her outdoor clothes on and waited for the flat to warm up. All the time she could hear the sound of running water. It was gradually turning into ice. She could tell by the sound. It was water running under frosty vapour and starting to turn to translucent ice. It was running more and more sluggishly. She put more wood on the stove to cope with all the cold.

The damper was open and the fire roared in the stove. It flashed on the surfaces of the old copper pans. She started moving about the kitchen at her usual tasks. She didn't even think about what her hands were doing. Then it struck her that whoever had taken all this trouble for her, who had chopped wood exactly the right length to fit the kitchen stove and piled it in the wood box, wished her harm. She was absolutely certain of it. She examined one of the pieces of firewood. It could have come from under the plaster facing of the house. No, this wasn't being helpful. It was some sort of mockery. She was in the act of burning up her house.

Now she didn't know what to do. It was still cold. She shut the damper to make it burn more slowly. There was a smell she didn't like in the room. It felt as if a door down to the cellar had been left open. But of course anything of the sort was quite impossible. No cellar smells could find their way up here. She lived on the first floor and there was a door to the cellar down at the bottom of the stairwell. For quite some time she went about in the vague smell of stone cellar, trying to ignore it.

Then she opened the door to the room she rented out. It smelt stronger in there. But she couldn't see anything unusual. Everything was in its place. She stood surveying the scene for a long time. Finally she went over and opened the sitting-room door. A puff of cold wind blew around her legs and she felt her skirt flapping in the draught. There was a smell of something raw and musty. She took a step forward into the gloomy room and at the last minute clung fast to the door post behind her to keep herself from falling. The floor had given way. A great abyss yawned at her feet.

Her only thought was that this was impossible. She wanted to turn back and shut the door on it all but she stayed, unable to move. There was a hole right through the building down to the rough stone walls of the cellar. That was where the smell was coming from. Around the walls there were just a few things left in the room. The tiled stove was still in place. But the table had gone through. The chandelier hung by three cords, its veined alabaster bowl swinging over the great hole in the building. Pipes and cables had been broken off and rugs dangled over the jagged edges of what had once been the floor.

She balanced her way carefully back to the door. She wanted to get out, out of this destruction, so totally inexplicable. She had troubles enough already. In fact, looking back, she thought things had been quite tolerable until now. She had sat out there in the kitchen worrying about the cold and about burning the wood of the building on her stove. She wished herself back and sat down at the kitchen table, resting her forehead on the cold oilcloth. She tried to concentrate on willing everything to be as it had been a little while before: fire, building, angels, stones and the sound of running water.

Ebba Julin had got fat. When she needed to climb some stairs, she had to declare war on them. She would haul herself up by the banisters, stub her swollen foot in its black lace-up shoe on a step and then swear. If Cis was with her, she would follow behind, lamenting Ebba's lot. Oh dear oh dear, she would say.

This time, Ebba was doing battle with the stairs up to Tora Otter's flat all alone. At last she reached the top and stood puffing painfully by the table with the marble slab where Tora cut her sweets.

She knocked on the door once she'd got her breath back. No one answered. But Tora's galoshes were on the coconut mat by the kitchen door, so she was there. Ebba went in. The stove had gone out and the kitchen was cold. She went over to the bedroom door and looked in. It was empty in there of course, because Tora rented it out to a lady teacher. It was almost eleven on this Tuesday morning in February. She paused a moment to look at the teacher's things in the neat room. Then she opened the door to the sitting room.

Between the two bay windows was a sofa upholstered in brown shagreen and on it lay Tora. She seemed to be asleep. Her face was pale and a little trickle of saliva ran from her mouth down onto a black silk cushion she had put under her cheek. She's sick, thought Ebba. A watering can stood beside her and a duster lay on the arm of the sofa. Ebba went over and touched her.

'Are you all right?' she asked, and Tora gave a start. She sat up and ran her hand over her hair. She seemed confused.

'Bless my soul,' she said. 'You here?'

Ebba had been going to ask her again how she felt but was afraid it would seem an intrusion. It was bad enough having taken her by surprise.

'You seem a bit dazed,' was all she said. 'Shall we go out into the kitchen and light the stove?'

'Christ, has it gone out?' said Tora. 'What's the time?'

When she looked up and caught sight of the yellow-veined bowl of the alabaster lamp she put one hand over her eyes.

'Are you feeling dizzy?' asked Ebba.

'I felt so tired all of a sudden. Thought I'd have a rest and then I dropped off,' said Tora. 'Must've been dreaming.'

Ebba wasn't really an especially warm person. Her voice had a harsh, rough quality. People generally said she had a good sense of humour. Now she went across to get the crocheted rug from the rocking chair and put it over Tora. She felt rather embarrassed doing it but Tora didn't notice. She took hold of the edge of the rug and pulled it up to her chin.

'I only came up to show you what it looked like,' Ebba said.

'What what looked like?'

Tora's gaze travelled the length of the rag rug across the floor to the tiled stove. She still seemed to be freezing cold.

'The medal.'

'What?'

'The Red Cross medal,' said Ebba gruffly.

'Blow me, yes. Can I see?'

'I've got it on,' replied Ebba calmly. She unbuttoned her big, black plush coat and loosened her scarf. Her breast swelled, a mighty hill of beige-coloured silk. The medal was pinned a little to the left. It looked rather small.

'Well,' said Tora, 'it all went all right then? Your trip to Stockholm. Was it the King giving them out?'

'No, Prince Carl.'

'Well, he's royal too.'

'Yes, if he's not royal,' said Ebba hotly, 'then I am!'

'All right, I know,' said Tora. 'Was Ingeborg there too?'

'Oh yes.'

Ebba described Princess Ingeborg and her dress and then she described the prince, his long legs and slender hands, his rounded eyelids and the gemstones in his cravat.

'What did he say?'

'Well I think it sounded like congratulations - yes, I'm sure he said congratulations.'

Tora looked at the medal. Her eyes narrowed and wrinkled up at the corners.

'Oh no,' she said, 'you've taken the wrong medal.'

Ebba took hold of the little brass badge and pulled it away from the fabric of her blouse to try to see it.

'Don't be daft,' she said. 'I got it from Prince Carl, you know. He put it into my hand himself. Soon as I'd sat back down I pinned it on my blouse.'

'The medal says Hildur Johansson,' Tora said.

Ebba wrenched at her blouse and got the little safety pin undone. She didn't say anything once she had it in her hand because she had to hunt for her handbag and find her glasses.

'My eyes are good,' said Tora. 'It says Hildur Johansson on it, plain as a pikestaff. You've got the wrong medal.'

She seemed a bit more lively than before and sat up on the sofa while Ebba was putting on her glasses and reading the medal. For a moment it almost seemed as if Ebba's eyes were moist but it wasn't easy to tell because the whites were all cloudy and bloodshot.

'Come on, we'll go out and light the stove and have some coffee,' said Tora. 'You know they'll sort it out for you eventually.'

Ebba put down her glasses.

'Hildur Johansson!' she said. What an...'

'What?'

Their eyes met and Tora gave a snort.

'Arsehole of a prince,' Ebba said.

They went out and put on the coffee.

They had a few things to talk about. Hillevi Lindén, known to them as Cis, was coming up to her fiftieth birthday. They were buying her a present from the home furnishing stores. Four of them were going to club together. Apart from the Tora and Ebba, there were Tekla Johansson and Frida Eriksson.

'And Tekla thought the same as me,' said Ebba. 'We'll get a crystal vase.'

'Can't you think of anything else?' asked Tora. 'It's just more old clutter. You end up with cupboards full.'

'No, we'll stick to what we said,' answered Ebba sternly. They'd given Tora a crystal bowl five years ago, but she'd obviously forgotten about that for the time being.

Ebba had finished her coffee so she got up. She would have liked to ask Tora if she was feeling better but she felt awkward. People are pale in February, she thought. Tora's hand kept plucking at the cloth.

'Well I'll be going then,' said Ebba. 'Bye for now.'

It was dark in the kitchen with its window onto the courtyard. Outside, the daylight was gloomy and meagre. Even so, Tora didn't seem to be going to put a light on. Ebba took her time buttoning up her plush coat but still didn't really know if she should say anything else.

'Don't forget to feed the stove,' she said at the door and Tora looked at her in surprise.

Tora had been finding it difficult to sleep at night for quite some time. She had a bedtime drink of hot water and honey and found it easy enough to get to sleep in the evening, when she was tired. But then she woke up. Objects in the room gleamed coldly. She scarcely recognised her own alarm clock and the pot plants on the window sill looked stiff and strange. At first it had only happened towards morning, but now she sometimes woke up after only an hour. Her body ached. She couldn't find a position to give her any rest and relief. When she closed her smarting eyes and reached the oblivion of sleep, reality was ripped into meaningless shreds, with pictures that were sometimes cruel.

What's the point? What's the point, she lay there repeating to herself. But she didn't even know what she meant by her question. Trying to sleep? Seeing the pictures before her eyes, those shreds of life, cut into pieces?

She always seemed to be cold these days and she supposed it was because of being tired. Now she wasn't sleeping properly at nights, she sometimes had to lie down in the middle of the day and then she would fall asleep and have dreams. Then the stove would go out, like it had the time Ebba Julin had come round and it had got so cold in the flat. She felt permanently chilled.

She would go and see Dr Henkel, at any rate, and have her chest X-rayed. Not that she thought she had a spot on her lungs, but she'd go anyway. Sister Frideborg the welfare visitor said you ought to. When Tora got there she felt guilty, taking up a place other people needed. There were so many people there, coughing.

She didn't feel her usual self at all. When she heard the rattle of the plate as it slid across and felt the cold metal on her skin, her heart began to pound and she had to shut her eyes for a moment.

'Keep still!' said the nurse. 'Now hold your breath.'

She shut her eyes and heard steps receding. She saw the blue flash in the room even so, and when she opened her eyes in the half-light her mouth felt all dry. She would have liked to ask for a glass of water but didn't say anything because she couldn't trust her voice.

The doctor told her there were no spots on her lungs.

'Would anything else show?' she said.

'Anything else?'

'Yes,' said Tora. 'If I had a growth in my breast, say, would that show?'

'In your breast? You mean in one of your breasts?'

She swallowed and could feel that her top lip was all sweaty. So he wouldn't notice, she ran her finger over it. Henkel stood there with tufts of black hair in his nostrils, looking at her over his spectacles.

'Is there a lump?'

'No-oo, I don't really know,' Tora said. 'Sometimes I think I can feel something.'

'Come here.'

So she had to go up to him and undo her blouse and he palpated her breast with his cold fingers. It was embarrassing. She hadn't shown anyone her breasts for years. He smelt of tobacco and that made it so obvious he was a man even though he had a white coat and an absent-minded look behind his spectacles. Though now it wasn't absent-minded any longer.

'How long has this been here?'

He had found it. Hard to say how long she'd been aware of it. A

60

growth in her breast. It had been there and it hadn't. Pain? Well yes, but that was just her rheumatism. She'd stood in the market place for almost thirty years, in all weathers. It rubbed in one place if she was wearing a tight blouse. It had been a slight discomfort, that was all. A daily reminder. Though she hadn't thought about it much.

'Why didn't you get this looked at?'

What should she answer?

'We'll have to get it X-rayed. I'll write a referral.'

They were new words. Tumour. Referral and X-ray. She collected them in the bowl of her memory. And then: Radiology Clinic. She heard the word and she said it herself. Yet when she finally got to Stockholm and saw it inscribed in the plaster on the wall she was still surprised that it looked as it did.

She took the train up to Stockholm and the bus to the Radiology Clinic. There she had radiotherapy in a bare room. She lay on a narrow, oilcloth-covered bed feeling terrified of the great machine above her. She thought it would burn her, maybe destroy her deep inside.

Other people were handling her body now. Mostly they were young girls with warm, soft breasts under their apron bibs and blue dress material. They were kind and cheerful and took hold of her with no embarrassment. She felt as if she had become a little child again, an important child with a big body. Yes, their hands gave her a body.

It was a long time since she had given it a thought. Activity was what had bound together her days and hours: bustle and duties and worry about running out of time. Her body had been a tool of work and a means of locomotion.

Now she realised that it was her. Lying here idle, it was the hand

and not the grip of the hand that was real. Then she remembered other times when her body had seemed very real to her. She remembered the fear in her whole body when the pain of the first contraction went shooting through the nerves in the small of her back, the fear she would break. She could still feel that fear though she could no longer remember the pains. She could think that her nipple was wet with saliva, going cold. Her body was filled with memories of heaviness and pain and fear and rare delight.

This body in which she had lived for so long had been alien to her. Where had she been? So long since she had gone about in here. Not even the heartbeats were familiar to her. They frightened her when she heard them amplified by the night and the silence, resonating through a mattress. They were like footsteps echoing in a strange house.

Now she was obliged to move into her body. Slowly she became acquainted with its terror and secrets, little discomforts and fleeting urges.

I exist in the world by no other means. The buzzing in my left ear, the one I can't sleep on, is the most familiar of all sounds. And yet it's so long since I really heard it, because it's such a long time since it was new. My body has been living its own life for so long that growths and marks and ruptures have come without me noticing them. Now I stare at them as if they had appeared overnight and wonder whether they bode ill, whether they are symptoms of some still-hidden process inside me, where I am at my softest and most helpless.

Now came a time when it was easier to be in Stockholm than at home. Up at the Radiology Clinic it was quite natural to have a growth in your breast, that was why you were there. The girls were no less cheerful for that. None of them looked at her as if they were scared of catching what's inside a lump like that or scared of showing her their real faces, because they didn't have disgust, curiosity and sympathy all battling to get uppermost inside them.

She felt nothing but hatred and cold as she walked the streets at home these days. She preferred not to have visitors in her flat. She just wanted to be left in peace.

She had already been up to the Radiology Clinic three times before she was able to see the Professor. It was only a short conversation, even then. She would have to have an operation.

If she had at least been dressed. But there she sat in front of him on a stool, her dress and petticoat rolled down to her waist. She tried to pull them up while he was talking, with ice-cold fingers she tried to pull her dress over the breasts he was studying as objects unconnected with her body. Then she felt afraid the hateful word would come creeping over his lips, so she forestalled him with a breathless query:

'Can't it be taken out then?'

He looked up.

'Indeed it can,' he said. As I said, we'll operate. We'll remove the tumour.'

New words. There were growths, nodules, tumours, abscesses in her collecting bowl now.

She'd arranged for some help with the market stall without saying what was the matter. Tests, she had said and no one had asked again. She had an ordinary lump on her wrist and she had shown the professor that too, of course. It was just cartilage, he said. But at home she pretended the tests were for that.

Tekla Johansson and Linnea Holm normally helped out at the stall anyway. They stood there together now, while Tora was in Stockholm.

It was a Saturday at the very end of March. They had been very busy but now it had eased off for a while. They hadn't got round to sitting down on the cases behind the stall but were still standing watching for customers. There was a slight slope on the far side of the street and at the top stood a shop selling all sorts of cut-price goods and a barber's. Behind them, a tower of dark blue cloud vapour was building up. Within a few minutes, the air went the ash-grey colour of a solar eclipse and then a gust of air came scudding across the gravel of the square, followed by a squally blast that instantly lifted the canvas of cheesemonger Färman's stall and stretched it as taut as a square sail. The supports twisted sideways, the pegs came out and the pole came crashing down onto the cheesemonger's head. As he sat stunned on one of the packing cases behind his stall, the first fully-formed and almost hot raindrops fell on Tora's roof canvas, which was flapping wildly along with all the others in the market place. It looked like a fleet putting out to sea, an armada sailing to the sound of roaring canons and the muffled crack of grey sailcloth. There was a great flapping and rattling and Linnea and Tekla didn't notice the rain starting to fall straight into their boxes, preoccupied as they were by checking to see if the cheesemonger was all right.

But as they dabbed at the back of Färman's head with a wet handkerchief and looked for blood on the lard-white scalp beneath his black hair, the canvas had been forced back by the wind and was no longer flapping. The stall was open to the sky, the grey fabric was pressed back taut and the rain poured down into the boxes of sweets, quickly filling them.

They realised that several of the market stalls had gone over; grey canvas had been ripped where it was mended or worn and people were trying to salvage their wrecked stalls while cabbages rolled underfoot and paper bags whirled about before plastering themselves soddenly onto a lamp post or the hindquarters of a horse. For now the horses too were coming from somewhere; heads bent against the rain, bowed deep under their heavy collars and with water cascading down the fringes of their hooves, they struggled up with the open-sided carts so people could begin to load.

Tekla and Linnea abandoned the cheesemonger, who at any rate hadn't been knocked out, though he was dazed. They tried to salvage the roof canvas before their stall went over too. As they pulled out the pegs that held the supports in place, the rain ran straight down their arms and they were soaked to the skin.

Here was Charlie Bira at last. He loomed up, high on the driver's seat, out of the horizontal rain that turned grey and muddy as it bounced off the ground. He started wrenching down poles and canvas while they packed boxes, first emptying out the water as best they could. Most of the contents was dissolving and the water was pink with caramel colouring. They hadn't managed to get a single lid on. Tekla nearly wept when she saw the state of the cashbox, but Linnea resolutely held a tin lid over it and drained the water off the notes and coins as if it were a saucepan of boiled potatoes.

The worst thing was that the two big packing cases had to have everything stowed away in them very skilfully if there was to be room for it all and Tekla couldn't remember how it went. Tora always took charge when they were packing up. Charlie Bira with his drayman's hands and snuff-stained chin would certainly never have been allowed anywhere near the boxes of sweets. Now he was hurling in boxes that landed on end and there wasn't room for the half of it. All the time the rain was pouring down in a solid wall. But the storm was over and the sharp thunderclaps and white flashes had stopped.

In the end Charlie Bira hurled boxes and tins straight onto the cart, put the sheet of canvas over the lot and jumped up himself. He lashed the horse's backs with the reins and they were off, jolting along the disintegrating street. Tekla and Linnea pulled their hats as far down over their eyes as they could and sat hunched on the back of the cart as the horse, blinded by the rain, waded home to Store Street.

Back at Tora's they didn't bother putting anything away in the shed except the tent poles, trestles and counter top. Charlie helped them get the rest of it up into the kitchen. They took the key out from under the coconut mat and lit the stove to get it warm and help dry out as much as possible. They draped the canvas over the banisters, because if it stayed crumpled up in a wet bundle it would go mouldy. They could hear that the rain had stopped. It was brightening up outside and there was the sound of running water in the gutters.

They set to work drying the tins and boxes and seeing whether any of the sweets could be salvaged. Everything that didn't look as though it could be dried out got scraped onto the marble slab on the landing. Not that it could be used, but they didn't dare throw it straight into the slop pail, it didn't feel right. Soon there was a collection of melting, disintegrating sticks of fruit jelly, cherry softies that had turned back into sugary slush and a gooey red mass of burnt almonds. They laid sticky lollipops of peppermint rock to dry in rows on baking sheets and picked out the delicate marzipan shapes one by one and inspected them before discarding the remains of little peapods, yellow mushrooms, strawberries, pears, new potatoes dusted with cocoa powder. They were still at it when Tora came.

They had forgotten the Stockholm train. The time had flown by. She stood at the bottom of the stairs and stared at the wet canvas.

Then she came up and stood observing their work. The sticky mass on the marble slab startled her.

She went slowly into the kitchen and saw the tins propped up around the stove and the settee on which there was an untidy pile of boxes whose sugary contents they had not yet had time to sort through. The weights from the scales lay scattered on the floor.

They noticed she was pale and perspiring, as if the walk from the station had been an effort. She listened in silence to their account. Absently, ashen-faced, she pushed aside a cardboard box and sat down on the settee.

'Well, you could at least've tried to get the lids on.'

She looked as if she would have liked to lie down but there was no room. Several of the glass lids of the colourful tin boxes had got smashed. They had been in a rush and Charlie Bira was heavy-handed.

'Well,' she said. 'So this is the way you pack up?'

They said nothing.

'You could've got the lids on when it started raining. Were you standing gossiping?'

'I told you, we had to see if Mr Färman was all right,' Linnea said. She took no notice of their explanation.

'Thirty years I've been doing the market and this has never happened before. But it's all the same to me. You'd better go now.'

There was silence in the kitchen and she shut her eyes.

'But we ought to clear up first,' said Tekla.

'No, just be off.'

At that, Linnea lost her temper. She hadn't straightened her back since three o'clock when the storm blew up and now it was five thirty.

'All right, no need to treat us like children,' she said. 'We did what we could.'

'I can see that,' said Tora and her voice was full of scorn. 'I should have known to expect no better from the likes of you.'

She regarded the waterlogged boxes with their sticky contents and poked at the marzipan shapes Tekla had laid out on a tray, six little pieces in a row.

'Damn you, Tora, this time you've gone too far!' said Linnea, slamming the lid onto a box and starting to untie her wet apron. 'What makes you think you can treat other people like this? Have you ever thought about that, Tora Otter? Eh?'

'Just go,' said Tora, closing her eyes.

'Oh no, I'm going to tidy up here. I'm not leaving the place like this, whatever you say. I'm not a child!'

Then Tora shouted at them.

'Go! Get out! D'you hear? The nerve of you!'

She started to sob and brought her fist down on a lid so hard that the glass broke.

'Go, I say. Can't you leave me in peace in my own kitchen? Leave me alone, I say. Look at all this stuff you've ruined! You've not a clue how much this all costs. Don't you realise it's work and that costs money, eh? All my stock's ruined. When d'you think I'm going to be able to make a new lot of sweets? Not that it's any of your business. Get out! Get out I say!'

Tekla tried to get out of her wet apron but its long strings had tightened into a hard knot. She gave a sob. Linnea was as white as chalk and said nothing.

'I don't ever want your help again, d'you hear!' shouted Tora. And don't go calling it help either, you get paid. Don't you?'

She shouted at Tekla who was halfway out of the door:

'Answer me! Haven't you always got paid? What've you ever done for me that you didn't get paid for? And good money as well! But I don't need you! I'm never asking you for anything again - do you hear? Not on your life. Come hell or high water. Get out of here!'

And she drove Linnea out, shoving her with hard hands. Tekla was already well down the stairs. Linnea stayed outside the shut door and tried to hear what was happening in the kitchen. It was deadly silent. After a long while came the sound of raking and rummaging as if Tora were trying to clear up the boxes. Then it all went quiet again and they heard her start to cry with awful, gulping breaths.

'Oh my God,' whispered Tekla. 'Shouldn't we go in and try talking her round?'

'No,' said Linnea, still looking white. 'Let her be. You heard what she said, and no one's paying us to go in and get our heads bitten off.' So they went, Tekla still in two minds all the way out to the street, stepping gingerly in her leaking galoshes. Linnea was furious; she walked fast.

Now she was alone. She moved a few tins and covers at random, got the sticky residue on her fingers and tried to wipe it off on a sackcloth towel, feeling nauseous. It was only gooey sugar, dyed red with caramel colouring, but it made her feel sick.

Not much got done. She was so tired that she had to lie down for a bit and then she fell asleep on the settee she had cleared. Bad dreams soon woke her again and she padded about in her stockinged feet, trying to tidy up a bit. It was late in the evening now, almost night. She felt strange. Was it the radiation treatment?

She ought to get changed, have a wash. She drank a little water and a while later a bit of cold coffee. So they found time to make coffee, did they? She felt peculiar and decided she might be hungry. In the pantry there were a couple of bits of batter pudding with ham, which she picked up in her fingers and ate cold. After a while they gave her stomach ache.

She didn't get as far with the mess in the kitchen as she'd hoped. She dropped off to sleep before midnight and slept uneasily for a few hours. Then she was up, tugging at the wet canvas sheet again, beside herself with weariness and irritation. It fell to the ground. Bugger it, she said to herself. It's so heavy and disgusting. It'll go mouldy if I leave it like that. Well, go mouldy then. See if I care.

She didn't even get it all finished on Sunday, though she stayed in all day. As she got the boxes clean, she just piled them in the hall. She took lots of rests, lying on the settee with a shawl over her. I'm tired of it all, she thought. Tired of myself too.

Her fatigue was standing over there by the door. Standing waiting for dusk, when it was time to come shuffling out.

Rubbish. There's no big, heavy body in the dark. It's just the way you feel when something's too much for you. It's the furred coating on your tongue, the bitter taste in your mouth. It's the sluggishness, the constipation of your life forces. The grey light.

She'd known a painter called the Cock. He got lead poisoning and then died. But before he died he grew heavy and tired.

Fatigue is when time stands still. Though you were in such a hurry before and didn't know how you could ever get it all done. Now the whole lot has capsized into the pool of time and a film is forming on top of it. Weariness is when you know it all. When everything that happens merely confirms what you already knew.

Tora, now you know. You who had such a healthy body. It had been something to be proud of too! It had been an absolute necessity. You could never have managed otherwise.

But you've grown so tired. You can't manage any longer even though you want to and you've made your mind up. Things don't get done. And it doesn't matter. You're the only one affected now. You're on your own and the boys are grown up.

If they had just left her in peace. Even on Sunday there were several knocks at the kitchen door, but she didn't answer and kept quite still. She was obliged to go out and move the canvas sheet so people wouldn't ask questions. The teacher who rented one of Tora's rooms returned. She looked around the messy landing as she went in and through the sitting room with her little suitcase. Every weekend she went to visit her parents, not returning until four o'clock on Sunday, when the bus got in.

That evening Tora finished off, carrying boxes and cartons across the yard in the dark and piling them in the shed, where there was a sweet smell of confectionery and rotting wood. Then she just wanted to be left in peace. It was still a few days until she had to go to Stockholm for the operation. But the others wouldn't let her alone. She took no notice of the knocking but even so, one afternoon, Fredrik and Jenny were standing there. They had come in with the teacher.

They didn't ask many questions and she tried to avoid looking at their faces. She said she was going to have an operation but without mentioning the tumour in her breast. She was afraid she would frighten them and make them back off and feel sorry for her at the same time. Fear might create a vacuum around her. She showed Fredrik and Jenny the lump on her wrist the professor had said she needn't worry about. She let them think what they liked. It wasn't for her to say. It would have been better if they had left her in peace.

There was no sign of Linnea and Tekla, thank heavens. News must have got round that she'd fallen out with them, because Ebba didn't get come round either. Cis and Frida must have heard what had happened, of course, but they were too scared to come and see her.

Well, let them be then. They needn't bother. I want to be on my own, anyway. She started putting things in order and sorting out drawers and cupboards, because she wanted everything tidy at home before the operation. Then it was Sunday and she was supposed to go up to the grave. She generally went there every Sunday afternoon. But she hadn't the energy now. She would wait until evening.

Jenny came up and said people had been asking after her at the market on Saturday.

'We'll do the market stall for you next Saturday, Tekla and I,' she said.

'I've nothing to sell there,' replied Tora, 'so you can save yourselves the trouble. The whole lot got spoilt in the rain.'

She hadn't made any new sweets. Jenny looked down and after a while she went. Dusk came before Tora had been up to the grave and then it was dark.

On the Monday morning it was drizzling and windy so there was no risk people would be going up to the cemetery. That made her decide to go. She had to make sure it looked nice and tidy. Clear away the fir twigs and see whether the pearl hyacinths had started peeping through. On the way there, she stopped outside her old café. It was called the Cosy Corner now. There were flower-sprigged curtains at the window and a coffee pot on a sign. Oh well, if they thought that would make it more popular. It was all the same to her. They were welcome to get rich on the café if they wanted to.

The building next door to it had been demolished and they were in the process of digging the foundations for something new and much larger. It was apparently going to have a full-size basement, because the excavation was deep and they had been blasting. The rainwater was collecting down there in mud-yellow puddles that glistened without reflecting anything.

She trudged the length of Vanstorp Way, up to the cemetery,

carrying a little bag with a pair of scissors and some sticks because she was going to prune the rose and perhaps give it a bit of support. As she stood looking at the headstone paid for by F. A. Otter's colleagues on the railway, it struck her that the trees all around had grown a lot in the course of those almost thirty years. She remembered a tasteless joke. Someone had said they got plenty of fertiliser up here. It was horrid to say that sort of thing to someone who had a relation lying under one of the well-raked little mounds. And surely they almost all had. Even so, she couldn't put it out of her mind like she usually did. She wondered what vulgar person it had been who said it, but couldn't remember.

Then she thought of the ground she had just seen excavated down on the building site in Hovlunda Road. The yellow subsoil had been gleaming in the fine rain. The layer of soil and roots from the old garden they had dug up was so thin.

Whoever it was who had said it, they'd been wrong. The roots of the trees didn't go that deep. So the person had been wrong. It's only subsoil under here and nothing grows there. However hard you try, you can never become nourishment for a tree.

Nothing happens down there. Nothing at all. Nothing, nothing happens even if a hundred years go by. And she didn't know whether she felt terrified or relieved. You ought not to think about things like that. But thoughts occur to you at a graveside. If your beloved lay there. Is still lying there. *What* is it that's lying there? Thoughts like that.

She hadn't been alone up here since the very early days and she was used to chatting to the others, not thinking, when she was up here raking. Drips were falling from the black branches of the trees and the smell of dog urine lingered round the stones. Then the thought came to her that it had been a long time since she'd experienced grief as she stood here before the stone bearing F. A.

Otter's name. Now she sometimes even felt a sort of ill will towards him, the young man who would never change.

Life had worn her out and now her body was failing her. But nothing had happened to *him*. He was at rest down there in the subsoil, out of time's reach.

In some ways you were a real beast, she thought. No, that's not fair. She wanted to be fair even though she was tired and fed up. You might have felt like treating me in a beastly way if you'd dared. I suppose being kind can sometimes be just - well, almost the same as being weak.

He was always there and never more than twenty-eight years old. If she ever visualised his face, his eyes were always looking past her.

She was to have her operation on Tuesday and went to Stockholm on the Monday to be admitted to the hospital. But the operation had to be postponed for a day because they hadn't done all the tests, which meant she'd had an enema for nothing. It made her wearier still. She lay blinking in her bed because her eyes were constantly smarting.

She found the glare from the ceiling lamp so bright. It was in the middle of the ward. There were eight women lying there. The one on her right wanted to talk but Tora wasn't so keen. To her left was someone who smelt of ether. She wasn't awake much. Tora looked at her most. She didn't moan or groan at all.

She hadn't taken much with her because she wasn't sure what you were allowed to have in your locker. Her clock of course. A bag of burnt almonds that had survived the disaster. She planned to offer them round. And then she had packed a book bound in black oilcloth in which she'd jotted various things down over the years. She'd noted when the boys were ill. That was to help her remember which childhood diseases they'd had. Before that there had only been a few sweet recipes in the book. Then she decided it would be tasteless to put recipes alongside details of when Fredrik and Adam had measles and German measles. So after that she had mainly written little things that were useful to remember. There was a good preparation for cleaning sinks, oxalic acid and chalk. There were the proportions for alum and powdered dye to soak wool in. Whenever she'd gone away she'd kept a record of the weather and the sights they'd seen. Stockholm was on the list, so were Gripsholm and Mårbacka.

She didn't really know what she was going to put in the book now, but she wetted the tip of her indelible pencil and wrote that she was ill and going to have an operation. And she wrote that day's date. Then she lay thinking or pretending to sleep for the rest of the afternoon.

When they postponed the operation, she took it as a bad omen. The Tuesday morning passed quickly because they took her for a heart X-ray and a lung X-ray and then she had to have another enema. She wasn't allowed anything to eat either, so now she'd been fasting for two days and nights. She drank a little now and then and didn't miss the food. But her head had started to ache. In the afternoon she mostly lay pretending to be asleep so the woman in the next bed wouldn't ask her anything. But as she lay there she was worrying about whether to write anything else in her book. The next morning when they'd woken her at six and she'd no idea how long she would have to wait, she got it out again and wetted the short, stubby pencil again. She wrote:

'They're going to take a lump out of my breast.'

It had struck her that she'd let Jenny and Fredrik think it was her wrist that was being operated on. What if they never found out, she thought. You never know how much doctors will tell people.

She lay for a long while, pencil in hand, listening to the big doors slamming out in the corridor. The window panes shivered and the metal bedpans clanged against each other. The nurses spoke in low voices and usually looked stern. But the auxiliaries didn't drop their voices unless there was a nurse nearby. The place echoed like a huge industrial shop floor.

'It will be all right,' she wrote. 'I hope my time here goes quickly. I'm lying here trying to read the newspaper. I shall read until they come to fetch me.'

She hadn't started reading yet, of course. But she closed her book and put it with the pencil in the drawer. She must remember to put the clock away too before they wheeled her out. But for now she wanted to have it beside her and see the hands reaching eight and then half past. They gave her an injection in the thigh. The nurse didn't say anything about what time it would be. But she told Tora to take out her teeth and had brought a glass for her to put them in. As soon as she had gone, Tora got out two newspapers she'd brought with her from home. They were from Friday and Saturday, unread. She began reading them from the beginning and her forearms shook violently as she lay on her back, turning the pages. At last she had to shift over to a trolley they brought in, and they manoeuvred her as if she were unable to do it for herself. They wheeled her, two auxiliaries who only spoke to each other, along the long corridor with people standing on both sides, looking at her face. At last they stopped in front of a pair of huge, white painted steel doors. Then her heart began to pound so violently it hurt her chest and she tried to sit up. But they told her to lie down so she wouldn't fall off the narrow trolley as it went along.

Perhaps my heart's not so strong, she thought. It had never pounded this way before. The palms of her hands went hot and prickly and she could think of nothing but her heart as they wheeled her into the operating theatre. It was still beating fiercely, fit to burst, and her lips felt stiff. She saw a large group of people in there and instruments set out on towels. Then she shut her eyes so as not to see any more and tried to make her heartbeat calm down. As she smelt the ether she felt panic grip her.

'Count to ten,' said a voice that had spoken to her before, though she hadn't been able to make out the words. Her tongue stuck to the roof of her mouth. Someone took her arm and straightened it out. She could sense the white all around her, although her eyes were closed.

She woke up on the ward. Saw folds of material, buff-coloured. Eventually, the second or third time she came to, she realised it was a screen they had put in front of her bed. By the afternoon she could see large clouds in the sky instead but it was too tiring to look out of the window for long. They must have moved the screen a bit because they could hardly have turned her over. She couldn't lie on her left side, it was starting to hurt.

That night she slept, dreaming she had been assaulted, run over. Someone was whimpering like a puppy, and a nurse with a veil with a red cross on it came and gave her an injection in her much-punctured thigh.

'Do try to be quiet,' she said. 'The injection will start to work soon. The other patients are trying to sleep.'

She woke up and her breast and arm were very painful. Why does my arm hurt so much? she thought.

Strangely enough, Jenny was sitting there when she opened her eyes. She didn't say a thing about it not being Tora's wrist that had been operated on. She asked how she was feeling. But then Tora had to throw up in an enamel bowl and Jenny held her head and made sure the bowl didn't tip off the bed. She had her hat and coat on and looked nervous whenever the nurses went past outside in the corridor.

'You'll soon be up and about again, you know,' she said softly.

'You came all this way?' said Tora.

But she was too tired to ask any more questions.

'Tekla and I are going to do the market stall for you,' said Jenny suddenly, looking a bit more cheerful. 'Linnea doesn't want to. She's sulking, I suppose.'

'But there's nothing to sell. Everything was ruined.'

'Oh, Fredrik's making some more. He knows how.'

That made Tora almost smile.

'He can, you know, think how often he's helped you! He'll manage. He's doing it in the evenings.'

Jenny suddenly took hold of her hand and held it for a moment.

'It'll be all right,' she said. You'll soon be home again and standing in the square yourself. Adam sends his love too. And he gave me this for you.'

It was difficult for her to lift her head so Jenny took a big box of chocolates from the bedside locker and held it where she could see. It was from Anker's. There was a mauve silk ribbon and bow diagonally round it. It was so like him. Chocolate for *her*. And from Anker's. She looked into Jenny's eyes and saw she too was trying not to laugh.

'You could always use the bow to trim a hat,' she said with a little giggle.

Tora closed her eyes for a moment.

'Is the pain bad? Can you move your arm?'

So she did know, after all. Tora felt suddenly ashamed.

The day after, when Jenny had gone back home, the Professor came in. In his wake came the whole flock of white coats, and the sister who always checked everything in the ward before the rounds stood there holding a book open for him. He reminded Tora of a vicar.

There were no detectable odours in the room now; it was freshly aired and all the bowls and bedpans had been taken out to a sluice room. The patients lay there between taut, starched sheets, listening attentively to what the Professor mumbled at each bedside. The nurses in their stiff caps with a black velvet band leant forward occasionally to draw aside a sheet, so he could see the body underneath.

The crowd was advancing on her, their clothes rustling. There was a bell with a yellow, bone press-button fastened on her bedspread so she could reach it and without realising what she was doing, she fingered it, and it rang out in the corridor. The sister with the book gave a nod and one of the younger ones went out into the corridor. Later, Tora worked out that it was to stop the nurse who would be coming to answer the bell. None of the auxiliaries were allowed to come in or be visible in the corridor while the rounds were in progress. She also realised they all thought she had made a fool of herself.

Then the Professor told her they had removed her left breast and the lymph glands in her armpit.

She couldn't take it in at first. She lay there all afternoon, hearing his words inside her but thinking there must be some sort of mistake. Maybe he'd got her mixed up with someone else. Then she thought about the bell and their faces when she rang it. There was no continuity to her thoughts.

In the evening, she asked the Red Cross sister if they had really taken her whole breast away. She said they had.

'But why didn't they tell me?' Tora asked.

'So you think they should have asked you first?' said the nurse with a severe, sneering smile.

Tora was afraid of her. She hadn't felt afraid of anybody for as long as she could remember. This one had such a strange, protruding top lip and fixed, pale blue eyes under blonde eyebrows. Her eyelashes were fair too, almost white. You couldn't see much of her hair.

We forget, as we go about our daily business among ordinary people who are kind and careless and occasionally tiresome, hurting others with their thoughtlessness and egoism as we all do, that dangerous, evil people do exist. She felt she could have used that insight when she was setting off on this long journey for her operation and it frightened her to think how easily we forget things that are important to know, things that could save your life.

It turned out that the woman in the next bed, the one behind the draped folds of yellow cloth, had heard everything. She started talking to Tora. She told her you couldn't take a lump out of a breast without removing the whole thing. The tumour had long roots, she said, and you had to cut them off and pull them out.

'They go right up into your armpit,' she said. 'That's why they cut it all out. So it's a good thing they've done it. You should be glad, really.'

They carried on talking. She couldn't see the woman's face and it was just as well. Tora could tell from the way she spoke that she was from Småland. She had had a stomach operation, she said. She wasn't allowed up yet, but she didn't feel too bad. Then she described how she'd been in pain with it ever since Christmas, with diarrhoea all the time. By the evening, Tora knew she was a crofter's wife and worried about being away too long. Her children were called Olof and Gertrud. Tora told her the boys' names and said yes, it was her daughter-in-law who had come the day before.

'She looked smart,' said the woman from Småland. 'And such a nice hat.'

Tora had never thought about whether Jenny looked smart.

'Have they got children?'

'No, I don't know if they can have any.'

So here she was, aching where she had been cut, with pain right up under her arm. She was telling an eager voice with a Småland accent that she could hear from behind the yellowish, pleated screen things that she didn't usually talk about. She said she'd been worried about the lump in her breast, in case it was anything serious. She told her about the rain storm on market day and the ruined sweets.

'I gave them a real piece of my mind,' she said.

'Oh dear, oh dear,' said the woman.

Tora tried to tell from her tone of voice what she was thinking.

Just before they went to sleep that night, the woman said something remarkable. The lights had been off for some time and they had to whisper. But there were whispers coming from several other parts of the huge, bare ward and light from the night sky of springtime fell on them through the tall windows.

'Don't be too upset about losing your breast,' she whispered. 'You should be grateful. Even though it seems hard.'

'It doesn't matter to me,' Tora tried to whisper back. Her voice came out squeaky. 'I'm an old woman, after all. On my own.'

'Ah well,' said the low voice with its distinctive Småland 'r's. 'You may be right, you may be right.'

What a curious person, thought Tora. She knows so much about me already. But we'll never meet again.

The next morning they were both embarrassed when the nurses moved the screen and folded it away.

'Well, I suppose we should say hello properly,' said the woman in the bed, in the same voice she'd had during the night, when the light had cast white rectangles from the windows onto the blue dark of the room. Now the sun was shining, even on the beds by the farthest wall. They couldn't shake hands because Tora was lying with her left side facing the woman.

'I'm Signe Ekström.'

Tora mumbled that she was Mrs Otter. Perhaps the other woman couldn't hear.

'Now Småland, that's a place I'd like to go,' she said. 'They say it's beautiful there.'

She remembered the burnt almonds she'd brought and decided to give them to the woman as soon as she could get a nurse to open the bedside locker for her.

Now she was at home again. She could move her arm, though it pulled of course. She'd had a look at the scar: black surgical clips in a long curve. It looked like a mouth, grinning with its lips pulled back. The edges of the actual incision were thin, almost black. She couldn't really visualise how she must look without her left breast. She had only peeped under the bandage, not seen her top half as a whole.

April with April light. For a while, glimpses of the sun in a cold blue sky. Then suddenly it would cloud over and rain or spit for a bit. It was just the way it should be. It annoyed her to see dogs coming into the courtyard and peeing on the brown tufts of perennials in the border. It smelt bad enough anyway when the snow had just melted.

Jenny and Tekla (were going to do the market stall for her and that was all right. But she didn't want to see anybody. She'd have to thank them. She couldn't pay Jenny anything, either, so she'd have to think of something to give her. It was so hard to bear them being there, running around all eager and chatty. All she wanted was to be left in peace. She would often go and lie down on the sofa in the sitting-room although it was cold in there, lie down quietly and hope they would think she was) out when she didn't respond to their knock. She didn't know what to say to them.

You were used to talking and moving. You knew how to do it right. Then suddenly you didn't know any more. You had to plan every sentence before you said it. You couldn't even go and put coffee on for somebody without wondering how you'd just been behaving, what you had really said. Whether or not you were friendly. How much you showed.

Did they know she had one breast missing? Well, she wasn't going to say anything. It wasn't anybody's business. And anyway, she was an old woman. And all on her own, so no one need see it.

Blast, she seemed to feel like crying. But it didn't help so there was no point. It must be because she was tired. You weren't yourself after an operation.

A few weeks later she really was feeling well enough to make a batch of sweets. Not peppermint rock though, because that took a good kneading and then you had to throw it over the hook on the landing wall. She couldn't do that, with her arm. She could make up some cherry softie mix though, and cut it into pieces.

But she didn't do it. She let day after day go by. It seemed so pointless.

Tomorrow I'll do the cherry softies, she thought. It's just a matter of making your mind up. I'll go to bed in good time this evening and get up early tomorrow and make a batch. Everything will be back to normal. Mum's always up with the lark, Adam used to say. This little episode wasn't going to switch off her whole life. And anyway, the curtains needed changing.

She went to bed early, determined that the next day would be totally different. It was a Tuesday. When she got up in the morning, she hadn't had much sleep. She felt as if the very word Tuesday had an unpleasant, unreal taste to it. In fact, as if all this was part of her: the grey light, the constant grey light and the sound of motor cars and horse-drawn carts from the street, the clatter of tin and the distant sound of dogs barking. Damn and blast, she said to herself. Why is it all so vivid to me?

She started weighing out sugar but lost count of the number of scoops and stopped short. She ought to pour it all back into the sugar sack and start again. But she hadn't the energy.

Then she was seized by an irrational sense of dread. For no particular reason. But it was as if what she wanted no longer counted for anything. It was like being scared of somebody who was standing outside the door on the draughty landing, deciding everything she was to do and say without uttering a word.

I didn't want them to operate! But what good did that do? Yet it was still the only thing that mattered, wasn't it: the fact that you wanted something? Just this one day she would take it easy. Then she would begin in earnest. She would doze away one more afternoon on the sitting-room sofa and then find it hard to sleep at night.

Everything was going to be all right now. The lump was gone. Everything was sorted out as well as it could be. She had her flat, here in this building. She was lucky to have the shed. No rats where she kept the sweets. And, good, big dustbins she shared with the shop next door. The arbour. She stood thinking about the green swing in the arbour while she heated some milk for herself. It was a big, wooden swing where you could sit facing each other. There was room for the whole whist gang in that big swing, Tekla and Ebba and Cis and her. She'd make sure to invite Frida for coffee out there as soon as the warm, sunny weather came. When the lilacs were out. I might even have grandchildren, she thought. The Janssons in the flat downstairs sometimes sat in the swing with their grandchild and the little boy fed the squirrels with rusks.

Nothing was too insignificant as her thoughts circled round everything she had to be grateful for, not even the balcony facing into the yard. It was such a good place to put your saucepans to cool. Yes, this was a good building to live in and when she was in it she was at peace. She had no particular expectations of what was outside. Frida Eriksson's Konrad had said society was a heart pulsating with people's thoughts and deeds. Things like that meant nothing to her. She remembered it because it had actually originated from Ebon Johansson whom she'd known when she was young. She had thought he was talking about love.

She wasn't the kind of person who saw a heart when she heard the word society. She saw a local government office where you went, dragging your feet, to fulfil your obligations and she certainly expected nothing back from it. Here in the Angel House was where she lived her real life; from here she was occasionally obliged to emerge to earn some money. It was a struggle and a slog here in the world and even at the market there was competition. Some old woman selling sweets had moved in from Vanstorp and you could see from her fruit jellies and cherry softies that she was filthy. Tora couldn't stand there and point it out, either. You just had to hope people would notice the cat hairs.

No, in here she was fine. The children came to see her. Things had gone well for them. Fredrik and Jenny were good, decent people. There was nothing wrong with Adam either, really. Even if his money did burn a hole in his pocket and he had rather too many girlfriends. But they were good boys, both of them. They didn't drink. At any rate, no more than most people.

There was nothing to be scared of. Seven hundred kronor in the bank. If anything were to happen. And she was in the health insurance scheme. But still this fear and this feeling of being sick of it all. Where's it come from, she wondered, half asleep. How was it different before? She knew, really. There can always be some little tumour in your body, hidden, enclosed in a cyst. There's so much death in the world. Having harboured her little share of it shouldn't weigh so heavily on her. It had been cut out, after all.

But the question was: had the tumour already spread? Was death creeping through her body even now? Reason told her it had been doing that all along. Death is there from the start like the eye of a bird deep inside the new-born body's curtains of blood and dark, sharp and blinking, a little node of certainty and destiny. But somehow you are unaware of it. Until suddenly you find out, as clearly and unambiguously as if the district council sent you a notice in a brown envelope.

You. You are really going to die. Everyone else seems to have known - that you are going to die, that they are going to die, that Charlie Bira's horse is going to the knacker's and that everyone who's died really is dead. But as for you, you knew nothing about it. How else can you explain the fact that the realisation hit you so hard they could have knocked you down with a feather? Now you really are going to die.

Maybe not this year, not next year. Maybe not even ten years from now. But die you will. Your body will go pale and mottled. Then it will disintegrate and it will be no different from a dead dog rotting under a snowdrift in the spring. The worst of it is that everybody seemed to know - except you. Now Tora, it's your turn to die.

And at the very moment you grasp the fact, you start to feel sick of life. It certainly is strange. Shouldn't you be living all the more intensely and carefully now? Shouldn't you be able to see more clearly? Things you may never really have seen before: the clouds of pollen round the hazel catkins, how deep the shine is on the copper pot when you burnish it, the rounded shape of that loaf under the cloth, how strong your neck still is. But you see none of it. The lead poisoning of being sick of life filters through your system, makes your gaze heavy and weak. Everything loses focus.

You think you've behaved yourself. Conducted your life well enough. You didn't deserve to be punished like this. You've done your bit as well as you could. The boys. You let Fredrik get himself an education though times were hard and so many were unemployed. Just because he wanted to. You certainly did your bit. Behaved as you should. Were never a burden to anybody. Always worked. And now this happens to you.

It was dawn. The smooth leaves of the wax plant were shining. The air was cold and the smell of ashes from the stove distressing. It's just awful. You never imagined it could be like this. You wandered round, up in the cemetery, raking and tidying. But you simply didn't ever think - well, later of course. Much, much later. When you're old. But not now. Though the boys are big now, with their own lives. It could be worse. If they'd been little and this had happened. A couple of poor little lads with no mother.

She started sobbing, as if it were really true that the boys were little and would have to get along without her. She touched her cheeks and was scared and startled. Was she crying? It was as if there was blood on her cheeks, warm and salty in the cold air. Her feet were getting cold on the floor but it felt as if they belonged to someone else. She had knocked over a white mug of milk that had gone cold without her noticing. When? It was incredible.

Crying was no good. Giving up. Then she started thinking about the two little boys again, the poor little children. Their soft faces, small hands. Back then - all that time ago. And she started sobbing so violently that it racked her body and she was afraid of being torn loose, tugged from her moorings by the crying.

It wasn't only them, all that time ago, the two little boys she could see as clearly as if they were in the room at her side. The young woman was there too, when her husband died. She thought she could see herself but only in fragments, in glimpses of skin. The rosy nipples. She remembered plainly: he sometimes felt them with his fingers. On those rare occasions when he overcame his shame. She gave a cry and felt herself land on the floor. Reality: the cold cork matting against her forehead.

Since then, everything had been dead like this. Everything went cold. Work. Getting up. Having the will to do it. An effort of will, every day. No more getting up because you wanted to And he was rotting up there. His slim hands, the soft hairs on his chest, the delicate feet with their curving arches and thin toenails. No, never again since he died and all that was destroyed had she got up and begun a new day with enthusiasm. But she hadn't realised. She had thought this was living. Work. Will.

She cried out again without being able to stop herself and started to crawl towards the bed, feeling on the chair beside it for a piece of clothing. She could feel that it was something rough and stuffed it into her mouth, clenched her teeth shut over the wail.

I'm that young person over at Chapel Street. And I'm bleeding! He doesn't exist. He isn't anywhere any longer. He's dead. What's it like being dead? God - it's sickening, revolting! It's stench and decay. Being dead is a stiff, stinking, grimacing thing. Lips drawn back, cut up, split open. The smile smashed, the warm look, the trust.

The little boys have already started on death. They have no defences. You can't tuck them in against death, nourish them, warm them. They will go cold, their eyes glazed.

The little boys, she could see them before her quite plainly. The way Adam's little hand with the dimples below the first finger joint closed round her index finger, the dribble from his damp mouth, Fredrik's way of putting his head in her lap, a bristly, short-cropped head with a warm crown, his way of sighing as if he already had troubles. What troubles can you have, little man? The children's faces, those open flowers, will perish in death, go pale and stiff, tainted and mottled and disintegrating. The soft breasts will perish, one has already been cut off and thrown in a pail. Death has begun to suffocate me. It's a coating on my skin, a stench in my nostrils, a nasty taste in my mouth.

Slowly the hours passed. She had come through the night fully conscious and now it was light. She lay on the bed, mind empty of thoughts, as the everyday sounds began to come up from the street. She felt tired and flushed through, like a gutted fish, an opened belly without intestines, rinsed and scoured. Finally morning was here and with it the realisation that her life would never be the same again, that there was too much fear.

Ebba was coming up. She could hear her uneven tread on the stairs and the groan that escaped her each time she heaved herself up another step. Tora went silently through the teacher's empty room and lay down in the sitting room. Ebba was knocking. She was still breathing heavily and puffing. That Ebba, she's like a big cow, Tora thought. She suddenly felt like being cruel.

Just go away. You've no business here. All that's lying here is someone finished and done for. No, Ebba was opening the door to the teacher's room. Standing there trying to sniff things out, probably. Oh yes, she's a nosy one and no mistake, who'd be quite keen to poke into this and that if she could be sure she was alone.

But Ebba came straight across the room and opened the sitting room door without knocking.

'So you're lying in here?'

She didn't answer. It was obvious, after all. She was lying in here.

Ebba came over to her and stood with her handbag on her stomach in front of her. On her head she had her old, black hat with the agate clip at the front. You couldn't exactly say she'd smartened herself up for her visit.

She sat down on the sofa. She simply shifted Tora aside to make room, and Tora winced at her touch. It was an intrusion. But Ebba had never had any manners, for all she'd come up in the world. Brewer Julin had made a fortune, they said. But Ebba was just the same as when they served together in the third-class dining room at the railway hotel. Only the fox furs and the medal were different.

Then Ebba Julin took her icy hands in her own and rubbed them and afterwards Tora could never remember what she'd said but she could recall her deep, hoarse voice, droning on and on. A very strange voice for a woman. Maybe it was like that because she'd smoked cigarillos. Yes, she'd smoked them ever since she was a young woman, more or less covertly at first. She'd come to like the taste of the fine gentlemen's cigars when she was out with them. The hoarse voice with its veils of smoke talked and talked, and here and there a word bobbed to the surface of the flood: Tora dear - in such pain - won't show - not a bit. Tora began to cry.

She cried with her face pressed to Ebba's blouse and the breasts inside it heaved because Ebba was extremely agitated. Tora knew very well that Ebba was all those things people said about her. She sought out sensation and craved enjoyment. She not only smoked but drank a bit as well, and not such a little bit, either. That was presumably the one pleasure she and the brewer had shared when he was still well enough to have a conversation with. Now he had senile dementia. There was no doubt she was selfish and a gossip, Tora knew that. But she was kind as well. It was funny really: if you were kind you just were. Yes, there were kind people.

When she'd had a long cry and got cramp in her midriff, she made

90

an effort to sit up and Ebba helped her.

'I've got cancer,' she said.

But nothing dramatic happened just because that sickening word had crept out between them at last. Ebba carried on with her handkerchief, wiping Tora's face and her own blouse in turn. It seemed as if she had known all along. In fact, as if they'd all known. Nothing happened in the grey light of the room just because she'd let slip that hateful word. Ebba just went droning on in her deep, hoarse voice, saying loads of things Tora actually already knew, loads of things every grown-up person knows. But there is nothing else you can say, after all. It would be unreasonable to expect anything else, it would be completely out of the question.

A giant had a washbowl which he set down in the forest at the base of a moraine. It was made of granite and deeply indented, and he filled it with clear, amber water which looked like solidified resin when the sun shone on it on a summer's afternoon.

In winter, the top layer of the water froze into a lid and the entire bowl went very still, just like the forest around it. Then, down at its deepest point, a pattern of stripes and dashes would move. A pike, if there had been one, would have seen that it was not broken lengths of hollow reed swaying there but thousands of his brothers the perch, sluggishly and cautiously changing positions.

Across the top of the lid spun a rope-covered ball and after it, heavy but fast, skated men with clubs in their hands. They were dressed in black knee breeches and grey woollen sweaters. About half of them had black, peaked caps with both earflaps turned up and kept in place with two thin shoelaces knotted on top of their heads. Half had red knitted hats with tassels. Sometimes one of the ones in peaked caps went whizzing off with long blade strokes, feet inclining inwards, guiding the ball in front of him with his club. If a tassel-hat got in his way, both of them would go crashing onto the rough ice near the shore, flattening the broken reeds and sending ice and coarse snow spraying round their metal blades.

Round the edge of the Giant's Washbowl, people stood watching, virtually all men, coming so far out of town. But Ingrid Eriksson was standing there too. She stood there every winter Sunday, whenever there was a match on.

One of the players had a white cap, a big, rather bushy-looking one with a button on top. Ingrid's eyes were glued to it. Under that button was Arne Johansson. He was the reason she was here.

He was best. That was why he was allowed to wear a white cap. He often skated backwards with his bottom leading and swivelled back as he marked another player who was trying to dribble the ball past him. Then he made an unexpected move. His opponent lost the ball and it somehow hooked itself onto Arne Johansson's club and stayed fixed there as if with invisible string, a rubber band round the bottom of the club. He broke away. He skated vigorously, cutting into the thin covering of powdery snow on the ice, up to the other goal. There was a short skirmish right by it. She couldn't make out a thing, not even his cap. Everyone was yelling, but she wasn't. She didn't often yell. She chewed the thumb of her mitten, though, and after each attacking move she had a mouthful of wet, woolly fluff.

If he scored they yelled even louder and then everyone calmed down again as he skated back to the middle with long, leisurely strides. He did an extra turn, his bottom sticking out again.

To tell the truth, she spent a lot of time looking at his backside. It was so surprising. It was both compact and muscular, heavy, firm and slim. She couldn't find words to describe it to herself, which may have been why she stared at it incessantly in the hope of being able to discover its secret in the end.

He had strong legs with slightly rounded calves in the thick, ribbed oversocks that he wore turned up. She didn't get to see much of his face out on the ice. There was usually a cloud of steam coming out of his mouth. She would hear a panting as he went past, a hoarse cry, almost terrifyingly close:

'Hey Pete! Now, you bugger. My ball, my ball!'

Sometimes it sounded like a dog barking. He had quite a high voice. Whenever he scored, they all talked about him for a bit, everyone on the reedy edges of the little, round lake.

'Blimey, that Arne,' they said. 'Bloody unbeatable.'

And they took a swig and passed their bottles round.

She wasn't even remotely interested in bandy. To start with she had thought she was, for a while. She'd worked herself up, squeezed Maud's hand when he got near the goal, almost screamed when the little ball went rolling in.

But now she knew she wasn't. She was only interested in Arne Johansson. She who had once learnt the names of all the players in the teams that came to town to play against them and the ones they went by bus to play against! She had known the function and position of every player and why they awarded penalties and what was off-side. And now it had all gone. She didn't give a damn. It was quite a relief to admit it. Though it made her feel wistful.

Arne Johansson.

You're the only one.

Me standing here.

Club, ice, ball. Hard, abrupt blows to the ice. Sometimes he was far away, leaning forward with his backside out. His club poking out in front of him. Bandy's beautiful, said the supporters round the lake. It's the most beautiful game. Then suddenly all the players were coming towards her: a caked mass of meat and wool. Clubs went flailing around the pudding of men chasing a single little raisin, the rope ball. The thing it was all about. She stared at it.

All of a sudden it was exchanged for another. A new ball came thudding in, red and unused. So it wasn't that first one that mattered, after all. The old ball went bouncing out onto the snowy shore. It settled there. A boy picked it up, so now it would bounce and shoot about some pavement or improvised pitch in an icy school playground.

Naturally she understood. But there was something magical all the same about that little bundle that could suddenly be exchanged for another. So really this was about an assumption, an agreement. It was totally theoretical. When she started thinking along those lines, her old liking for doing sums came back to her. Once she used to find it very easy to do sums and took pleasure in it. Doing sums was like this: throw in a rope ball and let us assume!

Arne scored. She had been standing thinking about something else and felt suddenly embarrassed. What if he'd looked at her just as he swung out from the goal over on the other side and came gliding back to the middle with one foot in front of the other and the blades of his skates in a straight line, his club trailing along the ice behind him. His head was slightly bowed. Steam was coming from his mouth and as his glide brought him closer she could see the deep heaving of his diaphragm. He had his tongue far back and his mouth wide open, as he so often did out here on the ice. His lips were formed as if he was about to say awww...

He put the little finger of his right hand to his left nostril, pressed it, bent forward a little and blew straight out through his other nostril. The phlegm or snot or whatever it was glittered in the sun. Then she saw him raise his hand to the cheering at the shore's edge and skate off with heavy, accelerating strides after the ball that was already in motion again.

If this had been the summer, the ball would be bobbing in amber water now. She remembered the feel of the lake water on her body one really warm summer's evening.

It must be almost over, she thought. It was four-one now, wasn't it? So another win. Tomorrow the newspaper will say the plucky lads of the local team were like combine harvesters mowing down the startled tassel-hats from Nässjö. Was it Nässjö they were from?

What's got into me? she thought. If I don't pay attention at matches, he'll catch me out. But to herself she didn't bother pretending it was exciting any more. And she knew why, too. One of the teams would win. Nothing unforeseen would happen, nothing she could never have imagined.

It was like cycling home from town and getting worked up about whether or not Assar would be there first. That would be just about as exciting. But what if she came into the kitchen semi-aware of reality like people usually are, somehow aloof and insulated from it, and there stood someone who wasn't Assar at all, some unthinkable figure in Ingeborg's kitchen? Giggling to herself as the whole knot of players swept past her at high speed like a huge horde of maddened army ants, she imagined Ingeborg rocking large-breasted in the arms of a man with dark stubble, a thin moustache and smart, punch-patterned, pale yellow shoes. That would really be something. What made something exciting was if you never could have imagined it and the fact that it could happen absolutely any time.

But she wasn't bored. She was perfectly happy just to look at his backside. Her feet were freezing now, though, and she stamped her boot-clad feet over and over again. She'd acquired a sports outfit so she could go to bandy matches. It consisted of ski boots with thick socks turned over the tops; pants that were full at the ankles. You pulled them tight with a cord. She had a black jacket of wool felt, double breasted with a big collar you could turn up, a knitted scarf in the same wool as the socks and a leather hat to round it off. The leather was shiny and the earflaps and front flap were lined with curly sheepskin. She always wore the flap turned up like the brim of a hat and there was a flower crocheted on the sheepskin.

She could afford her sporty outfit because she didn't have to pay Assar and Ingeborg anything for her board. Most of the workers at the Tin Can lived at home. She knew she was spoilt. Assar and

Ingeborg indulged her. They were quite happy with her at the moment. Though Ingeborg had wanted her to take a domestic job with a family and learn some skills she could make use of in the future. Neither she nor Assar had the faintest idea what it was like at the factory, or what they said in the lunch room or exactly what she and Maud got up to in their free time, for that matter. So Ingeborg was happy. Though she sometimes told Ingrid to remember she was grown up now. She found it strange that her foster-daughter still lived like a seventeen-year-old.

The hard smacks of clubs on the ice and the screeching skate blades reminded her of the Tin Can, the band saw and the pressing moulds. Then they were shouting again: 'Arne, Arne, Arne!' She looked up, identified him among the flailing crowd of players and saw him break away towards the goal. But one of the tassel-hats must have hooked a skate round his club, because he didn't make it. A howl went up round the shore but the ref hadn't seen a thing. The tassel-hat cursed, stony-faced, as he untangled himself and went gliding away, leaning forward, heavy on the ice with his club sweeping in front of him. But a few minutes later they clashed again. Arne was well known for playing a clean game. She couldn't see that he was lifting his club or doing anything wrong. Even so, the tassel-hat hooked his skate again and gave a jerk. Arne, clubbed and culled, fell hard onto the ice and the tip of his opponent's skate. As the ref and a couple of teammates helped him sit up, there was blood coming from his mouth. They applied some snow and it was stained bright red.

She wanted to go to him. The palms of her hands were sticky. For a minute or two it all felt as if the whole thing was a bloody charade. Why was she just standing here with her arms held stiffly at her sides and her mouth gone dry, if he was badly injured? Was that part of the game too? She ought to hurl herself onto the ice in her boots, screaming, and put her arms round him. If he was dead or seriously injured she ought to hurl herself at the lot of them, as many tassel-hats and caps as she could get at to bury her teeth in their sides until she found their livers, stick her thumbs in their eyes and squeeze, kick them in the balls, over and over. She should be able to catch quite a few of them while they were still dozily circling with their clubs, shocked and confused, before they had the presence of mind to overpower her.

She'd closed her eyes. The excited shouts and whistles, the hoarse words of abuse became a mumble. They were just a growl along the reedy shore. She looked up and saw they'd got him on his feet. He wiped his mouth, leaving blood and snot on the arm of his sweater. He spat hard, and something went flying in an arc over quite a distance. A tooth? She heard him swear. Two men in galoshes came running and slithering onto the ice and took him under the arms. It looked comical because his skates made him much taller than them. She saw them taking him to one of the buses. Ingrid didn't dare follow them. She was scared of a man called Melkersson, the team coach.

Out on the ice, the game was underway again but everyone seemed aimless and listless. The tassel-hat had been sent off. The others kept straying to the edge, where the lumpy ice gave them a rough ride.

Then a murmur ran through the crowd. Arne came skating in with a plaster running from the corner of his mouth across his cheek. Cheers of triumph. He raised his club a little in salute and smiled. No gap in his teeth as far as she could see when he parted his lips. He took a run and went skating off.

He was angry now. He'd pile in goal after goal. He'd sweep the ice with them now.

'Come on Arne! Get your teeth in their fucking faces!' shouted a man, bottle in hand. The sun glinted on the glass of the bottle, sending out a sudden flash. How beautiful, thought Ingrid. I must be mad. I've lost all sense of judgement.

Arne was panting away over there. He had the whole team working right behind him, eleven times seventy kilos, a machine of almost a tonne of steaming muscle power working its way towards the little goal, thrust by thrust. He was in the lead. He raised his club and the ball went scorching up from the ice in an arc. Where was the goalie? Had they tricked him away? The ball went straight in and suddenly it was just lying there, stock still on the ice, round and red. Up went people's hands, their mouths gaping. They were nothing but coarse organ pipes of flesh for the air that went streaming up into a raucous bellowing note, a roar around the lake. She suddenly realised that she was screaming too. She was roaring open-mouthed and pounding her mittened hands, clapping and roaring, clapping and roaring. And suddenly falling silent.

They were on the move again, circling, heavy and solemn. Issuing steam in intermittent snorts. God, when would it end? She felt an inward pang of shame. It was a long time since she'd got carried away like that. Not since the early days, when she thought she really was interested in bandy. Stood here stamping because it was exciting. That was when she used to bring Maud along and they egged each other on and squeezed each other's arms so hard they were blue and bruised afterwards.

But to start roaring now, when she knew perfectly well why she was here. It must have been the blood on the snow. She blew her nose on a clean hankie, unfolding it carefully first, and didn't allow herself to look out over the ice as she did it. Fancy her behaving like this over a bloke. She wouldn't have thought it of herself. And Ingeborg wouldn't have thought it either, prone as she was to sighing and saying:

'You're still like a seventeen-year-old.'

Starting to long for grandchildren, probably. Little Assar wasn't ripe for that yet. In Ingeborg's world, people ripened like big cucumbers or pumpkins for pickling, and started producing little silverskin onions when the time was right. Ingrid had always laughed at her. Yet at the same time she had gradually begun to think there must be something wrong with her, Ingrid. Because, after all, love was what it was all about. Not for her. She thought it was fun to go dancing, fun to ride her bike, to kiss and tease. But she wasn't in love with a single one of those cycling caps as they passed the cemetery, not even on the dark evenings when she was a little tipsy with sweet vermouth.

She'd always thought that if anyone did ever get her, it would be because he was persistent, so she'd finally have to admit defeat in the game, make some gesture more significant than she realised, say something crucial some admirer had been waiting for with the gentle patience of an ox. And she would promise to produce him little pumpkins and onions and to that end put a ring on her finger and move into a flat. Some of them were good-looking and pleasant enough. It was bound to be one of them, she'd thought. Just not yet.

Then she took up watching bandy and stamping her feet loyally on the ice. But Arne Johansson hadn't even noticed her. She had the idea most people thought she was quite pretty, at least when her hair was looking nice. Yet he went panting round the training track. The only people he seemed bothered about were his Mum and Melkersson.

It hadn't been that easy to get to know him without letting on to Maud. This was something she couldn't talk about. It was completely different from the way you usually fancied someone. It was that particular way he looked, his backside, his legs, his thin lips. It wasn't that they were attractive exactly. He wasn't even

100

specially good-looking. It was the fact that it was him. It was his voice.

He went to dances but didn't often ask anyone to dance. He mostly leant on the railings, talking bandy. Summer wasn't his season. He did a lot of training, though, people said. He went running.

Since he didn't ask her to dance and she wasn't sure he even knew she was alive, she did the one thing you're not supposed to. She asked him for the ladies' excuse-me, even though he'd never asked her to dance. He looked surprised. She danced doggedly. Took in the smell of him. Explored the feel of his shoulder. What's got into me? shc thought. What's going on? Then he danced the last one with her and took her home to the railway workers' houses They didn't have much to say to each other. He kissed her before she went in. His lips were thin and a little hard. He didn't say anything about their seeing each other again. She knew he was two years younger than her and wondered if that mattered to him.

Then he seemed to drop her. She saw him occasionally in town and he would nod and look vaguely pleased. Ingrid would go home and try to interpret his smile. Why am I like this?

She had no answer but set to work to get him, and it turned out she wasn't seventeen any longer but an adult, strong and capable. After two weeks' hard work - she amazed herself - he was hers.

During this process she sometimes thought she must be sick in the head. She scarcely even looked about her if he wasn't present. Within herself she started to use the word love to describe this condition. It was a word that existed all around her anyway, and it eased the sense of shame, emptiness and urgency that she had whenever she wasn't near him. She didn't know if she was sorry she wasn't getting him quickly enough or if in her heart of hearts she wanted it to be like this.

She told herself that she loved him, that the very air was saturated with the taste of him, that life was now and only now when he was there. She couldn't claim to love him for his ideas or for how he treated her. It was his very essence she loved, his aroma. She loved the marrow of his bones, the smell of his breath, even the way he put his hand on a door handle. Seeing him take a shot at goal or tie his shoelace were both equally glorious. He did everything with the same exquisite precision, that is, he did it the way only he could. No one else smelt of Arne, no one had that voice.

It struck her for the first time that every human being is unique and particular; each person is one of a kind. Why, even people she'd never thought about or noticed before were special. She stared at Jansson the fishmonger and at her mother Frida. Good Lord, it simply wasn't true that there were thousands like them, as she had wearily assumed. There was only one Jansson the fishmonger and only one Frida and their time was now, just before death swallowed them up.

Then she got scared he'd die. She suffered anguish and hypochondria on his behalf. She was alert to his every cough but could hardly have a made a better choice if she was going to be a worrier: he was a miracle of physical magnificence, a male construction the Creator could easily have used as a prototype. She didn't bother much with what he said, because his way of moving and being was enough to embody warmth, strength and concentration. His lungs filled calmly and regularly to capacity with air, his heart pumped trustily and steadily and would go on pumping for seventy-two years. This man was a pillar of flesh and blood, a tower of muscle clad in smoothest skin. The little hairs on his forearms and round his wristwatch gleamed golden yellow. He had a wristwatch, not a pocket watch; and he wore shoes, not boots. The shoes enclosed his strong, arched feet and moulded themselves to them. She had never seen a pair of shoes more personal. When he took them off and put them aside they were almost a purer distillation of Arne than he was himself, lying in bed with his eyes closed. His broad ankles had stretched the top leather. Strength. She always thought of strength when she saw him. But his voice was weak. Yes, oddly enough, the strong airstream that seemed to pass unimpeded straight through him when he was running or skating didn't flow as easily when he spoke. His voice was high and strained. Only when he was alone with her could it sometimes change into a humming or buzzing or powerful purring, and at times like that she luxuriated in it. But he didn't say very much.

That was the aim of the battle: to make him talk. It had sometimes seemed to her that desire, raw and concentrated, was all she felt for him, that there was nothing more to her interest in him than this: to feel him wet under her tongue, to swap saliva with him, bite and tear him and taste the taste of him so she was virtually consuming his smooth skin; to smell the scent of him, that scent of skin and shirt collar mixed. She truly was lovesick. She had read it somewhere; I am lovesick. That was right. Think if Konrad knew! Tepid Konrad, the only thing that set him alight was the revolution. It struck her that Konrad was an old woman, a real old woman.

She desired Arne but when she finally had him in her hands, between her legs, under her tongue and inside her slippery vagina, she realised it hadn't been that after all. Not only that. It was something else too. The aroma of his being, the core and essence of what was him, was elsewhere. She couldn't crack his bones and scrape out the marrow, so she started to grope for his soul instead. Or whatever it's called. She was one hundred percent convinced he had one. The idea probably wouldn't have occurred to anyone else, but it came to her. She'd get him to talk. She was used to Konrad, after all. He was the only man she had really taken any notice of in her formative years. That was why she believed a soul expresses itself in speech. Thus began the long and futile task of getting the centre forward to talk.

So here she stood now, on the ice, staring at one man. She didn't understand it at all. What have I to do with him? she would sometimes think. He seems the most unfamiliar of all people. The distance between her and everyone else created its little illusions. They seemed to move and speak in agreed patterns, they weren't in the least enigmatic. But he got so close to her that he became a real person for her and she was frightened. And that fear made her explore words and pictures, fill herself with them and taste them: my beloved, my beloved how I love you, I hardly dare breathe when I feel your arms around me, that kiss was totally unlike anything I've ever experienced before, this is just how I've always wanted to be kissed though I didn't know it, your kisses are hot and tender, they give all your love, my beloved, you hold me hard against you and the whole universe is a wonderful symphony around us and the rain is sighing its soft sympathy with our love, beloved.

Love was supposed to explain everything but instead things just got murkier than ever. She threw her magazines under the bed, with balls of fluff and a blue-rimmed chamber pot for company. You didn't find love in *Ladies' Home Journal* or in the lily of the valley woods. Love was sudden silence and closeness, more than you could bear. It wasn't a bridal bed of meadowsweet. Though the sawdust in the cold attic had a strong scent too.

She decided her first hunch had been right: this was an illness of the mind, a mental illness in other words, something she had invented herself and was carrying round with her. He hadn't the slightest idea what was really going on inside her and he wasn't responsive to it. He was simply playing a game, just as he did on the ice in a bandy match. He knew what he had to do and, if strictly necessary, say; soon they would have baby cucumbers and baby pumpkins and everything would be as it should be.

To prove to herself she wasn't ill, she had to get him to talk. Three words she needed. Or even if he just said he liked her a lot. Those words would prove it wasn't just her who had this storm of madness advancing through her heart. But first she had to get past his stiff timidity. She had to melt the ice on his cheeks, the frost round his mouth when he asked:

'Doing anything special on Saturday evening?'

His timidity was a tough membrane, a hymen of the soul it would take more than one evening to split. She gnawed and strained and drilled but his mouth remained just as stiff, his voice just as neutral.

'Oh hello. It's you.'

Surprised. Hadn't he been keeping an eye on her here on the street corner? Didn't he realise she'd been standing here or pacing up and down for over an hour now? Shouldn't they have thrown themselves into each other's arms like water spilling recklessly over a cliff edge?

'I'm going your way,' he said. 'We can walk together for a bit.'

And this in spite of the fact that they'd long been sharing the sawdust bed up in the attic of the block of flats where the Swedish Motors workers lived, the middle block called South House. He never asked her about anything. Was he simply not interested or was it just shyness? She never found out. She told him eagerly about herself, about Assar and Ingeborg and Little Assar, about the Tin Can and Maud and absolutely anything she hoped might make her intimate and familiar to him. She wanted to be someone he'd known all his life. But the only thing that made any impact on him was the fact that she smoked. When she wanted him to go up the hill with her so she could have a fag out of sight, he refused.

He lectured her about lungs and breathing. Smoking wasn't good for you. For him, a human being was a physical phenomenon. He knew a lot about breathing. He told her about lung capacity and cilia and oxygen absorption. She revelled in it. Perhaps he wasn't as unintelligent as she'd thought. I've misjudged him, she thought happily. Because in actual fact it had pained her to find him a bit dim. She enthused about breathing.

'That's really interesting,' she said in an ingratiating tone, quite out of character for her. She did it to get him to say more.

She wouldn't be able to penetrate his shyness of course. But she could tell she was getting closer to him; he often smiled at her. As for those three little words, however, she could shelve all hopes of them. Of course it hurt. I'm a fool, she said to herself. All the magazines are foolish. And all those bits of songs. But it hurt all the same. The words would have been proof of something important.

She was more or less his official consort now in any case, since she was allowed to come on the bus when they played away matches. She saw a lot of little towns with the same bulbous petrol pumps as at home and the same windows of sausages and cooked meat, with running water silently striping the inside of the pane. It was when she got a place on the bus that she bought her ski boots and pants.

After matches they went drinking and she went along too. She got rather a kick out of seeing him knock back the aquavit and undergo a transformation. The shyness she had tried to gnaw and dig into shrivelled and fell off. He got quite crude. He wasn't really like that. He wasn't one of the actively crude gang but he laughed at those who were. She didn't mind much. He's only twenty, she thought. A young man. He's as raw as a raw potato, of course. She didn't know where all this wisdom was coming from, but it seemed to her she was carrying round enough wisdom for both of them. She had gathered it up with her two-year head start. They celebrated one of their away wins at a house in District Road and that time the booze made her sick, too. Three of them stood in a row to throw up over the balcony rail and all the mess landed on the balcony below and three bikes. He never forgot it. It struck him as funny. She thought: it doesn't matter. This isn't the point. These are just incidentals. We'll get past this stage. But on our way where? Where are we heading?

Out on the ice, something had happened, but she didn't know what. The players were in the middle, circling round as if someone had put one in. What was the score? She couldn't very well ask. Out here she was Arne Johansson's girl, his sweetheart. They'll soon be engaged, just you see. That meant obligations on her part. She always showed an interest. It was the most convenient ploy and indeed the condition on which she was allowed to go on the bus with them. Otherwise she'd have had nothing but the sawdust bed up in the South House attic.

She decided to pay proper attention to the closing minutes. But all at once there was a longer blast on the whistle and they stopped their circling. She saw Arne skate over to where the trainer was standing. He blew his nose into the cold air and then Melkersson was slapping him. It was over.

They went back into town on the bus. The windows were steamed up and the floor was littered with skates. Quite a few of them were already getting loud and taking swigs from their hip flasks. But the real celebration wouldn't begin until later that

107

evening. Arne was sitting right up close to her. The cut at the corner of his mouth wasn't deep. The sticking plaster had stopped the bleeding.

They asked to be let off in District Road and then walked the little bit to South House; she was nervous because she didn't know how the match had ended.

They had Sunday dinner with his parents. It was for her sake, she knew, that they ate in the best room among the black furniture with painted veining of a lighter colour. His mother had put out the nickel tray and a crystal vase. She wasn't really quite used to Ingrid yet and imagined she came from a posher background than she actually did, because she could afford those sports clothes. Ingrid was embarrassed by them when she was here and would have liked to explain: I don't have to pay anything at home, you see. But that wouldn't have been a good thing to say either. They didn't usually talk much.

His father's hair was thinning and his nails were outlined in black by the factory grime. He'd been at the match of course, and talked about nothing else. Arne's mother put pale, stringy beef with little slices of gherkin in front of them. She lovingly drowned Arne's potatoes in pale brown gravy.

'Steady on, Mum!'

'Eat up now. You must be hungry. My word.'

She had an exaggerated notion of how much he could put away. In actual fact, he ate quite sparingly. But he had to have meat. Ingrid sometimes thought of all the sacrifices they must make to afford that wretched, stringy beef. Ingrid hardly dared to eat any. It felt like eating a piece of Mrs Johansson herself, who grew thinner by the day.

His Mum and Dad were happy with them; they were even proud of her. His Mum didn't seem at all resentful of Ingrid. Maybe she's dense? thought Ingrid. Maybe she doesn't realise what we're up to. I expect she doesn't think he knows how.

Then they'd have bottled apples or conserved pears with thin cream and afterwards Dad would have a short nap, while Ingrid helped wash up and Arne read yesterday's paper, having spent the whole day training and mentally preparing himself. He missed out on Saturdays entirely. He had the day off work, too. Like most people, he'd started on the shop floor at Swedish Motors. But the managing director was keen to see things going well for the local team and was a regular donor to the club. So Arne had been given lighter work in the store. There was less risk of injury there and it wasn't so obvious if he was given the occasional Monday morning off for a pulled muscle or a hangover from the celebrations.

The January sun shone on the table as Ingrid folded the cloth. In the kitchen, Arne's mother was getting a bowl of hot water ready for him. He would change properly now. Before, he'd just wiped the sweat off his top half and changed his shirt. He splashed energetically all over the kitchen worktop and his mother was on hand with more hot water and big, waffled towels. She hadn't shut the kitchen door, just pulled across the curtain she kept there to foil the draughts. Ingrid sat in the rocking chair reading *Allers Illustrated Family Magazine*. Now and then she looked up at the brown and rust striped curtain and listened to his Mum's voice and the sound of water. It gave her a funny feeling to think of him naked out there and his Mum so scared she might see something. And in fact she hadn't actually seen him entirely naked. It had been too dark and cold.

Soon they'd go off to celebrate at the Urdar Lodge, which you could hire for private functions. She'd have to go home and change first. It was important that she looked right. After all, she was more than just Ingrid. She was Arne Johansson's girl and people looked at her more than before.

But the finale to this long day with cold and stamping of feet, beef, a full stomach and toiling along icy streets in stockings far too thin would be up in the attic in the sawdust bed. It was cold as the devil there and everything was so close and so tangible that it seemed to her they were crawling back into the dark, musky caves of childhood, where everything smelt and tasted so intense. At one point his finger, that had been inside her, chanced to brush his face, just touching his nose. It made him blush profusely. He couldn't have smelt such a scent since he was little, standing on a chair and leaning over the saucepan of melted butter, sugar, syrup, cinnamon, ginger and ground cloves, not since his mother stirred the little iron pan of simmering spices and syrup with a wooden spoon. He clearly remembered the wooden spoon being dark brown, in fact it had gone almost completely black at the bottom with the hot, spicy brew that would be turned into ginger biscuits. He looked at his finger now as if he thought it might go black, too.

They sat there like two children, or even smaller creatures, like wood sprites or elves in their cave full of spiders' webs. In here, ordinary water glittered like crystal. With just one tug of their hands, the long, drab, everyday drapes, the webs of life-weariness, fell instantly to shreds. They made secret passages under the others' paths and met whispering, foreheads burning.

Weren't they always a bit feverish in here? In here it no longer mattered that she was the one who spoke, while he remained silent. The fever was in them both. She felt his heart pounding as if it wanted to pump its way out of the cramped cage of gristle, muscle and bone, wanted to pump its way into her.

On the wondrous light in the forest above Louse Point one afternoon before Christmas in the winter of 1906:

Frida had seen that light.

She came trudging through the forest, down towards her old childhood home. The croft was nothing but a vague circle because the foundations had sunk and rowan shoots, leafless now, were sprouting everywhere in the layer of dead grass as if children had been playing with some sticks. The stones had been almost worn away by her gaze. She had come past here so many times over the years. When she went and stood inside the circle of sunken foundation stones, it was only to see if the bed they used to have in the kitchen really had fitted along the short wall. But it didn't seem possible that there could once have been a floor and furniture here. The dish of memory had been worn shallow by tired eyes and would soon contain nothing. Embankment Brita's empty face, children's cries, worry, coarse voices. It all seemed buried and unchangeable.

Frida's shoes weren't really stout enough for walking in the forest. But the snow hadn't come yet. Her boots didn't leak either, or at least not much. All around her, the forest was a dark, spice-scented, healthy green. She was utterly amazed. After all, in town everything was grey at this time of year: the mud in the streets, the plaster on the buildings, people's faces, shawls and bundles. In that setting, a heap of browny-yellow horse droppings was a real splash of colour. And the forest she had expected to find leafless and grim - here it stood, greener than ever with damp star moss and shiny clumps of lingonberry leaves, with lichens on the stones, cheekily holding up their little cups to the sky and demanding a share of whatever there was.

Once, as a child, she'd seen a picture called 'Find the Green Hunter!' It looked like that picture here above Louse Point just now, green on green and the hunter's jerkin was impossible to spot. There was a green shimmer in the little pools and the moisture had freshened all the moss into shaggy softness. She was hunting for clubmoss, at least that was what she'd say if anyone asked. If she found a bit of wood she'd put it in her basket with the clubmoss over the top. No one need know she was that short of fuel. There was no harm in taking a bit of kindling home with you, after all. It needn't bother anybody. How lush and healthy the clubmoss was looking! If only she could have filled a kindling basket with it, to sell in the market for Christmas decorations. But the news would get about. Now Frida Eriksson's reduced to standing in the market trying to sell clubmoss, poor thing. Eriksson must be out of work again. No, she'd only take enough to decorate the hood of her own stove.

As she moved forward, doubled over to pull up the long strands of stiff, coiled clubmoss, she started to feel dizzy. All she'd had to eat was two slices of bun loaf with a cup of rye coffee. She felt a sudden rush to her head and almost fell headlong, but managed to sit down on a tree stump in time with her head between her knees, as the surging sensation gradually receded and her cold nostrils went back to normal. But when she sat up and opened her eyes, the forest had been transformed.

It was filled with a soft, golden light she at first took to be filtering between the trunks of the trees. She took a few tentative steps, then came to a halt. It seemed to her that she, too, was suffused with light. All the leaves, every lobe of every stalk of the clubmoss had such intensity and lustre she could see each one in finest detail. Nothing escaped her in this mild and intimate light which neither blinded nor frightened her. At first she tried to fathom what could have caused it and decided the light seemed to be coming from hidden sources behind the stones, turning the moss into a shimmering border along their old, grey backbones. But there didn't appear to be any normal explanation for this light. The sun had long been hidden behind the wet veils and drapes of November and there couldn't be a fire beyond the trees and stones. Nor was there anything shining behind them, she saw now. There was no illumination falling on tired ridges of grey stone or rough, fallen trunks. Everything was light, and the light came from inside. Every growing or decaying thing, every stone in this heavy forest was being borne aloft by light, and that light was coming from the stone itself, as if it had suddenly reached such concentration it became radiant. The same applied to every branch, every fircone underfoot. Frida patted herself and knew she, too, was luminous.

She dared not move. Her eyes seemed to have been rinsed in the clearest of waters. They knew everything in the forest and every conscious moment. Everything ugly and shameful seemed to her transfigured; her actions were as pure as water and as basic as bread. She knew, too, that she was living for all time, that there was no time beyond time. For a moment she felt herself trembling with fatigue, felt she simply could not carry on looking at all this unless she bowed her head and closed her eyes for a little while. She only stayed that way for half a second, but when she looked up, the forest had gone back to normal again, and it was nearly dark.

She walked home with the clubmoss. She forgot about the kindling. All through 1907 she kept thinking about what she had seen in the forest. It was hard to remember everything exactly. Eventually, the light started to look like a wall hanging; she saw the forest before her eyes, embroidered in gold. She knew full well it wasn't the same as the real thing. She gradually stopped thinking about it so much. There was nothing to compare it with, and it never happened again. She didn't know of anybody else who'd seen a forest bathed in a strange sort of light like that.

The only time she ever really recalled what it had felt like was when she was standing at the window at night. The open window; it would be a summer's night with no need to think about keeping in the heat from the stove. She would be standing with a glass of cold water in her hand, having just taken a sip. She would see nothing remarkable. Only the yard outside and the trees in the garden beyond the dustbins, nothing else. It was just that feeling of time and inevitability and peace of mind.

She would often think, when she felt anxious: if I could just have peace of mind for once. If I could just have peace of mind about wood and paraffin and milk and shoe repairs. Just for once. She wasn't asking anyone in particular. Just wishing someone like her could have peace of mind for once.

But she never thought anything like that as she stood there at the window. Her mind was empty and that moment of peaceful recollection was not a fruit that had flowered, swelled and ripened in her own life. It seemed simply to have come rolling in, by chance and without any connection to the Frida Eriksson in this life, at number 60, Hovlunda Road. Sometimes she stood at the window, lips still moist with the water from the glass, and was at peace. Then morning would come again and it would be impossible to mention a thing like that to anyone. Year after year went by that way. She remembered the light in the forest, right enough, but the way you remember from a photograph or a story someone else has told.

She had relations in Muddy Lake who were religious. She found it awkward but they didn't talk about it. They were nonconformists, members of the a Swedish missionary society, and it didn't seem an especially pushy sort of religiousness, as far as Frida could tell. She went to visit them sometimes. She would go on the Norrköping train. It only took twenty minutes; then she would get off and her cousin Hilma would be standing there in her black coat and hat in front of the little station house that had red walls and black paintwork.

She could hardly refuse to go to chapel with Hilma and Ludvig. But it always made her feel sleepy. She wasn't used to sitting still for so long; the mumble and the squeaking of the organ were soporific. Hilma wasn't very exciting and neither was Ludvig, for that matter. But they were kindly, respectable people and didn't ask nosy questions about the children, about David and Anna who were causing her such concern. The food was good at their house too. Though she always brought something for them, of course, a couple of loaves of bread or an apple cake. When she got the job at the laundry and had enough coming in to be able to afford a train ticket, she was keen to go and see them. She thought it only right and proper that you had relations out in the country to exchange visits with. Most people had. Though Hilma and Ludvig weren't very exciting. That was what Tora Otter said. I'm not very exciting myself, Frida retorted.

She was there one summer Sunday in 1929. It completely changed her life. Afterwards she recalled it had been so hot she had been reluctant to make the train journey. She'd been afraid of getting sweat stains on her best dress and nearly hadn't gone.

But she did go. Ludvig and Hilma were both there to meet her. It was almost eleven o'clock and they were on their way to the

115

service. They were quite eager, for once. There was going to be a marvellous preacher. One of those travelling preachers. Everybody was talking about him.

The village was silent. They walked among the little groups of houses like black flies in a sugar bowl and reached the white wooden chapel just as the bell pealed. It was no bigger than a farmyard bell and sounded like the tinkling signal at a railway crossing.

Everything started normally. She felt even sleepier than usual because it was so hot. She watched the wild chervil swaying outside the window. It must be very tall. The sun advanced by degrees across the wooden benches, steaming open the pores in the varnish, or so it seemed, to release the smell into the chapel.

The preacher wasn't particularly tall or imposing. His voice wasn't resounding, as she'd expected it to be when they said he was a marvellous preacher. It was a low drone and you had to strain to hear everything he was saying. A strange sort of preacher, she would have said. But he seemed to be keeping his eyes fixed on her the whole time. She could see him shifting his gaze to other people. Yet still he held her fast. He came back to her and left her again. Their faces were like open blooms and he was their buzzing visitor. Not once did anyone turn away or drop their eyes.

He spoke of the light. She didn't understand all he was saying to begin with. It might have been that she was too busy studying his black outfit and his powerful, white hands that were never still. Then she was suddenly aware that he was in the middle of describing the very thing that had happened to her so long ago, before Christmas in the winter of 1906 in the forest above Louse Point.

At first she was just taken aback. How could he know? Then she heard him say it was always like that. The light was all around

116

them constantly, constantly, and he didn't mention Louse Point or the forest up there. Confused, she looked around the chapel with its smell of varnish. But nowhere could she see anything resembling a light from within the body of the world. HOLY, HOLY IS THE LORD OF HOSTS THE WHOLE EARTH IS FILLED WITH HIS GLORY, it said in gold letters above the door, and she realised she was embarrassing Hilma by turning round like that. She felt she'd been making bit of a fool of herself, and stood very quiet and upright.

He went on speaking and there were no two ways about it, he knew exactly what had happened to her that time. It was even more than that: the memory that had sunk and got silted over by twenty-three years of living and rushing and eating and talking resurfaced for her again, just as it had in those first days after her walk at Louse Point. She was suffused with the same melancholy sweetness and clarity. She could find no other way of putting it: he knew exactly. That time in the forest she, too, had known it all and been quite calm, and it would have been asking a lot to expect to feel like that again. But that man standing in front of them with the incessantly droning, buzzing voice, he knew. He couldn't have spoken the way he did, otherwise.

They had coffee afterwards and she observed him from a distance as he talked. He didn't seem at all ordinary, although he helped himself to sponge cake and stirred his coffee.

She wanted to speak to him, but Hilma and Ludvig would have been embarrassed by her if she'd asked to do anything of the kind. She wasn't even a proper member of the congregation and it would make people talk in Muddy Lake. They might even think she had some terrible sin to confess. So she just watched him as they all had coffee. The question she wanted to ask him was:

'What is that light?'

Though she knew he had already asked and answered it in his sermon. What manner of thing was it? What manner of light?

'It was Jesus,' he had said.

She felt rather stupid, too, because she had always thought Jesus looked like a person and she somehow she still believed it. But that was when you thought about Him, not when you actually saw Him.

'It was Jesus.'

For a moment she felt tempted to go up to him anyway, because all of a sudden it came home to her that her experience was very special. It was something that only happened to a few people. But then she decided it would set too many tongues wagging after all. Some people might not even believe her. Things were bad enough as it was. Hilma was staring fixedly at a single point on the floor, as if the gold lettering had fallen off the wall and landed there; neither she nor Ludvig said a word to Frida while they were having coffee. So she realised she wasn't her usual self, but didn't know exactly what was different. When they sang 'O perfect love', that feeling of peace came over her, the one that had occasionally touched her at the window on summer nights. This time it was a voluntary peace, as if she'd gone into a house and shut the door on herself.

They had Sunday dinner at Ludvig and Hilma's, chewing the pale pork in silence. It was a relief to be sitting on the train at last, looking forward to an evening at home on her own.

So in the summer of 1929, she'd joined the Swedish Missionary Society. She'd done it in her home town, of course. They had a proper church there, where she went every Sunday. She went to group meetings too, and to the sewing circle. She made a lot of new friends, though not intimate ones. When the chips were down, it was still Tora Otter, Tekla Johansson and that loudmouthed Ebba Julin she was closest to. They didn't take the slightest notice of her religiousness. They said no more about it than if she had got herself a new vegetable masher. Perhaps they were embarrassed. She didn't really know about Tekla, but both Tora and Ebba were down-to-earth types and wouldn't have been the least impressed by visions. What was more, Ebba was furious with the clergy. The vicar who'd once married her to well-heeled old Brewer Julin had made some provocative comment. If he'd had any idea how long the old dodderer was going to be around, Ebba said now.

What surprised Frida most about her new friends in the Mission Society was that they lived a life totally free from drink. Fancy grown men putting up with that. She would simply never have imagined it possible. Christmas and Easter, outings, birthdays, midsummer, payday - they all passed without a drop of aquavit.

It seemed a gentle, compassionate sort of world. A world with music played on guitars and organs and a bit of singing. They gossiped. But they didn't drink. A lot of them were important men. Wärnström himself, the factory owner, had had the chapel built, and later the church. It was what they called an offering. She made offerings herself these days. But she had so little to give. So she made over old clothes instead. There were so many needy people, she hadn't really realised until now.

From Greenland's icy mountains
From India's coral strand,
Where Afric's sunny fountains,
Roll down their golden sand,
From many an ancient river,
From many a palmy plain
They call us to deliver
Their land from famine's chain

119

So far she'd only tried to do her bit for the needy in the north of Sweden. She made children's clothes. But there were so many other people. Not all creatures were getting enough to eat at His table. In vain the mildest gifts are strewn, from Heavn's all-loving arms. It was all the squabbling that made it in vain, said the pastor. Maybe he was right. It was beyond her experience.

She liked making offerings because being there always reminded her of that time up at Louse Point. And she found out lots of things nobody had ever told her before. But it still sometimes felt as if she was growing further away from the memory of the light in the forest. Then she would have to go to Muddy Lake to visit cousin Hilma and go with her to the little wooden chapel. She hoped one day the light might again come as close to her as it had that day the marvellous preacher had spoken.

She usually went in winter, when it was hardest to remember. She no longer presented her loaves of bread or the cake made of sour apples and rusk crumbs to Hilma, but bore them into the chapel kitchen where the smell of damp teatowels mingled with the aroma of freshly ground coffee. Hilma stood bent over the coffee pot, wiping it out. Not a single ground must be left, nor a greasy ring from coffee left to stand and go stale before reheating. Frida put her bread on the kitchen worktop and covered it with a teatowel like the others had done. The still-secret mounds lay nestled beneath their checked cloths, and the place still smelt of nothing but wet teatowels drying and the aroma of ground coffee beans that always made Frida think: how lucky I am. But she rarely said anything out there. She was filled with anticipation.

Then she took in the cups and saucers and helped to set them out on the linen tablecloths. There was a sound of stamping from the entrance hall. Those winter days were full of grey light and creakings now. It was often so cold Frida didn't know how to keep her cheeks and nose from frostbite as she walked from the station. She had grown so thin, the blood in her veins so readily slowed to a standstill. Whenever she lost the feeling in her face she was scared and rubbed at it vigorously. The best thing would have been to run but she didn't dare, didn't even know if she could any more.

Here, inside, the flames of the twenty-four candles were flickering. They fluttered weakly, flapping in the wintry light like little wings, blue and pale yellow. They heard the preacher arriving. Their voices fell quiet, but soon there was a murmur of greetings and Frida felt tense. How rough his chin was as he arrived, how humanly chapped and naked and prey to the cold. He would just have shaved, of course. But thinking things like that made her blush.

Someone had arranged yellow chrysanthemums in the vase at the front; he would bend over them when he got there. He had already noticed them and was commending everything: the vanilla crescents Hilma had made and the cloths with inset lace and the children with beige stockings wrinkled round their podgy knees.

They fell quiet. Frida sat down on the bench next to Hilma and Ludvig, shuffling discreetly to get comfortable. The bones in her bottom cut right down into the varnished wood and she would soon be in agony.

This segment of humanity, sitting here with their backs to the cold draught, turning the thin pages of the hymn book, their fingers stiff with the cold from outside, was now supposed to be enveloped in God's presence. And they were supposed to enfold God within them as a seed encases life as yet unwoken and an apple encases pips and a core. The woman at the organ pulled out the vox celestis, principal and forte stops with little thumps of felt-covered wood. Easing apart the swell levers with her knees, she began to play the harmonium, that oversized, foot-pumped harmonica.

Light's abode, celestial Salem,
Vision whence true peace doth spring,
Brighter than the heart can fancy
Mansion of the Highest King

Some of them sang, others mumbled and growled, moving their lips to the words as if they had gone stiff. Gold shone dully on woollen dresses and the posters on the walls paled in the winter light. Egypt's and Canaan's land were on the verge of being wiped out, rendered infinitely distant, almost non-existent.

Endless noon-day, glorious noon-day,
From the Sun of suns is there

And now this congregation, this little human assembly in Muddy Lake, was supposed to seek God with its most refined organs: ganglia, neurons and papillae, transmitters, fine ossicles and everything that could possibly serve to absorb and register in some super-normal memory. Smells were to be expunged, any smell other than that of God's own body in the world. Voices were to die down, the scraping of children's legs along the varnished benches was to cease, and with it the piping of the organ. There was to be silence. Above the wafer-thin, untouchable membrane of the cerebral cortex, there was to be winter light and blindness.

The preacher looked over the top of his service-book as if to make sure this had all happened. But they were covered vessels. They did not receive God in the silence of this January Sunday, despite their preparation. They were too rough and unfinished. For those He had once touched, the words had the effect of commendation for the patience they nurtured. Abide in your longing. You are keepers of the faith. Said he who had just been commending their vanilla crescents, yellow flowers and the delicate lacework of their cloths.

So here they were, thirty or forty men and women who had swept the porches with brooms for each other, lit the fire, baked cakes and biscuits, and brewed that good, strong coffee for each other; who had come together with low voices and clean clothes. They must bear this sadness a little longer. The preacher spoke so carefully. He did not say THE LORD LIVETH in his holy temple. He spoke softly and quite informally of their obligations, as if to intensify the sadness that would soon be over.

It was probably still there, like a wisp of smoke from thin flames in the draught from the door when they had got to their feet. Then the preacher smiled and turned to the table. And there was a quick thudding of shoes as a little boy ran across the cork floor. They had held their service in the chapel, while outside the snow waited, and the winter sky in its blindness, shedding light on people who would soon be going home, going their separate ways.

A cobbler, a foundryman known as the damn Bolshie, a bakery worker and a heavily pregnant woman were sitting in the kitchen of a flat above an old theatre, where the wind whistled through the weather-boarding and the paint was flaking off the window ledges like greyish snow. They were drinking coffee, ground and brewed for them by a dark, silent woman called Agnes. There was a bandy player sitting with them.

The Bolshie was sucking his coffee through a sugar lump clenched in his teeth. He started to sweat, the sweat exuding gases that the old cupola furnace and the passage of years had steam-blasted into his body as if it were filtering pulp. The baker's long, white hands, his protruding shoulderblades and round, bony head made him look like a wooden angel over the altar in a medieval church. The woman carrying a new little Bolshie or bandy player in her abdomen, taut as a balloon, watched the bandy player eating sponge cake and wished he'd say something. They were talking about the church council elections.

'We Communists aren't against Christianity,' said the cobbler. 'We're the only ones who respect the principle of freedom of religion.'

It all went quiet round the table. There was no sound but the crackle of wood burning. They used spruce for fuel here, puny little logs that didn't even need splitting. The twiggy bits caught in the narrow opening of a burnt-out Näfvekvarn stove. 'Bloody hell,' thought the bandy player, 'isn't there anyone here who knows how to chop a proper bit of wood and put a new grate in that stove?'

On the table was a bundle of leaflets: *Has Truth been a Victim in the Church Council Election?* The surface was greasy, almost steaming. The foundryman's fingers were gleaming with its blackness.

'Do you all believe this?' asked Ingrid, who had come waddling in to them in her galoshes, making her way past the packing cases and cycle racks in the yard, expecting any minute to feel a pain in the small of her back and a trickle of water between her thighs.

'What's the church council election to you? What's God to you?'

'It's not about God,' said the cobbler. It's about freedom of religion.'

'It's about cleansing the community,' said the Bolshie. 'About justice. About the truth for once.'

It is the most despicable lie ever to appear in print, she read on the leaflet; her brother - bakery worker, caretaker, church angel and admirer of Victor Hugo - put the sugar bowl down on top of the words.

'Have some more buns,' said dark Agnes in the hope they might not eat all the sponge cake.

'Who wrote that?' asked Ingrid. 'Who wrote: *If any voter doubts that the editor is anything but a blatant liar*? Was it Ljung? He usually writes your leaflets, doesn't he?'

'He's gone over to Kilbom,' her brother said.

'Ah yes, peace be with him,' said the cobbler.

'Amazing how religious you've all got,' said the woman waiting for a contraction, a terrible pain, bearable or unbearable, like a knife or a white-hot poker, the squeeze of a cold hand or just an icy nail in your belly. She had no idea because it was the first time. She remembered back to when *Das Kapital* finally came out in Swedish some years before; she had put it on the back of her bike, strapped it to the carrier, planned to have it with her all summer

125

and read it until she knew everything. But he had laughed at her, that tall, pale, angelic-looking bakery worker who was her brother, and told her you didn't sit down and read *Das Kapital* the way you would a novel by Selma Lagerlöf or Victor Rydberg. You study it in groups. A single person can't expect to absorb the whole thing. 'You've always been quite brainy,' he'd said, laughing, 'But *Das Kapital*. That's priceless.' And she had felt silly.

But now she wished she'd read *Das Kapital* from cover to cover instead of rolling around in the grass and pressing herself against another body in sweaty embraces on the sawdust in an attic, minor misdemeanours for which the imminent punishment seemed out of all proportion.

The cobbler asked for the sugar and took four lumps, turning the coffee that was left in his cup to golden sludge. He stirred and stirred, but the coffee was so cold the sugar wouldn't dissolve. The bakery worker elbowed aside the leaflets they'd paid for out of their own pockets. The metal cashbox under the bed was long since empty. But the pregnant woman was reading the words in extra-bold type: *Who really were the two hundred voters who stormed the polling station at dusk?*

'It's all lies,' said the cobbler. 'Same as that stuff about us turning down the offer of a joint list. It's a lie. We were never even asked. That's the truth.'

The bakery worker didn't really want to look at his sister but he couldn't help it. He thought it looked obscene, her being pregnant. He hated bandy. He tried to be fair in all other respects, but he hated sport and bandy. The lamplight scarcely penetrated to the corners of the little kitchen. The wind shook the wooden walls and when the broken window panes rattled, it sounded as if the building's teeth were chattering.

'Would you have agreed if they had?' said cumbersome Ingrid

who sat at the head of the table, finding it hard to accept that she was grown up now, wanting to run away from the burden that would grow into a coffee maker, a bandy player, a Bolshie or a girl in the grass with a thick book and a bike thrown down beside her.

When Konrad got to his feet and went over to the cupboard, his brother-in-law the bandy player thought he was fetching out a bottle. But he wasn't. There were no bottles here, except the sort with blackcurrant cordial and small beer in them. He was just getting some more milk for the coffee.

'Would you have, then?' said Ingrid, 'If the Social Democrats had asked?'

'We've never ruled it out,' said the cobbler doggedly, as the damn Bolshie helped himself to the last piece of sponge.

'But would you've said yes? That's my question.'

'A hypothetical question,' said the cobbler, with a sallow, colluding smile to the foundryman. Cumbersome Ingrid was feeling that if you're about to face a pain which will probably turn out to be unendurable, a bit of aggravation beforehand makes no odds. So she said:

'I know what hypothetical means. So that's not enough of an answer. Not enough to shut me up. I want you to tell me if you would've cooperated in a joint list.'

Having thus sown a good deal of aggravation round the table, she leant back. Wind was rumbling in her taut belly. Her body was unreliable these days. She never knew what it was going to do next. Let wind escape, through her throat or her bowels. Be wracked by that pain, feel a numbness or a prickling sensation. Or would her breasts suddenly be all sticky? And as the cobbler explained to her that none of them could reply to a question that hadn't yet been put to a full meeting of the Communist Party of this town - of this nest of Social Democrat vipers, he thought to himself, glowering at the bandy player, who was staring vacantly at the cupboard - and put to the vote.

'How would you have voted yourself?' she asked.

'Do you think it's right,' he said, 'to have twenty candidates on a two-party list and not give the voters the right to choose between them? What sort of freedom's that?'

'You're not answering my question,' said Ingrid, having struggled to control the air flow inside her, both upwards and downwards. She was still so afraid of breaking wind that she shifted a little on her chair, so the noise would distract them if anything happened.

'Everything you're saying is in here.'

She pulled the bundle of leaflets towards her and read in a monotone:

Has not your noble talk of a one party system in fact turned into a boomerang harming no one but yourself, Mr Editor?'

The bandy player shifted his gaze from the cupboard to Ingrid and her index finger, poised on *Give the Editor his just deserts! Vote Communist next time!*, then back to the cupboard again. But the peaceful state in which he had been held, a gentle lapping of boredom and a sort of semi-involuntary contentment, was suddenly shattered by an attack from the cobbler:

'How I would have voted is totally irrelevant. I am a servant of the masses. But ask an ordinary worker. Ask Arne.'

It went quiet, all the faces turned to the bandy player like pansies to the sun and he said:

'Uh?'

With the patience of a true servant of the masses, the cobbler said;

'The joint list.'

And Ingrid wished so fervently for him to say something, show them his silence had been significant, that she didn't notice the cobbler's evasion strategy.

'How would you have voted?'

'I dunno,' said Arne. 'I don't give a toss for the church council elections.'

That made Ingrid laugh out loud like a man.

'See, you lot!'

From the foot of the stairs came the sound of children, the voices and footsteps and nudgings of a whole group of children, plus one wailing. The foundryman was on his feet and into his coat before the children got to the door. He took the cobbler and a pile of leaflets with him and was gone. Ingrid leant back on a spindly chair and took a pride that was probably groundless in the fact that the foundryman, big as he was and accustomed to an infernal din in his job, was actually more scared of children than of anything else.

'We'd better be going too,' Ingrid said. The bandy player suddenly came to life and smiled at the provider of the coffee, his smile like that of a suddenly roused and rather guilty member of the public at a lecture or in church.

'But first you can have your book back,' she said. She brought out a paper bag and produced a book from it, quite a thick book, which she put on top of the bundle of leaflets. The children had scattered in all directions. They were tugging at their mother, using the logs as building bricks, begging for a sugar lump from the bowl and scrambling up onto Konrad's knee to ask for a sandwich. One of them had wet his pants.

'I suppose you thought this was just the sort of thing for me to sit at home reading, now I'm this big,' Ingrid said. Two ruddy spots flared on her brother's cheeks, the cheeks of the wooden angel as pale as flour. He would never have said anything so personal, nor had he thought it. Why did she have to talk about her condition? She seemed provocative, out for vengeance. The bandy player blushed in his turn.

'And I read it. Listen to this!'

She really had the bit between her teeth now. She was really angry. Arne had seen it before. They'd been married for four months. But how could she get so worked up about leaflets and things in books? How could the atmosphere in the kitchen get so tense just because she read out a passage of Ivar Lo-Johansson?

'We're going now.'

'Thanks for the coffee.'

'That's all right, come again soon.'

This from kindly Agnes, busy putting clean pants on a bottom covered in a rash from being wet and out in the evening chill. They went. She waddling and he impatient to escape the confined space. The heavy book was still there on the table and the printing ink staining her finger had left an oily mark on the passage she'd just been reading out. Agnes read it softly, in quite a different tone of voice:

'A woman grows slowly, cell by cell, for the short moments when she is to love and give birth. Her days of work and dreams bind these bright moments together like a reinforcing glue.'

The children fretted and whined. They didn't like their mother turning away and looking out of the window.

'Fancy her getting so angry about it,' said Agnes. Konrad cleared his throat.

'Well. Obviously. A human being grows in a different way, after all. She's not an animal. A woman is - something else.'

The kitchen was engulfed in storm of crying. Scratched cheeks.

Open mouths. It was time for Konrad to take the two who had been born at the same time with such high, lopsided foreheads and put them to bed in the next room, where it was quiet and peaceful, the mauve and golden-yellow of the wallpaper enfolded them and they felt safe in the high, brown bed. He wiped their hands and faces with a damp flannel. That would have to do, since it was so late. They were two very tired children. They hadn't the same stamina as the others. You had to take it easy with them, let them be on their own to get their strength back and keep up with the rest. He remembered the stories Ingrid had wanted to hear as a girl, about the troll with eyes like fiery coals and long, pointy teeth. You couldn't tell these children stories like that. It would scare them so much they wouldn't be able to sleep.

He told them the story of a boy called Karl and a girl called Sissa, whose father was a poor woodcutter in the forest. When they were on their way to the shop to buy sausage and sugar for their mother, he said, they found a squirrel with a broken leg under a spruce tree. He limped so pitifully as he tried to run away and his black eyes bulged, stony and blank with fear. Sissa took him up in her hands and Karl stroked his head with one finger. They took him back home. They forgot to buy the sugar. But it didn't matter. They made a bed for the little creature with the broken leg, that dangled behind him as he tried to take a flying jump onto the curtain and fell onto the dresser in a clatter of dishes. They made his bed in a shoebox, with two mittens and a pot-holder to keep him warm. They splinted his leg with a little stick that their father split from a log. And he got better again. But he would have to tell them next time and the time after how they managed it, what their father said, how tame the squirrel grew, how much milk he drank and how many morsels of rusk and pancake he ate. It was time for them to go to sleep.

He stayed there with them in the quiet room, shaken by the gale blowing in from outside, and listened to them sleeping with little whistlings and the occasional whimper after a sudden spasm that might have been fear. He thought how hard it is to really know anything about a person, to understand somebody else's life and why they live it as they do. As the thuds of little bodies on the seat of the wooden settle the other side of the door and the scraping of spoons round plates of gruel gradually died away, he felt exhausted. There were now seven hours until he had to be at the bakery mixing dough.

When he went out into the kitchen, picked up his bundle of leaflets and put them in his briefcase, Agnes studied his face.

'You're tired,' she said. 'Go to bed, love.'

'I've got to deliver these.'

She took off her apron. The only sound from the settle and the beds was a snuffle now and then.

'I'll come with you if you like,' she said. 'They'll be fine. Vera's so big now. She can help Knut if he needs a pee. It'll be all right. Nothing can happen to them.' But deep inside she was petrified of fire. She took his hand. He bowed his head.

'You needn't come upstairs in any of the blocks. Not a single one. Just keep me company.'

But he still wasn't entirely happy because he was thinking the whole time about how he was going to tell her they'd paid for the printing of the leaflets out of their own money.

'Agnes,' he said. 'Agnes, there's something I've got to tell you.'

To a daughter

Children are born without wanting to be. Their mothers generally can't do anything about it either. To tell the truth, it's a fact that many children would have been welcome miscarriages. Many children would have been got rid of if their mothers had dared or known where to turn. I think it's horrible.

No one's ever told me the whole truth about childbirth. I feel very alone.

I go to the pictures every week, sometimes several times. I've seen Marlene Dietrich in *Morocco* and Greta Garbo in *Romance* and South Sea island films with beauty queens from Samoa. I read in the paper about one film, it said you couldn't imagine a more splendid subject, so I went to see it. It was *A Woman's Tomorrow* with Vera Schmiterlöw and it was about a prostitute who repented and started a better life. In *Dangerous Curves*, Clara Bow was little and weak and she loved a villain and wouldn't see what he was really like. I've seen *Tarnished Lady* and *His House in Order* with Talulah Bankhead. They were all lies.

We're completely surrounded by lies and the worst of it is, they don't seem to serve any purpose. My brother says they're there to keep the masses in ignorance and dependence, to make them believe in fate and think there's nothing they can do to change their lives. But it seems to me some lies are completely meaningless. I don't see what good they could do anybody.

Being born is a question of fate. Giving birth is fate too. My foster-

133

mother can't see it like that. She's convinced everybody makes a conscious decision to conceive, or should do if they're healthy, wholesome people. That's what she calls people she likes: healthy and wholesome.

But you might be raped or get drunk. You might both be drunk. Some people are so refined and highbrow I can hardly believe they know how to do it. And yet, bits of their anatomies find their way to the right places. Maybe they don't even realise what they're doing and carry on talking about other things, how they love each other and so on, while it's happening. But that must be quite rare. Other times you might be so rushed you hardly think about what you're doing and still find you've conceived. You might think conception's disgusting. In fact, you might hate him, but it happens all the same.

I don't know when I conceived. I'm not especially bothered about it having been one particular time. There've been so many times. They've all been great. I didn't think about getting pregnant very much. If I had, I'd have been scared. And worried about the shame of being found out and my foster-mother's misery. Though that wasn't as bad as I expected.

The father is someone I liked very much. For some months I thought of nothing but him, day and night. It's no exaggeration to say I dreamt of him when I was asleep, too. But I never thought of us getting married. Everything was fine as it was. All I longed for was summer, so we could lie in the open air together. I never thought it might be us two getting married. What we were doing had nothing to do with anybody else or with the future. I never thought more than a few days ahead, and about the summer of course.

I used to think about marriage quite a lot, and about people who were married. But it doesn't seem possible for anyone to crawl in and hide from the lies all around us. There are no secret places to hide. My brother wants the world to be different. He wants all the oppression and exploitation to vanish. But whatever fair words he and his wife say to each other, they're still lies. She looks at him as if she were a servant, or his mother. I don't like her doing it.

We weren't married when I got pregnant. That's very common. Most people lie about it and lots of children don't know that's how it happened. They realise when they grow up and see the dates in their parents' wedding rings or something else that doesn't quite add up. But I'm not going to lie about this. I've decided.

At first I didn't believe it. I put it out of my mind, that's why it took us so long to decide what to do. My foster-mother was worried and kept going on about sanitary towels that must need washing. She was a lot more worried than I was.

When I finally realised, I nearly went mad. That's the hardest thing to be truthful about with your own child. It'll be really difficult. I didn't want to have babies at all. We weren't together any more by then, it was my choice. We didn't see each other for a long time and when we finally did, I just cried and came out with a load of insults and accusations. I was beside myself. I simply couldn't accept it. I forgot I'd ever liked him. I saw it as an invasion, an infringement of my rights, something so ancient and awful I couldn't understand him being happy and proud of it. I felt painted into a corner and the worst of it was, he thought things had turned out just the way they should. My foster-mother said I should be glad he wanted to accept his responsibility instead of trying to get out of it. He found us a little flat and she made me some skirts with expandable waistlines and jackets with lots of gathers so it didn't show so much. I had to give up my job.

The worst time wasn't when I was screaming and shouting and threatening to jump off the kitchen table and take hot baths until I got rid of it. That made him really panic and get cross with me. My foster-mother was afraid I'd do something foolish too. In fact the two of them got on very well. They were full of care and attention. I realised of course that the care and attention weren't for me. They were for that thing in my stomach. It's a harsh thing to be saying to someone who isn't to blame and may not want to be born at all. But it's the truth.

The worst time came when they thought they'd talked me round. I was left on my own in the flat. He started his preparations for the bandy season again and went training every evening he was free and at weekends. I was very isolated because the girls I used to go around with were all out dancing and whenever I went down to see them at the hairdresser's they seemed embarrassed.

There were a few others who'd had babies, and they were very keen to talk to me. They wanted to confide in me about placentas and prolapse of the womb and infant diarrhoea and engorgement. They said the baby could have birthmarks if I saw a fire, or a hare lip if I saw a hare. I preferred to be on my own.

Then the fear started growing inside me. It kept pace with the baby. At that stage I'd never have thought of the baby as someone you could talk to. I'd never have dreamt of it. I thought of it as a horrible animal, eating out my insides and threatening to kill me.

I didn't dare stay sitting at home on my own any longer and I started eating lots of sweets. He gave me housekeeping money. I used some of it to buy all the sweets I fancied and I expect I put on a lot more weight than I should have done. When he asked about the money and wondered where it had all gone, I didn't bother to lie. I just said I'd spent it. I'm sure I was a great disappointment to him. I had to borrow money from my foster-mother several times. She didn't want me to pay her back either. I think she felt embarrassed by me.

But it was all the same to me. I had no feelings left. Well, except fear. Everything else seemed pointless and absurd. I started going to all sorts of things, just so I didn't have to be on my own in the evenings. I went to absolutely anything, even to the Salvation Army when Lapp-Lisa was playing her guitar and singing. I went to talks at the Community Centre. There was Sten Bergman talking about travel and adventures in the Kuri Islands and showing his slides; and an engineer talking on 'Russia, Promised Land of World Industry'. That time, my brother was there and he looked pleased to see me. I suppose he thought I only went to the pictures and he was right, on the whole. I didn't care if they were love films any more. I went to anything. I saw Harold Lloyd in *Feet First* and a comedy from Denmark, *Full Tilt*. It was all the same to me.

When Dr Ada Nilsson was at the Community Centre speaking on the physiological side of marriage I was there, and it was good. She was proof you can talk about everything. It's just a matter of choosing the right words. But the next day she was giving a lecture called Birth Control and I didn't think I'd dare to go. I was afraid people would laugh at me and think: *she's* left it a bit late. But in the end I didn't let it bother me and went along all the same. I even sat quite near the front. And at least now I know I needn't ever be in the family way again. There are things you can do, even if it's hard to get the supplies. I'm not intending to get pregnant ever again.

My foster-mother kept on coming up and trying to get me to take an interest in cooking and the cost of food. She seemed not to dare to tell me off for not bothering to behave the way she'd hoped. Instead, she kept dropping little hints, like how you had to pay two kronor a kilo for pike at the moment but only sixty öre for herring. I've always found it easy to remember figures, so I ended up with a catalogue in my head despite myself. I knew a joint of beef cost two fifty a kilo and potatoes fifty öre a half peck and eggs had gone up to two kronor a score and a packet of Persil cost forty-eight öre. There was no escaping it. In the end I felt uncomfortable paying more for things than I needed to. Maybe that's why I stopped buying sweets as well. But I think it was mainly because I went right off everything I'd liked before. I had a craving for lots of strange things instead, like cress. It's summer now luckily, and I can go round looking for cress in the evenings. If anyone's got it in their garden I go and pick some when no one's looking and put it in my pockets. I eat it when I'm back out on the road.

I've gone all heavy and bloated. I have to walk with my legs wide apart. When I catch sight of myself in the mirror on the cupboard, I can't believe it's me. I feel as if my body's ruined. My stomach's all taut and covered in purplish blotches and streaks. It looks as if it might burst. It's hard to make yourself go and see anyone when you look as awful as this. And I don't trust my body any longer. The whole time it's doing things I can't control. I get heartburn and my feet go numb. There's air trying to escape from my guts nearly all the time. I get out of breath climbing stairs and it's hard to breathe even just sitting still.

A while back I noticed I'd got some big, blue knots on my calves. I could see the veins curling up and knotting themselves. I cried because it looked so revolting. My foster-mother told me I ought to go and buy support stockings for varicose veins. I went to a surgical appliance shop where I'd never been before. There were people queuing in front of me so I had ages to stand and stare at the shelves and read what was on them: back supports, health corsets, radium blankets, rubber ice packs, mattress pads, enema bags, sample bottles, bed-pans, spittoons, oiled taffeta, atomisers, stomach pumps, arch supports, trusses.

I thought about us lying together, him and me, and simply

couldn't understand what business I had in a shop like this. In fact, I still can't come to terms with it. But I had to buy an enema bag as well, because I was so constipated.

I sleep a lot these days. That's the best thing about it all. I often drop off again after he's gone to work and sleep half the morning. I hadn't given a thought to getting anything ready for the baby. There was plenty of time to do all that later, I thought. But I shall be having you any day now. My foster-mother's brought up a whole load of clothes for you. It feels embarrassing, talking to you.

She'd made gowns with embroidered collars and little drawstring fastenings. Tiny babies shouldn't have buttons, she says. There were little interlock vests too, but I expect she bought those. Then there were binders and matiné jackets and navel bandages and lots of hemmed muslin nappies and nappy inserts and little knitted pants. There was a white cotton blanket she'd finished round the edge with blue blanket-stitch.

'You'd better get a clothes basket ready for the baby to sleep in,' she said, 'Line it with material. Something dainty with little flowers.'

She asked if I'd got any sheets.

'Can't I just use the ordinary ones and fold them?' I said. She nearly had a fit and I had no choice but to say:

'Only joking. I've made some sheets.'

I don't know why I'm like this with her.

In the mornings I can't stop worrying about what's going to happen. I make a bit of breakfast and then go back to sleep. But it gets worse later in the day. The evenings are worst of all.

I'm so dreadfully scared. The worst of it is, there's nothing I can do about it now. Every single day I can feel little twinges in my belly, I get horrible cramps and think this must be it. Then I sit on a chair just waiting for it to come again. When I eventually realise it's not time yet, I start crying with relief. But I think about hardly anything else.

There are three people who could have told me what having a baby is like. But they've fed me lies. When my foster-mother had her baby I was standing behind a door, listening. She was about forty-five and it was her first time. She did a lot of awful screaming and one of the things she said was that the pain would drive her mad and they'd got to get her away from there. It went on for hours. I hid outside.

She was screaming and the midwife told her she'd got to try to help. She wasn't to tense up and resist each time she had a contraction. But each time she screamed as if she'd reached some high place and was looking down into the abyss and then she screamed like a person being tortured by someone more cruel than we can ever imagine. I hid in the walk-in cupboard in the kitchen and everyone thought I was out. Although she was in such pain, she asked about me several times. She didn't want me to hear her. I've wondered since whether it was because she wanted to spare me or because she didn't want me to be put off.

Hour after hour that torture went on, and in between she lay panting and dreading the next contraction. Then it was the bearing down. The midwife told her to keep her chin down and push. She screamed that it would tear her apart. Which it did. I know they had to stitch her up afterwards.

When I asked her what having a baby was like, she said it was a miracle and the most wonderful experience a woman can have in her life. I said surely it must have hurt. You don't really notice all that, she replied. You're so happy about the baby. But she whispered that the room doesn't smell very fresh when you're having a baby. I ought to make sure the midwife cleaned up and aired the place before she let the father come in, she said. I wonder if it's true. She's a bit on the fastidious side.

I asked my mother too. She said it was soon over and you didn't think about it much afterwards. But she must've been lying too; there was a scared look in her eyes. There was one other person I was able to ask and she said that for her it was all over and done with in a night and a morning and a day and an evening. She had two boys that way. But I know she had a baby long before she was married. That was her first time and maybe it hurt so much she didn't want to talk about it. She probably felt ashamed too.

She's very tough and thinks other people should be the same; I even thought she might be cross with me for being scared. But she wasn't. She just said there are so many things we don't want to do. And she looked sad.

People tell you a lot of strange things. They revel in telling you what breasts with abscesses and mastitis look like and how the placenta sometimes comes out covered in blistery swellings. They either want to be heroines themselves or to feel important because they know about those things. They come straight out with it in the middle of coffee.

Their stories are lies as well. I shall tell you the truth about your birth if you turn out to be a girl. I promise. But I shall never tell anyone else anything about it. It seems to me I'd be too embarrassed. Though perhaps people aren't?

It's not that long since I finally recognised that you were a child. I started feeling lumps and bumps on my stomach. I mean, I'd been feeling movements for a long time, so I can't explain why I didn't recognise it was a child with arms, legs and a head. I couldn't even remember what babies looked like. It's so long since I saw a newborn baby. I went up to see a girl who'd just had one. She was surprised to see me because we didn't know each other all that well. But I didn't care.

The baby was tiny and very red. He seemed so delicate that I found him rather horrible. When she put him to her breast he groped for her and started sucking the minute he got her nipple in his mouth. I asked her if he'd done that from the start and she said he had. I asked her again if it was really true that he'd groped for her at once and wanted to be near her.

'Of course,' she said.

'Wasn't he afraid of you to start with?' I asked.

That made her laugh.

'No,' she said. 'Babies aren't the least afraid of being near their mother.'

But that made me realise they aren't afraid of being near anyone. If you put a baby to a dirty, disgusting old man, even one who was drunk, it would grope for him. If you put a baby to a person who's planning to hit it or choke it or assault it, it would still grope towards that person. Babies don't understand that the rest of us are particular people. They think we all belong together.

After all, we like little babies, we generally find any roly-poly little creature sweet, any puppy or baby animal. I suppose that's their defence against us, just the way the hairless, pink belly a puppy displays to an adult male dog is his defence against him. I didn't think that baby I saw was particularly sweet. But I do know I shall feel that you put all your trust in me because the arms you were put into were mine.

I'm assuming it hurts dreadfully when you give birth, so dreadfully that it's a blank afterwards. I mean, I'm not altogether sure that those who've been through it are lying. They may not be untruthful, just unaware. Perhaps they don't remember because the pain has burnt away a patch of their consciousness. Perhaps there *is* no truth where this is concerned. It simply gets forgotten every time.

But carrying a child is heavy work, and giving birth to it is a great labour. I sometimes wonder whether every woman who's had a baby feels enormous reverence for human beings because they know how they get here. But it doesn't seem to work that way. The ones I know are more or less like everybody else. Yet I think they must have felt that way for a little while.

It's the last day of August and the Community Park will be closing for the season this evening. There's a dance of course, with the Roxy Band. They're really good. The WEA choir's going to perform too, it said in the paper, but people usually just snigger when they're on.

It's already over I expect. It's dark now. I can see fireworks, rockets in the sky. From the Park, I dare say. I'm waiting to feel something that hurts or water starting to trickle down my legs. I'm scared the whole time.

Carlsborg opens its mouth onto Cobbler's Row, a wide jaw with an extended lower lip of concrete. The whole building is of brick and as red as meat. Square and squat, it lurks among the cedars at the top of the rise. This being the only high ground in the whole area, it put itself there to maintain the hierarchical distinction between itself and the home of the Lindh family, and to a lesser extent between itself and the spindly church on the other side of the railway, the Post Office that is a second-rate copy of the Swedish House of Nobility, and the building with stepped gables that houses the Register Office.

An old building like that can swallow almost anything: God's children and types reeking of cheap aquavit, railway folk, joiners, foundrymen and schoolteachers, nervous academics who come bearing higher education certificates, and great, coarse lumps like Fabian Bärj. Its mouth, as mentioned above, yawns onto Cobbler's Row where it intersects Industrial Road; they walk in that way, its well-oiled jaws close over them (Do not shut the door! It will shut itself with Norton's patent silent door-closing device) and if they ever emerge again after their sluggish journey round its corridors, being rendered acceptable to Carlsborg's gloomy bowels, they all look pretty much the same.

You come first into a relatively bright entrance hall, where a great elk raises its muzzle over all who enter and little moths swarm around him like flakes of gold in the lamplight. The further you go, the darker it gets. The walls are panelled in a wood that resembles, and is supposed to resemble, oak. Here are the marks left by the cast-iron umbrella stand. It had huge, sturdy feet like eagle's claws. Here there was once a picture called 'Island of Death' and this is where the former owner's harmonium used to stand. He was a simple man in spite of being rich. He pumped the foot pedal of his harmonium and sang songs about longing for the afterlife. Here, by the window looking out on the Co-Educational Intermediate School, his wife would sit darning socks in all her wealth, a good example to the unpropertied classes who often live like crickets and butterflies and get chilblains from going about with their heels poking out of their socks. This is where they ate porridge and this was where they had their first telephone. On a shelf are a silver-plated palm frond and a stone from the Mount of Olives with emblems of Christ Crucified. They go back to the time Wärnström the factory owner and his wife went on a trip to the Holy Land. But Oscar II has been taken down. He used to be here above the shelf, painted on silk, a handsome, harmonious image in pale blue, silver and gold. He's in the cellar now.

Of course there have been changes. The drawing room and the gentlemen's' study have been combined into one. The wall has been knocked down and now there is a counter running the length of both rooms, where payments to the local government are received behind glass panels. Female cashiers with all their pension entitlements in order look out through gilt-edged openings. Typewriters and manual adding machines clatter and whirr, telephones ring and the oak parquet creaks beneath endless feet. Marks are left by rough boots dripping melted snow, and the dust from the archives collects in the folds of the heavy, brown velvet curtains. But Mrs Wärnström worries no longer. She has departed this land of sin, taking nothing with her.

The town council meets on the first floor. A great beam of dust lies across the table in a ray of sunshine and there are cigar burns on the tabletop. Round the walls there are portraits of the fathers of the community: station inspector Baron Gustaf Adolf Cederfalk has the look of a man suffering terrible colic; Holger Iverson-Lindh, flaming red in the face, flanks his father-in-law Alexander Lindh, merchant and Knight of the Vasa Order. Petrus Wilhelmsson who started the joinery is undecorated and looks like an elk, and manufacturer Wärnström is depicted beneath the palm frond and emblems of Christ Crucified we passed just now. Of the former chairmen of the municipal council and members of the town council, long turned to ashes just as their cigars have done, there are many with the same troubled expression as old Cederfalk. But presumably it is the artist who is at fault, because high living doesn't tend to lead to the sort of spontaneous combustion Cederfalk appears about to experience.

All in good time, a bust of Per Albin Hansson will appear in the window, mounted on a pedestal of polished oak. The proposal has already been put forward. Where should he stand if not here, with his drive to make Sweden into a People's Home, a welfare state as egalitarian and democratic as any good home? Stationed here, he will look out from the place where the lady of the house put her wool basket as she sat darning socks as a lesson to those who live like butterflies and drink aquavit in bowers of lilacs. The man who created the idea of the People's Home was no tribal chief of the Caucasus with glinting toecaps to his boots but a family man, used to being served and obeyed in the gentle, informally disciplined way fathers are in good families. What father would want his children standing to attention when he addressed them? Lingering inside the brown velvet curtains here is the atmosphere of those snug evening counsels round the lamp, when the children were encouraged to open their little beaks and say frankly what was on their minds, but also to learn, to realise that he who wields power has responsibility and knowledge as well, and everyone's best interests at heart.

How rosy their faces were in the warm, yellow light, how dark and dreadful the shadows in the corners. The dream of bringing democracy to the state in the way it already existed in the family could only have been the dream of a patriarch by the light of an evening lamp.

The community's former fathers have withdrawn to their walls and graves; those mighty elks, those kings of warehouses and forges, knights of the martyr to indigestion, have abdicated. So have many of the devoted and unpaid. The town now has a municipal finance director who is also the chairman of the town council in receipt of a large salary. The new fathers meet in the town council chamber, allied across all petty class and party divisions: the building contractor, the town architect, the senior doctor, the irrepressible Fabian Bärj, the chapel-going business-men and shop owners, the foundry boss and the owner of the pattern-making business, the editor-in-chief and of course Wolfgang Altmeyer from Austria, taken in as a foster child by Holger Iversen-Lindh and now wielding the power that Patrik, son and heir, was in a hurry to exchange for bawling orders across a barrack square, which was more straightforward and less likely to upset his stomach.

The Correspondent takes back views of these men standing in the bustle of the town square and publishes them for the public to win prizes by guessing who they are. They nearly all help collect money for needy children and hand out the presents at the Christmas party they give for them.

This building, though, where the strong smell of old men has accumulated, is where they carry out the sombre, worthy element of their duties. In these rooms, claustrophobic with cigar smoke and the reek of rubber galoshes drying by radiators, the aura of mothballs surrounding heavy overcoats, the slight odour of spirits from duplicating machines and evening grogs, the smell of dust from dark studies and meeting rooms, the old men move sluggishly along Carlsborg's corridors until they are expelled. Quite a few of them have already started making arrangements for epitaphs and inscriptions on plinths and pedestals.

Death pulls down all decorations and barriers, rots chains, turns ribbons to ashes and silences grand words, writes Magnus Swärd, news editor of *The Correspondent*, on the occasion of the opening of the new crematorium. But it's not entirely true and he probably doesn't mean it literally anyway, being himself a specialist in grand epitaphs, before and after death. He's a nervous, excessively thin man with thick, prematurely grey hair. He used to spend his days in the public record office up in Carlsborg, now known as the town hall. Then the editor-in-chief took him under his wing to secure the succession. Wallin only has two daughters, Ada and Lisa, of whom one is married and the other religious, so now Swärd writes his obituaries in working hours. He's a true poet in the old Swedish tradition, waxing lyrical about Vikings when the archeologists find a ship burial, and about shoe-shop proprietors turning fifty, whenever the occasion arises. He has a mechanism in his head which always produces the right word or phrase. 'Land arisen from the seas!' he declaims in his ceremonial cantata for the Co-Educational Intermediate School's celebration of the Ice Age (which is where he usually starts). 'Hail Erik Johansson!' runs his fiftieth birthday ode.

He is skilled in the art of the subtle insinuation. Blessed is he who has had a well-established position and has not shifted from his chosen path. All hail to him if he has combined practical competence, clear-sightedness and thoroughness in his work with strength of will and at the same time been a loyal friend, forceful and unstoppable.

But if he has gone quietly and carefully through life, we may suspect that the individual in question was a wimp, and if he left behind him sound labour and unstinting effort he had of course achieved little in the community. If he is a humanist and philanthropist that's all well and good as far as it goes, and likewise if he was far-sighted, but we soon realise he left much undone; and if it says straight out that he was a dreamer and idealist then he was a benevolent drunkard.

But if he's a forceful donor, founder and gentleman, albeit starting small in humble circumstances and working his way up with his own hands to the world of granite plinths where consecrated bells ring out to the eternal glory of work and zeal, then he can rest assured that Magnus Swärd would have declared 'Hero, depart for Valhalla!' over his mortal remains, were it not for the unfortunate fact that the new Chancellor of the German Reich had already used it for the remains of old Hindenburg. Finding that someone else got there first is a misfortune which does occasionally befall Magnus Swärd in the exercise of his profession.

It is the second of January 1938. The park round Carlsborg with its cedars, yews and oaks is what news editor Magnus Swärd would have called arrayed in frosted splendour. It's very early in the morning. Not yet seven.

Here comes Fabian Bärj, who will in time come to be called The Irrepressible. He is in a grey overcoat and a black hat with a rolled, rib-edged brim and his enormous stomach fills out his coat. He's blonde, with a solid, red face. He has bent, corn-plastered toes, but they don't show of course; he's no savage, he's wearing shoes and black galoshes. Today he takes up his position as municipal finance director. Last autumn he became chairman of the town council. His Social Democratic party now has a qualified majority on all the committees and boards. Housing is being built for large families, local-authority-sponsored cottages are springing up on reclaimed land in meadows and in boggy areas of sparse pine forest, drained for the purpose. Unemployment is non-existent, there's no need to struggle any longer to get five more men from the local district onto the relief work scheme; there are plans for a proper swimming area and an extension to the Community Centre.

He's come early today. We don't know why. He knows the building well, after all. But now he's going to belong to it in the same way as the cashiers behind the glass and the elk head the moths will soon have reduced to powder.

He's not alone in the frosty park. There's a queue outside Carlsborg, a queue of people and dogs. There's Berlin the chemist with his yellowish Welsh corgi, Jenny Otter with a black, rather overweight schnauzer and Miss Lisa Wallin whose father owns *The Correspondent*. She's got a standard poodle whose strength exceeds her own and she has wound its lead round a lamp post to get a better grip. There are the two old Blixt sisters as well, both attempting to manoeuvre their heavy, misanthropic rottweiler. There's Modlund the carpenter, hopping mad with a mongrel cur that insists on trying to force himself on the peke belonging to Miss Thorin from Elfvenberg's Drapery and Knitwear. Her way of putting it is that the cur is bothering her bitch, which drives Modlund mad. And that's just the head of the queue; there are lots more of them, the dogs growling and peeing, pretending to be indifferent or in some cases hanging furious and half-strangled on their leads.

To one side of the queue but right at its head is Mrs Severin, the schoolmaster's wife, with their beloved Irish sheepdog Shoulder, and Lisen Severin is angry. She's accusing the chemist of not letting her back into the queue after she took Shoulder to the man-made mound of rocks, designed as a viewing point, for him to answer the call of nature, or relieve himself as the chemist so crudely puts it. The chemist utters not a syllable more. He stares like factory owner Wärnström on his granite plinth with ice forming in his eyebrows, and the queue stamps its feet and says nothing.

The dog owners are all queuing to get a low number on their dog-licence disks. They bid good morning to Fabian Bärj who is now passing them on his way into the building. It swallows him with the sigh Norton's automatic door-closing device breathes these days after forty years of swinging on its oiled rod. The elk regards the queue while the door is open and seems to be observing, just before it disintegrates into grey powder, that mankind hasn't found any new forms of folly but is sticking to the old ones.

It's quiet in the great building. There's a ticking sound behind the panelling. His galoshes slither as he walks across the black-and-white squared floor. He came here to deliver some cheese in 1901. Does he remember? He'd got a job as errand boy at the dairy. In 1913 he started as a brakesman on the railway but he left before he was promoted to temporary station hand. It was in the Young Social Democrats he started spelling his name Bärj instead of the common Berg. There wasn't a lot of union activity in the railway company, the old men were cautious liberals. But he was bold and joined the local union branch when he was still only a brakesman. The station master hadn't liked it. Bärj would write in to the paper, signing himself Young Social Democrat and Onward and Upward.

Having left the railway, he filed moulded cast iron at the Wärnström foundry for a while and then progressed to the shop floor. There he stayed until his local public duties took up all his time. He was first secretary and then chairman of the union branch, volunteered for office in the Co-operative movement, sat on the town council and the temperance board.

And here he is now, standing on the cold, shiny stone floor under the elk, but this time without a box of smelly, porous cheese, without red ears and cold-numbed hands. Yet still he stands there as he has always stood there, as if those shamelessly squelching galoshes grew on his body along with the grey overcoat and the hat with the rib-edged brim, keeping pace with his beard and corns and the brown spots on the backs of his hands. Here he has stood and become The Irrepressible, a man who is prepared to listen without batting an eyelid to a speech in his own honour, who has in actual fact already done it: he recently had his fiftieth birthday and was presented with a smoking table by his local Social Democrat branch.

His heart's in the right place where this, his community, is concerned. He came early, although he is so familiar with this dark building and knows how heavily the chairman's gavel weighs in the hand. It is hard to understand what he is really doing here at this early hour. There may not even be any mystery to it, though that's how it looks as lamp after lamp goes on in the great building and we catch glimpses of his shadow. Has he come to settle up with himself? Is this his day for promises and firm intentions? What in God's name is the fellow doing there? Is he just fiddling with the inkwells and stamp pads or is there something real and important going on as he bends over the desks? Is he having doubts? Is he turning something over in his mind?

No! It's out of the question. He knows very well that now he has power there are only two things to fight for: getting more of it and validating the conviction that it's ended up in the right hands.

152

Buildings like Carlsborg are not designed for spiritual exercises, meditation, mental agonising and self-criticism. Look at old Sterkell, one-time railway engineer, sitting at home writing a handbook for amateur bird-watchers. Anyone who stepped forward as he did and said, 'I'm a useless laundry director and when it comes to running a bathhouse I'm totally incompetent' might as well devote himself to literature, birds and private life.

So what *is* the fellow doing there in the cold white lamplight, watched from outside by ten or fifteen frozen dog owners and their pets? Is he dreaming? Will you ever be able to partake of his dreams?

It was the only sunny day they'd had. And now it was over. They pedalled. In the service of death, in the service of death, pulsed the message in Jenny's head, loose words plucked from the heat and noise and oily smells of their afternoon. She didn't know where they were going any longer. Never in her life had she felt so tired; all she saw was Fredrik's back with a big sweaty mark between the shoulders, plastering his rayon shirt to his skin. His bike was loaded down with a tent and blankets, a cast-iron frying pan, a coffee pan, a saucepan for potatoes and a rucksack of food. Their wellingtons were tied to the saddlebags. He had taken almost everything when he saw how exhausted she was. She only had the suitcase of clothes on her carrier.

It was the summer of 1938 and he had four days' holiday. Taking them along with the midsummer holiday, it was long enough for them to go by rail north-west to Kristinehamn and do a cycling tour.

Värmland was incredible, the whole province was like a decorative wall poster. So steep, so blue - and they saw eagles! Jenny had grown up by a flat field in a little village called the Ridge with a lake for swimming a few kilometres away and a forest where you could throw bottles and dump old bedsteads. But now they were discovering Nature.

It was a clergyman who had said that to them. They met him in an old-fashioned gig with cracked and mildewed leather seats. He had reined in his horse with polite ceremony in order to greet them. When he heard that they hadn't seen Alster Manor House or the one at Mårbacka, he had amiably offered that comment about nature which had stuck in Jenny's mind. Later on, for instance reaching a lake, she caught herself thinking the clergyman had been right. They had discovered Nature. Here it was.

They pitched their tent overnight by vast lakes that were silent except for a little chat with the stones on the shoreline at dawn, slept on brushy fir in blankets sewn into bags; mournful, warbling birdsong from out in the drizzle followed them right into their slumbers. They had never been so close to each other, ever. But the rain kept on.

This was their one day of sunshine and they had spent it indoors, on factory floors smelling of hot grease and metal. Fredrik had wanted to see Bofors. There had been two things he wanted to see in Värmland: Johan Ericsson's eagle-crowned grave by Lake Daglösen and the Bofors works.

His day-to-day work was turning bearings for a 40 millimetre automatic anti-aircraft gun. It was work subcontracted to his factory by the ordnance foundry at Möckeln. He'd wondered about the gun and tried to visualise it as he stood at the lathe. Now he'd seen it.

They had made their way round foundry and cooling tower as the sun cast all its strength onto the flat roofs and gravel crunched beneath the soles of their sandals. They had been shown the grey powder that was Sweden's treasure and pride, an iron ore virtually free from sulphur and phosphorus, being sintered and split in two once more. Then they had climbed up inside the tall, dark blast furnace, still with the dressed ore of Tuollavara on their fingers, and seen a combination of iron ore, coke and limestone crashing down the furnace stack, which roared with fire as if trained to frighten them into respect.

The furnaces of the steelworks had produced the hard yet ductile

155

mixture of chrome nickel steel with tungsten and molybdenum alloys, which had been drawn off into a chill mould where it had set into a vast ingot and then been heated to white-hot. This they had seen after trudging along endless gritty walkways with the deafening blows of the drop-hammers ringing in their ears. The white-hot ingot was forged in an 1800 tonne press which squashed and kneaded it like a mad baker's wife until it was a long, thin shape you could begin to recognise as the barrel of a gun. You could also begin to imagine the ductility and strength of the renowned Bofors 40 that had blown so many human beings to bits, yet never harmed its gun crew or any monitoring commission member, which indeed it was designed to avoid.

The barrel was jacketed in several layers of the material, which would all be subjected to the same pain and pressure when the projectile was eventually launched, rotating in the heat.

Finally the barrel was immersed in simmering oil in a tall cooling tower and Jenny had given a sigh of relief when their guide merely pointed to it. She had been afraid they would have to climb it. Bofors owned gunpowder factories and mines, sintering works, chemical plants, blast furnaces, machine and electrosteel works, steel foundries, rolling-mills, forges, pressing works and engineering factories. For a while she'd been afraid they were going to have to see it all, except the mines, because they were in Lapland.

But Fredrik had been aglow with passion and interest. He'd been first in the group all the way round, first as the mandrel bar roughly bored out the gun barrel, first at the turning lathe and so close he'd been able to take a curling metal shaving, bluish black, as a souvenir. He was proud. He had heard and read time and again that you could be proud of the Swedish engineering industry.

Now here they were, pedalling. The uphill sections were long and the forest was silent. Isn't he ever going to stop, she wondered, feeling a sharp jab of resentment as she caught her breath painfully. She was saddle sore but couldn't tell him because the chafing was in a place you mustn't talk about. He might laugh.

'How about here?'

He turned round but got no reply. She followed him mutely along a small, bumpy track past fields where silent cows stared at them in the dusk. Their jaws worked and subterranean rumblings came from their ruminating paunches.

'Here.'

'The cows,' she said.

'They won't come over this way.'

'Well, I'm not staying here,' she said.

She could sense his scorn as they jolted on along the track, rutted with barely dried mud. The bikes wobbled and the saucepans clashed.

'Here, then?'

She made no reply, just got off her bike. The tent was tightly rolled and damp. Its musty smell made her feel sick as they opened it out. They started bickering about where to pitch it. They'd had words on the subject every evening, lighthearted banter. But this time he was impatient and thought her slow and stupid. His almost paternal joking about her technical incompetence had suddenly turned to scorn.

'For Christ's sake,' he said, seizing the bag of tent pegs. 'Can't you at least keep hold of the guy rope? Hold it, I said!'

Then she started to cry. She sat down on a tree stump without even checking if it was crawling with ants. She just wept, not knowing whether he could see. He didn't touch her, at any rate. When she eventually looked up, he'd put the tent back on his carrier, tightly rolled.

'Come on.'

He offered no explanation. It wasn't until they were back on the road that he said:

'You can sleep indoors tonight.'

They pedalled on. She was crying and those words from the afternoon were pounding in her head again, torn adrift from a context that had eluded her: in the service of death, in the service of death. He didn't utter a sound. They rode until they came to a school with the date 1905 on the wall, a solid stone edifice. She didn't even know what town or village they were in. They must be on the outskirts of somewhere. There was a tangle of grass round their feet and a worn football pitch to cross. She felt too ashamed to ask. It was awful, but she was so tired she'd just followed him dully and now she'd no idea where they were. But she didn't ask. No, she wasn't going to give him that pleasure. They were still on the verge of quarrelling as they went into the echoing building.

'Swearing is rude, crude and ignorant,' read a notice on the wall, and Jenny immediately felt that unpleasant school feeling. A large gymnasium had been fitted out as a hostel for walkers and there were six people there, who looked up as they entered. They didn't know what greeting to offer.

Two elderly men were over by one bed, burrowing in a rucksack for long johns which they perhaps intended wearing for the night. A lady was stuffing newspaper into a pair of wet and muddy gym shoes, and on the next bed sat a man who was presumably her husband. He looked like a staff sergeant and continued nonchalantly sculpting his corns as he greeted them. There were two girls as well, young and blonde. Jenny was immediately aware of how she looked after the cycle ride and of being a tall woman, still slim for her thirty-six years, with long, strong legs that were now

158

weak and shaky with pedalling. Oh yes, she could see those two flighty young things with their white blouses and their hair that was quite probably bleached, peroxide blonde. It wasn't always much fun being the tallest woman in the room. But Fredrik was tall, after all. Jenny's hair was blonde, a dreary, ratty colour when it was unwashed like now. It was the most boring hair colour of all. She had blue eyes and when she looked at her face in the mirror it just seemed ordinary, but the lawyer had said she was pretty. Before they were married she'd been in domestic service and the last two years she'd kept house for a lawyer, a widower. Fredrik had never been jealous about it later, he hadn't the imagination. Often, when she looked at herself in the mirror, she ached with longing for something, for children, adventure, knowledge, ecstasy. When she combed her hair down and let it fall over her eyes, she looked younger.

The flighty young things had shorts, but she didn't. In winter she sometimes wore a divided skirt.

There was a rustling of straw-filled mattresses and sandwich wrappers. They had a guarded conversation with the staff sergeant about where they'd been. Fredrik was quite reserved and Jenny was shy. The staff sergeant's wife pulled across the curtain that separated the men's and women's beds and the two girls unzipped their clothes. They were the height of modernity. Whizzz! Zzipp! they went. Jenny did surreptitious battle with hooks and eyes. She had safety pins in her underwear and it wasn't easy to get undressed in here without being seen. Sounds of gargling and throat clearing came from the washbasin in the corridor; then the staff sergeant came jogging in doing his breathing exercises and threw himself backwards against a set of wall bars, head down. They heard him puffing and panting for a while, then gradually it went quiet. The two elderly brothers, who had now pulled on the long, warming undergarments they had brought with them, wrapped up their smoked bacon and tucked it away in their rucksacks. They wiped their knife clean and said goodnight. And just as the staff sergeant was going to tell Fredrik to put the light out on his way back in - he was just going out for a pee - they heard someone whistling in the corridor, the door opened, a rucksack thumped onto the old, thickly-varnished, evil-smelling, brown floor and a voice said:

'Buenas tardes, señoras y señores!'

At first they really did think he was a foreigner. He had jet-black hair and couldn't have been more than twenty-five. The blonde girls peeped through the curtain. Then he laughed at them all and asked in plain, ordinary Swedish whether there was a bed left for him. He introduced himself and went round saying hello to everybody. There was no longer any question of turning the light off, despite the notice saying lights had to be out by ten o'clock.

'All in bed already?'

They were embarrassed; after all, the light of the summer evening was still outside the window and they'd been thinking of going to sleep simply to abide by the regulations.

'Hasn't the party started yet?' he asked, and the staff sergeant's wife looked disapprovingly over the edge of her blanket. But then she surreptitiously pulled the chamois-leather rollers out of her hair, for it was no longer quiet like it had been, and the two girls were up and getting into their clothes with a great deal of loud zipping.

It took a quarter of an hour or so, but then hunks of bacon were balanced on suitcases and they were buttering bread and hearing that the staff sergeant was not a staff sergeant at all but a grocer from Kumla and the two brothers owned a little sawmill. The girls worked at the Luma lightbulb factory in Stockholm. They spoke

160

with Stockholm accents and pretended to make a fuss when Meijer, the one with black hair, produced some aquavit from his rucksack. A notice on the wall said that the possession and consumption of alcoholic beverages on these premises was strictly forbidden. Eventually though, with much giggling, they accepted a mug of lemonade with a dash of aquavit. Jenny shook her head at first, but when Fredrik's bottle came out too, she accepted some in a rosy coffee cup. Meijer wanted to hear where they'd all been; he'd been in Spain himself, he said, and it went very quiet. The brothers chewed on some sausage. Just for a minute, both girls had their hands on the mug. Then Fredrik cleared his throat and asked:

'International Brigade?'

Meijer nodded and no more was said on the subject. But Jenny had never seen anyone who'd been in the Spanish Civil War and she could hardly take her eyes off him. She wondered if he'd come straight from there and thought his hands and his rucksack looked different to other people's.

They weren't at all the feeble lot they'd seemed when they all went to bed half an hour before. And Meijer was by no means the liveliest of the crew. That honour went to the old brothers. They had a harmonica and a set of clattersticks among their things and they sang and played:

> To Stockholm went Heppi Teppi Nepp
> To Stockholm went I
> To Stockholm went Amali-ay
> and told us to drink it dry!

The girls from Luma didn't seem to have bleached their hair after all. Jenny was sitting so close to them she could see the colour went right down to the roots. They looked like sisters, but they weren't. They just dressed alike for fun. And they admitted they came from Arboga originally, despite their strong Stockholm accents. Jenny had started chatting to them and that was why she never knew how the discussion between Fredrik and Meijer began. But it must have been Fredrik of course, saying that they'd been to Bofors and that his job was turning bearings for the Model 40. He tended to get a bit excited when he'd had a drink. He liked to be the one doing the talking, without interruptions. He was no conversationalist in the sense of keeping up when the repartee was bouncing around like a ping-pong ball. With one part of her mind she heard him delivering a lecture on gun manufacture, most of it in words borrowed from their guide. In the service not of death but of life, for example.

'How the hell d'you work that out - gun manufacture in the service of life?' said Meijer.

Fredrik told him about the field-gun's elbow-joint design that was also used in cars, but Meijer just laughed in his face. Fredrik didn't like it.

'The 40's one hundred percent defensive,' he roared. 'It's got a reflex sightline that can aim at moving targets and track them as it fires. It's so effective no one believes bombers would ever dare come in low enough these days to actually hit their target. They'd be shot down inside ten seconds! So - in the service of life, you see, not death!'

'How touching,' said Meijer.

It seemed strange that he could treat Fredrik so contemptuously, thought Jenny, how did he dare? After all, Fredrik was no dozy idiot who stood at his shift doing what he was told and waiting for the working day to end. His brain was active as he worked and he had come all the way to Värmland to see exactly what he was making; that must be why he had lost his temper with Meijer.

162

Though Jenny hadn't noticed it happening. All she heard were the usual tirades, all those things men talked about these days: mustard gas and civil defence precautions and ultimatums. The old brothers were peaceable and probably didn't really know much about it. The grocer, though, got quite heated. He spoke of the face of our age, calling it a gas mask. And all of a sudden Fredrik was on his feet, shouting that enough was enough. It wasn't the staff sergeant he was shouting at, but Meijer, who had claimed Axel Wenner-Gren was nothing but Krupp's lapdog. He was the one who'd saved Bofors when the law banning foreign interests in the Swedish arms industry came into force.

'With Krupp's money, that's for sure!' said Meijer.

'Right, that's it!' shouted Fredrik.

The Clatterstick Brothers immediately offered to sing another song, but they were halted by the staff sergeant, whose wife was snivelling and gulping for breath. She was scared no doubt, and Jenny felt ashamed. But Meijer just looked amused. Fredrik said it was ludicrous trying to convince him the world was a seething hell of vice and crime.

'With a smart, shiny exterior like the front of the Bofors hotel,' Meijer put in. He was quick as a snake in his replies. Fredrik turned, heavy as a tank, and Meijer lit a cigarette as he listened to him. But then the staff sergeant who was a grocer put his foot down. Whatever else they did, they weren't going to smoke in here.

'God almighty,' said Meijer, making no move to put out his cigarette, 'Krupp goes sailing in the South Pacific with Wenner-Gren; then Wenner-Gren goes sailing with Wingquist. And you read all about it in the magazines. Don't you ever think?'

Jenny had seen a portrait of Wingquist, the managing director of Bofors; his eyes in lead-grey oil paint had rested on her and she hadn't listened much to what the guide was saying but rather experienced a general sense of God and Sweden and how it felt when the male-voice choir sang. But Fredrik had been paying attention to what the guide said about the man who saved Bofors from nationalisation.

The main fact Fredrik knew about Wingquist was that he was the genius who had invented the ball-bearing. An engineering design like that gave Fredrik a sense of almost physical pleasure. He delighted in the thought of those beautiful spheres mysteriously rolling in oil. Without being fully conscious of it, he had a fundamental conviction that a world which runs on ball-bearings must be a good and rational world. He admired the great design engineers and had dreamed of being one of them when he was younger. John Ericsson's mausoleum was the first monument they had visited on their cycling tour. He had as little time for the great cultural figures of Värmland as he did for royalty. But he revered the design engineers. He simply couldn't imagine that the world could be rushing headlong to perdition on ball-bearings or hydraulic systems.

Jenny, knowing hardly anything about bearings and guns, was intimidated by them. She was in fact suspicious of all complicated constructions that could go wrong if you interfered with them. Remarkable people made her wish only that she need never encounter or be addressed by them. If evolution had been left up to you, Fredrik once said, we'd never have got further than Henscroft.

That was the site of the first Stone Age finds in his home area. Road-makers had discovered a settlement with shards of bulbous clay pots bearing impressions of grains of wheat and grape pips. Henscroft Man was described in the schoolbooks as a potter beside a warm sea which deposited shells on the sand. Fredrik, who hated schoolteachers and all their pronouncements, found Henscroft Man

164

and his crew clad in animal skins merely ridiculous. But Jenny saw a woman rolling lengths of clay in front of her and assembling them into the shape of a pot. She moulded them together and smoothed the surface with wetted hands. Then she carefully pressed a pear-shaped grape pip all along the edge to make a pattern. Inside her, unseen by schoolteachers and Fredrik, Jenny had a secret room. Inside her was not only Henscroft Woman but also a lot of other ideas about the world and its history.

A big gun is born in fire and heat as the semifinished steel pours down into a mould. But it is conceived at a drawing board in an office that is quiet and cool. Drawing offices and laboratories are the brains of a company. There, reason and order prevail. There, calculations are made scientifically and logically, the guide at Bofors had said, pointing up to the rows of windows in the empty, white noon light, without any interference from emotion or self-interest, in order to set a heavy mass in motion and find a form for it. (And form is joy! Even Henscroft Woman knew that.) There is a link between the order that prevails in drawing offices and world order itself. (And order is beauty!) It could be expressed in complex terms or simple ones, like the way Fredrik whistled it as he snorted and splashed in the washbowl on a Saturday afternoon: things are getting better and better with every passing day.

'Better guns in a better world!' said Meijer sarcastically.

But if he'd listened to Fredrik he'd have grasped the fact that he wasn't talking to some idiot with no idea what he was making parts for, nor some crazy fool or grumbler who believed in the excesses put about by a propaganda merchant like Konrad Eriksson.

'I'm afraid I don't know him,' said the smiling Meijer.

'Or that the world outside Sweden is nothing but a great bag of shit!' roared Fredrik.

It was awful! The staff sergeant's wife withdrew, pulling the curtain across behind her. The Luma girls finished their spiked lemonade and said they were going to bed. Everything was spoilt.

'Go outside if you want to argue,' said the peaceable harmonica player and he and his brother started taking off their trousers again, yawning widely.

Meijer talked and talked. Jenny could hear his droning, purring voice through the curtain. Fredrik had decided to go quiet. He tended to lose confidence when people tried to talk him down. Or perhaps it was merely that Meijer had to go out for a pee, so Fredrik didn't manage to get his answer in.

While he was gone, the staff sergeant sat up in bed and said a horse-dealer and gypsy king had died at New Year. He came from Ornäs and his name was Meijer. He died in a fight in the churchyard at Tuna.

'Where did this fellow say he was from?'

Then his wife sat up too. She had her hair wound back into the chamois leather rolls, each twisted round so one end could be inserted in the other, but she didn't let that bother her this time. She peeped through the curtain and said she'd plainly heard him say he was called Geijer.

'Geijer,' said one of the girls reverently. They could reach no consensus on the matter. Three had heard it as Meijer and three as Geijer. They debated it hotly. Fredrik said nothing. He lay in bed feeling angry.

Geijer/Meijer was whistling as he came in and got undressed. The grocer who had been doing breathing exercises asked him to switch off the light. The room went more or less quiet except for the rustle of mattresses, and the brothers at once began to snore gently. The bedsteads were sturdy iron. Fredrik had identified them as military issue.

Jenny dozed off and was woken by a violent creaking of bed springs. She saw the staff sergeant, as she still somehow thought of him, bending over his wife in the gloom, letting out dreadful groans. Jenny lay stock still and didn't know whether to shut her eyes or stare at them, cough or pretend to be asleep. Then he manoeuvred her up off the bed, laid her flat on the floor and made her stretch her arms out backwards and hold onto some wall bars while he carefully pulled on her feet, at which point Jenny realised she had one of those backs where something slips out of place and he had just been trying to help her with it.

It was hard to get to sleep after that. She wasn't used to communal sleeping arrangements. The straw rustled whenever anyone turned over and their breathing was insistent, as if they were trying to pant unwelcome confidences into her ear. The smell in the room made her feel queasy.

There was already some light in the sky when she decided she was definitively awake, and hungry as well. She took her bag of food and tiptoed carefully out to try to heat some water on the spirit stove for some cocoa. A chill had spread through the stone building in the course of the long, cold, rainy night.

There were puddles on the schoolyard and the football pitch. It must be early. She hadn't got a watch but the sun still wasn't up. And yet there were some boys coming cycling along the road, half-grown lads who threw their bikes down at the edge of the road and ran onto the football pitch.

She didn't pay much attention to them as she made her cocoa. When she looked out again, they were lined up in the grey, dawn light. They hadn't got a football with them. In front stood a man in plus-fours, giving orders. She almost forgot her cocoa. They had sticks in their hands and kept a firm grip on them, even as they threw themselves to the ground. They extended the sticks in front of them and held them aloft, stood at ease with them, shouldered them and stood to attention, erect and eager. They turned and marched and their forelocks blew in the wind that whistled round the tall schoolhouse, thrown carelessly down as it was in the middle of a plain.

'They don't care about their clothes,' she thought. 'Imagine, getting up so early, youngsters like that.' They threw themselves down on the worn, rain-soaked football pitch at a bark from the short man. Frozen through, she drank her watery cocoa and cautiously warmed her hands on the hot mug. It was utterly grey outside.

She didn't understand what the boys were doing. There were so many things she didn't understand. She tried not to think about it, there was no point. She had enough to do as it was: fingermarks on the pedestal table's grained surface of polished birch; the fact that brown beans went hard if you added the salt at the start of cooking, whereas peas softened quicker if you salted the soaking water; how hard you had to wind the wool when you unpicked something, so it didn't stay all curly - whole days were filled for her with this anxiety. It came tumbling out of the wardrobes when she opened them, the floor crunched with everything she had to worry about, it drifted into heaps in the bottom of the larder, accumulated in the turn-ups of Fredrik's trousers and formed tidemarks in washbowls and buckets; it boiled over as a dirty grey scum and settled on everything as greasy deposits and fine dust. It settled on her energy and initiative too. She wasn't one of those people who get things done in good time. Many months of the year had elapsed before she finally decided to air out the wardrobes; in fact, it was early summer and she had to give up the idea. The other women, her neighbours, might make embarrassing comments.

Her routine preoccupations sometimes turned into a sort of

extreme absent-mindedness that couldn't be explained, least of all by Fredrik, who always had his mind on the job where work was concerned. He would have had every justification for reminding her: this is your work! All you've got to remember is that the food needs to be on the table. I've got ten minutes to eat, then I have to cycle back to the factory. That takes a quarter of an hour. Work it out and you'll see. If I'm to have time for a ten-minute rest after dinner, it's got to be ready when I get home.

But he didn't say it, and that was worse. He looked at the stove. Once he even went over to it and lifted the potato saucepan and felt the ring, which was scarcely lukewarm. It took fifteen minutes to heat up, so his gesture said everything; he had no need to scold her or get cross. No, she knew what she was worth.

She didn't want to think about it. It was as pointless as dwelling on all the things she didn't understand. Sometimes she would decide she ought to read all the news in the *Social Democrat* more closely and pay attention to everything Fredrik said, to try to keep up. But she was already so far behind that it was a hopeless task. Meijer had asked Fredrik if he didn't feel uncomfortable as the volume of orders swelled like a pregnant boa because the world was arming itself, and she could see the distended snake before her. But when he said it was swelling because Adolf Hitler had invaded Austria and because the Sudeten Germans were hooting and demonstrating down in Czechoslovakia, she lost the thread of what all that had to do with Bofors and Swedish Engineering Ltd. It was popularly believed that the risk of war was creating a boom in the armaments industry, Fredrik had replied. But in fact it was a little more complicated than that.

'There's a technical and scientific trade cycle; the technical innovation we need is implemented in cycles, so to speak. Military expertise dictates that we find ourselves witnessing an intensification of trade, driven by the need for technical development, every thirty years.'

Good heavens! What a memory. She recognised the words: they had been spoken by the Bofors guide. For her part she had been more or less stupefied by the blows of the drop-hammers, by the heat and the gloomy atmosphere, and had only perceived them as the string of noises they still were for her. But Fredrik had been able to reproduce them almost word for word for Meijer.

Sometimes she thought she might have asked more questions if she'd been married to someone other than Fredrik, who knew it all.

She leant her forehead against the cold glass. Up-down-up-down-up-down went the boys' bodies in the dirt out there. She heard the door open behind her and turned, startled, to see Meijer. He already had his hand on his flies, so she knew where he was going. He was pale from sleep and looking more like a gypsy than ever in the dull light. He stopped short when he heard the shouted orders from outside and came to stand beside her.

Jenny could discern the boys' grey faces as blurs in the pale daylight. Were they scouts of some kind? But their brown shirts had neither badges nor armbands.

She might have asked Meijer what he thought but she couldn't get a word out, she felt too embarrassed standing there alone with him while the others were all asleep, after he had emerged with his hand on his flies.

They marched closer; now they were standing right under the window on the gravel and the patient, trampled wild chamomile growing in it. She could see the thin features and weak-chinned profiles of the younger ones and their seniors' coarse noses and cheeks getting rough with the growth of facial hair. She could even hear their breathing as he barked: up-down-up-down! They were quite literally crawling across the wet pitch; he praised them when

170

they reached the goalpost with its rotting net flapping in the wind, praised them in their degradation and they got up and ran on, their panting harsh and heavy. The youngest already had red cheeks and necks.

Meijer leant his forehead against the window as she had done a short time before and whispered that it was appalling, as if he understood what he was seeing. And though she had no idea who they were or why they were running and marching and throwing themselves up and down out there, she knew he was right.

'Yes, appalling,' she whispered back.

Then he moved off and she went quickly back into the dormitory on cold feet and crept down into her blanket sleeping bag. She was frightened, without being able to put a name to what frightened her.

'Clubs!'

That isn't a final bid in preference whist. A thoughtful silence falls over the four women sitting under the !amp. There is warmth between them but a draught at floor level. Store Street is generally a good place to live, though. They're gathered round the sitting room table. Outside, there's a war on. Yes, war and winter and cold, and inside there's warmth from a tiled stove and yellow light under the lamp. All four of them are between sixty and seventy. Tora's sixty-two. Ebba's the eldest. She often draws their attention to the fact, too. The lino is green and reflects dimly onto their faces. The light from the alabaster bowl on the ceiling is thick and as yellow as honey. There's a slight creaking of chairs and the occasional exploding spark behind the closed doors of the stove. The counters rattle in their boxes when they pay up. They are old counters and have yellowed, like bone. Sometimes tricks and forfeits need working out, so Tora takes a newspaper with the headline 'National Gallery treasures removed to place of safety' and does her calculations in the margin with a stump of indelible pencil. All the objects in the room are silent and unseen. Their time and metabolism are imperceptible. True, the wood sighs and gives a stretch, the pieces of furniture go wandering, but mostly at night. The damper cord with honeysuckle embroidered in satin stitch and stem stitch is a very lovely piece of work in a style known as art nouveau, but it's faded and the Jap silk backing has split. The pale 'Dance of the Fairies' on the wall breathes a hint of summer-night mist into the room with the yellow light. The wax plant is asleep at the moment. Sleep has spread to the very tips of its longest branches. It's an enormous plant, trailing like the Tree of the World across the top of the bay window and not falling asleep until late because the room faces west. The red gleam of the sunset dims only slowly over the foundry.

'Clubs.'

And since clubs isn't a final bid, something needed to be said or done. Otherwise it would force a no game.

When Frida Eriksson used to play whist, she seldom dared bid any of the high suits. She usually passed, and her suit was low-ranking clubs. She would lay clubs even on quite high cards, the sort that would have made Ebba Julin flash: hearts! But of course even clubs can offer cautious encouragement to your partner if he's thinking of playing out his hand.

This time it's Tora who's made a cautious bid. She's calculating and cautious, but she can make unexpected moves. She's not as interested in the game as she used to be. Tora's one of those people who likes calling misère and she often forces a no game by passing on the last hand after she's laid. But that won't do here. Her 'pass' comes distractedly.

But Tora's a diamonds sort of person really, without a doubt. They all know what to expect of each other, generally speaking and with one exception. Tekla Johansson's busy counting, her full lips moving.

'Come on, bid,' says Ebba. 'Counting won't make it come to any more.'

'Spades,' says Tekla, who has her bolder moments. And she can defend her decisions stubbornly, especially the ill-considered ones. Ebba's always convinced there must be a way to win. One way or another they can make their contract. Hearts or play out! A no

173

game or lie in ambush for a revoke. She sits tapping the table top with the knuckle of her index finger, stretching and tending her wide mouth as if that's the organ she uses for thinking, and for once she's quiet. It's a strong bid, Tekla's spades. But there's always the unpredictable element: Cis. It's not easy to tell what she means by bidding clubs.

'Oh, play out!'

Ebba's reached a decision. Cis looks indignant. She hasn't got any good no trumps, the clubs were a sequence.

'We'll win this one, all right,' says Tekla.

'Don't get too cocky!'

Ebba deals and they start playing the sixth contract. And as sure as the kitchen clock will soon be striking nine, they hear a scuffling at the sitting room door and know it's Frida out there. They no longer laugh softly at her before she comes in, because her mild hypocrisy has been going on for so many years that mocking her has completely lost its point. Because she comes out of love, after all.

Obviously Frida Eriksson hasn't been allowed to play cards since she found religion in 1929. But she usually looks in and shares their sandwiches when that time of the evening comes. At first she claimed it was just coincidence. They'd gone and changed to Thursdays. And Cis was invited instead of her. That had hurt a bit, of course. Tora was so wrapped up in Cis, always talking about her. So now she'd presumably got what she wanted, said Frida, and made herself scarce for a long time. Today she holds back a little behind the door as she looks in.

'Ah Frida, hello!' says Tora. 'Good timing. I was going to put the kettle on as soon as we'd played this hand.'

She always makes silver tea for Cis, just milk and hot water, then coffee for the rest of them. They have beer with their sandwiches and a little nip of the hard stuff. It's something Ebba introduced a year or two back. Frida sticks to coffee, of course.

Ebba buys drink with Julin's liquor ration book. He's so far gone these days it's as much as he can do to sign his name. Tora and Tekla are both living alone so they have ration books of their own. But though Ebba's got Julin's book and a man-sized entitlement, she finds it harder to manage than the others. She often has to buy extra with the coupons Tekla doesn't need. Julin drinks aquavit every day of his advanced and shaky old age. It's the only thing that can inject a bit of life into him now his whole body's gone into stagnation. Sometimes he stays there, pale and still, lying on the bed settee of a morning without so much as a quivering of his white eyelids.

Ebba drinks a fair amount herself. The others are extremely moderate in their consumption. Though last time they went round to Cis's to play, they had some Benedictine her son in Stockholm had given her. She had thought it was some type of posh cough mixture until they taught her otherwise.

Tora gets to her feet. She's going to put the kettle on and Frida will hold her cards in the meantime. They secretly find that a bit amusing. As Tora goes out, you can see her left hip's crooked. She walks with effort. They're here now, the evil days, about which people usually say: I have no pleasure in them. They came early. But she offers no resistance. The sun, the moon and the alabaster lamp have moved further away. The brooks beneath the ground, the rain on the roof and the little grasshoppers are silent.

She goes to grind the coffee. She takes off the damp cloths covering the sandwiches and stirs a spiced, potted cheese to which she's added a few drops of aquavit. She's shorter than she used to be. And less bad-tempered too. She often wakes early in the morning, at dawn when the floor's cold, and can't get back to sleep. In the past she would have got up and tired herself out with work. She would have made a big batch of dough or filled a washtub, just to show herself a hard worker jolly well has no trouble sleeping when evening comes! But she hasn't the energy these days. She puts on her glasses and reads bits of the newspaper, then makes herself some coffee or sits looking out of the window.

Outside, the squirrel darts off round the trunk of a tree, its tail twitching and billowing. Its little head with those pointy ears peeps out on the other side. The stove is starting to give off some warmth and the pack of cards lies so temptingly to hand from her game of patience the evening before that she can't help picking it up, cutting the deck and laying out a Harp. The sun comes up. It fills the skies with gold, as she remembers they used to sing at school, and some of that gold spreads over the woodshed's snowy contours. The coffee tastes fresh and strong. Why should she heat up watered-down leftovers for herself, even if it is early morning? The evil days aren't as bad as she thought they were going to be. The pitcher is not yet to be broken and discarded in the fountain. But there is still a lot to lose.

You have to resign yourself to losing a bit. Ebba's always said so. She used to own a brewery, after all, a big business. But actually, she said it even back when she was running on strong legs between the dining room and kitchen at the Hotel de Winther. She said it when Clarén left her in the lurch and she miscarried. Tora didn't like her talking about it like that, and Tekla cried. But hadn't they said it countless times themselves? And laughed. The years go by.

Ebba had lost some teeth too. Yes, you have to resign yourself to losing a bit. Though her teeth have always been so strong she's never needed a set of dentures. Hers are brown from cigarillos now and she finds chewing difficult. But while Tora's cutting down, the steeper the descent and the more stretched the cord that will suddenly be pulled away, the more Ebba seems to want. Her mouth, always wide and untidy with shameless lips, wants to bolt down more than ever now, and what those poor, tender-rooted teeth can no longer grind up is passed on for her stomach to cope with. She's getting pot-bellied and bloated. Her stomach has turned into a barrel over which the silk has to strain. Her eyes are still brown and fresh, and wrinkles crisscross the dry skin of her face. They lay bare the same sort of pattern as on a skeleton leaf, its brown fabric disintegrating between the fine threads of its veins. So only the most important part is left, the part that has evolved into Ebba Julin from the soft, wide-mouthed girl, tense and sweaty, who ran with a tray through the third-class dining room.

She doesn't like her hands, brown and dry. They are the part of her she sees most, after all, and so she ornaments them with a large number of rings, gifts from her brewer husband. This can make her look like some awful old duchess. But they know her.

She's not afraid of anything. She's no longer scared of what might be lurking along the roadside. Nor is Frida, strangely enough, though she's so thin you could blow her out like a candle. Frida walks home alone on even the darkest of nights. She's got nothing left for anyone to take, she's scarcely visible.

Tekla's got large and stout, her feet worn out after a lifetime of use, her hands work-roughened, with shiny skin stretched over the joints. Things have turned out well for her. Her rent's low and she's got a little pension and a bit in the bank. She's saved some of the money from the market stall. Yes, everyone says things have turned out well for Tekla and she deserves it after working so hard all her life.

Then came an afternoon when they went up to see her but she didn't answer their knock. They knew she was in. There was a pair of shoes outside the door, size forty-sevens reported Ebba when

177

she told Cis about it. Well, then they knew what to expect, of course.

He was a pensioned-off railway worker, not in good health. Tekla waited on him and saw to his needs.

'Why? Why, for Heaven's sake?' they asked her. 'What's he to you? He only wants to get at your savings and have his meals cooked for him and be looked after.' He was a widower, after all, used to having someone chasing round after him, and finding it hard to cope on his own.

They got married. Why, for God's sake? She had no answer to that. It just felt the right thing to do. She was fifty-nine at the time. She cared for him for four years. He got worse and worse until he depended on her like a little child. But in a body that was heavy to lift and turn.

'He's on his way out, clear enough,' said Ebba. 'I bet he knew it would turn out like this when he married her. And he won't leave her so much as a copper, mark my words. A suit of clothes and a watch.'

Tekla cared conscientiously for the sick man until he died. Then she was alone again. But she knew a lot she hadn't known before, carried it inside herself; it wasn't bitter. And they remembered what she'd said when they reproached her for throwing herself away:

'Things don't always come out fair. It can't be helped.'

Ebba gave a snort, but Tora thought about those words and found they were true: things don't always come out fair, not by any means.

Cis had moved into town about then. Her name was Hillevi really, the most beautiful name Tora knew. She wished they could call her that too, but didn't dare be the one to start.

Cis had been married to a junior station officer down Norrköping

178

way. When he died, her son in Stockholm helped her get a flat in the town. She'd never really liked it in the country. She found it hard to be natural with the ordinary country people and she'd felt everyone was staring at her. She held herself so erect, her walk was so dainty. You just couldn't help looking at her.

'Oh yes, Cis is always so special,' hissed Ebba, who thought Tora always made too much of a fuss of her. Tora didn't reflect on it much herself, though, at least not until that time in the apple season. She'd taken her a basket of windfalls that Krantz the watchmaker had let her collect. She'd put aside all the best apples, the unblemished ones, for Hillevi. It was early in the morning, but she didn't think. She just walked straight in. The door was open; Cis must already have been out onto the landing for the newspaper. She was sitting in bed reading, without her teeth in. Tora had always assumed she had her own teeth, but she hadn't. Hillevi had just been more reluctant to admit it than other people, and had a very good set of dentures. Her son had paid for them. You couldn't tell at all, they just looked lovely and even. And why shouldn't she have even teeth? After all, she had a straight back and such small feet, with no chilblains. A delicate scent lingered about her and she had her hair in a thin plait which she wound into a little coil, high on her head. But Tora didn't feel she'd caught her out, sitting there in bed with a puckered, sunken mouth. She just felt an even greater affection for her than before. It was so great her heart started beating faster, and that was the first time she suspected there might be something special about Hillevi, the fact she felt like this about her and was giving her unbruised apples which no slug had touched. But Cis was cross with her for coming in without knocking. They were so unlike each other.

Tora used to walk her home after their whist evenings because Hillevi was scared of the dark under the trees and of the long,

179

rustling shadows there. Tora herself suffered from claustrophobia, which she'd admitted to Hillevi but no one else. Going past the wardrobe door in the evening could bring her out in a cold sweat, and she sometimes had to turn her back quickly on the tiled stove in the corner and the damper's pointing, knowing finger. This terror had come over her in latter years and wasn't actually in the wardrobes or under the beds. You couldn't reach to sweep it up, it haunted the chilled outer rooms of the heart and was cruel. She had to get out, away from this building with its corners and shadows. Standing at the edge of the forest by the ridge, with the darkness around her like a cloak, she finally felt safe and her heart stopped wanting to burst.

'We're certainly different, you and me.'

She looked at her closely, more closely than she'd looked at most people in her life. We love that which we are not. That other, missing half of me which would have made a human being of me. My feet should have been dainty. And your hands work-roughened. We should have been each other, our own potential brought to life. Everything that didn't happen in my life is you. My knobbly, aching feet cry out for your delicacy, for it to rise up in me. Your fear cries out for my security.

She had experienced that other love too, on occasions. But it was a cloaked impostor. It was nothing but the urge to see your own reflection, the desire to see images of yourself and to beget self-images with your own self-image: we are as like as two peas in a pod. If I belch, you belch. Let's beget a little monkey with a mirror in its hand that we can dandle in sweetest narcissism.

She looked at her closely and thought: were we so different right from the beginning? Yes, of course. But the coarsening and wearying were also the result of work. They were the stumps of opportunity left after heavy axe blows in the forest of work. And

180

then there were torpor and sleep: the birds that flew by without your even raising your head. The lark who sang every spring while the sweat stung your face, sang without your giving her a name. And indeed who did? Some elegant person out for a gentle stroll, following the ruts your workload has made in the path across the fields.

There have been times, of course, standing over the peppermint-scented marble slab of an evening, when your hands came to rest in the sweet mixture and you thought: look, what stars outside the window! How far can we go? How vast is the darkness beyond? Oh yes, many times. And the moon. There's certainly something strange about the moon. One night he's big and red and close, then he's cold and white and far, far away in the sky. Can it be the same moon? Then you start throwing the sticky mass over the hook in the wall, with harsh little blows. By the time it's as white and glossy as you want it, the soles of your feet are stinging and seared with pain and the joints of your fingers will only straighten out in hot water. And the moon? Oh, he set long ago.

Perhaps Hillevi doesn't know that much about the moon in actual fact, but her feet are so dainty. It's as if she's permanently walking on soft, indoor carpets. Her mouth forms words much more distinctly, makes you think: this is a word. How my knobbly, aching feet are crying out for your delicacy, for it to rise in me! Cursed work that coarsens us and makes us blind and dumb and weary.

Cis's elder son works for the railway like his father, though he took his higher school certificate and works in Swedish Railways' head office in Stockholm. He sends her money. Each day, she goes to the station with *The Correspondent* and gives it to one of the engine drivers to take to him. She marks in red pen anything she thinks might interest him. After all, he's far too busy to read the whole paper. But she overestimates his interest. Sometimes as much as half the paper is marked in red. The rolled newspapers with elastic bands round them pile up in her son's office. Hillevi sleeps a little, gets up early and gets out her red pen. While the others are still toiling and bustling in spite of encroaching old age, this is her most important task.

They've woven rugs together, too. It always used to be Tora who set up the loom and prepared the warp. Things are different now. No one quite knows how it happened and the first she knew of it was when she came across them one evening in the upholstery workshop they'd borrowed. Ebba, who always used to hold the plait of threads while they wound the warp onto the roller, had a steady grip on the handles of the wooden wheel and was winding the warp threads calmly and evenly onto the roller. Cis was the one feeding in the end of the plait and she looked a bit scared when Tora opened the door.

'O-ho,' was all Tora said.

'Well, we thought we might as well get on with it.'

Benches and chairs were littered with paper bags torn down the sides and opened flat, which they'd been using to work out the warp. There were lots of crossings out and scribbles. Cis had been crying most of the day and Ebba was hoarse with shouting at her. But they'd worked out the warp and put it on the loom. And without saying a thing, although it felt very peculiar, Tora sat down and started to help them thread the heddles.

It wasn't exactly her first piece of weaving. Fredrik and Adam came clattering in, smelling of after-shave and clean white shirts and cracking jokes with Cis and Ebba. Then Fredrik decided he was going to work out how many miles of rag rugs she'd woven in her life. A rough estimate, at any rate, as he put it. All those runners might stretch as far as Rome if you laid them end to end. He was always glad of an excuse to pull out the slide rule he kept in the breast pocket of his jacket, however smart his outfit. He started interrogating her. But she wasn't having any of it.

'Off you go, the pair of you. Don't just hang round here.'

'But Mum! I really could work it out.'

No, what business was it of his how far her rugs would stretch? Most of them were worn out, in any case, worn down to the bare warp years ago. Sometimes she felt they were usurping her power, those gentlemen who were her sons. They were stuffed with knowledge from the Tiden dictionary they'd sent for by mail order, from the songs they sang to the guitar, from crosswords and magazines and the books circulating down at Rosenholm, where they all went swimming in those out-of-work years. They wanted to cover the Caliphate of Baghdad with her rugs or lay them out as far as the Pope in Rome. But she had tramped up and down them herself and she knew they led nowhere but from the stove to the sink and back again.

'Be off with you. We've things to do.'

What was there to cry about, anyway? No, blessed be the work there had always been plenty of! And there's nothing like weaving to take your mind off things.

'Except maybe a rubber of whist,' is Ebba's stock response.

She stares at the ten of hearts on the table and has the king in her hand, but can't make her mind up. She can't really afford to let Tekla or Cis in now. There's still the jack, of course. So she slaps the king down hard on the table after all.

'Yes!'

She picks up the trick.

'Though this cost me dearer than the fun I got, as the old man said when he buried his wife. Now let's try for the clubs.'

'What a cheek!'

'Come on. I know your game.'

'Nope, I'll just have to throw a no-trump. There's nothing else I can do.'

'Well where have all the clubs gone, then?'

Cis's sequence of clubs comes to light on the other side of the table.

They play for money. What they lose goes into a cigar box that locks with a crooked pin. They carry it like the Ark of the Covenant between their homes every Thursday. The money will eventually be used for a trip. They've only ever had the one trip so far, to Mariefred. That was a few years ago now; it takes time for their little losses to mount up to cover the cost. Ebba once suggested they could all share the extra expense, but no one else thought that was a good idea.

They often talk amongst themselves about what fun the trip to Mariefred was. Frida went with them too, because they'd collected some of the money before 1929.

They had to take the bus to Hjälmarsund because the boats of the Örebro Shipping Line didn't put in at little landing stages like Hampetorp and Läppe any more. How they laughed at Ebba, who had so much clutter with her she had to get it off the bus in two stages. Carrier bags and umbrella, suitcase, shawl and the basket with the coffee things. Her handbag made a clucking sound. You guessed it! She had a bottle of brandy with her, in case it got chilly on the water.

It was a fine, clear Sunday in early August. The ore baskets hung motionless from the cable lift up to the mine. They found they'd actually put on rather too many clothes: light-coloured summer coats with sweaters underneath, silk scarves crossed over at the neck and hats of lacquered, plaited straw with elastic bands at the nape of the neck and an extra hat pin to be on the safe side, so the hats didn't go sailing away like white seagulls over some open stretch of water.

The white *Gustaf Lagerbielke* was already alongside; its engines were throbbing and there were ducks and coots bobbing in the water churned up by its propeller. They stepped cautiously down onto the gangplank and Frida kept her eyes straight ahead so as not to be tempted to look down into the green, eddying water and feel dizzy. A member of the crew wanted them to pay before they had even set foot on board.

'What a stickler,' said Ebba. 'He could at least wait till we'd found somewhere to sit.'

But he insisted. Then the Captain came along. It wasn't the actual Klintwall, about whom they'd heard so much, but this one was very smartly turned-out too. He gave a salute.

'Allow the ladies to take their seats!' he commanded, and the crewman had to close his round satchel. The Captain saluted once again, his hand to the gold braid on his cap, and went up onto the bridge. A few minutes later they put out from the shore.

At last they had time to look. They hadn't far to go across Lake Hjälmaren. The *Gustaf Lagerbielke* gave a hoot and a hoarse cough of black smoke as they reached the other side and entered the Hjälmar Canal. The meadows and fields and bending alders were so close they could have stepped onto the bank and walked alongside. The pace was gentle, too. They had nine locks to negotiate in the morning sun and tried to keep count as they sat there on the brown-painted benches, rough with thick paint. It looked wet, with long drips where the paint had run, making Frida get to her feet in alarm and check the back of her coat. But there was no need to worry.

They emerged into the channel of the Arboga River. Time was

standing still along the banks. They saw a flat-bottomed rowing boat that had sunk so long ago it was cradling water full of water-lily leaves and algae. They got to Kungsör, where the air rang with the silence. Nothing disturbed it but the sound of horses' hooves clattering on wood far away; a lingering aroma told them someone had been busy at a baker's this Sunday morning. The delicious smell of baking made them exchange looks and get out the coffee basket. There were so many things to sort out, the cups, the bag of sugar and the soft, sweet crescent buns from Anker's, that they didn't look up again until they were right out in the open water at Galten.

Yes, now they were in Lake Mälaren, where the small islands swam with caps of green. White castles and manor houses stepped down to the meadows by the shore and regarded the watery reflections of their faces, windows dark with misfortune. Although it was broad daylight, they started telling each other their ghost stories: horses and carriages that drove up to the front steps leaving no trace of wheelmarks in the gravel; restless, wandering ladies who had had their hair brushed until their scalps bled as a punishment for their hardness and vanity; lords whose horses' hindquarters had been branded by the devil as they rode to safety in the nick of time.

They went on through the straits at Kvicksund, where the water was full of rowing boats propelled by silent, bent-backed men. They came to the open water again at Blackenfjärden and a huge, mahogany motor boat passed them, heading for the grand summer villas where the glassed-in verandahs glinted as brightly in the sun as the anglers' bottles had done. They came in sight of Ridö Island at about dinner time and went down to eat. They had prime roast beef with a cream sauce and gherkins. They couldn't have done better at home, they thought. The Captain came down as they were having their coffee and said hello again; he had some coffee himself, with a half bottle of arrack punch. It was already open and had been chilled for him. He said it was special for Sundays. Then he told them all about the real Gustaf Lagerbielke, who was the County Governor of Södermanland and said those famous words when the old parliament, the Diet of the Four Estates, assembled for the last time. They'd all read them in school, but couldn't remember them of course. The Captain could recite them from memory and the way he did it brought tears to their eyes. That was true nobility and no mistake. But there was a nasty little shock at the end. Makes you feel tatty and worthless, being told something like that, thought Tora, but didn't say anything.

When they went back up on deck, the open waters of Granfjärden were already behind them. The *Gustaf Lagerbielke* was fine, despite the captain having sat with them for so long. They were making their way safely through a cluster of islands, some of them so deep and fir-scented they almost blocked out the light, turning it green in the narrower passages. They stretched out their hands to the branches, but couldn't reach them of course. At Hjulsta, the ferry was on its way across the water as they passed, with a cartload of furniture on board. Perhaps it was some estate workers, moving to a new place right in the middle of harvest and everything. You couldn't help wondering what had happened. They could make out a bed settee and a tall chest of drawers as plain as anything. The people were standing quietly beside their meagre possessions, staring at them and making them feel most peculiar, as if by being on the deck of the white boat they'd joined a different class of people.

The water looked increasingly glassy as afternoon advanced towards evening. The pike started to rise, shoals of bleak set the water quivering and sprats jumped and writhed in droplets of silver by the reeds and stones. The islands lost their colour, looking magnified and heavier in the water. There was a slight but chilly breeze and they went down into the aft saloon for a while. They found themselves quite alone there, strangely enough, and could even have had a quick game of whist. But it would look bad if anyone came, which they were bound to do before long. People were just staying out to watch the water going as dark and heavy as bronze across Prästfjärd Bay as the sun went down. They had to go up again because they didn't want to miss anything. Ah, that's grand, they sighed, staring straight at the red disc, and could still see it even when they closed their eyes. They were so starved of beauty there was every risk they'd stare dangerously long. Afterwards it grieved them sometimes that they couldn't remember every detail. But one of them remembered the ducks with golden heads swimming in the light of the setting sun; and another the little gardens hanging out to dip their flowering, fruit-laden fingers into the green water, close enough to touch as they passed by. One of them would always remember the scent of the waterlilies lingering on the breeze in an inlet.

Deep in Gripsholm Bay lay Mariefred. Long before they got there they could see the castle where royal widows had lived, its mass solid as a rock. They would hear the next day all about thrifty Queen Kristina who made Ebba Brahe so unhappy; about Queen Maria Eleonora, that bewildered and desperate creature Gustavus Adolphus left behind; and about Queen Hedvig Eleonora, mother of Karl XI. She might well have joined them in a game of whist, because she loved playing cards.

Now the main thing was to disembark and find the guest house. They were excited even as the *Gustaf Lagerbielke* rounded the open-air swimming pool. The houses adjoined shops and each other; some of them even seemed at one with the honeysuckle covering entire walls and extending across from neighbour to neighbour. The smaller buildings, too, were woven together by birthwort and Virginia creeper which overhung their low windows.

They had to ask the way and received a courteous reply. After all, they were in fact five travelling ladies even if they had an awful lot of bags and parcels and giggled when Tora got the name of the boarding house wrong. But it had been chillier on the water than they'd realised, after all. Cis could feel it in her chest and they had to stop and fasten her scarf at the front with a safety pin before they continued their evening walk through the jasmine scented streets with phlox and roses drooping over the fences.

'Fancy,' said Frida. 'Fancy there being somewhere as lovely as Mariefred.'

Tora awoke in the night to the sound of a nasty cough in the dark. They had two rooms but the connecting door was open. She could hear that the coughing was coming from Cis and Ebba's room. It sounded so painful it hurt. In the end, Tora got up, put on her shoes and a sweater over her nightdress and felt her way downstairs. She couldn't find the light switch so she kept hold of the fire hose that was hanging along the wall.

Down in the kitchen she looked for the milk and found it. She moved quietly and wasn't particularly worried about being caught there, although it would be a bit awkward if the landlady came out into the kitchen. She'd tell her what had happened the next morning in any case and there was really no need to disturb her. She couldn't find any honey, but put some sugar in the milk when it was hot enough. Up in their room, Ebba had left the bottle of cognac on the chest of drawers. She felt around until she found it and poured a generous drop into the milk. The cough was still hacking away in there. Dear oh dear, how it must be hurting her chest.

She carefully picked her way across to the bed in the dark.

'Here you are,' she whispered. 'Sit up, Hillevi, I've brought you some hot milk.'

'What?' said a hoarse voice in the middle of a coughing fit.

189

'So it's you, you old dodderer!' said Tora.

It was Ebba. She put on the light and hung a petticoat over it so it wouldn't disturb the peacefully sleeping Cis. And Ebba coughed and said you'd never have got up to make hot milk if you'd known it was me!

'No, you're right there,' said Tora, and they both laughed so much they almost woke Cis. She shifted uneasily under her covers.

It tickled them because Tora's partiality for Cis had created a certain amount of tension amongst them. It had made Frida in particular quite miserable. But being able to joke about it eased the tension. And time and again on their way home, Ebba recounted the whole story and how Tora had looked when she caught sight of her under the light.

'So it's you, you old dodderer!' they would say when they happened to meet each other in the street or at a moment like this, when Tekla's claiming a jack Ebba's forgotten all about. And when Cis finally takes a trick with her ace of clubs because Tekla hasn't discarded her last club, Ebba pulls a face and blows smoke through her nostrils. Now it's Cis's turn and she's got two low clubs left, making Ebba say with reverence:

'Still waters run deep and no mistake.'

They can't secure the final contract and they all scrabble in their boxes of counters when Tora's worked out the penalties.

They gather up the cards and put a cloth on the table. It's time for a little sandwich and a chat about the trip they're planning for the summer. It won't be the same as the wonderful trip to Mariefred of course. They're older now. Nobody mentions that, though. Summer's still a long way off, outside there's winter and war. Yet the *Gustaf Lagerbielke* must still be making its way between the swimming green islands, they can't imagine otherwise.

190

'**I**n times of peace, crack shot Simo Häyhä had farmed his home land in the parish of Rautjärvi, but he had also perfected his readiness to fight, in case bad times should come. As a marksman he had won a whole cupboardful of trophies, taken the championship and become acquainted with Uukko Pekka as he went round the rifle ranges. He enlisted for active service as a corporal.

Then war came. In the intense trench warfare on the static defence line on the border, the marksman felled huge numbers of Russians with his own 'Pystykorva' rifle. He killed more than anyone could count. The quiet man from Rautjärvi never fired at random. Every single shot claimed an enemy life. Then someone suggested the marksman should keep a tally of the number he had killed. He began to keep a book where he listed every definite hit, verified by witnesses, and every day he stepped up to the 'Father' of the company in the command tent to report his score for the day. The total grew quickly although the days were short. At dawn, the crack shot hurried off - sometimes taking with him a Russian rifle with telescopic sights, although his real preference was for his own weapon - and headed for a look-out point in terrain favoured by his prey. He often remained there until night began to fall. The total passed one hundred. 23 definite hits was his best daily total, with a number of possible hits besides. Over Christmas the record score of 24 was reached.

At all events, before two months had passed the crack shot had single-handedly felled a whole company of his country's enemies, and that did not include the wholesale slaughter when the two sides were at stalemate.

As the second hundred began to add up, Simo Häyhä received evidence of appreciation from quarters other than his company commander and fellow soldiers. The corporal was promoted to platoon leader. The Supreme Commander's orders of the day confirmed that the man had been awarded the Freedom Medal. He was also presented with a watch; the next prize a luxury rifle, Sako model, which arrived via various command levels, reaching first the division and then the marksman himself, who now had 219 Russians on his list and was considered the most deserving recipient.

One cold and beautiful day in February when Corporal Häyhä was out at the front line, he received orders to present himself at the Chief of Staff's office. He had been fighting the Russians for over 21/2 months but was now obliged to leave the combat zone for the first time. Life in the support lines filled him with diffidence and surprise and he was a little shy of the high-ups, but he comported himself with the military discipline urged on him by the 'Father' of the company. He slept in a proper room above ground for the first night in a long time; and the following day in the presence of the staff officers he received from the Colonel's hand both the splendid weapon and a letter of commendation bearing the divisional seal, which said, among other things:

'This weapon of honour, gift of Sweden, is presented to Corporal Simo Häyhä, Platoon Leader, in recognition of his excellent service as marksman and armed soldier in combat. His contribution shows what can be achieved by a sharp-eyed Finnish man of decisive actions, who stays calm and does not let his hand tremble. This weapon of honour is to be considered equivalent in value to a distinguished service medal. As an heirloom passed from father to son, it will tell generations yet unborn of the deeds carried out by Simo Häyhä in the great war in which Finnish men fought for their country's freedom, their people's future and the highest ideals of humanity.'

The corporal slung his new rifle over his shoulder beside his trusty old Pystykorva. The simple military ceremony was over, but there was still a photograph to be taken of the platoon leader at his General's side. Then Simo Häyhä returned to the lines - to set the sights of his new rifle adorned with its silver plaque.'

(*The Courier*, 29 February 1940)

The old cinema known as the Casino Theatre was in half-darkness because it was overcast and Konrad Eriksson hadn't put the lights on. He was alone with General von Döbeln and was supposed to be shifting old clothes, shoes and skis, gift parcels of toys and carrier bags full of bandage material up to the gallery. He hadn't started yet. He stood for a long time, staring at the great log jam of skis on the floor. He had just counted them and had made it a hundred and thirty-one pairs. But there weren't enough poles for them all. The leather of the bindings had cracked and the metal had rusted. People wanted an excuse to get rid of them. They weren't all gifts of love. He moved about in the sparse daylight, fingering the heaps of knitting wool. A strange, musty smell surrounded the piles of clothes. Some of them must have been washed. But most of them smelt as if they'd been lying around in attics, and some of the items had a distinctly medicinal odour. Old clothes lay everything bare. Their owners have gone hurrying on, but there are the trousers with all their stains and baggy knees. Shoes with heels worn down on one side and sweater sleeves stretched out of shape and now too short speak with total candour of the person who has just left. In the middle of the pile of clothes was a newish looking radio and he twiddled the dial, moving the pointer along the stations. London, Vilna, Coventry, Kalundborg. His thoughts went wandering off and for a few moments he forgot his repugnance.

Döbeln was pinned up below the gallery. He was standing in front of the Finnish flag with arms folded and a rapier at his side.

194

A PEOPLE IN JEOPARDY, CAN YOU HELP? read the caption. For a whole week down here he had met Döbeln's eyes whenever he turned round. Honour, duty, willpower. Though that wasn't on the poster. He'd looked it up. In the end he'd felt obliged to read up on him.

He was the grandson of the physician Johan Jacob Döbelius who recommends the excellent spa water on the Ramlösa bottles as well as the son of Johan Jacob von Döbeln, Professor of Medicine at Lund University. Konrad himself was the son of a plank carrier at Wilhelmsson's Joinery, who lost his job after the big strike and got run over by a tram when he was drunk in Norrköping the following year. They had both been about the same age when they lost their fathers, fifteen. Döbeln went to the naval academy in Karlskrona, Konrad to Berta Göhlin's pastry shop and café where he learnt to be a baker. Döbeln became a mercenary and fought for the French army in India. He fought against the Russians at Savolaks, suffered a head injury and was taken captive at Porrasalmi. As a result of this he was trepanned and Konrad assumed it was the terrible scar left by the procedure that had made him adopt the black headband. Perhaps he had a big hole or dent in his skull. That was an unnerving thought for Konrad Eriksson, who wasn't physically brave. He couldn't bear the sight of blood and if anybody aimed a blow in his direction he would recoil, even if the lunge was only meant in jest. He was a Communist, yet had never been beaten up, not even when Stalin signed the pact of friendship with Hitler and Finland was bombed by the Russians. But he didn't go out much.

He suspected Döbeln had found life fairly tedious during those thirteen years he spent at the Captain's House in Dalsland. Though he was interested in agriculture, of course. Then came the Russian campaign of 1808. At Lappo village and church, in defiance of the clear orders of the supreme commander, Adjutant General

Adlerkreutz, General Döbeln led an assault so successful that the Adjutant General later had to sit down with his obstinate General and doctor the report. The figures for the respective strengths of the two sides were also adjusted so the Russian troops appeared to have outnumbered the Swedes two to one. The Swedish brigade had in actual fact been numerically superior. The report was well received in the highest quarters. The hero of Lappo was made a Knight of the Order of the Sword, First Class, and his superior was elevated to the rank of baron.

Döbeln fell ill when the Swedish forces were surrounded at Jutas, but it is said he swept aside the doctor's medicine bottles, got out of bed and won the battle. That was something Konrad had thought about a great deal, because he suffered from gastric problems. They weren't so debilitating that he couldn't stand on his own two feet in the mornings. No, it was more a constant, vague discomfort, an insistent churning, burning and grumbling in his stomach that sometimes intensified into actual pain. It sapped all his fighting spirit. There had been a time when he counted himself a professional revolutionary. Mixing dough had just been a way of getting by until the revolution was over. Later he became caretaker at the Casino, and occasionally filled in as projectionist at Franzon's other cinemas. Only yesterday evening, guts burning, he had shown *That's the Life* with Irene Dunne. The usual projectionist had been called up. Konrad had been exempted for reasons of poor health.

Georg Carl von Döbeln was a professional soldier whose career didn't end with Jutas. He became Supreme Commander of the Swedish forces on the Åland Islands and marched them across the frozen Kvark to the mainland, a risky operation. He fought the Norwegians in Jämtland and formally discharged the veterans who were all that remained of the decimated, dysentery-plagued

Finnish army in Umeå, with a very moving speech. His private life was complicated, with political considerations dictating his choice of wife and extended legal battles to legitimise the son he had fathered before marriage. Konrad had never had the slightest difficulty begetting children. He had six of them, though only the twin boys and the youngest girl lived at home these days. He was fond of Agnes but had always felt rather guilty where she was concerned; he would never have been capable of marrying for political reasons.

Döbeln's last war was against Napoleon. He fought as pig-headedly in Germany as he had done at Lappo, but on this occasion he was court-martialled for his actions, instead of receiving renewed honours. He was condemned to death, then pardoned, and in the end died of old age after a whole life spent longing for peaceful, happy professions. Posthumously, his name became synonymous with the Lappo movement and the Winter War.

There was to be a Finland Benefit Evening at Franzon's old cinema. He had kindly put the premises at their disposal, said *The Correspondent*. The paper had given them free publicity. Konrad had had two days to take all the well-meant donations and products of the Women's Defence Volunteers' coordinated knitting operation up to the gallery, and he should have lit the stoves first thing that morning. He hadn't. He had spent most of the time sitting on the hard, brown-painted wooden benches with Döbeln behind him, those eyes and folded arms. He had wandered to and fro in the huge, chilly auditorium, sometimes hunched over with stomach cramps. He had done nothing more with the clothing and the old ski boots and skis than to deliver the occasional kick to a pair of shoes or wind a shoelace round his finger so hard that it turned his fingertip purple.

He was employed as caretaker and it was his responsibility to get the premises ready for the various purposes of the hirers. Franzon had been called up. His wife had given the instructions. And Konrad had stayed silent. It struck him that what he was brooding about as he wandered around there was honour, duty, willpower. But when he tripped over the pile of ski poles in the gloom, he realised he had left the lights off because he didn't want to be seen in here with Döbeln if any of his party comrades happened to come by. He felt a traitor.

He ought to take the boxes and piles of clothes up to the gallery and get the fires going in the stoves so the place warmed up, then quietly and calmly withdraw before they started to arrive and let them have their Finland Benefit Evening in peace. But the idea was repugnant to him. He sat there thinking he simply could not face mounting the steps to the gallery with an armful of old clothes. He had counted the skis as she asked him. That was all.

He was still sitting there when Gerda Franzon came in. He heard her stamping. She obviously had slush on her shoes. She blew her nose. It was a cheerful sound. She hadn't got a cold, he thought, just a runny nose. She opened the big double doors right at the back of the auditorium and he heard her catch her breath. It was cold in there, of course, she hadn't been expecting that. Then she turned the overhead lights on. Another sharp intake of breath. Ski boots, sweaters, toys and old coats everywhere. The gallery piled high with boxes. Skis in the aisles.

'Oh dear,' she said.

And blew her nose again. He could hear her clearly, wiping her nose briskly, taking fast little breaths.

'Eriksson, are you unwell?'

Cautiously, prepared to show instant sympathy and start to make other arrangements if it turned out he was poorly. It would have been easy to say he wasn't well. But he maintained his position.

'No,' he said, 'I'm not.'

It wasn't strictly true. But what is actually strictly true? He got up as she came down the aisle. She was wearing a winter suit with a leather collar and a tall fur hat in pale grey Persian lamb. Just as he'd thought when he heard her blowing her nose, her cheeks were red and her hair had gone curly in the damp. He studied her very carefully. He was behaving as if he were feverish. She had a bundle of posters and a sheaf of sheet music under her arm. Döbeln stared at Konrad. And Gerda stared too.

'Ericsson, haven't you...'

No. He hadn't. He had to draw the line somewhere.

'I don't understand.'

'It's just I can't,' said Konrad. 'I've got to draw the line somewhere.'

'Draw the line?'

Then she said quietly:

'Is it - political considerations? Political considerations make it impossible for you to help Finland, Mr Ericsson?'

He said nothing.

'Good God, of course that's it,' said Gerda. 'Good God!'

And suddenly she started shifting clothes. It happened before he had a chance to grasp what she was up to. She tossed the bundle of posters and music down onto the bench beside him, picked up a huge armful of old dresses and coats and headed for the gallery. He couldn't stop thinking about how awful they smelt and had to sit down again, weak at the knees. The sheet music was lying there beside him, with a poem cut out of a newspaper. He read:

You fell on snow in Finland's deepest forests
Our duty is clear: to honour you with deeds.

199

We claim the right to keep the spruces sighing
from year to year the song your country needs.

Others advance where you fell for the Northlands.
Our path is clear, for us there is no choice
Even in death you still march on before us
Defending dales resounding to your voice.

His stomach was burning. Gerda Franzon charged up the steps to
the gallery with her burden, her heels rapping on the wood. Konrad
felt light-headed. He had no idea what he'd been reading. He read
the verses over again to calm himself. His weakness was that he
found himself overwhelmed by a sense of unreality whenever
things got particularly stressful. When he most needed all his
presence of mind, it would completely desert him. His thoughts
went jumping around, playful and panic-stricken, as they do in the
moment before sleep. He felt sleepy, too.

Gerda carried armload after armload up to the gallery. She was out
of breath now. He didn't know if she looked at him as she passed
because he was sitting bent double with his face in his hands. Then
he heard the pile of skis come crashing down. But she obviously
decided to give up on those. They were terribly heavy. He heard the
stove door slam open and the rustling of paper. He didn't realise at
first; it was the smoke that made him leap to his feet.

'No, let me,' he said. 'I'll do that.'

'Oh, will you?'

Did she sound scornful? He opened the damper. She passed him
the box of matches.

'It's seven o'clock,' she said. 'But maybe there's time to warm it
up a bit in here. And you will help me with the clothes and things,
won't you?'

He shook his head.

'I'll light the stoves,' he said.

She wasn't angry any more. She tugged at his jacket sleeve and asked him to sit down again.

'We're in such a rush anyway that it can hardly make any difference,' she said. 'I must talk to you, Mr Eriksson. This just isn't possible.'

'Oh yes it is,' he said.

'This sort of behaviour isn't like you. You could at least say something. I can't seriously believe you want nothing to do with sending these things, the clothes, the teddy bears, all the things people have knitted, to Finnish children and civilians who've been bombed out of their homes. I simply can't believe it.'

'It's not that,' said Konrad. I just can't.'

He wasn't himself; his words came slowly. His mouth felt swollen. Gerda looked at him and he turned his back on her and started putting wood in the stove. Just as he'd read 'Even in death you still march on before us', he found himself reading and re-reading the name on the stove: *Näfvekvarn, Näfvekvarn*.

'Mr Eriksson,' said Gerda. 'Do turn round.'

He didn't.

'At least listen to me.'

She sat down on the bench, rubbing her hands, which were red from the chill in the hall. In a quiet voice, she started telling him she'd been up in Stockholm with the Women's Defence Volunteers to receive the Finnish children arriving from the war zones. The reception centre had been at the Maria Hospital in Södermalm.

'Do you know it?'

He nodded without turning round as he knelt in front of the stove. He fiddled with the damper.

'They were suffering from starvation,' she whispered. 'Eating gave them stomach ache, we had to take it very gradually and they couldn't understand. It was dreadful having to say no to them. We couldn't talk to them, either. The interpreters couldn't be everywhere.'

She rubbed her hands on the fabric of her dress and blew on them.

I've never seen anything like it,' she said. 'I'm afraid I've led a very sheltered life. Very comfortable. It's hard to imagine the poverty. And the fear. They were so afraid, Mr Eriksson. Do you understand? What had happened to them was inexplicable. They thought we were evil, too. When we had to delouse them and bath them. They thought we wanted to harm them. There was hardly a single one who really trusted us. I had no idea it would be like that. I, well, I thought perhaps they might be grateful or at least glad we were looking after them. Do you understand? Do you think that was ridiculous of me?'

'No, no.'

He shook his head violently.

'Some of them were really *hard*, you know. There was one girl who had a little brother. She had those high cheekbones, in a thin face. Never smiled. Not once. She was on her guard the whole time and no one was allowed to touch her little brother. When he had to have an injection, she forced her way to the front and made us do her first. She was afraid we would... you know what I mean?' Konrad wondered if she was crying but he dared not turn round to see.

'They were put in different families, she and her brother. They were split up. It's hard to find placements for those older children and people don't want to take two. At least I wasn't there to see when they split them up.'

She sat in silence for a moment. He almost thought she'd finished what she had to tell him.

'And then there was a little boy who had to have a bath,' she said suddenly, flatly. 'He dared not even come up to me. Maybe he'd never seen a bathtub or a shower. I could see he thought it was something terrible, something that could hurt him, maybe kill him. He went down on his knees. He was asking me to spare him. He begged and begged in his language, looking at me, whimpering. It was so heart-rending, the way he begged me. It was horrible, I tell you. I wanted to run out. I felt I was the person he thought I was. I simply didn't know what to do next. I couldn't force him into the bathtub when he was beside himself with terror.'

She fell silent. After a while he turned round and looked at her. She was sitting there, leaning forward in the glare of the ceiling lights, and had covered her face with her hands. Her Persian hat was askew. Konrad got up slowly. He had been on his knees by the stove for so long he'd lost all feeling in his feet. Cautiously, he started to move them. He seemed to be hurting all over, now.

'So what did you do, Mrs Franzon?' he asked. 'Did you let him off his bath?'

'Oh no. I couldn't. You don't realise how dirty and neglected they were. Their parents were all dead or had disappeared. No, they had to be bathed. All of them.'

He was looking her straight in the eye now.

'What I did,' she began, but then caught her breath and stopped. 'Do you want to know what I did?'

He nodded.

'I got undressed.'

That made Konrad turn away. He could feel himself going as red as she was.

'Yes, I took off my clothes and got into the bathtub myself and washed from top to toe. Then I had a shower. He stood watching me from the furthest corner of the bathroom. At the start he was

203

trembling with terror, especially when I touched the shower. But then he came over to me. And when I'd finished and got dressed again, he let me bath him.'

Hearing she had finished, Konrad walked across the hall to the other stove, pulled open the door and began stuffing in sticks and newspaper. Not a single sound came from over there. Good God, what had she done to them both? If he didn't help now...

She said not another word. And she was clearly sitting quite still. She had stripped for him. And he was making her feel she'd done it from sheer calculation. But that wasn't true!

What was truly true? Thank God the fire caught straight away. He picked up the log basket and made for the door, looking at her from the side without turning his head as he passed her. She was still sitting hunched forward, her hands over her face.

When he came back with the wood, she was gone. Clothes and skis lay untouched. The stoves were burning but she had turned off the lights. Perhaps she's going to cancel the whole Finland Evening, he thought. He went upstairs to the flat and it was deserted there too. Agnes must have gone out with the girl and the twins were at school. It was quiet in the Casino Theatre, so quiet he could hear sounds that were entirely unfamiliar to him.

The building was not really standing there silent. The porous, semi-decayed weather boarding had soaked up the autumn rain. While autumn lasted, the old cinema had been like a half-rotted fungus. Then it froze and stabilised. Now the sun was starting to get stronger in the middle of the day. The building dripped and dribbled rusty water from defective gutters. Perhaps it would disintegrate in the spring floods like the old cadaver it was, rushing off in pieces with the mucky brown water along the gutters in the street. That would be a relief. Then he'd lose his job here with Franzon. Then he'd have to get up at four each morning and set dough to rise and scrape baking sheets clean at Anker's. If he got a job at all, now Stalin had joined forces with Hitler and Finland had been invaded. Mrs Anker was a widow, old and appalling. He was quite scared of old women and he'd never be able to convince her he was right. She didn't know a thing about the Finnish officers' flirtation with Hitler, about the border that ran 35 kilometres from Leningrad or the Hangö Pensinsula. His job would be borne away from him on a torrent of meltwater. Let it go then! At least he wouldn't have to make bun dough from powdered eggs, synthetic margarine, mock marzipan, artificial sweetener and all that infernal rubbish.

Don't take on so, Agnes would say. There must be something you can do. That was her philosophy. There must be because there had to be. Agnes always tried to stop him taking on so. That was how she put it.

But down there just now, with Gerda Franzon, he had felt out of his mind. Not just the way you sometimes say you are, but really insane. For a few moments he had stood down there in the aisle and heard her crying for the Finnish children's sake and because she had told him, the caretaker of the Casino Theatre, that she had stripped naked and yet he had still refused to help her. Then he felt he must be truly insane, not caring about anything. He didn't want to help a single human being. Then, for an instant, everything was totally true. And it was just as well Agnes wasn't at home.

He thought he heard another sound. This time he didn't go down, but made his way to the gallery through the attic. The cinema was almost in darkness now with its grey mass of clothes, scarcely discernible, for the light had withdrawn and left the place to its mustiness, to the clicking of rotten planks and the slurping of the meltwater. In the muddle of clothes on the benches and the floor and the sagging stage, his mind could fill in the dark mass with a collar shiny with grease, stained trouser flies and the shapeless little sweater sleeve, with tiny arms, feet and legs, distorted bodies, faces struck with terror.

It was all still and quiet as he emerged into the gallery and leant over it. There was time down there, stagnant time. There were pools of spilt time and time fossilised, with children's faces grinning in pretty patterns like the imprints of shells in stone, the little noses, the rounded foreheads, the lips drawn back over the rows of teeth.

It was time rotting and it was stinking garments left here in heaps for rags, for ripping into shreds and being re-used. Perhaps someone would sleep on pillows stuffed with all this time, make love on mattresses of solid time, turn these garments and brush the unpicked seams clean of dust and dirt, cut out the pieces for new clothes to be removed at some railway station just before the silence.

There were skis and poles protruding in all directions in solidified snow and dust, weapons laid down with cold-numbed hands, the course of the river gorged with meltwater and rotten planks, cracked boots, feet swollen up like clubs and bleeding from frost, blood and oil on snow. And here on the stage lay a corpse that had swelled up and dried again, gone cold and developed skin like parchment, turned dusty and stiff. It was a statue that could be put away in a cupboard and dusted down for the next anniversary; that swelled up again for the failed coup at Mäntsälä; that was carried at the head of a great procession of farmers and sat grimacing in the car at every abduction, at every assault and death on every patch of frozen pine forest and worn wooded hillside and in every muddy ditch. He lifted his split brow again at the word Lappo, as he would raise it at Savolaks and Porrasalmi like a dog catching the scent of a bird. But he caught the scent of corpses, the smell of death in the brushwood.

There he lies, on the catafalque of old suitcases on the stage, with a torn headband because old silk bandages always split in the end; the hole is showing and the cheeks are stuffed with unbleached cotton wool, the mouth made up to look pink and the claw that grips the hilt of his sword, its jewels lost and its silver blackened, is covered in a glove and the glove is stuffed with the yellow cotton wool, plump, yes, swelling up again. It's time once more. He lifts his brow, soon he'll be scenting corpses again. It's completely quiet now. Time is petrified. The dust won't come off. It's a coating, branded with shadows. The clothes can't be moved, it's quite impossible. The trousers and sweaters have turned to stone. Here, a few paces from the silence, the heaps are clothes of stone.

The Women's Defence Volunteers had arrived. They already had their uniforms on, ready for the evening. He could see them through the kitchen window and hear their voices. They were carrying things and dragging things and the whole theatre echoed with brisk calls and commands. Some of them had their maids with them. Gerda's clear voice often rose above the rest, directing WDV's with tall, teetering piles of clothes up to the gallery. She was apparently herself again. But how she would hate him, Konrad Eriksson, caretaker, traitor and voyeur. Assuming, that is, she thought about him at all.

He ought to stoke up the stoves but couldn't face going down. Agnes came home and gave him some bicarb. He knew they had as much wood as they needed downstairs. They'd keep the stoves going all right. They were competent; they'd had field kitchen training, a week's course last summer in Malmköping. He lay on the settle, listlessly reading 'The Joy of Labour' by Josef Kellgren in a magazine. Agnes heated some milk, put a few rusks to soak in it and sprinkled sugar on top for him, as if he were a child. Some people can't take milk when their guts are playing up, but for him it was salvation.

'Poor old you,' said Agnes. 'What rotten luck.'

But she knew very well. There was no need for them to discuss it. His restless pacing of the wooden floor down there all morning had alerted her, then the thud of logs and the long silence.

The carrier arrived with the piano. He should probably go down and help. He knew the doorway was a few millimetres too narrow but you could just do it if you lifted off one side of the double doors. Nothing happened so presumably they had worked it out for themselves. There came a tinkling sound. Just two hours left and the tinkling went on and on. It must be the piano tuner. Konrad went out onto the gallery and looked down. New posters. SWEDISH MEN, DON'T HESITATE! The Swedish and Finnish flags on the stage and big, bushy pot plants from the florist's, a lectern trimmed with blue and white ribbon, carnations, a carafe of water. He crept among the debris up there, couldn't keep away. He wanted to see Gerda Franzon. And right enough, she was herself again. Her Persian hat sat straight on her head, her cheeks were glowing, her hair was curling. She set out a large pair of silver candelabra on the stage. They flanked the lectern. Tall, yellowish candles. Were they wax?

The WDV's gathered round her and she told them she had inherited the candelabras but generally kept them packed away.

'We used to have them in the library,' she said. 'On my father's desk, where he had his altar. He used to perform marriages in there and then we'd light the candles in the candelabras. But they're just impossible in a normal home, they're too big. I've polished them specially. Imagine - it took me two hours!'

She laughed. Yes, she was herself again and he was glad of it. Let her forget him, forget he existed, forget him as completely as a little girl forgets a bird that once crashed into a pane of the greenhouse, beak first. Or doesn't forget.

She'd undoubtedly had tears in her eyes as she told them about the candelabras. Perhaps she could produce them to order. Perhaps they were there, ready and glistening in her soft brown eyelashes at the mere thought of certain subjects. Children and war. Döbeln at Jutas. Papa's candelabras.

People started arriving, lots of them. There was no need to worry about the heating. The hall would heat up with the warmth of their bodies and their breathing. It wouldn't do them any harm to freeze on hard wooden benches for a little while for Finland and the Cause. Gerda Franzon couldn't have had anything to eat all day. She'd been here virtually all the time. And how cold she must be in her thin-soled shoes.

The guests of honour had arrived. Among them the Finland-Swedish writer who was also an officer. So pink at the back of his neck, such soft hair. And there was the Swedish press attaché, also in uniform, advancing slowly with the actress on his arm. There was a rustling at Konrad's side - Agnes wanted to get a look at her. That was understandable. She was a famous actress. She had a fur collar and little fur-trimmed galoshes. So elegant. They went up onto the stage and everyone clapped for an awfully long time. But the actress must be used to it. He wondered what she was thinking.

Gerda Franzon sat at the piano with her hat on. The guests of honour took their seats on stage after the blue-eyed writer-cum-officer had pulled out a chair for the actress, then everyone went quiet and Gerda played a patriotic Finnish march on the newly-tuned piano. She played emphatically with small, energetic hands, red with cold.

Konrad withdrew through the attic. He went and lay down on the kitchen settle again. The building was so unsound he could hear almost everything they said down in the auditorium. The press attaché thundered and the actress's clear voice was as incisive as glass file. She was no doubt reading that poem about Finland's deepest forests that Gerda Franzon had put down on the bench earlier. He could visualise the expression in Gerda Franzon's face as she asked for it to be read. What is truth? Is there such a thing?

'Do you want a bit more milk?' Agnes asked. Then there was a lot of deliberate, bad-mannered tramping on the stairs down below as the writer was speaking about Finland. That would be the foundryman called Möller who the people in town called that damn Bolshie, along with Wickman the cobbler. It was hardly surprising they were feeling aggrieved. Ten years ago there would never have been a Finland Benefit Evening here, even if one had been asked for. The premises had belonged to the Reds even though Franzon was technically the owner. But the local branch of the Communist Workers' Party had been wound up five years ago and the middle classes had forgotten their suspicion of the Casino.

When Möller and Wickman came in, Konrad felt a genuine and angry burning sensation in the pit of his stomach, as a change from the dull griping. They had come to check he wasn't on duty downstairs, he was convinced of it. He lay on the settle with his magazine on his chest and barely answered when they addressed him. He was irritated by Agnes boasting about his strike as if it amounted to some great act of sabotage, a deed of real heroism down there in the cold cinema. He felt he could see Döbeln raising his head again, a male voice resumed its thundering from the stage below and he told Agnes to shut up. He had never said anything like that to her in his life. The kitchen went totally quiet.

The voice started reading out the names of the companies that were donating a day's income to Finland and they sat in silence listening to the list: Anker's Café, Automobile & Tractor Company

Limited, Rudolf Landström Workshops Ltd, Persson's Cold Meats, Aina's Ladies' Hairdressers, Hedberg's Gold and Silver, Sports Trophies and Presentation Gifts; then suddenly Wickman cleared his throat and started telling them all the latest rumours to blot out the sound.

Everybody was at it, Konrad thought. 'Anxious times call for community spirit, vigilance and silence' announced all the billboards in town, but everyone was spreading rumours. About Per Albin Hansson and Günther and rationing and bombers and shutting all the Communists up in concentration camps. It hadn't struck him before, but suddenly he was sick and tired of rumours. Möller announced that their friend and party comrade Ljung, who worked down at the station, had been helping load crates that had ended up in the wrong place the other night back onto a goods train.

'Heavy blighters, full of sub-machine guns and nine millimetre ammunition, German, the lot of it. Can you credit it? We're getting German arms. Not much risk of us having to fire at the Germans with them, then. That must be what they're thinking.'

'Rumours, I'm tired of rumours,' said Konrad.

'They're not bloody rumours. They prised open some of the crates over by the engine sheds where it was dark and saw what was in them, plain as could be.'

'But if that's true,' said Konrad, 'why did he carry on loading them, then? Why didn't he refuse? Why did he help?'

'Well,' said Möller, 'I don't know as that would've been a very good idea.'

'But you have to draw the line somewhere! Don't you? Don't you agree with me? *You've got to draw the line somewhere.*'

'Well, yes,' mumbled Wickman, who was usually so ready for an argument, and Konrad sensed they were treating him like an invalid. It annoyed him. He relapsed into silence. After a while they left.

211

'There we are,' he said. 'That's the inspection over and done with.'
'But Konrad,' said Agnes. 'They're your friends. You do take on so.'

He went out into the attic again and peered round the weatherboard door to the gallery. They were clapping down there. Then the actress stepped forward. She had her arms at her sides. Her hands were slightly turned so the palms showed. She raised her head. There wasn't a sound in the theatre. Slowly, with suppressed emotion but a melancholy jubilation in her voice, she recited the words of the Swedish national anthem, 'Thou ancient, thou freeborn, thou mountainous North.' He stared at her white, upturned face. She began on the second verse; her voice had risen, intensified:

Thy throne rests on memories from great days of yore,
When worldwide renown spread over the earth.
I know to thy name thou art true as before.
Oh, I would live and die here in the North!

There's nobody sane left, thought Konrad. If I had a tiny child again. Or even a dog. He heard them singing 'Our land, our land' as he carefully closed the door behind him.

The next day, Gerda Franzon came to fetch her candelabras. He'd put them in the pantry wrapped up in towels. It was the only storage space tall enough. She'd seen that everything had been cleared up, down in the theatre.

'I saw you'd tidied up after the Finland Evening, Mr Ericsson,' she said. He didn't reply, but brought out the candelabras that had belonged to the Gerda's father the Dean, and unwrapped them from the kitchen towels.

'I put them up here,' he said. You can't trust the locks down there.'

'I forgot them,' said Gerda.

She must have been in a state of agitation and distraction when she left. Perhaps she'd invited the actress, the writer who was an officer and the Swedish press attaché to take tea afterwards. He could imagine them all sitting drinking tea together.

She was ready. She wanted to be off and she was in a hurry as usual. She had to go down to the train for the send-off ceremony for the Finland volunteer force. She thanked him stiffly again and then said, unexpectedly:

'You suffer from gastritis, don't you?'

He looked at her in amazement. Did it show that his belly was aching? No, she'd heard about his affliction long ago. She wasn't even looking at him, but at the kitchen curtains where children's sticky fingers had been.

'When my husband comes home on leave I won't mention what happened yesterday,' she said. 'I just wanted you to know. I told the WDV's you were ill. Suffering from gastritis.'

She held her neck and back as straight as a ramrod as she went.

He read in *The Correspondent* the next day that there had been five hundred people at the station to see the volunteers off. Thirteen men from the town and the surrounding countryside were going. They were given gifts. The senior doctor presented them with a bag of bandage material and the chairman of the town council made a speech. He said they were doing the district an everlasting honour by volunteering to go. Then he loudly proposed three cheers.

Konrad found it hard to visualise Gerda Franzon cheering, or singing 'Our God is a fortress strong' with the rest. The train departed. But shortly afterwards it came back again, this time slowly, jolting. Somebody seemed to have changed the points and sent it into a siding over by the engine sheds. There must have been a lot of confusion. He wondered whether the any of the pale, long-faced volunteers at the window had laughed. Or maybe they hadn't even bothered to look out of the windows the second time.

Finally, someone had the presence of mind to start singing 'Thou ancient, thou freeborn, thou mountainous North' and they all joined in as the train pulled out again, this time for good. He had little doubt it was Gerda Franzon who thought of it.

What is labour?
It is a cave in the mountain with a boulder thrown aside from the mouth.
What is the joy of labour?
It is when the horse dreams he is leaping up after rolling all over in the morning dew.
What is exhaustion?
It is a salty smack of blood on your tongue.
What is tedium?
It is the creak of the walk-mill, wood on iron.
What is the reward for drudgery?
More drudgery.
What is the labourer?
A blind horse.
Why does he labour?
Because someone more cunning than he has blocked the cave-mouth with a boulder.
Why does he not leave his labour?
Because he must go round and round.
What is the point of labour?
To draw the walk-mill round in the mine.
Who can see the light?
The master. He is outside. He can see the light of the sun.

Suddenly, everyone wanted a trenchcoat. They used the English name. The men left behind at home didn't want to look like rejects, flatfoots and civilians. They took out the fabric belts and put in leather ones with buckles and double rows of punched holes. They looked almost the same as officers' belts. Even small children wore trenchcoats. They were army surplus grey. The men still at home rode their bikes between huge stacks of wood, on their way to the factories in trenchcoats and berets. Crystal chandeliers sprouted on the ceilings in the home of Curt Carlsson, founder of Curre's Clothes.

Ingrid Johansson did epaulettes. They were double, with sturdy linen interfacing, buttonholes and a double row of top stitching round the edge. Some weeks she was on belts and occasionally she did linings, at piecework rates. That was the best. She sometimes got on so well that she would save the coupon she had torn off the order form until the following week, so as not to run down the piecework rates.

Nothing would have induced her to put on a trenchcoat. But they were quality products, even so. Swedish quality.

Swedish quality is closely-spaced, dead-straight stitching, even seam widths, impeccably fitted linings, hems that stay in place. It's tempo. It's two hundred and twenty-five women bent over the fabric, pulling threads, sewing napes, cutting and notching. It's dust and fluff and banging. It's the cutting room with quick men and better pay. It's the terrible accident in the pressing shop in 1938 when two men were burned in the hot steam. It's strong pockets, buttons that stay done up, poor ventilation, banging, a constant drone and rogue draughts. It's well-sewn napes, tired backs, level collar ends, dumb tedium, glazed eyes, snide remarks at the lunch table, tears and refusals. It's tempo, tempo, tempo. It's the lunch rooms where the cleaning ladies sweep up the rat droppings every evening, it's the white globe lamps hanging from the ceiling. It's tempo, which means time. Swedish quality is director Curt Carlsson who studied professional tailoring in France and England, who comes from the province of Västergötland where his father owned a cap factory, who made a cap for his own teddy at the ripe old age of two point five years and a little waistcoat a year later, who travels in person all over central Sweden with his trenchcoats and overcoats, men's and ladies' suits in huge, ingenious cases, and introduced the term 'tempo' at his factory. It's Johansson in the cutting section and Forsander the stockroom boss who have grasped it so well. It's amazing machines that make buttonholes and sew on the buttons. It's everything inspected in minute detail, it's tempo, tempo and an assembly line that runs, stops, runs, stops. It's blazer lapels that lie flat against the fabric underneath and trousers with even turn-ups, closely-spaced and invisibly fastening fly-buttons and careful pressing. Swedish quality is Luther's catechism and explains the Fourth Commandment. It's Genesis chapter 3, verse 19, share capital of one hundred thousand kronor and a time clock.

Ingrid had been working at Curre's Clothes since 1935. At first she had sat picking loose threads out of jackets for 27 öre an hour. There was a long row of girls in those days, sitting at tables unpicking tacking stitches when the tailors had done the seams. They sat on backless stools, but they had footrests. When there was a big order to finish, they had to do two hours overtime every evening, for which they got 32 öre an hour. In 1938 the new factory was built, a flat-roofed, four-storey building in the functionalist style. The idea had been to have a roof garden for the workers' recreation; the architect designed it and *The Correspondent.* reported it. But it was never built. There was an anti-aircraft gun on the roof now.

Ingrid had picked threads until she was promoted to the cutting room, where her task was to lay a cardboard pattern with perforated holes over the fabric, make a few marks with a bit of tailor's chalk and send the fabric on down the line. Then she had moved to the big sewing hall with its long rows of windows and white globe lamps, where the sewing machines stood packed tightly together but the noise built a barrier round each one. There she had stayed and was now quite a skilful parts seamstress. But she knew other girls who had gone flashing round the factory like ball lightning, chopped and changed, choked on the dust when they worked on shoulder pads and asked to be moved, transferred to the packing room and got backache from standing. Others seemed to have been set down at their sewing machines sometime in the thirties and stayed there, hunched and short-sighted. The production line ran on. Stopped and ran on. This building was designed for the product. Not for the incidental, stooped, coughing, short-sighted people who happened to get marooned there as the years went by. The fabric came in lorries to the delivery point in the basement where the bomb shelter and cardboard box supplies were. It was then taken up to the attic stockroom, and from there to the cutting room where it was cut with hand-held electric shears or in the automated system where fifteen suits could be cut out at one go. The pieces continued along their conveyor belts to the third-floor trouser shop. On the second floor was the big sewing room where trenchcoats, jackets, waistcoats and ladies' suits were tailored. The garments were pressed and checked on the first floor and finally ran back down to the storeroom where they were packed into cardboard boxes with tissue paper between the folds and driven out for delivery.

Not until Ingrid was moved to the sewing room did she realise there were women who had grown old at Curre's. She had barely reached thirty herself at the time. She saw that their bottoms had grown broad and flattened with sitting, their backs bowed and their eyes short-sighted and peering. She had never thought before about how you get old, only that some time, some other time, you do. One evening she took down the hall mirror and propped it on a kitchen chair to have a look at her bare backside - Arne had been called up - and didn't think it had gone flat. Not yet. She often heard the older women complaining of backache. She never said anything about hers, and assumed it was the same for many of the younger women. They kept it to themselves and tried to pretend it was just a passing discomfort.

Yet though they grew older and had aches and pains, though they had a time-clock, piecework rates, conveyor belts, foremen, dust and fluff and the bloody rat droppings in the lunchroom that had come along with them to the new factory, there weren't many who said they didn't like it. Especially not the older ones. On the contrary, the flattest backsides, the most stooped backs said they were very happy at Curre's. Their all-time best, they said it was. Better than the Tin Can, twenty times better than the apple sauce factory and a hundred times better than the way things used to be. There'd been no choice then but to go and work on a farm, they said. That was when Ingrid always walked out of the room. Most of the younger ones did, when the old dears started going on about milking and how to work the separator. But perhaps she should have stayed. She should have stayed and asked Greta Hjelm, who did linings and had been here for eighteen years, what the joy of labour meant. Actually, Ingrid knew the answer. She'd heard it plenty of times.

'I'm just glad to have a job,' Greta would say. 'And I like the company. I've always been happy, really. Though it's been hard work, and tedious. I've always been lucky with my workmates. You do hear people saying: I couldn't stay here, not on your life! Not for more than a week, at any rate. But they stay. The years go by. You need a job. And there isn't anything else. No, I'm just thankful I'm not on jackets on the production line and can do pocket flaps and ticket pockets and little bits like that. I could never learn those new ways, I'm too old. I ribbon-edge these linings, I do, and I earn quite decent money some weeks. So I can put aside a coupon off the order form now and then. You're not supposed to do that really, but then you don't want to run down the piecework rates. So I can't complain really. But it's been hard work, all right.'

Ingrid was still left trying to make sense of it all. Most of the people she knew hated their jobs. They didn't get worked up about it and they wouldn't have wanted to lose those jobs at any price. But they hated in that nagging way you might hate in a warped old marriage; they were affected by the same slowly-spreading poison you find there, growing accustomed to the unbearable and to the knowledge that life exists to be suffered, time to be killed and you just have to be grateful as long as you can still tie your own shoes and dress yourself.

She told this to her brother Konrad, who was the only person you could say things like that to. She told him, too, that she'd come to the conclusion most people didn't think like that. Most people didn't think at all. They just went and sat where they were supposed to sit until their bottoms were flat and their spines were bent and their eyes went on strike, when they were replaced by a firm, round bottom and a good pair of eyes while the garments ran

220

past on the conveyor belt in a never-ending stream.

'Oh, they think,' said Konrad, 'They just don't think the way you do.'

He said it quite curtly, which was unlike him, and she could hear from his tone of voice that he didn't like what she'd said. Then he asked her how often she went to union meetings.

'How often?' she said. 'What are you getting at? It varies, I suppose. I always have to get a babysitter for Ulf, you know.'

He said nothing.

'But I do go. I'm not the kind who couldn't care less about the union, if that's what you think!'

'Well how often do you say anything at meetings?'

'Whenever I need to,' she snapped.

But she'd never said a word. And he seemed to know.

'They have such a funny way of saying things,' she said. 'They all get so obsessed, the ones who speak there. They talk all stiff and strange. And they go on and on. About joint piecework agreements and pay rises and all that.'

'What would you like to talk about, then?'

'Job satisfaction.'

'Well, do it,' said Konrad.

He got up and fetched a piece of paper that had been tucked inside a book.

'I had this returned a little while ago,' he said. 'It's about what you said.'

She read it.

'What's this?' she asked.

'A poem.'

She couldn't see that it was in verse, so it wasn't easy to tell. After reading it again, carefully, she said:

'I'd like to copy it out.'

'Keep it,' said Konrad. 'It was rejected by a magazine. I'm not going to bother trying anywhere else.'

That gave her an idea.

She went to the union meeting in Hall B of the Community Centre with the poem in her handbag. But as soon as she heard the gravel on the forecourt crunching under the soles of the women's shoes as they emerged out of the dark and rain, her courage began to ebb away.

They had their sectional meeting on the fourth Tuesday of every month and the chairman, a man called Evald Ström who worked as a presser at Curre's, always started by welcoming 'the few of you who are here'. That made Ingrid feel awkward and stare down at her boots. She suspected everyone sitting in the back rows was feeling the same. The ones who said things sat up at the front. They were the committee members, the keepers of statistics, the shop stewards and a few more. White globe lamps, like the ones in the sewing room but slightly smaller, hung from the ceiling. She kept looking at them, and at the walls, which were empty.

The acceptance of the draft agenda and the approval of the minutes of the previous meeting were the start of a ritual she found as soporific as the sound of sleety rain running slowly down the windows. Evald Ström presented reports and official letters, reading at top speed. Their section had donated suits and trenchcoats to Belgian children and the letter of thanks, translated by the central committee of the union, was read out. The committee recommended rejection of a request from the Belgium committee to raise money by selling Queen Astrid badges. The communication was put on file. They opted instead for Rosa Axelsson's proposal of a collection for Save the Children. Each time the hammer fell, Ingrid gave a start and felt a pang of conscience she couldn't explain.

Rosa Axelsson was one of those sitting near the front. She was another one who spoke softly and quickly when she got to her feet and asked to speak. She faced the front, addressing herself to the chairman.

Ingrid knew Rosa was one of the thirteen women who had set up the section. She was just nineteen at the time. But she'd been involved in the union ever since she was fourteen, when she'd written to the Norrköping branch of the Swedish Garment Manufacturing Workers' Union to ask advice about a supervisor who had sworn at her. She sat on her yellow-varnished chair just below the platform with no trace of insecurity or guilty conscience. It was her birthright to sit there because her father was the chairman of the foundry workers' union and he'd been one of those who took the initiative in setting up the local branch of the Social Democratic Party.

Next to her sat Nancy Pettersson who had originally been the section secretary and had filled oilcloth-covered exercise books with that upright handwriting so unusual for a woman. She had written in language that was impulsive, forceful and misspelt. She had wanted to abolish God, the bosses and the lists of piecework rates, but now she wasn't secretary any more. The black exercise books had given way to loose sheets of minutes with punched holes for filing in ring binders, and you had to elect people who could use a typewriter to the secretary's post now. But they said Curt Carlsson was scared of her. He was in the habit of cancelling or postponing piecework negotiations if Nancy was going to be there.

The chairman read the last official letter: the union's central committee was proposing immediate action to root out all Nazi-Communist traitors to the national cause.

'Since our section has fortunately been spared these scum,' said the treasurer without looking up from his papers, 'the proposal is that this communication be put on file.'

'Can we move to a resolution on that?' asked Evald Ström.

'Yes.'

'Is this section resolved to file the central committee's communication?'

'Yes.'

Instantly, the hammer fell. Ingrid knew there was a particular procedure for getting in with your request to speak at the right moment. When the chairman decided a point had been debated long enough, he moved on swiftly. The front rows assisted him with their promptly chanted responses. They needed to push on and they did.

In the time remaining, the meeting went through the lists of piecework rates for underpressing, buttons and plus-fours. The last of these took longest. The plus-fours had formerly had loose linings, but the factory directors maintained the number of procedures had been cut down by the change to fixed linings and the price should therefore be adjusted. Ingrid's heart had started thumping. She opened her handbag. She started feeling all hot round the middle. The voices went droning and creaking on, but she could no longer make out the words. She sat waiting for the chairman to say Any Other Business. When he finally did, she was so quick it seemed silly.

'I'd like to raise the question of job satisfaction,' she said.

It went very quiet. The people at the front turned round. She could see Rosa Axelsson looking, the whole committee. The treasurer whispered to Evald Ström, who obviously didn't know who she was.

'I call Ingrid Johansson.'

'I think there isn't enough job satisfaction at Curre's,' she said, 'and I wonder if anybody else agrees with me, and at the other places too.' All the faces froze. Ingrid wasn't looking at the committee all turning to face her, but at Greta Hjelm who was sitting in the same row. Greta was embarrassed, she was doing funny things with her mouth. She would have turned away if she could.

Ingrid was sure she could have said the same thing to Greta while they were sitting having their sandwiches in the lunch break, and she wouldn't have been at all embarrassed. She forgot everything else she'd been meaning to say and just pulled the sheet of paper out of her open handbag and began to read. She'd been going to say: I'd like to read a poem by Konrad Eriksson about job satisfaction or the joy of labour, and maybe we could use it as a basis for discussion. But she forgot.

'What is labour?' she read, thinking it had been a terrible mistake to forget to say this was a poem, since it wasn't in verse.

'What is the joy of labour?' she went on, trying to raise her faltering voice but only making it go higher and thinner.

'It is when the horse dreams he is leaping up,' she read, not looking at the committee. She tried to catch Greta's eye but couldn't, because Greta was looking down at the space between her feet and still doing that thing with her mouth. Had she got something stuck in her teeth? Inga-Maj from the suit line was picking at a ragged cuticle, seemed to be focusing all her concentration on it.

'Who can see the light?' asked Ingrid in a thin voice. 'The master. He is outside. He can see the light of the sun.'

There was a moment's silence. Since nobody was saying anything, Ingrid sat down. It was over.

'Well,' said Evald Ström, then cleared his throat. 'Maybe there's something there. Something to think about.'

He cleared his throat loudly again and when he went on, his voice was back to normal.

'The committee has in fact discussed strenuous measures that could be taken to attract the membership to meetings,' he said. 'We could consider having some item of this nature on the agenda in future.'

'Mr Chairman,' said Albin Eklund, getting to his feet. 'In that case, I would like to suggest it would be more appropriate and have a wider appeal if we included some singing in the programme.'

Albin was a member of the male voice choir. There was a brief discussion but Ingrid found it hard to hear what was going on. Her ears seemed to have closed up. All she could hear was the blood surging and pulsing. Though she was aware of Evald Ström's voice as he decisively summarised the exchange.

'I find there are several proposals for the next meeting to be conducted less formally with singing, music, coffee, plus some time for instruction in the correct interpretation of a contract. Can we move to a resolution on the formation of a working party?'

Ingrid was still trembling slightly as they finished and she took her coat from the hook.

'So you didn't think I was right?' she said to Inga-Maj.

'Course I did, for heaven's sake.'

'Seems to me all we ever talk about is piecework,' said Ingrid.

'Yeah, s'pose so.'

'We're always going on about what we get paid.'

'Well, you may not need the extra,' said Inga-Maj.

Greta was kinder. On the way home, Ingrid asked what she'd honestly thought of her contribution.

'It was unusual,' said Greta.

And she was a kindly soul. Ingrid didn't say another word. Hellfire and damnation, that bloody Konrad. Never again. Back home, she had to make her excuses to Arne's mother. She'd been babysitting for Ulf and thought they were going to have coffee together before she went over to her flat.

'I've got to get to bed. I've such a headache,' Ingrid lied.

But she couldn't sleep. It was all going round and round in her head. What is labour? A cave in the mountain with a boulder thrown aside from the mouth. What is the joy of labour?

But seriously, Ingrid. What is labour? Three hundred epaulettes on a moving conveyor belt.

What is the joy of labour? Three hundred epaulettes on a moving conveyor belt.

What is exhaustion? Three hundred epaulettes on a moving conveyor belt.

Tedium? Three hundred epaulettes.

The reward for drudgery, what's that? Three hundred epaulettes tomorrow.

What is the labourer? Three hundred epaulettes and a coupon to tear off.

Why does he labour? Because there are three hundred epaulettes moving towards him on a conveyor belt.

What is the point of labour? To make three hundred epaulettes today, to make three hundred epaulettes tomorrow, to make...

Who can see the light? Curre Carlsson. He can see the light of the chandeliers.

Ingrid got a letter from Arne. When he wrote it he was lying in a big room with windows overlooking the wide Klarälven River. Round three of its walls ran a platform of rough planks with a layer of straw bedding. In the middle of the floor was the stove and a margarine crate for the fire watch to sit on. They had knocked nails into the ceiling beams to hang cooking pots and clothes on. In the evenings, the playing cards would slap against the margarine crate and the draughts would run along behind the bulging wallpaper, making it ripple where it was coming loose from the wall. All this, the yellow light of the paraffin lamps, the straw that rustled whenever they turned over and the bad smells in the crowded quarters, she could perhaps conceive of. But she didn't realise the letter had already been read. She would never have believed it even if there had been someone who could have told her.

It had been steamed open in the secret department at the main post office in Stockholm, where thorough men and women read letters written in the reeking fumes of red-hot metal stoves. Many of them were ashamed of what they were doing and called it a squalid job. The letters were about anxiety. They were written by people anxious about companies and farms and children and rivals. The men round the stoves had visions as soon as they closed their eyes. They wrote heartfelt letters, jealous and agitated letters, but most of all they were anxious.

Most of them found the inactivity and waiting hard to bear. They wanted to get back to their jobs and their women. Arne was one of those who was also slightly anxious about coming back.

He was a former bandy player and was still well known in his home town. Swedish Motors had been sold off and merged with Swedish Engineering, but he still worked in the stockroom and might find himself staying there all his life. That thought had struck him now he was far from home and it made him uneasy in some way he couldn't define. When Ingrid had read his letter, she felt worried without knowing why. He hadn't really put much in the letter about what he was thinking. He hadn't put that he missed her and Ulf. He hadn't put that he'd soon be home.

She knew he needn't worry about losing his job. She thought he ought to be grateful for that. He never wrote so much as a word about Swedish Engineering or the stockroom. But then, it hadn't really got much to do with his life, his real life.

His real life was lived on the other side of District Road, behind a fence that extended far into the forest of small pines. He was the coach of the local bandy team. We won, he would say, or: we had too many injuries to qualify this season.

She remembered his old coach Melkersson, the one she'd hated, and didn't know whether to laugh or cry. There had been nothing she'd wanted more fervently or ruthlessly then than to get him from Melkersson. And she'd thought she'd done it.

Send me a photo, he wrote. I haven't got one of you.

So he did miss her, after all. Maybe he wanted to show it to people too. She imagined them showing each other pictures of their fiancées and wives.

Ingrid folded up the letter and went over to the mirror. She had a headscarf on, with the ends twisted into a turban. You couldn't see her hair. But when she pulled off the turban, which she always wore for work at Curre's, it fell down round her face. It wasn't quite shoulder length. It needed washing. Most of the blocks of rented flats had hot water twice a week now there was a fuel

229

shortage, but in the old South House owned by Swedish Engineering there was only cold running water. She'd have to heat up some water and stand with her head bent over a washbowl, rinse her hair in ice-cold tap water and put it in bulky curlers. She couldn't face it very often. But when she saw her sallow face and her lank, flattened-down hair and thought how it would look in a photo, she felt the urge to do something about it.

She put on her coat to cycle down to Maud Backlund's ladies' hairdressing salon in Lunda Road. She couldn't see Ulf down in the courtyard. But she expected he'd go in to his Gran. It was convenient living the next staircase along from your parents-in-law. But it could be eerie, too. Sometimes, when she saw Arne's mother coming out with her shopping bag to go up District Road to the Co-op, she felt as though she was seeing herself in twenty-five or thirty years' time. She could remember how it felt to be twenty, when nothing was permanent. Real life hadn't started properly. You were just trying things out because there was plenty of time. Now she was over thirty and had had the strangest experience. She'd come on foot over the brow of the hill and across the open ground where they generally improvised a skating rink in winter, down towards South House which looked brightly illuminated that November evening. The lights were on in their flat because she'd just popped out to call Ulf and hadn't switched them off. Reaching their block, she had stood at the window and looked in at the lamp hanging over the kitchen table, at the checked oilcloth with the marks left by Ulf's fork and at a chair with a green cardigan hung over the back. There was a coffeepot on the stove. It felt to her as though she had never seen it before. It suddenly revealed its form. It was a yellow enamel coffeepot with a pale green stripe round the edge of the lid. The enamel was damaged, a round black spot. At that moment she found it quite impossible to believe that in just a couple of minutes she would be coming into that kitchen, going over to the coffeepot with the black, iron blemish in the enamel and picking it up, putting it under the cold water tap and filling it like absolutely any other fully-grown woman in a kitchen in a town. Because she was the one standing out here. It was inconceivable that she was a grown-up wife and mother who went to work every day, did her job fairly competently, came home, stood in the queue in the Co-op, bought three litres of milk for eighty-one öre, cooked meals in that stove corner, darned the heels of boys' socks of brown wool, made herself coffee, cleared the kitchen table and got out the writing paper, wrote to a man in a requisitioned farmhouse with floral wallpaper on land sloping down to Klarälven River. It was inconceivable, yet it was absolutely true. Her form was as fixed as the form of the coffeepot over there in the stove corner; she was as solid as cast iron, as shiny as enamel and she'd had no idea of it until this evening. She had neither thought nor believed it, yet had seen herself as one sees a child still out playing in the dark, who someone will call in and look after in a while, a child who may not come, because she happens to feel like doing something else.

She didn't really want that sensation coming back again, but it did, prompted simply by the sight of those everyday objects in the kitchen, and it made her restless. She would get on her bike and ride off as she was doing now in the dark evening, from streetlight to streetlight, feeling the bumpy road jolting her from beneath. She would often go and see Maud, who was happy for her to come for a shampoo and set after the salon closed or on a Sunday afternoon, although you might have expected her to be too tired. Maud had reserves of energy, and Ingrid sometimes wondered where she got them from.

Ingrid was pretty much convinced that most women's existences were just as colourless as her own. Perhaps a few really were having the sort of exciting time their menfolk imagined when they shut their eyes. Maud had certainly had a bit of fun when the troops were in town. But that had been right at the start of the war. Now she was self-employed and working terribly hard.

She rented a three-roomed flat in a big, new, four-entrance block and had fitted it out as a ladies' hairdressers. She had kept the kitchen and the smaller room for herself and her little girl but the hairdressing had a tendency to spread, with bottles and jars and hairbrushes full of brown or blonde hair. The smell even found its way out onto the stairs. But Maud liked it. She called her business Salon Maud and had a sign in the window with brick-red lettering on a pale green background. She had decided at the very start that pale green and brick were the salon colours. She had pale green net curtains at the windows, modestly drawn. She wore a green overall and the imitation leather seats on the chairs were red. It was a fashionable flat in the new functionalist style, with a fireplace for an open fire in the hallway. She hadn't used it because she was afraid of it getting sooty.

She bought electric permanent wave equipment, hairdryers and a basin for shampooing. For the first time in her life, she felt free and relatively secure. She wasn't worried about the mortgage repayments because the customers kept coming. She didn't spend much money to speak of, and even if it was a bit quiet during the week, there was always a rush on Friday afternoons and Saturdays. Particularly when the men were expected home on leave, the women would come to her with their hair tied up and scarves wound round their heads. She let the shampooist wash their lifeless, flattened hair and she permed it and set it with curlers and clips. They left the salon with ears and cheeks glowing from the heat of the hairdryers and heads covered in waves, curls and rolls, like Jeanette MacDonald or Greer Garson. But they didn't keep their hair like that between appointments, of course. She would meet them in the shop and they would adjust their headscarves and tuck back any escaping strands and be embarrassed when she looked at them.

The first time Ingrid sat on one of the imitation leather chairs with curved, tubular steel legs, she had asked:

'So how did you manage to buy all this?'

'Took out a loan, of course!'

'But what about the surety...or whatever they call it.'

Maud hadn't answered at first.

'D'you think I'm being nosey?'

'Hell's bells, you're no nosier than the rest of them. Only difference is, you ask straight out.'

She wound a terry towel into a turban round Ingrid's head. Then she lit a cigarette. She still smoked her flat De Resques.

'Old Maudie's come up in the world. And I know you don't begrudge it me. So I'll tell you how it happened. Cause I know you won't tell anyone.' And she explained about Sigurd K. That was what she called him.

'And please note I've never told his name to a living soul,' she said.

It was 1939. He had signed up for officer duty in the town's veteran reserve training scheme but God knew he was regretting it; he couldn't stop thinking about his business. Sigurd K. was approaching fifty at the time, quite stout with curly black hair that was beginning to turn grey. He wasn't exactly jovial, but terribly kind and tender-hearted. She'd felt a bit sorry for him. too. It seemed pretty ludicrous now, but that's how she'd felt. He'd looked helpless in his over-tight uniform jacket, with trouser legs that had to be turned up at the bottom. But he had a totally civilian wallet in his inside pocket and he treated her lavishly. They'd had great fun together but he was still undoubtedly glad when it was time to get back to Eskilstuna.

Maud was expecting Yvonne by then. She hadn't planned for that to happen. She didn't notice she was expecting until after he'd gone, either. She knew very well he was married. They hadn't talked about it much. Sigurd K. wasn't the type to run his wife down. Maud thought he was quite attached to her, but even more attached to his cement works.

As for her, she'd had to leave Aina's salon and move back in with Mum and Dad again. It hadn't been much fun and God, what a fuss! She didn't want to think about it. But in the end she put her foot down. She was nearly thirty, after all.

'That's enough,' she said. 'I'll handle this myself.'

But it wasn't so easy being plucky because she still had to rely on Mum to look after Yvonne while she was at work. She'd started at the Tin Can again after a bit. And Sigurd K., whose name she'd loyally kept out of the inquisition down at the child welfare board, wasn't paying as much as she'd hoped. It was the business, first one thing and then another. She'd believed him, actually. Times were hard. But in the end she lost her temper. It was after she heard through the grapevine that he was doing very well for himself. She'd burnt the ends of the dried blonde hair she had in her hands when she heard he had a detached house and a Volvo V8 as well. She was past thirty by then and starting to get varicose veins from being on her feet all day. She was afraid she'd have to spend her whole life standing in Aina's salon if she didn't find a fellow willing to take on the girl as well, when they got married. Assuming the sort of fellow existed who would treat Yvonne right. She wasn't sure he did.

Granny and Grandpa were very attached to the girl by this time.

She was their little sunbeam, they said. But what a life, under their watchful eyes year after year. Maud had always assumed it would change of its own accord in the end, but now she realised it probably wouldn't. She had to do something about it.

She'd written to Sigurd K. to say she needed more money so she and Yvonne could get a place of their own. But he said she wasn't to write. His wife might get hold of the letters and his life would be ruined. So she rang him at the office instead. She only managed two sentences before he hung up. She must on no account ring like that. There was a switchboard at his company these days. Did she want to ruin his life?

That made her livid. Yvonne was flipping well just as much his kid as those two in Eskilstuna!

She decided to go there in person. She was there four Sundays in a row before she worked out the lie of the land. He went out for a walk with the family on Sundays, like everybody else. And they went to the pastry shop with the café nearly every time. Sometimes they just bought buns of course, to take home. But on the fifth visit to Eskilstuna, she was in luck.

She was very smartly dressed and her hair was nicely done. Yvonne had a new pale blue coat, white overshoes and gaiters. Her cap was trimmed with rabbit fur. She always looked pretty. Maud hadn't taken out the ringlets at the back of her neck until they were on the train, so they'd be sure to stay in shape. They were sitting eating cakes when he came in with his wife and two sons, proper louts in school caps, incidentally. They had red ears and baggy plus-fours. Maud held her head a little higher.

His wife had silver fox fur on her coat and a hat, built up high and draped with silk jersey. It stood proud from her forehead like a runestone, only asymmetrical. She was chic and expensive right enough, but quite heavily built, and she must have been ten years older than Maud. They sat down right next to her and he didn't notice her until it was too late. Then she thought he was going to have a heart attack and for a few seconds she regretted the whole idea. He went deathly pale and pressed his hand to his heart. Then he stopped staring their way and his wife asked him considerately if he was feeling all right. Maud breathed again. She truly did not want him dropping dead on the spot. In fact, she wished him no ill at all, as long as he paid his way. Perhaps it had been a bit cruel bringing Yvonne so close to him, she could see that now, looking back. But it worked.

It was interesting to hear what his wife had to say. She was pretty spoilt, it was clear. And inclined to boast. He must be sweating now. The boys were nothing more than spoilt oafs; on that score she frankly felt sorry for him. She wiped Yvonne's mouth with a handkerchief and asked her if she'd like another cake.

'Yes please,' said the little girl, who had always been placid and docile.

He hurried the louts in their grammar school caps and he hurried his wife so she got irritated and the silver fox furs rose and fell wildly. He hustled them out so briskly when they'd finished their cakes that they almost tripped over each other in the doorway. But he came back in. She hadn't miscalculated.

She slowly enjoyed the bit of Napoleon slice she had on her fork and watched him puffing and blowing as he bent down to hunt under tables and chairs.

'Forgot my gloves,' he explained. But when he came shuffling round the table and hissed that he would meet her in a park, she hissed back that she didn't want to put the little girl through such a thing.

'But I'll ring you tomorrow at twelve,' she said. 'You can always send the switchboard operator out for a minute.'

She carried on with her Napoleon slice, which admittedly only had mock cream between the layers of pastry but was still one of the best things she'd ever tasted.

'This won't do,' he said on the phone. 'You must see that, Maud! I'm risking everything here. I haven't done you any harm!'

She was standing ringing from a public telephone. There was a cold draught whistling round her legs. She stood waiting for him to say he couldn't even be sure he was the girl's father. But he didn't. That prompted her to think quite well of him in spite of everything.

'Perhaps what you'd really like is to be rid of the responsibility for me and the girl for good.'

'Don't get me wrong, Maud! But try to see things from my point of view.'

'Give me five thousand in cash and stand surety for me to borrow money to open a hairdressing salon,' she said.

He went very quiet. Then he said he'd have to think it over. She must see that. He'd be in touch.

'No,' she said. 'I'll come to Eskilstuna.'

He agreed to stand surety. He even brought the five thousand kronor personally, in an envelope. Maud even introduced him to Yvonne.

'This is Uncle Sigurd,' she said. 'He's coming for a walk with us.'

Sigurd K. had tears in his eyes. As they parted, she said:

'Thank you, Sigurd. I think this is the best way for both of us. You won't hear from me again.'

The way she told it, Maud made getting yourself a hairdressing salon sound so easy. That was the way she was as she worked, too, everything seemed easy. Ingrid sat with her head tilted backwards for shampooing and let Maud massage her scalp and work up a good lather with hot water.

'Is that nice?'

'Mmm.'

'Oh sweetie,' said Maud, 'Yours gets greasy so quickly, doesn't it?'

She began rinsing and the warm water flowed though Ingrid's hair. It suddenly got hotter.

'Ow, it's scalding!'

'Know what? It's darkened to a sort of ash blonde now. You should bleach it a bit.'

'Not on your life.'

'What's wrong with that?' laughed Maud, starting to comb though the thin, wet strands. Ingrid's face looked pale and grey beneath hers in the mirror.

'What a sight I am!'

'No worse than most of them after a day at Curre's. We'll soon have you looking yourself again.'

'It's not worth it. I mean, I'm not going anywhere. Just couldn't face standing washing my hair in the bowl, that's all.'

'I've had an idea,' said Maud. 'Henna! We'll use a bit of henna.'

'Are you out of your mind? The last thing I want is red hair! What d'you think Arne would say when he got home?'

'No, I mean natural henna. It adds a bit of body, makes it more manageable And gives it a hint of gold. Just what you need. Go on, let me try a bit of henna.'

Ingrid looked at herself and Maud in the mirror. Maud had henna-dyed, reddish-black hair with a rim of curls across her forehead and another at the back of her neck. It was fastened with combs at the sides. She did her own hair early in the mornings, before the customers came. Now she was putting a couple of dessertspoons of henna powder into a dish and mixing it with water to make a paste.

'It has to stand for a bit,' she said. 'Shall I give you a cut while we wait?'

'No! I don't want my hair short.'

'You've got split ends, see. It won't grow any length at all, it's too brittle. It'll keep breaking off before it gets down to your shoulders. We'll just take a bit off. Just the ends.'

'All right, but not too much, you hear?'

'Lord, how they all treasure their tatty old rats' tails! Dried-out hair and split ends that'll never come to anything anyway.'

Maud laughed at her and Ingrid felt caught out, unmasked even in her own eyes. Oh yes, she still cherished that dream of long, billowing locks. She had thought she didn't care much about her appearance these days. Perhaps deep inside she still did want to look like Veronica Lake after all, hiding at least one of those eyes with its moody, critical expression behind a curtain of thick, wavy hair.

'What're you laughing at?'

'I'm not laughing,' said Ingrid, 'I just thought of something.'

Maud had started applying the henna methodically to one strand of hair after another.

'We'll have a coffee while this starts to work,' she said. 'Want to go dancing at the hotel later?'

'Don't be daft.'

Ingrid's scalp was dark brown by this time, with the strands of hair clipped up on top. Maud wrapped her head in a terry towel dipped in hot water and they had coffee in the kitchen. Yvonne was asleep in the other room. She had some dolls on the bed and it looked as though she'd fallen asleep playing with them. Ingrid wondered if young Ulf was in yet, if he'd gone to look for her at Gran's. She sometimes felt guilty about him. When school was over he was supposed to go to Gran's for a sandwich and a glass of milk. He usually did, but never stayed long. When Ingrid got away from Curre's she would go and look for him. He could be gone for ages without her having a clue what he'd been up to. Sometimes he had raw knees, sometimes he had bruises that could only be the result of a beating-up. Or did he get into fights? She didn't know. He seemed to think it wise to keep his business to himself.

Maud set Ingrid's hair using aluminium curlers and clips and then it was time to go under the dryer and read *Woman's Weekly*. She was cut off from her surroundings by the roar and the heat and had no idea what Maud was doing or how long she was there. When she finally lifted the dryer and felt that her hair was dry, the warmth had almost sent her to sleep and she let Maud do whatever she wanted with her hair. She fixed it up in a couple of big combs at the back of her neck, and on top she made careful finger curls and teased them into place with the handle of the comb. The henna had turned her hair a full, reddish gold. Ingrid felt apologetic at having to put her headscarf back on and flatten the work of art Maud had created on the top of her head.

When she got home, she puffed the curls back up again and stared at her face in the mirror. She looked different with her hair done. She was quite pretty if she smoothed out her features and tried to temper that sharp look. She longed for Arne when she saw that oval face beneath the soft, newly-washed hair, but it was a longing that sapped her spirit. She felt she might just as well take out the hairpins fastening the curls and let down the whole glorious creation, combs and all, and brush her hair straight.

She could sit down and write to him instead. The pad of writing paper was on the kitchen table, headed with the previous day's date and 'Dear Arne'. She didn't know what else to write. She couldn't very well tell him she'd been to Maud's and had her hair done. Then he'd think they'd been out somewhere, gone dancing perhaps. He'd brood about the hairdo, she knew it. What if she wrote about Ulf? That he was out somewhere although it was past nine o'clock. That he picked his scabs too soon and made them bleed and got the sheets messy. She could only think of little details like that, things that would worry or irritate him. She couldn't write: I miss you. When he came home she wouldn't be particularly nice to him. She'd be bad-tempered and he was bound to notice.

She didn't know that she genuinely missed him, either. Staring at her reflection, that sallow, thin-lipped woman with the critical, almost cross expression in her eyes and the crown of red-gold hair with a coiffure of artful curls, she realised she wanted Arne to love that image and say he did. She wanted a worshipper of the oval face and the hair, of these soft breasts and this stomach, still rounded under the waistband of her skirt. Time was short. Soon she would be angular, bony and dry.

She wondered what he wanted. A woman willing to affirm him, to tell the same lies? Did they really care about each other? She'd never considered it before, not while he was there. Did they touch each other? Were they there to look at each other's external appearance, critical if it was sallow, flabby and worried? Proud and devoted if it was as shiny as enamel, smooth and mysterious?

She'd been to the cinema and learnt how to love. She'd always known that was the wrong way, but had learnt nonetheless, as a left-handed person learns to write with their right hand at school. She was to be a framework covered with sleek skin and bouncing curls and sometimes she was indeed just that, and took pleasure in it. She exhibited her framework before a hungry man, to lure him into a confession. She had given up on words, but by his deeds he could confess that he loved her. If she felt the urge to come to him with greasy hair, with tired, dangling arms and a stooping back and say: be with me, console me for my aches and pains, for the rush and the pointlessness - would he take her to him then? Did she dare to try? She dolled herself up for him. Yes, that was what she did, though she hated the very word when she heard someone else saying it. Was it for him, even? Wasn't she in fact truer to herself as she sat here by the mirror?

If she were to write: I want to live in the same world as you. I want to lie by your side now, on rustling straw, to freeze if I have to, to be unwashed like you. I want to go out there with you and put my hand on your arm as you're about to fire. I'd scream: never shoot at a human being, Arne! Never shoot at a human being. But it seems so pathetic I keep quiet and put a brave face on it. I knit knee-warmers instead of screaming.

We each live in our own world. You don't know much about mine and I don't know anything at all about yours. I've never been in the stockroom at Swedish Engineering. You've never been to Maud's or inside Curre's.

I shall soon look like your Mum when she goes to the Co-op. I should try to get used to it, the sooner the better. But I can't. I feel frayed, pulled in too many different directions. Do you think there's something wrong with me, the way I can't get used to things or defend my life to other people?

My days consist of work, rush and a sort of strange waiting. I'd like to scream HALT THE PRODUCTION LINE! Stop! Stop! I'd like to simplify everything. Life should be like potatoes and fish, like water and stone. It should be like soil and autumn air! Halt! Stop! SLOW DOWN THE PRODUCTION LINE! I want to stand back.

I'm out of step when it comes to living with other people, always have been. I love life, let me tell you. And yet most of the time I feel fed up with it. The circular saw's screeching outside and the

242

sky's the colour of cabbage soup. Do you know I'm afraid of the war even though the Germans are coming off worst all over the place now? I'm afraid of the bombs and the poison gas. I'm just not part of the brave home front and I wouldn't want to be scanning the sky for planes from a watchtower. I don't even look after the allotment, although feeding the country's so important. The last potatoes froze and now the spade won't go through the clods of earth.

What are these attacks of exhaustion and crying and abandonment and hysteria? Will I ever understand? This feeling that life's got too hard and the demands have multiplied and there's work, nothing but work, poking its grey snout up wherever I look; every surface is covered in dust, the cupboards are bulging with junk, with clothes that need mending. I should be doing something about it all. I should have gone over and got the allotment sorted out before it turned into a rubbish tip.

Most of all I'd like to do something nobody knows about and nobody's expecting. In this rain. In this time. In this poisonous fog. In this death.

D ear Arne, she wrote. Everything's much as usual here. Our Ulf sends his love. He had Joseph's brothers for homework on Friday and sat down and learnt the whole thing off by heart. Then the teacher didn't ask him. You bet he was cross.

We've killed the pig and I'm going to start the curing tomorrow. I've got a whole box of meat waiting in Tora's shed. It was terrible though, because Eriksson's wife phoned and said they couldn't have the pig there any more. The neighbours had reported them to the police and they were going to come and count the pigs as soon as it was light. Right, kill it, we said. But Eriksson had been called up and wasn't there. She didn't care what we did as long as it was gone before the police came. Well, there was nothing to do but pump up my bike tyres and get over there and kill it! I thought Fredrik could have done it, since he's at home, but Jenny didn't want him to know about it, because he's against hoarding and all that. He thought we'd registered the pig and given in the coupons for it. And anyway, he's so squeamish he can't bear the sight of blood or guts or anything.

Tora was cursing and screaming at us the whole time and Jenny was crying and the pig was squealing. He suffered, all right. It was awful. I'm not sure I'll be able to get down a single mouthful of that Christmas ham, we'll have to see. And Jenny's hopeless, by the way. She was useless even for holding the belly or whisking the blood. I sat on the pig and Tora clubbed it with the back of an axe. She'd slaughtered a pig before, she said, but if so it must have been fifty years ago. She was in a wicked temper. The worst bit was the scalding and scraping off the bristles. But it's done now and there'll be pork when you come home.

Today Mrs Andersson next door was shouting for Morgan. But he didn't come, of course. In the end she shouted, 'Morgan, if you come in, you can have some pork!' That made him come. I wonder if it was black market pork. I I don't suppose she would have yelled about it if it had been.

The weather's dreadful, but otherwise all's well here. I feel like going to Maud for a shampoo and set. I'll do it for when you're coming home. Hope that's soon! Love to my dear boy from your own Ingrid.

Arne Johansson had been called up. He lay on his back trying to swat midges and horseflies and on his front on a straw mattress that was getting lumpier and less substantial all the time. He stood up and hung about sometimes as well. But he really did spend most of his time horizontal. After five weeks quartered up north by the Klarälven River, he got friendly with a woman who worked in the café they used to go to in the evenings. She lived on the other side of the wide river in a big, grey wooden house with a front porch overgrown with hop vine. Her husband had been called up and was stationed down south, outside Oxelösund. They had to all intents and purposes switched the parts of their native country they were supposed to be defending, and presumably the other bloke was slumped down or propped up just as miserably as he was, waiting for the action or for it all to end.

The woman's father-in-law was a constable and lived in the same house. There were a lot of regulations to be enforced in these uncertain times. Sometimes he was called away and had to stay overnight. Then she would hang out a lantern and he could see the light, coming and going in the shifting shadows of the wind-tossed hop vine on the porch. Arne would swim across and lie with her on a yellow bed-settee. She also gave him real coffee from confiscated supplies and made him swear, whatever else he told people about his experiences in military service, never to breathe a word about that coffee.

In the farmhouse that was their base, and full of sounds and smells very different from those awaiting him on the other side of the river, he would get up about half past eleven in the evening and mutter that he was going out for a pee. Then he would go down to the bank and if the lantern light was flickering over there in the late summer darkness he would put his underpants and vest down by an alder root and wade out into the river where the bottom was soft, muddy sand. He swam in water warmer than the night air and weeds tangled themselves round his body.

She towelled him dry once he was indoors and it was a wonderful, fitting prelude to their intercourse in the yellow bed-settee. She was cheerful and had a shock of dark, rigidly permed hair and little breasts as pale as almond buns. They had a lovely time. In fact he felt romantic for the first time in his life as he rose from the black river water, dripping wet with goose grass caught in the hairs on his stomach, and made a crouching dash for the hop-covered porch with the yellow light. He couldn't be gone long. But luck was with him right through August and most of September; he wasn't missed. The others would be snoring when he got back to his quarters. If anyone did open a sleep-fuddled eye and ask where he'd been, he would say he was constipated. The constable didn't arrive home unexpectedly and the Germans didn't come so there was no sudden order to fall in - he saw her nine times in all without a single soul other than themselves having an inkling.

Then it was October. The water in the river was growing colder by the day, but he was not aware of it because a week and a half had gone by since the lantern had last been hung out in the now leafless hop vine. Then one evening it was there, flickering in the strong wind as he stood longing for sleep and fumbling with the opening in his underpants. It was so cold he curled up his toes as he stood there in the coarse, wet grass that was just beginning to rot in the rain and raw fog of late autumn.

As he stepped down into the water he almost cried out. But he restrained himself and waded bravely on. His feet began to ache with the cold; this wasn't water, it was red-hot iron and ice. He took a breath and threw himself headlong, heedless of all caution in the pitch-black night that howled its song in the tops of the firs. That evening he had really been longing for home. He hadn't only been longing for freedom and meaning and home baking with his coffee, but longing because he was somehow terrified of the strange fir-forest soul of this steeply landscaped province. He had longed for water lilies and leafy shade, pale lilacs by a leaning gate and the still, black water of a pond; houses with white paintwork and railway tracks shining and singing in the heat; the roses that often bloomed right into October outside the laundry, the rustling of tall maples, bicycle wheels slithering on a dusty, sun-baked track and the smell of pork through an open window; he was longing for his province, for Sörmland. As he pulled himself out on the far bank, his numbed fingers found it difficult to get a grip on the rocks and he thought with horror of the necessity of re-entering the water to get back. For a moment he toyed with the idea of walking naked across the bridge and giving himself up to the sentry, whatever the cost. He abandoned the idea. But he would go home next weekend, even if the water lilies had rotted and the frost had nipped the roses.

When he had got into the house and down into the warmed bed, it transpired that his male member had shrunk in the cold. It had as good as disappeared. However much she teased it and played with it as she usually did after his intercourse with the cold water from the north, it remained no more than an embryonic knob. Her laughter cooled and he struggled desperately to make his feigned passion light a real fire. Nothing helped. He didn't get any coffee either, and as he cast himself once more into the black liquid ice from the high bogs and fells he cursed her.

The next time he didn't go over, and said at the café that there'd been an emergency exercise in the middle of the night. He wondered if she believed him.

'I see,' she had said.

He ate a bun with the cloying taste of synthetic margarine, finished up his so-called coffee and went. The lantern didn't appear again. In the end he gave up bothering to go down and look. It was deep, late autumn. He slept.

The others went on with their talk of women. It hadn't bothered him before because they started about the time he normally went down to the river to see if there was a lantern out for him. They talked women in three categories. First they talked about the ones they'd had, or claimed they'd had. They reported on how tight their pussies were, the hair on their stomachs, the shape and size of their breasts. They often compared them to food: marrows, loaves, fried eggs. They also noted whether she bonked them back or lay there like a block of wood. None of this was relevant to him. He wasn't starving for women. He would lie there dozing until it was time to get up and see if the yellow lantern was lit.

They moved on to the second category of women, the ones they fancied having. He'd found it quite amusing hearing their inflamed fantasies about the woman he was in the habit of swimming over to, whose breasts had got pondweed stuck to them on one occasion. Her name was Maj-Lis. Every time he heard her name, he would be roused from his semi-slumber. Now it irritated him to hear them taking about her backside. They'd stopped saying Maj-Lis and rechristened her Cuddly Bum. One of them said he'd had her. Arne was sure he was lying but his irritation turned to distaste. He was wide awake now.

'Put a bloody sock in it for once,' he said. 'Some of us are trying to sleep.'

Some of them really were sleeping, sleeping or dreaming silent dreams in the borderland between sleep and consciousness. There were some who never said anything about women. They just gave awkward laughs.

Among those they fancied having, some were as unattainable as film stars. They were the bright, luminous apples right at the top of the tree. There was the daughter of a district medical officer, often seen on aircraft defence duty. The young wife of one of the battalion doctors had rented a room on a nearby farm so she could be with her husband. One of them had chanced to meet her in the autumn woods. It was plain she was lost. He mimicked her refined, cut-glass pronunciation, her cheery, friendly greeting. What a lovely day! Yes, she'd been out for a walk. And strayed a little far from the path. Could he show her the way back to the village? And they'd strolled along together. A gorgeous autumn, wasn't it? But she hadn't seen any lingonberries, she said. Blimey, all she had to do was look between her own legs. It caused salvos of laughter round the quarters when he said that's what he'd thought, nearly said. But on the walk itself he'd been consumed by a venomous resentment of the bitch with the Persian lamb collar who seemed totally oblivious to the fact that she was walking beside a man. He was just a private, a thing her husband could make crawl through the autumn mud with a single command. In her twitterings beneath the dark firs there wasn't the slightest hint of fear he might rape her.

The third category of women were those at home. They said the lot of them were at it, all the time. But no one said this about his own woman. And when you got back off leave, you didn't give anything away.

'Well, did you get one in or was it occupied?'

'Strewth, no,' you said. 'No problem at all.'

'You were lucky. Lindberg hadn't beaten you to it with his great prick, then?'

'Maybe she was the lucky one!'

Laughter.

'Hell no, I won't hear a thing against the home front. It's hard work for them, no doubt about it.'

'True, true.'

And the tales of how the home front had been caught at it were legion. He knew the scene where they were caught at it. He'd nearly laughed himself to death hearing it, many a time. God knows who was the most comical sight, the civilian standing there in the gloom of the bedroom shielding himself with his hand, or the indignant warrior in his over-sized tunic, having to shake back the sleeves to get his fists out. And the woman in the bed, sitting howling of course, wearing the silky nightie she'd had for Christmas. That was life. It was true.

'Make a note,' they said. 'You can never be too sure. Still waters...'

Ingrid, though. He'd never have believed it, never even entertained the thought. She was so firm, somehow. She didn't like playing about. At Evert Kjällström's summer cottage she'd lifted the host's hands from her bosom. Arne had seen it. He could picture it still, the whole scene with the dark leaves of the lilac, Chinese lanterns strung across from the woodshed door to the verandah and gnawed slices of melon skin on the plates. Evert Kjällström's hands had been there on her bosom but they had been removed, politely but firmly.

He would have gone mad if she'd been up to anything. In the foul-smelling darkness with the laughter and low voices around him, he lay thinking he just wouldn't be able to stand it. He didn't know why. That's just the way he felt. Good job she was the sort of woman she was.

251

The relationship with Maj-Lis was over. He would never say anything to Ingrid; it would only hurt her and in no respect did it have anything to do with them, not remotely. Christ, no. It was an entirely different affair. Apart from the last icy swim and its consequences, it had been a wild, dark, romantic fir-forest affair, the sort you have one of in your life and never tell anybody.

He would go home. Write before you go, they said. Otherwise you never know. He smiled at them. Inside he was thinking it was impossible. Not Ingrid, not in their bed. With coffee in the kitchen after. It was simply unthinkable.

That evening, one of the men was telling them about a foreman's wife who let the conscripts in town have her up against a fence.

'Her bloke thought she was a paragon of virtue.'

'Maybe she was, too. Before the war!'

'Oh God, this bloody war,' they said.

'And it's not over yet, either.'

And they started talking about Stalingrad.

He lay awake. In less than twenty-four hours he would be home. And he hadn't written.

H e's on the train now. Outside are the dark and the war. Well actually, the closest things are isolated cottages, dim yellow lights in the darkness, flicking into sight and disappearing backwards. He's on his way home, to their town. For him there's only one light that counts in this world and that's the kitchen light in their flat in South House. It's a white globe fixed high up on the ceiling with a seventy-five watt bulb. But his memory and longing benevolently transform it into something close and golden. It hovers over the heads of Ulf and Ingrid.

He looks at his watch, sees he'll soon be there and presses his face to the dirty window pane to try to make out where he is. He thinks he recognises a pile of planks, or rather its location, its highly familiar and proper location in this darkness all around. He sees buildings and has arrived.

There's a lot of noisy activity when the train stops and the bustle of footsteps on the platform, but then it pulls out and everything goes quiet. Trains travel fast and mysteriously in these times; they can be stuck, just as mysteriously and inscrutably, for hours somewhere with nothing but a bit of forest and a steep gravelly embankment to stare at. It's so quiet at the station now, and he regrets not having written home to say he was coming. She would have come down to meet him and they could have put his case on her carrier.

As he walks past the City Hotel he can hear music through the cream-coloured curtains. A window is slightly open and he can smell food and tobacco smoke. He stops for a minute and listens to the shuffle of feet and a woman's voice singing: 'Now it's here at last, the moment I've been waiting for.' Tears come into his eyes. He doesn't know what's come over him these days. He's gone soft as a child. But he's glad to be home, dammit. That's nothing to be ashamed of. He only wishes he could stay. It's no life, cooped up with twenty-five blokes, propped or slumped on his bed, lolling there till evening and the semi-intoxication of sleep. And he's had quite enough of sighing firs and wild northern romance. What the hell, Ingrid's got a sense of humour, and she'd laugh all right if she knew what her old man had been up to. Maybe.

He walks over the concrete bridge on Highway Road. The detached houses on the other side are blacked out and silent. There's a rural smell of frozen, rotting potatoes in the raw, misty air. The stacks of planks in the middle of town are as they always were, the street is slightly potholed and the downhill stretch to the Co-op and the kiosk as long as ever. He recognises it all, but takes no pleasure in the recognition because there's no light or sound anywhere and it seems to him the town is sullen and has turned its back on him. It wants to sleep. It doesn't want to hear about war and conscripted soldiers. What an idiot he was not to write home, or ring in advance and have a message taken over. What the hell had he been thinking? He was sorry now. The bicycles were packed together outside the hotel, some leaning against others. He saw an old black Hermes with pale grey tyres there. But then there were lots of those.

He's home. The whole of South House is in darkness. There's no light shining from their kitchen window, golden or white. There's no black Hermes in the bike rack either. But it could be parked anywhere, he thinks, nothing so odd in that.

In the flat it's quiet and smells of home. He stands there just inside the door for a moment before he puts on the hall light. Then he goes over and opens the door to the other room a fraction and sees young Ulf lying asleep. He's in Ingrid's bed. The other bed hasn't been put up. The kitchen's empty. He's confused, feels his bowels turning to water. He runs himself a little water from the tap and is surprised how bad it tastes. He's never noticed it before. This bloody town, he thinks, tossing the water down the sink.

In his brown case he's got half a litre of aquavit. He gets it out and pours himself some. He doesn't bother with a proper spirit glass because he's not drinking for pleasure. It's for his stomach.

As he's sitting there, Ulf suddenly appears in the doorway. My God, the lad. Arne clears his throat.

'I could hear it was you,' says Ulf. 'When you coughed.'

But before he heard Dad coughing over the tap in the kitchen he hadn't known. He'd been lying there stiff and tense, pretending to be asleep. He thinks there are spies out there. They steal along the fence round the town football pitch and then, when the lamps suspended above the street are set swinging and their capsules of light are hidden in the tattered, gale-tossed crown of the lime tree, they run across the road to South House. There they part the branches of the elder and run their fingers over the kitchen window, making the glass tremble.

The spies are like the nasty old drunks only taller and thinner. They have black armbands.

When he heard the key in the lock he froze, because it didn't sound like Mum. He heard the footsteps coming over to the door and squeezed his eyes tight shut when it opened. Whoever it was stood there looking at him. Breathing, there in the room.

He went. Then came the sound of the tap running in the kitchen and that cough when he tasted something he didn't like. It was Dad.

'Where's Mum?' he asks Ulf.

'I don't know.'

Dad stares. But empty-eyed, as if he's looking straight through him.

'Well anyway, hello,' he says eventually. It sounds as if he's saying it while he's doing something else, something much more important. But he's not doing anything. He's just sitting there. He's got a baggy uniform. Grey cloth, baggy all over, over the top of his boots, over his leather belt. He can smell the clothes from the door.

'Don't you know where Mum is?'

'No. She was at Auntie Maud's. But that was before.'

'When was that?'

He's not sure. Earlier this evening.

'Didn't she say where she was going?'

'Yes, but I was nearly asleep,' says Ulf. 'I'm taking my bike,' she said.

'What did she do at Maud's? Have her hair done?'

'Yeah.'

Dad shifts his glass. Then he sits staring at it for a while.

'Get to bed now,' he says suddenly.

Ulf wants to go over to him instead, but he daren't because of that voice. It's a peculiar voice. It's like the window pane. There's nothing to see in the shiny black glass which the elder keeps scraping with its branches, invisible from inside.

So he goes back to bed. He creeps backward through the years, down into the twisted sheets. He picks the scabs off his knees so they sting and bleed, bright red. That'll make her cross. So he puts the light on and tries to rub away the spots of blood on the sheets with spit.

'Turn the light off now,' says Dad from the next room.

He sits with legs wide apart, arms resting on thighs clad in coarse grey homespun that looks as if it has been made of compressed rags. She still isn't here. High on the pale green paint of the tongue-and-groove boards, the hands of the wall clock jerk their way through time, minute by minute. He can hear it behind him, in fact he can feel it in his whole body. His hands hang down like lead weights towards the cork floor. He is paralysed with disappointment.

It strikes him that many a thing idly and lightly dismissed as the way of the world is atrocious. For an instant he finds himself staring down into the abyss of total disillusion with life, but draws back quickly and takes a gulp from the glass on the kitchen table.

But his thoughts go on, asserting there must at the very least be other ways to live. Or must have been. Too late now. But when did it get too late? When did he take that final turning?

He can well imagine there being other people to share a whole life with. More cheerful. More easy-going in an ordinary, everyday sort of way. There really are people who don't take everything so deadly seriously.

A picture of a completely different type of woman comes briefly into his mind. But dimly. It's not a face, not pure physicality. More a sort of sugary haze smelling of sponge cake. Good-natured laughter. Calm movements. *Forgiveness.* Or at any rate understanding.

Why can't the person you're married to just be nice?

He's poured some aquavit into a tumbler now, the first one he came across when he opened the cupboard. He's sitting staring down into the clear spirits.

'What's the bloody point of coming home?' he says in a half-whisper.

So this is what it's like to come home: an empty bed, a dance at the City Hotel and a kitchen left chilled and desolate. There's a draught from the hall and he sits and has a little cry. If Sweden had been taken by the Germans and the town pulverised and reduced to ashes by bombs, it couldn't have felt any worse for him than what has happened or is happening at this very moment.

Military service or Swedish Engineering, it all comes down to the same thing. There's tedium and good humour in both places and it's his prime duty to obey, to follow the instructions given. But in here it's different, he's always been the ruler, the one for whom herrings have been put to soak and cabbage parboiled, ruler of the main room, the kitchen and the hall, and of her private parts, concealed in their mid-length interlock knickers. He was the one who decided what was to be stuffed into them. He was the one responsible for what emerged from them.

But now. He doesn't even know if he's been deposed. If he shuts his eyes, he can see the white knickers, the beige, ribbed silk slip and a wool skirt of pre-war quality in a heap on a floor. Then he drinks a bit more aquavit so he doesn't have to see and the spirits, clear as water, warm him from the stomach outwards, beginning to cradle him like nice, hot bathwater. He sees himself as the ruler again when he closes his eyes. It's that time when his coronation robes were wine-coloured wedding pyjamas. His summer-scented kingdom rises up willingly beneath him and asks: be my destiny. Tell me what will emerge from my most secret places and how you will shape my life, forty years' Babylonian captivity in a bed-settee as the gruel turns sour on the dishcloth; or a decent-sized flat and a summer cottage by a lake, sweet-scented children, a playful dog, pot marigolds and a flag. I shall ripen like a field of wheat under your sun, smelling of food and clean sheets, I shall be its winter resting period and comforting hum. See the polish on all the king's things, the radio set with gold weave over the front and its friendly stations, Stockholm-Motala, the arm of the settee, the coffeepot, the white china of the lamp and the heavy, nickel-silver cutlery.

And now the king arises from his kingdom, which turns on its side to slumber in anticipation of his return to the things and their friendly sheen.

This is an aquavit-induced dream. In reality the only smells are of sleeping child and empty flat. The arm of the settee has only had a rudimentary wipe and there's greasy dust on the china globe of the lamp. There's a dance at the City Hotel tonight and the kingdom has been overturned by anyone you like from anywhere you like, Dalarna or Skelleftehamn, and the power has passed from him and his robes have been dragged in dirt and melancholy until they resemble nothing more than a grubby old pair of underpants. She seems tired of the whole damn thing because she hasn't even bothered to wash his civilian ones. There's not a single pair in the drawer. He gives up the idea of changing after rummaging around in the chest of drawers for a while; life is an indescribably soured and boring business, for which he takes aquavit as you might for the runs or a bad earache.

At which point she comes home.

He starts on her the minute she's put the black Hermes with the slightly buckled front wheel in the rack and come in through the door, taken aback. He starts on her gold-dyed - yes, dyed - pinned up, rolled and curled hair, goes close to see if she's got lipstick on and whether he can detect the smell of drink and asks her why their child is sleeping alone. In the other room, Ulf lifts his head from the pillow and listens to their voices, which are raised and upset.

It only lasts a few minutes, then they fall silent. They're sitting opposite one another now, each on a kitchen chair, each with a kitchen wall to stare at.

'Pour me a glass too,' she says.

So they sat opposite each other, drinking, each sunk in a private well of sourness, and there was no joy to be had anywhere, from the film of dust on the lamp to the coat of yellow varnish on the cork floor. Which had dried uneven because it always had to be so damn quick whenever she decided to do anything.

He sank deeper and deeper into his well and wondered whether the time hadn't come to shut up. She didn't accept that she was a hussy with gold-dyed curls and a mouth gleaming like a half-healed wound, sticky with make-up. She gave a humourless laugh and said:

'I haven't time for any of that.'

She got up at six every morning and went to Curre's and sewed. She bought food and cigarettes with her own money and she'd no time to go out dancing. She'd no time to let the varnish dry between coats either, or to wash anything more than the urgent things. Last night she'd helped slaughter a pig, tonight she'd written a letter and the last thing she'd been doing before bed was going down on her bike to post it. To him.

And her hair? Her hair! To him she seemed as strongly perfumed and loose-fleshed as an over-ripe banana, he couldn't help it. He was talking to her as if she were someone else. He was talking to a lot of women, and to Maj-Lis. If he'd really decided to get it all off his chest he would have asked them not to be so done up and covered in permed curls. Why couldn't they love just one? Wasn't that beautiful? That was all he wanted, intimacy and warmth and the faint smell of blood-suffused skin on a neck just below the ear, nothing more. Why couldn't they be modest and take their underclothes off under their nightdresses? Why couldn't they sleep alone and dream on these dark autumn nights? He would have liked to tell her about a girl he once played with in a big packing case. A long time ago, but it had never got any better than that. Why couldn't they be on their own, finding refuge from the raging storm, playing a game with little pebbles and bits of broken pot for cups and saucers, with wild chervil leaves for parsley and the brown seeds of the curly dock for coffee?

Warmth and trust were what he asked and would give a hundredfold, no, ten thousandfold in return. He wanted to be cuddled, nothing more (not least because much of the bottle's clear contents had vanished, spreading like lead through his testicles), be cuddled and give his warmth, that he'd multiplied ten thousandfold and stored up in his breast like a badger set under a wintry cairn of stones. He didn't manage to say all he wanted. But some of it.

'One might wonder what you've been up to recently', said Ingrid.

Then he knew it really was time to shut up. Because the thing with Ingrid, and in fact all Konrad Eriksson's mob, was that they knew how to talk and turn things against you. Either with lots of words and clever remarks that they mostly laughed at themselves or, like now, with bald, hurtful brutality.

He said nothing and refused to look her in the eye. Then she felt the panic rising in her. It hadn't reached danger level yet. It was just making its presence felt. She got up and switched on the radio, and what came out was lovely and symphonic. She went on round the kitchen, to and fro, with defiant, everyday steps, tidying until there was nothing left to tidy. Finally she suggested he took his things off so she could put his underclothes and shirt to soak.

Maybe she could hang his tunic and trousers out of the window to air overnight. He had been oblivious of the smell of aquavit and the filth of mobilisation reaching right out into the hall as she came in, but now became aware of it and turned away from her, his spine a long, tired curve. He wanted to go and lie down but he would damn well sit here. He'd show her.

She tried to tidy the last things in the kitchen, collected up the bottle and glasses and was about to take them to the sink. Then he said:

'Don't you bloody touch those!'

And she let go of them in sheer surprise at his having spoken. He drank a little. Then the radio played the national anthem and the home service closed down. For a moment the radio sounded as if it had a fire crackling inside and then it quietly started its monotone nighttime howl, its suicide song. She had decided not to switch it off, because he was sitting nearest, but her nerves couldn't stand it. She rushed over and turned the knob.

'And you say nothing! she screamed. 'Nothing!'

She had gone around in her loneliness and wondered, as he had, when you reach the absolutely last crossroads in your life. How did it turn out like this? But the idea of going anywhere without him had never occurred to her, not even now.

She would never have denied that he'd been the great event in her life, even though it hurt, because she'd never found out if it had been the same for him. But for her it was before and after Arne, no other chronology counted, even when she hated her predicament. She had acquired a centre of gravity. Yes, he was a weight in her. It didn't have much to do with falling in love, although it had masqueraded as that in the beginning. She'd hardly recognised it as love, at any rate not the way love had been described to her. It was a feeling of being at home. Solidarity. Weight.

He was her ballast. It didn't matter what he himself was like. Sometimes she thought it was pure chemistry, sometimes she thought it must be something to do with their souls. Then she would laugh at herself, in lighter moments than this.

She'd never wanted to have a child by him. She'd have preferred to do without the Babylonian captivity as well. Getting pregnant had come as a shock. But she'd taken the decision always to treat the child fairly and it had created endless disagreements. He was jealous of the boy and she stood up for young Ulf's rights. It had been hard work through the years and there'd been quite a few scenes. She knew, too, that all her worry about Ulf and her touchy insistence on fairness came of love. Love, among other things. But she wasn't sure she was good at showing it. It wasn't that easy. And the last couple of years, Arne had been different with Ulf. He'd started seeing him. Starting from when he learnt to skate. It hadn't brought the three of them together. No, their love - if that was what it was - seemed to be the sort that meant they were happiest alone.

Acquiring this weight, becoming attached to Arne, hadn't been an easy kind of happiness, in fact it hadn't been happiness at all, not the way she'd expected it to be in those days when she went to tea dances at the Casino or stood waiting for him after the sports club bazaars. It was weight.

Weight, weight, weight. This cursed weight.

There was a lot she'd have like to say to him just now as the panic was rising and she'd begun with his dirty clothes that she'd been able to smell from the hall. But it wasn't a good start.

'Say something then!' she shouted. 'Can't you hear me? Did you come home to keep your mouth shut till you die from lack of oxygen?'

His saying nothing was part of the rules, and she knew that really. Because now they had in actual fact mounted a stage in a theatre with their scripts in their hands; everything was predictable and unalterable. She would speak, her voice growing shriller and shriller, while he stayed silent. She would dig deeper and deeper into the past, right back to that time of sawdust attics and icy bandy pitches long ago, where there were memories as tender as teeth with the nerve laid bare.

'I don't give a shit about you,' she said nastily. He didn't like women swearing, especially not her. It made him flinch. He gave her a look. She'd got at him after all! She swore again to get at him some more, be even nastier.

'I don't give a shit about you and your rules!'

Because the way she saw it, they were playing by his rules. His silent game governed the whole performance. If only he would move and speak, if his eyes would come back to life, she'd be able to say completely different things. She'd be able to throw down the script she was having to read.

She thought he lived in a world of rules. He always had done. Not just on the ice. But particularly there, of course. In fact, when he was a player, there were even rules for how much they ate and drank and how often they could see their girlfriends and rules for who were your mates and who were your enemies. Someone had decided for them who the enemy was, so he was the enemy. Someone had decided for them who was a team-mate, so then they were unswervingly loyal. They had middle-aged men as coaches and team leaders, middle-aged blokes in hard little hats, and they loved the boys. That wasn't a word they'd ever have used, but Ingrid had never been in the slightest doubt it was love.

There'd been a pale, frizzy-haired one called Melkersson. He'd tried to get Arne to think she was a bad for him, sucking him dry, leaving him inert. But she'd had an ally in Arne's lust. Melkersson had been powerless over that.

Somebody told Maud who passed it on to her that boys were sometimes propositioned by men and that they often struck out at the one making the proposal, recklessly, in fear and self-disgust. Perhaps Melkersson had been struck in that way and perhaps he didn't dare proposition anybody. But she had strong suspicions. They'd never pretended to be friends, he and Ingrid. They'd stared coldly, scarcely acknowledged each other.

'Oh, hello Arne,' Melkersson would say when they turned up together. As if she didn't exist. 'Come in, Arne.'

And Arne had ignored her too. Once, he'd left her outside the place where they trained while he went in to talk to Melkersson.

'Wait here a minute,' he said.

He was gone fifteen minutes. Which drew out to twenty. When nearly half an hour had gone by, she went off and left him. She wondered for a long time afterwards how long he'd forgotten her. But she would never find out, because she hadn't waited. She hated him for times like that, but in those days she'd transferred her hate to Melkersson, the frizzy-haired, ageing, bandy-legged bandy coach with the hard little hat.

Now Arne was a coach himself. He was a Melkersson. The boys were his. The team was his. They were a sort of magnification and extension of himself, his will and his skill. It was a wonder they didn't notice what lay behind his affectionate concern for their calf muscles and precious ankles. For him they were muscle power embodying an idea he had, an idea about how they should go about defeating the enemy, the tassel-hats. He polished them and trimmed them hour after hour to make their wills into perfect spools, spinning with a single purpose: to get their dicks out and come at those tassel-hats from behind and bugger them senseless. She'd been within earshot of the busses and the changing rooms before matches and heard him whipping them up into a frenzy. It would be wrong to say she was shocked or even surprised. She'd been to far too many of their parties by then. She was just glad she knew, now. This was how you viewed a defeated enemy. As an arse and a woman combined.

Sport was supposed to teach and foster comradeship, fighting spirit and idealism. But that idealism was a flag cracking in the wind. And that blank, flapping idealism was supposed to foster and teach and bridge over the hostility between classes and the egoism of the world. This was where the qualified engineer and the worker would meet, the baron and the young farm labourer, and may the best man win. Here, class distinctions would fade away and class struggle cease. Here, understanding and comradeship and international solidarity would put out shoots; and they put out shoots right enough and started to grow. But no one had any idea what was growing! There was a smell of old gym shoes clinging to this idealism. Their standard was blank but it cracked nicely in the wind. Forward, boys! She thought they were more honest on the bus and in the changing room, chanting their high mass of hate just as the local farm lads used to chant at the lads of the next village before their big fights at the crossroads. She told him as much. At regular intervals through the years she would come out with it, against her own will. If only he'd answer. The ridiculous thing was, she knew a good answer he could have given! She knew a plausible counter-argument. But since he never answered at all, she always ended up shouting.

'And Cuckoo Point's the worst of all!' she screamed.

The director of Swedish Motors had sponsored the building of a clubhouse for them out at Cuckoo Point, where they dumped their sweaty training gear in the firewood bin along with the newspaper and wood and the whole place smelt, in fact stank, of old gym shoes! They put up elk horns on the walls and fixed gymnastic rings to the fir trees and they took saunas and afterwards ran bellowing down to the lake so any living thing turned tail and fled. Red and heavy-limbed from the heat of the sauna, bellowing with inebriation and fighting spirit and the joy of living, they terrified cuckoo, elk and may-bug until they were totally alone out there with their idealism.

'Answer!' she screamed. 'Can't you hear? You've got to answer. I can't stand you not saying anything, you're driving me mad! At least look at me!'

She tried to force his face round towards her, strained to make him look her in the eye, but then he tensed all the muscles in his face to close it to her, and shut his eyes as well. His face was so tightly closed it was distorted, she couldn't recognise him and it scared her. In her panic, she hit him. She had to strike not once but twice before he opened up again, and then he fell sideways as if the blows had been very hard ones, and crawled across the floor towards the stove. He felt for the hook they used for lifting the lids but dropped it on the floor and got hold of the riddler instead. She shrank back from the weapon as he got to his feet. But he wasn't trying to attack her. He held out the riddler to her and said:

'Good. Hit me if you want. Hit me. I deserve it. To be hit.'

And without her knowing how they'd got there, she was standing with the riddler in her hand and he was crouched in front of her. She felt herself go cold and was filled with shame, dropped the tool. She went and wiped her sooty hand on a sacking towel by the sink.

'Get up,' she said, supporting him under the arms. 'Come with me.'

She dragged him to the door. He let his upper body hang heavy and immobile, but his feet obeyed. She left him lying across the armchair in the other room, crying.

She didn't need to wake Ulf because he was lying stiffly curled up in bed, listening.

'You can sleep in the kitchen now,' she said. 'In your usual bed. I'll get it out for you.'

She put her arms round him and his pyjamas were drenched with sweat and cold against his back.

'Dad's come home,' she said. 'We're going to put the other bed out so he can sleep there.'

She changed his pyjamas, and when she'd put him to bed and come back into the room, Arne was crying into one of the silk cushions his mother had crocheted.

Ingrid went through the well-rehearsed procedure with the lower section of the bed-settee: pulled it out, opened up the iron base and wedged the rocky bit with the book they always used because it fitted the space exactly. It was Ebba Theorin-Kolare's *The Man You Gave Me*, and that made her smile because she was feeling warm and strong again.

When she'd made the bed, he fell fast sleep without even bothering to pee first. She found she had cold feet when she got into bed and the chill spread to her whole body as she lay looking at him in the light from the streetlamp outside the window. Her strength and her courage deserted her, just as her hate had evaporated a little while before. She was frightened.

'Arne,' she said, taking hold of his arm. 'Arne!'

He grunted and went on sleeping; when she finally tried to wake him by shaking his arm and telling him she was scared, he stroked her cheek and turned over. She was alone again in the cold light from the street, which lay glittering on the artificial silk bedcover.

'Wake up, d'you hear! I can't take any more!'

Then he sat up in bed with the pillow as a support for his back against the headboard of the bed and his face was grey and pale.

'What are you doing?' she sobbed.

'Keeping myself awake,' he said, and sat rigid with his eyes open.

'Don't be daft!'

But he didn't move. And she started to cry, turned on her side and cried noisily, with her back to him. But he seemed not to notice. He made no attempt to touch her. So she rushed out to the toilet and curled up on the cork floor in the little room and carried on crying in the bad smell that came creeping across the floor, felt the cold spreading through her whole body from her arms and legs. He didn't come. Nobody came. She could cry her insides out without anybody coming to care for her. She was in hell, and knew it with a stiff, ice-cold middle that hurt whenever she tried to take a deep breath. So she rushed back into the bedroom and threw her arms around him, concerned only with the warmth of his body.

'Be nice to me,' she said. 'Be nice to me!'

She fought to loosen his rigid arms until she finally had them around her and could feel the warmth. She didn't care that she was begging and pleading, what did that matter?

'Come on now, don't cry,' he said. 'I'm here, you know.'

He had come through the shyness and the stony numbness and the self-loathing and he was speaking. She thought about everything they had come down through together over the years; the high-flown sentiments and the silliness, and the crudeness for that matter and the drinking and the ordinariness, and they had removed it from each other layer by layer, like undressing. The veils of sweet music and the stars around their brows were no more than scattered items now; they had discarded understanding and togetherness and fidelity, and all the explanations and meanings were like cast-off rags littering a hall floor. They had entered the chamber of closeness. Touch me, she begged. Touch me in the most secret places where no words and no explanations can reach. Words want to have a grubby finger in everything. But they can't reach in here. Here, we're alone with each another, skin to skin.

And the most unfathomable thing of all: why you? We're not even suited to each other. We can't live together without arguing. How can we touch?

She started to cry afterwards. But not like before; she was crying quietly now. She could see he was finding it hard to keep awake. But he managed nonetheless to ask her why she was sad. So she tried to tell him how she would stand outside the illuminated kitchen window and look into their empty kitchen without being able to accept that she was the woman who lived in there and handled all those objects. She told him about the coffeepot that looked so terrifying as you stood out there and saw how its shape was fixed and limited for all time.

'I'm scared of turning out like that,' she said.

'Scared of turning into a coffeepot?' he said with a little chuckle, and felt for her cheek in the darkness. 'You and your ideas.'

'No, I'm scared of turning out like your mother!'

At first she thought he might be angry, but he just said there wasn't much wrong with his Mum.

'But of course you needn't stay here all your life,' he said. And he asked her if she'd seen the new block of flats down past the hospital, the green one people called the Ice Palace, because there'd been something wrong with the heating in the first place. But now the heating system had been sorted out and it was as warm as the Fuel Commission would allow.

'I know the landlord's agent,' he said. We were posted to the same place and he's got the bit of floor next to mine. There's a flat free there at the moment and we can have it if we want. You needn't stay here.'

271

He patted her hand and said it again. You needn't stay here. Then she could hear from his breathing that he was falling asleep.

The next day was Sunday and they took a walk to the Ice Palace to have a look at the vacant flat. Ingrid had put on her smart blue coat. They went slowly, and long stretches of road were empty, a dirty grey colour but glistening after the autumn rain that had fallen early that morning while they were still asleep. Now and again the shining expanse was crossed by Sunday strollers, arm in arm or holding children by the hand. Some of them carried cake boxes. Ingrid and Arne said the occasional hello and paused to exchange a few words with someone Arne knew through the bandy club.

They passed the Salvation Army, Maud's salon and the allotments. Matted grass and seed heads still lined the ditches. The ground had been dug ready for winter, except on their plot. There, the potato tops were quietly rotting, and Ingrid felt ashamed she hadn't dug the potatoes up in time.

They went past the mortuary, closed and windowless below the hospital. Reaching the Ice Palace, they stopped to look at the green, rain-blotched walls.

'It must be that one,' said Arne, pointing two floors up. 'There aren't any curtains.'

As soon as she got into the entrance hall, Ingrid knew she would never like living in this block of flats. She couldn't stand the smell in the stairwell. It was hard to say what it was. She thought it smelt of stone. But that was so silly she couldn't tell Arne. Could it be the plaster?

She hadn't liked the knobbly green of the outside walls either, or the corrugated iron balconies. On the echoing stairs she took hold of the red-painted metal hand rail and felt as if she were in a factory or the engine room of a huge ship.

Arne, who had borrowed the key, opened a brown-painted door with an empty name plate. The hall was dark. In the kitchen he went over to the sink unit.

'Stainless steel!' he said. And then he showed her: an electric stove. Just a click and it's on.

'No, don't light it!'

'But you can just click it back - look.'

Hot and cold water in the taps, radiators under the windows, WC, a bathroom in the basement. A dining alcove where they could put the bed-settee. Ulf could sleep in the kitchen if they put his folding bed up against the wall during the day.

'And here's the other room.'

It was called the living room and the idea was for you to be in there most of the time. Listening to the radio, knitting and reading the paper. It had pale green wallpaper. There was a view over the field, and beyond it Ingrid could see the sawmill and the Tin Can where she had worked long ago. There was fir forest on the horizon.

'You could have yellow curtains here,' said Arne.

She suddenly had a picture of herself, standing ironing curtains in the room with pale green walls. It made her realise it wasn't as easy as Arne thought. They couldn't escape from anything by moving. The ironing board with its acrid, browny-yellow scorch marks would appear here, along with the evil-smelling vacuum cleaner with its fraying flex; the Singer machine with its noisy strap and wheel, its treadle worn bare of paint by her feet, Arne's slippers that had moulded themselves to the bulges as his feet, the coffeepot and the slop bucket would all come with them and year after year she would run the vacuum cleaner over the kitchen, the hall and the other room.

'I don't like the smell in this building,' she said.

He stood fiddling with the ventilator under the window.

'Smell? Is there a smell in here?'

'Seems to *me* there is.'

'I can't smell anything,' Arne said.

'It's there, all the same.'

'It's nothing serious,' he said confidently. 'You'll soon get used to it.'

'I don't want to get used to it!' she shouted.

Fredrik Otter had a dream and he made it come true on a concrete plinth. It was a dream of seclusion which he called freedom. He wasn't planning to fight his way out to freedom. Instead he intended shutting himself in with it and erecting a fence round it.

But before the cement could be poured into the wooden frames and the aggregate added, a plot of land had to be prepared. He bought twelve hundred square metres from Wolfgang Altmeyer.

Altmeyer, who had come to the Iversen-Lindhs as a war orphan from Austria in the last war, now had a business empire largely divorced from the mercantile dealings of the Lindh house. People reckoned he was very shrewd.

The old merchant, Alexander Lindh, had taken an interest in all the small craftsmen and owners of patches of forest round the station community where he had arrived some ten years after the railway, with no assets and virtually no credit. He had sold and exported things and been convinced that without him they would all still have been sitting on their home-made, rib-backed settles, reduced to mending each other's shafts and rakes when land reform did away with all the little farms. If the old man was something of a digger-wasp, with his enquiring proboscis stuck into most of the activities and assets of the small farmers and craftsmen, then his grandson and latterday heir Patrik Iversen-Lindh could sooner be likened to one of those simple-looking beetles known as a pill-roller, for his habit of pushing before him a round ball of dung, several times bigger than himself.

Patrik was struggling with a company that was growing quite elderly by the town's standards. From the start, an atmosphere of self-sacrifice had prevailed in old merchant Lindh's offices. That is to say, he had decided what would prevail there, and as far as he was concerned it was austerity and paternal benevolence. A number of ladies from better and tolerably better families had helped to give the whole concern, or at least the office, an idealistic, not-for-profit air. They were as unlikely to mention the hours they worked as their need to go to the toilet.

As long as the building was clattering and pinging and rustling with activity, as long as they kept on exporting ploughs and matchwood and plaster ceiling roses, the company had a use for their devotion and it was no exaggeration to talk of full-scale slave labour, at least in the case of the most idealistically inclined.

But the big stockroom of goods with its smell of wood and grain and rats grew increasingly bare, the office grew quieter and the former slaves had to draw the blinds to stop themselves falling asleep at their desks in the strong afternoon sun. Wolfgang Altmeyer, who had been making himself useful in the firm ever since he completed his college course in economics, told Patrik straight out that the whole place was like an institution for the support of elderly gentlewomen. The former slaves had become a drain on resources; they were bound to the company by those ribbons of tradition which Alexander Lindh had so ceremonially waved aloft every time he made a speech to the staff. They had to have birthday presents and anniversary presentations, and it seemed to Patrik six months seldom passed without the need to present some horrifying old slave with a watch or a vase for half a century's service on her swivel chair. The next Monday she would be there again, ready for new sacrifices, and on the last of the month she expected her salary. Patrik thus found himself caught in a disaster of business economics, with virtually non-negotiable salaries to pay out, traditional Christmas gratifications to motivate the staff, expensive Christmas parties, outings to the grounds of the estate in a hired bus, rolled gold watches and paid sick leave.

Altmeyer's prescription was to make the lot of them redundant. But since they had undergone premature menopauses as a result of their exertions for the house of Lindh, Patrik couldn't do it. He hadn't the nerve to do it, the heart to do it, or the stomach for it. So like that meek beetle he rolled the big company along in front of him and could see no way out.

Altmeyer would long since have fired the old praying mantises, male and female, who were well on their way to consuming their benefactor. He would have sold off the colossal building with its false and genuine antiques to the local authority. But Holger Iversen-Lindh was still alive. His head wobbled because of a burst blood vessel in his brain, his right foot wouldn't obey him, faltering in mid-air before it reached solid ground. His tongue moved stiffly when he spoke and he supported himself on his son Patrik's arm. He needed to live in the murky green darkness of old oil paintings and tarnished silver. Where else could he live?

So as soon as he started acquiring assets and creditworthiness of his own, Wolfgang Altmeyer began to separate his interests from those of the company. He had interests in the construction industry all though the 1930's. He was among the first on the spot when the dust rose high into the sky as derelict old Sweden was pulled down. He soon discovered it was practical and profitable to own sawmills and cementworks if you were going to be among those constructing the new kingdom of planking and pasteboard and wood pulp. It was impossible to keep track of what he owned any more, but nobody was surprised to discover a certain asphalt works was his, a gravel pit, a few patches of sandy, pine-dotted heath, a transport company with eight lorries or a little sulphite plant by a lake. Above all, though, he owned land.

Down past District Road he owned an area of land of that type which in the absence of any more adequate description is usually referred to as economically unprofitable. It yielded nothing: no timber or grain, no potatoes or gravel or tar. It was a stony bit of woodland consisting of birch and rowan, stunted alders and the occasional lanky spruce. It was relatively low-lying and mosquito larvae hatched each spring in the foul-smelling hollows. It was not rich in flora. The children knew not to look there for blue anemones and no cuckoos called from the sparse treetops.

Altmeyer had it divided into twenty-two plots with an average area of twelve hundred square metres. These he sold to people who worked for the Swedish Engineering Co. Ltd., Swedish Railways and the telegraph company, to a few self-employed craftsmen and one police officer. He left it to them to make building plots out of this far from promising, semi-acidic, scree-covered land that was neither forest nor town.

What people said, of course, was that Fredrik had bought his plot. He would be a home owner, all in good time. But he himself was very careful with terms and concepts, and he pointed out to Jenny that in fact the bank had bought it from Wolfgang Altmeyer. Between them stood Fredrik with his guarantors and his interest. For this price, plus the labour contributed by himself and his family in clearing and preparing the ground for building, he would be allowed to live there. Perhaps it was because he had pondered long and hard on this ownership, fundamentally far too symbolic for his taste, that Fredrik was more passionate than anyone else for the right of self-determination on his own twelve hundred square metres.

He chose the most elevated plot on the site, but it also had the biggest waterlogged hollow. It was indisputably the most rugged and stony of them all, but it had two tall and shapely spruces, together with a glacial boulder on which moss and wall fern grew. To enable their mailbox to be correctly situated for their address, Fredrik would have to blast an access way through a rocky hillock. This, in combination with the draining of the marshy depression, would level the whole plot and reduce it to a carrot patch, he thought. So he refused to do any blasting and said he was going to put his mailbox on the road behind, which the town planners said was incorrect. Then he did battle with the local authorities so noisily you could hear it right over at Carlsborg, and threw their letters into the rubbish pit. They came and poked about cautiously with the ferrules of their walking sticks in the clay and stump holes and he received them sweaty, angry and exhilarated. Jenny felt very uncomfortable about being in dispute with the authorities.

He didn't get on very well with the neighbours, either. It was less what he said than what he did that made them feel he thought himself superior. The Otters were the only ones on the whole site to opt for a single-family house, while all the others were being built with a kitchen upstairs so the top floor could be let out. Could he afford it? He offered no particulars. When he had thinned out the trees, the biggest rowans were left standing. The neighbours, who had been planning to plant little fruit trees, hinted that rowan moth grubs could get into their apples in years to come. On the contrary, said Fredrik. If a grub's got rowan to feed on, he doesn't bother with apples. It was his opinion against theirs. But no one argued with him since he'd defied the authorities on the mailbox question. He was considered a strong figure.

Like everyone else on the site, which had become known as the Upco Estate after the Unified Pricing Company, Fredrik and Jenny cleared their plot themselves. They worked on it in the evenings, on

Saturday afternoons and on Sundays. They kept their work clothes and their tools in a tent, where there was also a little spirit stove for making coffee. Making the coffee was the only time off Jenny could steal. To start with she looked quite smart and sporty as she stood there turning the handle of the stump-grubber once Fredrik had fixed on the heavy, rusty chains. She had a divided skirt of tweed and lovely black wellingtons. But she soon got so hot that she felt her feet were coming to the boil inside the rubber, and the wool of the divided skirt was too heavy. She began to resemble the other women battling to clear their jungles. They wore faded cotton frocks they were on the verge of throwing out and thin shoes with worn-down heels that had once been their best. They had bandannas wound into turbans, except the policeman's wife who wore a hat, with an elastic band round the bun at the back of her neck.

And so, in a wheelbarrow over springy, sagging planks, they carted away a hundred and twenty-five cubic metres of stiff clay and acidic, stony soil, matted with roots, before the people from the building firm came to put up the timber framework. They dug a ditch for the drainage pipes and the evening they finished it Fredrik stroked Jenny's cheek, although everyone could see. Disorientated mosquitoes and rowan moths fluttered over the filled-in hollows. It was all absolute hell and she cried in the tent when she was making the coffee. It was their holiday tent. Overnight it was full of pickaxes, crowbars and spades.

The foundations were laid and the flooring beams were mounted across the sills of the reinforced concrete base. Two by five joists were hammered up and an outer shell of one by seven weather-boarding with laths was added. The space between the outer boarding and the inside walls of planed tongue-and-groove boards was lined with sheathing paper and filled with sawdust for insulation.

When they got as far as the roof trusses, Jenny baked a cake and they put a good-luck wreath up on the ridge of the roof. By the first of April, the whole thing had been assembled into one hundred and five square metres of living space with internal walls of Treetex fibreboard. It was a house and no longer a dream. The water ran in the wastepipe, it gurgled quite beautifully and Jenny stood listening and thinking about where it ended up.

Now they had a stainless steel sink unit, a WC, bathroom appliances, yellow-varnished pine floorboards, linoleum in the kitchen, a laundry room, a boiler room, storage space for potatoes and coal, and a larder down in the cellar. The weather-boarding was painted pale green, the roof was tiled and the mailbox was at the back, just where Fredrik had wanted it.

He used his key to let himself in and stepped into the tiny enclosed porch they called the wind trap. He took off his galoshes there before opening the door to the hall. Two reedy voices were singing a hymn, accompanied by an organ. It was the morning service on the radio; the time was just before eight. As the voices sang the wailing words he saw in his mind's eye an old woman and a fisherman in a thick sweater. In Budapest, the hymns on the radio were sung by pupils from the conservatoire. He didn't know who did it here.

He had left the drilling machine and gone home from the engineering works because he had felt one of his asthma attacks coming on. Technically speaking, Fredrik Otter had sent him home. Fredrik was both his foreman and his landlord. The whole of Ferenc Krauth's life depended in one way or another on keeping on good terms with Fredrik Otter. Sometimes he reflected that if he had been in Budapest, Fredrik would have been employed as a turner at the Buda Works. He and Ferenc would in all probability never have met. The civil engineers and designers worked in an entirely separate building. It would have been unthinkable for him to have had Fredrik Otter lodging at his house. He and his mother would neither have needed a lodger nor been interested in having one. But he wasn't in Budapest. He looked out of the hall window at an exact replica of this two-storey detached house in pale green wood with a little balcony above the verandah.

The morning service was over. A man's voice began reading the weather forecast. It was a long one because this was a very elongated country. There was an awful lot of bad weather, fog, snowstorms, strong winds and disagreeableness of all kinds to be enumerated.

'Hello!' Ferenc called in the direction of the living room, but there was no answer. Jenny was presumably out. She had probably just forgotten the radio.

As he came into the room, he had a sensation of the house having turned all its window-eyes inwards to look at him. He had never been alone in here at this time of day before. The kangaroo vine twined its way up the wall, the same vine that framed their evening conversations. And yet not the same. He had a sudden urge to touch it and see if the leaves were dry and papery or whether it was still alive. When he switched off the radio and it went quiet, he felt he was the only person in all Sweden.

It was cold in there. He decided to check whether the boiler was still alight. If it was, he could put in a shovelful of coal briquettes.

The steps down to the cellar smelt of potatoes and damp sacking. He passed swiftly through the smell, trying to make himself impervious. There was no crackling sound from the boiler. When he opened the lid it was black inside. He had no idea what you were supposed to do with the damper or the regulator so he dared not try to light it. Once he had been lying on his bed when he heard explosions. Having eventually realised it wasn't the Germans invading, he could hear that the noise was coming from inside the house and had thought it was going to blow up, perhaps from the pressure of all the silence that had been building up in there minute by minute since it was built. It was the expansion tank booming as hot steam leaked out over the sawdust on the attic floor. No, best not to touch the boiler.

He looked at the ash can. It was over-full again. Fredrik never spared himself in his job at the engineering works. He often drove himself to headaches and insomnia for the sake of urgent defence orders. All he really wanted to do when he got home was sit in his worn brown leather armchair. If Jenny chose to say anything at that point, to the kitchen wall or to the dark outside the window pane, about the ash can not having been emptied, he would rest his head against the tall chair back and close his eyes with a pained look. Sometimes he punished her by getting up, exhausted as he was, and going straight down to the boiler room. Jenny and Ferenc would hear him thumping the ash can up the steps and outside in the dark, and would not meet each other's eyes.

Ferenc's urbanity suffered badly during these silent scenes. He would have liked to intervene. Had it been possible to do so without taking sides, he would have hauled out the ash can himself. He knew this was his weakness, a soul too urbane for a harsh climate, and wondered how deep it went, if it would have come with him to the concentration camp where he would now have been, and what burdens he would have been hauling there.

In the empty house he suddenly felt closer to Fredrik and Jenny than he ever did when they were at home. Instead of resisting the dry, polluted air in the boiler room, he inhaled it. Cautiously, as if about to commit a minor crime, he went out and opened the door of the larder a crack. He felt a strange curiosity. There was a brown stoneware jar of eggs preserved in isinglass, a gelatinous mass he would have been loath to touch if he had been asked to fetch a few eggs. Those sticking up out of the jelly had brown and grey patches on their shells. On the shelves there were glass jars of preserved meat. It looked grey and fibrous. The seal had gone on a couple of jars of mushrooms and the jar of lingonberry jam was sticky round the top. He felt how close he was to Jenny now, this everyday stranger with whom he was living an involuntary life.

The jars of mushrooms on the shelves included some he had

helped to fill himself. He couldn't bring himself to eat the contents. Jenny would take preserved elk meat and stir their whole ration of half-cream into the sauce with the browned mushrooms. Then Ferenc could eat neither meat nor sauce, because of the mushrooms. They had no hesitation in picking mushrooms that looked like big pigs' ears, scaly paws or inside-out cows' stomachs. No, he refused to eat such things.

Jenny meant well and was trying to be a good housewife in preparing such dishes, and she got upset. She would salvage pieces of meat from the sauce and put them on his plate. Fredrik looked disapproving. He clearly thought Ferenc was behaving like a spoilt child. But although the bits of mushroom had been removed, he still felt there was too much forest around them as they sat there. The first storms of autumn tore and whined at the pinewood timbers of the walls, making it seem as if they wanted to be tossing like the great trees outside, their living sisters. The wood did not seem dead, despite having been sawn and trimmed and planed. He felt there were knothole eyes staring at him from the birch furniture and he was petrified of finding bits of bone and shot as he chewed the elk meat. He imagined the elk as a vast creature. He thought he could hear the clatter of hooves and felt a violent longing for the indoor life. Yet he knew he would never be truly at home and indoors as long as he remained in this country.

There were little leaves in the bilberry compote and he deposited them carefully on the edge of his bowl. Jenny was blue about the mouth and her teeth looked peculiar, unsavoury. Fredrik didn't smile all that often, with him it didn't show so much. He ate the compote with milk in a deep bowl into which he broke pieces of crispbread. The whole procedure made a disgusting noise.

They lived close to the forest. It filled the jars on their larder shelves. Jenny's hands were purple as she made jams and cordials at the end of the summer. Their aroma was strong and appetising. Even so, Ferenc couldn't bring himself to appreciate the products. A spoonful of jam on a pastry for dessert, fine. Fruit conserves and compotes with a crisp little biscuit and thick, whipped cream like you got before the war. He could long for that sort of thing. But big, deep bowlfuls of runny red jam of the kind that always reminded him of Russia, topped with broken-up crispbread slowly going soggy in the cloudy pink milk, it was neither a dessert nor a main dish. He thought of berry-devouring bears in high Carpathian forests.

But the proximity of the forest helped them survive the winters in those years of meagre rations. The old woman whose name was Tora seemed to be the wisest of them in these matters. She had already organised their survival of one war, and it had been harder then. She dealt out empty milk jugs and baskets made of woven bark before they set off for the forest. Even Fredrik obeyed her. He lumbered round among the tussocks, getting purple fingers.

They looked for the blushing parasol mushroom near old mineshafts, and one Sunday Ferenc had seen a dead elk in black water. Its belly had swollen and burst and its legs looked like the broken fenceposts that littered this terrain, grey and rotting. He turned back and abandoned the hunt for the parasol mushroom, whose name they had taught him to pronounce in their language before they set out. He knew that this mushroom would have filled them with reverence even if they had found it growing on a rubbish tip.

They came home exhausted and sat down to pick over the lingonberries, spreading them out on a blanket that would trap the leaves and other debris. They spread newspaper to sort the mushrooms on. Fredrik meanwhile fell asleep on the sofa in the living room and out in the kitchen they could hear him snoring. But

Ferenc dared not abandon the two women. He cut out maggot holes and rotting yellow sponge that was hiding beneath wide caps of brown fungus. He found himself in trouble for not having been selective enough when he was picking. The old woman studied every mushroom he put in the cutting pile. Once she gave him a terrible telling off for one of them she claimed could have been the death of them all.

Fredrik's mother had long treated Ferenc as a child or feeble-minded because of his broken Swedish. But he won her respect when autumn came and he fetched out the overcoat he had brought with him when he fled. It was blue wool and made by a Budapest tailor. She felt the fabric and looked at him, and he was no longer the destitute wretch she had taken him for. He wished he might one day be able to show her the gold coins that were sewn into his leather belt. He still had four left after his escape.

They talked a lot about this woman's gastric problems, which sometimes meant she had to lie down on the sofa when she came to visit her son and daughter-in-law. They said she was resting because her digestion was playing her up again. But Ferenc was sure she had a different, more serious illness, and that she knew it. Sometimes she looked him in the eyes as if to confirm his knowledge.

It seemed to him that the illness and death casting a shadow over her short, windswept autumnal days made her doubly eager to teach them the art of survival. But Fredrik was already impatient. He was waiting for the war to end. Then no one on earth would get him out berrying in the forest again.

Ferenc thought of his own mother, his little mameh who hadn't been able to do much more than play her instrument and sew, but who had also taught him the art of survival, though in totally different circumstances, in a forest of stone. She had persuaded him to sell shares and government bonds sooner than he had thought necessary. She had had the gold coins sewn into his belt and before she died she had told him not to stay any longer, but to get away.

She had been buried almost in secret. He knew how urgent things were by then. He had been to the bank and tried to take out the remaining money in her account. There had been a delay. Since he didn't know what it might mean, he hadn't waited. He had forgotten a pair of suede pigskin gloves on the counter, pale grey, and he could still see them in front of him. He could see them lying on the polished oak counter. It felt a very long time ago.

His little mameh had never walked in a real forest, he was sure of it. But he somehow imagined that old Tora, who knew lots of places where the proud field mushroom Agaricus augustus grew, and the meaty-tasting saffron milk caps stood in circles in the grass, must have risen directly from of the forest before she gave birth to Fredrik.

Acrid steam from the mass of boiling fruit filled the kitchen and she stirred with a wooden ladle as discoloured as her hands. The mushrooms bubbled gently in the frying pans, the kitchen was hot and condensation formed on the windows. The condensation dripped in streaks down the panes and he wished they had let some air in. But they were eager to conserve the warmth generated by the crumbly briquettes.

The kitchen no longer felt human and pleasantly warm to him, as it did when Jenny made her bun loaves. They were frightening creatures, these possessors of kitchens with sour and pungent smells from bogs and sandy pinewoods. They kept themselves alert in the heat with thin, pale gold coffee and he finally had to take flight from the fumes and the swarming maggots.

He would lie on his bed in his room, not knowing what to do with his life through these wasted years. He had nothing to read in any of the languages familiar to him. Downstairs stood an old witch, stirring a potion his stomach refused to accept.

In the cellar larder in front of the shelf of conserves, that sense of being forsaken came over him again. But he didn't want to go and lie on his bed and let it grow. Still slightly ashamed of his undertaking, he passed on to the cold, dank mustiness of the laundry room and let his eyes travel over the wooden duckboards and the concrete floor to the rusty sludge of hairs and scraps of linen thread in the drain outlet.

He didn't see them as particularly hygienic. The laundry room always had a funny smell and the baskets overflowed with dirty clothes. Jenny did a big wash every two or three months. For that she would don boots, a rubber apron and a checked headscarf. When she was cooking the dinner or baking she would put on a big, white apron. But he didn't think she changed the sheets often enough and he didn't know how to ask for clean ones without offending her. He'd seen Fredrik's pillows. It looked as if the factory grime had sweated out of him and his mouth had left yellow rings. It might be his tobacco.

She vacuumed zealously. The big cleaner would be whining round down there when he came home short of breath with a tight chest. She didn't always think to switch it off, either.

She cleaned her house thoroughly all right, at least in bursts. She dusted, polished, vacuumed and scrubbed. He couldn't fault her hygiene where food was concerned and he gave her credit for the big white apron.

It struck him that he nearly always felt grateful to them. They didn't make him live like a common lodger. He joined them for a cup of tea in the evenings and they invited him along on their excursions. But here in the house alone, he suddenly felt overwhelmed by irritation with them. He felt furious with Jenny for leaving the radio on all through the Stockholm stock market report, without listening to it.

They lived in a little house and that construction of wood and millboard sometimes seemed very fragile to him. It enclosed their trivialities, their relative lack of cleanliness, the smell of cabbage soup and the things they fancied to be true, of which he should by rights have known nothing.

One of their fancies was that things had turned out splendidly for them. He knew he ought to consider himself extremely lucky he'd ended up with them. And he did. He'd grown quite fond of them, but just wished their lives were more aesthetically pleasing.

To teach himself more than just the spoken language, Ferenc had worked his way through a school anthology Jenny had lent him. There he'd read a saga about their ancestors. Though very much abridged, it had given him a good picture of their national temperament. In the story they knocked each other's teeth out with axes and torched their low huts to burn each other to death. His spirit, which was both Viennese and Hungarian-Jewish, revolted with almost physical symptoms of nausea against this history reeking of goat's hair and the smell of burning. Fredrik, however, found the stories both humorous and epic. He had felt something of their spirit in him when he was digging the drainage ditch and refusing to blast an access way and he was damned if the swastika would ever fly over the Swedish Engineering Company Limited. Ferenc found Jenny more ignorant but less naive.

He had come to a halt in front of the potato crate, where long, pale mauve shoots were sprouting through the chinks. He had a sudden feeling of not wanting to be this close to these people. Quickly, he left the cellar.

Upstairs he found the living room bathed in pale sunlight, and it felt cold. In the evenings the radiators would be glowing hot for a couple of hours. You couldn't touch them. They would sit round the smoking table, which was a solid, dark-brown piece of furniture with cupboards in the base and a glass top where they stood their cups of tea. Fredrik had a tobacco tin in one of the cupboards and he kept a slice of raw potato in it so the tobacco stayed moist. After filling his pipe he would always put the tin away in the cupboard. He literally hid it, as if he hoped to save tobacco that way. He smoked an enormous amount. Jenny had to give up coupons for him. They had taken to drinking tea since Ferenc came and he taught them you could use sweets instead of sugar to save on the sugar ration. Sometimes the sweets Tora gave them turned the tea bright red, sometimes it tasted of fruit or mint.

There were generally four of them sitting round the smoking table in the evening. The fourth was Ann-Marie, who always sat on the floor. She wasn't Fredrik and Jenny's little girl, but the daughter of an inventor Fredrik had got to know when he'd offered Swedish Engineering the production rights to one of his designs. Ann-Marie had no mother. She had long, thin legs and would sit with her back against the hot radiator and her chin on her knees. There wasn't a scrap of spare flesh on her body. She stayed with them when her father was on his travels, trying to sell an invention somewhere, or patent it. Ferenc suspected he was often away longer than he need be, out on a spree as Jenny put it. The girl would sometimes come when he was at home as well. She was blonde, with thin, flyaway hair she kept off her face with a brown hair slide. Tora would curl it for her with the tongs because it was dead straight.

She liked pulling faces. Ferenc kept urging her not to furrow her brow and pull her mouth out of shape. She'd never be beautiful if she did that.

There were only two armchairs and it distressed him that Jenny sat on one of the dining chairs. Not an evening went by without him offering her his place when she came out of the kitchen after the washing up was done. But she wanted both arms free when she was knitting. On Saturday evenings he sometimes managed to persuade her to sit in the saggy armchair. On those occasions she would put away her knitting and he would serve them the wine he'd bought from the state off-licence, where your purchases were registered in a brown book. She would listen with them, her hands in her lap, to the variety show on the radio. Fredrik tried to explain the Swedish jokes to Ferenc, who listened politely. Jenny would smoke a flat, Turkish-style cigarette from a metal case in the smoking cupboard. They were very old; she seldom smoked. She didn't think it right to use up any tobacco coupons when Fredrik's consumption knew no bounds. He exchanged his coffee ration for tobacco coupons and would get 90 points for a quarter kilo of coffee. He couldn't survive without his tobacco, Jenny used to say to Ferenc, and that was the only thing she ever told him in confidence about her husband. He understood more or less what she meant. There seemed to be some great, pounding fury deep inside Fredrik. Sometimes the very silence in the room seemed to be holding back a fury he would never allow himself to express. When there was a storm raging outside and the trees were tossing their crowns as the air tore through them, when evil spirits seemed to be shaking the sheet metal of the balcony and the halyard clacked furiously against the flagpole, he would sometimes look at Fredrik as if he expected something to happen to him. But he sat quiet in the warm room with his head bowed over the local paper as the radiators hummed.

Jenny, too, gave the impression of being semi-absent from this existence in which she should be so at home. Sometimes she forgot to water her houseplants. It was as if they had never existed for her.

She had a kangaroo vine growing in the arch that divided the living room in two. In the window niches she had hibiscus, Christmas-flowering cactus and abutilon. They always seemed to be dormant or ailing and their pots were flecked with white mould.

One big, repulsive cactus which even in its natural state had a sickly-looking white film on it suddenly produced a red flower, a rosette in the peculiar gap between its leaves. But then Jenny threw it out. She explained she'd recognised the flower from a picture of Hitler, who was making a speech from a podium surrounded by flowering cactuses just like that. She didn't want to be reminded of that madman, that savage beast whose fault it all was. Ferenc was taken aback. He'd had no idea she felt so strongly about the war. He'd got the impression she didn't know much about it.

The cactus lay on top of the compost heap, turned out of its pot. Its roots froze in the dry cold and it would sink with the first thaw. He wondered how anything could flower in the winter light.

Jenny didn't always seem to be with them. She stood absent-mindedly crushing a delicate brandy glass in the washing up bowl. It had belonged to Fredrik's father. He went in and sat down in the leather armchair without a word of reproach. Jenny stood looking at her bleeding fingers. How could that have happened?

There was an impatience in her Ferenc could never quite understand. She took up playing the piano but didn't get anywhere. They had a black piano that had come, like the big leather armchair, from the café her mother-in-law had owned. Jenny was musical and he bought her sheet music in the hope she might learn to play some Viennese waltzes. The photographs on top of the piano rattled when she played loudly. Now it was Ann-Marie tinkling away at the waltzes, which he regretted having bought, and she had taught herself to pick out 'Warsaw is the City I Love' as well.

Sometimes as they sat sipping their tea he would think of the Café Vörysmarty in Budapest. And he would try to tell them about it. But it was impossible to conjure up the buzz of voices in that soft language, the chink of coffee cups and the aroma of pastries and tobacco. He kept trying. He came to realise, however, that they couldn't imagine what people did in a café where you could stay on long after you'd finished your cake. That made him feel mean and impatient, and he thought that if only they'd known some German or French he could have explained. But they would have visualised their ludicrous town architect or the musical director with the beret and cycle-clips if he'd tried to tell them about the poets, architects and theatre directors, the journalists and the great conductor on whose entry people would rise to their feet, the idle old ladies with aristocratic names and thin, blue lips. He was ashamed of his meanness and impatience because he wanted to be kind and grateful. Which indeed he generally was as they sat in the living room in the evenings and the dog turned round in front of the radiator, warming its belly in the radiant heat. The demijohn of fermenting home-made wine gave a regular cluck as the bubble moved round the airlock. They made the wine from rye and ordinary baking yeast. He wanted to like it. There were times when he wanted to like it, with all his heart.

As he went upstairs he tried to avoid seeing. He didn't want to see anything else, he wanted to go and lie down until the pain and the pressure in his chest eased. But the miserly winter light up there on the landing caught him all the same and he automatically kept his elbow in to avoid knocking the much-mended bird that stood on the banister.

He went into his room and got into bed. He hadn't really any asthma symptoms now. That, too, filled him with feelings of shame. Outside the window, the great spruce rustled solemnly.

There were trains hammering through Sweden night and day; it wasn't exactly a tour of the country like *Nils Holgersson's Wonderful Journey*, but they did see a lot. Playing cards were slapped down on suitcase lids, toilet floors flooded and stank, they ran out of aquavit, their home-knitted things itched under the uniform cloth. They tried to sleep as the trains shrieked past blacked out towns, silent stretches of water and the black fir forest that was their soul.

The idea was for everybody to change place. At least, it seemed like that. Maybe there was no plan behind it all. The man used to staring at furrows ploughed in rich soil had to learn to negotiate treacherous upland bog country. Many of them saw a lot of things they never knew existed, and they would talk about them for the rest of their lives. They would tell tales of such far-flung places as Fårö Island and Stöllet and Valsjöbyn, how they built roads and rifle ranges and had to pull dead Norwegians, frozen stiff, on sledges across the high fells. They whiled away the empty hours in cafés, they wanked and played cards and wrote home and did deals in cigarettes and aquavit. Nothing was the same.

And there was something else. It was to do with their women. It had been starting here and there even before Europe exploded and the draught blew the Swedish cottage door wide open. It had started at the Ericsson and Luma factories and the Retail Ready-To-Wear Co. Ltd., with make-up, sweets and cigarettes, plus two pairs of silk stockings a week. Then it crept in at SKF Ballbearings and the aircraft watchtowers. You couldn't say anything was the same any more. Some of them said the devil had got into their women.

The solid middle-aged and elderly women didn't go clambering up into aircraft watchtowers, of course. They were too unwieldy and they didn't want to learn how to spot different types of plane. They had no shorthand or typing skills, spoke no foreign languages, hadn't a clue about nuts and bolts, most of them. What could they do?

Berta Söderkvist could bake melting moments. Ada Gustafsson had had a little restaurant for eighteen years, and what's more she'd been in charge of the catering when the Belgian giant Ferdinand visited the town with his funfair. Hilda Kjellén was known for her delicious sour cherry jam and Hulda Bergström could make Danish pastries that were lighter and flakier than anybody else's.

They became the WDV mess corps. The ones who cooked the food were known as kitchen volunteers, the ones who stood at the long tables on the station platforms to feed the troops were known as serving volunteers. After all, half of Sweden was on the move and longing for home. They poured out of their trains on black winter mornings, three or four hundred men at a time. It was bitterly cold and ice was forming in their beards by the time they had tramped the platforms for a while. There was a clatter of billycans, they talked and swore in low voices, but when they reached the serving volunteer with her soup ladle they would pull themselves together and make a humorous remark. Sometimes they just told the plain truth: this food's as good as Mother's. Why does there have to be a war?

The volunteers were well wrapped up, with white aprons on top and protective oversleeves. It wasn't easy to see what they really looked like, but the younger the appearance and the prettier the face, the more determinedly a man would pull himself together. They hadn't much time to talk though, none at all really. There were thirty-five of them to feed seven hundred and fifty men in seven minutes. Sometimes it was eight hundred men in ten minutes. Officers crunched around in the snow. One of them saluted Hilda Kjellén.

'Your hands must be freezing,' he said, sounding so human. People said some of them were Nazis, but Hilda didn't think this one could be. He asked her if she knew where the train had come from and if it was going to Värmland via Hallsberg. The volunteers worked irregular shifts to stop them getting too familiar with the timetables, but she'd picked up a few things even so. The Hallsberg train had already gone, with eleven hundred men on board. Hilda was plump, good-natured and obliging, and chattered the whole time as she ladled out the soup; she wasn't one to get flustered easily. But then she had to take the safety pins out of her oversleeves and go with the lieutenant to the station hotel. It was a serious matter; he was a security officer and had lured her into a trap.

They didn't take her out and shoot her in the green cold of dawn, but she was reprimanded and the head of the field kitchen, Ada Gustafsson, the one with the little restaurant, was given orders to put Hilda on cooking duty in the engine sheds where she couldn't talk out of turn.

'I knew he wasn't a Nazi,' said Hilda, who had never before been utterly wrong about anybody.

The engine shed was a semicircular building with a black roof on the edge of the railway yard. It was made of brick and of an artistic architectural design, but when they arrived on those winter nights it looked as if it had been hurled there from out of chaos; it was a mass of brick and solid weight over there in the dark, and they always found the echoing, soot-encrusted roofs above them oppressive to begin with, in spite of all the rush. During that worst time there were eight to ten long trains arriving at the station every night, which could mean eight thousand men to feed. They worked in groups, relieving each other at intervals. They were told the evening before when they would be on duty, always at different times so they wouldn't get to know the timetables of the secret trains thundering along the tracks.

Their previous activities had consisted of community parades, Festivals of Light in the church, sales of straw handicrafts and raffles of peppermint rock and hand knitting. Then came the National March for Health, air raid training days, Christmas present collections for the troops and field kitchen courses.

And then one night they found themselves there with 144 kilos of peas, 350 kilos of potatoes and 150 kilos of pork to be turned into meals for eleven hundred men. But the pork was in the form of long pigs lying cold and dead on an open cart. Berta Söderkvist who baked such lovely melting moments set to and ran the soaking water while Ada Gustafsson measured out scoops of salt. They had a fatigue-duty conscript to help them, and they gave him instructions on how to tackle the pale pigs. But they soon grew impatient and took the axe and saw into their own hands. The fatigue-duty helper was quite pathetic those first couple of years, when anything truly male was supposed to be bearing arms.

The helper had dungarees and an imitation fur cap and his fingers were swollen like sausages in the cold. The helper shuffled, he peeled thick, clumsy, soil-clogged chunks off the potatoes, sniffed up snot and glowered through pale blue eyes. It seemed improper and above all surprising to see him standing hunched over a snowdrift, peeing, because fatigue-duty conscripts weren't supposed to have anything between their legs, or at least not much.

299

But the very worst time passed, and it all became part of everyday life: hearing the hammering trains, being worn out and sick of strutting officers and brisk, hearty ones. Soon enough, all the troops had a shuffle just like the helper's. By then the volunteers had long since made friends with him. A friend in need is a friend indeed, they joked, and found him such a dab hand with the low-pressure boiler. And anyway, said Ada Gustafsson, there wouldn't be any wars if everyone was a reject like him. She brought the helper into the warm and made a fuss of him with coffee and cardamom buns.

Jenny Otter was in the group led by Gerda Franzon and there were ten of them in the group, ladies she found quite intimidating to begin with. She didn't know any women that well except those in her own family, and she'd been suspicious of them. Women can't keep quiet, Fredrik said. When they were working together round the Osby boiler, they were very informal about names, didn't call each other Mrs. Initially this intimacy had made her uncomfortable.

She and Fredrik had been married twelve years when the war broke out. There hadn't been any children. The shame and pain of the first childless years had silted over with time and tedium. She didn't put as much time and effort into cleaning as she used to at first, when she wanted to show everybody there was absolutely nothing wrong with her except that she hadn't produced any children. Then she began to forget what she was supposed to be doing, more and more often; she even forgot to get the potatoes on for when Fredrik came home. He made no reproaches. Nor did he need to. She thought it was eccentric behaviour herself.

For as long as the WDV's activities consisted of tombolas and communal peace parades, she didn't take them very seriously. She often forgot to go to meetings. She forgot to wash her collar, cuffs and armbands on the day of the Festival of Light in the church and had to iron them dry in a mad rush just before it was time to go.

The first time ten WDV's had to feed a thousand men in a fifteen-minute stop on the station platform, she was afraid she wouldn't be up to her part of the job. She was going to be in the engine sheds with Gerda Franzon's group, cooking pork and root vegetable mash. They arrived in unnecessarily good time one dark December evening, just as the delivery of vegetables and pork was coming in on a cart. Jenny looked at the mountain of swedes and the frozen pigs, then she looked at Gerda Franzon who had a maid at home and Hilda Kjellén who was known for her delicious Danish pastries. They were all talking in loud, shrill voices and were all just as nervous as she was. A few moments later they were hard at work, without her knowing quite how it had happened.

Then she discovered that, contrary to what she had thought, she was possessed of strong arms, stamina and punctuality. She discovered that fat little Hilda Kjellén was the most cold-blooded of them all; that Berta Söderkvist was quick-witted and what was more could get them to laugh in the midst of all the ghastly rush; and that Gerda Franzon knew how to organise and practically never allowed herself to feel tired. Jenny didn't care that no one else knew. As she came down to the engine sheds at night and heard their clear voices above the din she was happy.

The war was no longer so alarming as it had been at first. It hammered away like an old train. Jenny rarely read the war reports in the paper. She was sick of the very word.

One night they were on the platform gathering up the pots and pans after the latest contingent of troops when a long, darkened train pulled in. No one got out. Finally a few officers and men loomed out of the darkness and began patrolling in front of the carriages. But not once did the carriage doors open as the station employees busied themselves up at the front by the locomotive.

One officer grew irritated with the WDV's for taking so long to go. They carried on doing what they had to do at a steady pace, took away the now cold and empty canteens, dismantled the trestle tables and gathered up forgotten cutlery.

Then they saw the faces at the compartment windows. The platform lights illuminated them. They saw that one whole carriage was full of women and that their hair was very short, almost shaved. They stared out through the dirty glass but made no move to wave or give a sign.

A few minutes later, the train pulled away into the darkness. Frightened by what they had seen, they tried to think of explanations.

Ferenc often came home from the works complaining of a tight chest. It was hard to catch his breath, he said. Sometimes he was already there by the time she got back from the engine sheds, tired after her work alongside the low-pressure boilers and the rattling trains. They were short of fuel at home now, but she opened the damper to let the boiler burn up a bit for his sake.

Fredrik wanted them to live on their rations. It wasn't that he was stingy. He just hated hoarding and black market deals. Briquettes, butter and margarine, pork and coffee were supposed to be sufficient for their needs. They weren't, of course. But he didn't know so much about that.

She sometimes wished he could have been a bit less of a stickler for honesty. He could have been more like his mother. Tora fixed and fiddled her way through the grey years. She had a secret pig on a farm somewhere, sometimes two. She managed to get herring from Oxelösund. Brown parcels often arrived for her on the country buses, greasy packages, sometimes leaking or bloody, making the bus driver curse as he handed them over. There were eggs in them. Hens for boiling. Ox legs. Pig's trotters. A hare. Birds and pike.

Fredrik ate all this without knowing where it came from. If you want to go through life whiter than white, there are a lot of things you have to pretend not to notice. Jenny cleaned and prepared the hens and knew he would never have eaten them if he'd seen the intestines.

She ran the tap into the saucepan to boil water for tea and put her hand under the stream. But she felt it without feeling.

'What are you doing?' he asked.

I'm feeling to see if I can feel,' she wanted to answer. But she said nothing.

'We saw some Norwegian women on a train last night,' she told him. 'They'd had their heads shaved.'

She could see from his expression he found it nauseating. But she was telling him for the same reason as she was putting her hand in the gushing water.

'They were going to Germany,' she said. 'To a camp. They were Norwegians who'd been with German soldiers.'

'So they were being punished for that?'

'Why yes.'

'What did you all think when you saw them?'

What had she thought? She didn't know any longer.

'I suppose - we wondered what the devil they were doing there!'

That made him livid. This man who was usually so polite. Called her lots of things: a blonde giantess in gumboots! Said she was stupid, she was making herself seem stupid. He spoke a broken, childlike Swedish. His rage seemed comical. She stared at him. It was lucky for him Fredrik wasn't in.

His tone changed. Didn't she realise? They were Norwegian Jewesses and women who had worked for the resistance. Why should the Germans send their whores to camps?

'Right, that's enough,' she said sharply. 'None of that language.'

'Jenny!'

She turned her back on him.

'That was what an officer told us, anyway,' she mumbled. But she realised now it had been a blatant lie and began to blush. The blood went pulsing up from her neck, it wouldn't stop. He put his hand on hers but she wouldn't look at him. God, let this all be over!

'What sort of tea would you like?' she asked stiffly.

During the summer he had picked herbs and asked her to dry them in a low oven. He had taught her to use them to make teas. One of them helped him with his asthma.

But this time she could see the attack had gone too far. She had to get him a bowl of hot water and a towel to put over his head and shoulders. As he sat inhaling the steam, the balance between them was restored; he was polite and grateful once more.

She felt like his mother when she placed the towel over his head of wavy, ash-coloured hair. The hair was silky, she had happened to feel it as she brushed against his head. She didn't move away but stood behind him listening to the laborious, wheezy breaths inside the steam tent. She was resting one hand on the kitchen table. It lay on the yellow oilcloth and she looked at it as if it had nothing to do with her body. It looked like some object she had put down there. In sudden horror she jerked it back and put it in her apron pocket.

'What is it?' he asked from under the towel.

'Nothing.'

Why was everything so awful sometimes?

'Jenny?'

But she didn't answer. She started getting cups and saucers out of the cupboard.

Autumn had arrived, with persistent grey rain. It rained at night as they were feeding the men beside the troop trains, it rained on Europe's muddy fields and ruins, on the faces of the children and on the graves.

More and more often, Ferenc would come home during the morning with breathing difficulties and sit in the kitchen with her, sipping the yellow tea that smelt of mint.

'It will soon be Sukkoth,' he said.

She didn't know what that was. How could he explain: the branches with their leaves on, the wine, the fragrant fruit and the voices mumbling blessings.

'I didn't know you were religious,' Jenny said in surprise.

'I'm not orthodox,' he said. 'My father didn't like religion. But my mother's father used to build a *sukkah*.'

He didn't really know how to explain why he should be thinking about it now. Traditions? It's part of my culture. Would she understand?

Sometimes he looked round and wondered what her traditions were. Christmas. Pork meat. Cleaning, cooking, baking. Duty. Work. Punctuality. He wanted to tell her about the *sukkah* his grandfather had built and the delightful experiences inside it, sweet cakes with wine, those few days of decampment when nothing was normal and grandfather not stern but affectionate and jolly.

'And you could see the stars through the branches of the roof,' he murmured, making her turn round in astonishment, for he had spoken another language.

'*Mama-loschen*,' he said. 'I'm talking *mama-loschen* again.'

His father hadn't liked it. It had been heard less and less frequently at home. His father was an architect who had studied in Vienna and was eager for his son to learn German impeccably. In the end, Ferenc had been embarrassed if his mother said anything to him in the old tongue, and the end result was that they only spoke Hungarian at home.

So it was decades since he had heard it, but it started coming back to him, the old nursery language, and it seemed to him he could feel his mother's lips against the back of his neck: Oy oy oy! he was little and had burnt his hand on the stove, out there with the maids. She had bandaged the hand with a strip of linen with *schmaltz* and rocked him to and fro and talked *mama-loschen*, mothers' soft language for the little things that happen, for people and their tears, for what is fun for boys and grandfathers. Oy oy oy!

He wondered if Jenny could lend him a Bible and an almanac. She turned away to hide a smile. What was she laughing at? Well, it was just his funny way of pronouncing things. She should have been very angry with him a few days ago for saying a very bad word about a certain group of girls. But he had called them hurs and that had made her want to laugh at the same time. Now he was calling the Bible the Hily Scriptures. She would bring him a Bible, nonetheless.

Having taken it out of the bookshelf, she opened a page or two, then looked embarrassed as she handed it to him. He soon saw why. It was pristine and obviously unread. Jenny Lans. On the Occasion of your Confirmation in Vallmsta Church. John 4:7-15.

'Here's the almanac,' she said. 'That's been used a bit more.'

He took the Bible up to his room with him and worked his way doggedly through the mass of text in Deuteronomy. He used the Swedish-German dictionary Fredrik had bought for his evening classes. It took him all afternoon, but then he came down beaming with joy.

'Tubbernaclies!' he cried.

She was standing at the sink with her hands in the cloudy water and regarded him in amazement.

'Tubbernaclies!'

He showed her the Bible. Jenny dried her hands on her apron, sat down with the book and read the passage he indicated.

'The Feast of the Tabernacles,' she said quietly.

'Aah!'

How lovely it sounded. Yes, it was a lovely-sounding name. She agreed with him, but went back to the washing up.

Then came a time when he was often out in the afternoons. He went somewhere straight after work and only came home well past dusk, when darkness had fallen. She wondered if it was a good idea, with his constrained airways. But he laughed off her worries and called her his little mother. He was always rosy-cheeked and healthy when he got back home on those evenings.

One morning he came home from the works with no sign of shortness of breath. On the contrary, he was in high spirits. If she would come with him, he had something to show her. She realised he had deceived Fredrik and the thought unsettled her. In fact it scared her. She truly didn't want to come with him!

He couldn't take her fear seriously. He tugged at her arm as she sat stitching the waistband of a skirt and she wished she might have had some huge, overwhelmingly dull and messy household task to use as an excuse.

Wouldn't she come out into the forest with him? Into the forest! Yes. His face was like that of a child. The soft, ash-toned hair had fallen across his forehead. He was like a flame flickering round a sullenly smouldering lump of wood, and in the end he conquered her. She put on black rubber boots so short that her thick oversocks protruded over the tops. She took her old coat with the imitation leather collar. She felt well and truly frumpy. She wound Fredrik's checked scarf into a turban, having now decided she wanted to be a frump when she went out with Ferenc. She would be utterly hopeless, grey and brown, drab and heavy. She would make him see her as she was.

But he went dancing along at her side. His boots splashed in the puddles and he laughed uproariously at a Swedish word for 'puddle' being the same as that for 'kiss'. He took three or four steps to every two of hers; he talked and talked. Jenny wondered where he was taking her as they walked to the end of District Road and on as far as Heavenside Gates, then turned straight into the woods. They went along the well-worn path and she was just thinking that perhaps they were heading up to the high viewing point, when suddenly he left the path and plunged in amongst the trees. He helped her over tree trunks blown down by the wind. There was a sharp, fresh smell around them. The little rowans were standing bolt upright, almost bare of leaves and with bunches of bright red berries. They went further in, under tall spruces, then the ground sloped uphill and it grew lighter again. They were standing on a hillock.

'Here,' he said. 'Look Jenny! This is my Tabernacle. My *sukkah*. You are very welcome, my lady. Tread carefully.'

He took her arm.

'Isn't it beautiful?' he asked rather anxiously.

'Yees...'

It was no mere brushwood den. No hut or hovel either. It was beautiful, he was right. She stumbled over some tufts of lingonberry on her way down and he caught her as she fell. After that he kept tight hold of her hand.

He must have had to search for a long time to find so many branches with their leaves still on. Some were even green.

'These are cherry leaves,' she said, feeling them. 'Where did you get them? At the Gatehouse? Good Lord, they didn't see you I hope?'

He shook his head.

'I took the things from there after dark.'

It was all painstakingly woven together and he explained he had made the shelter the traditional way. But as there were no palms, myrtle, cedar, vineleaves or willow branches to be had in this forest, he had taken used the species she was familiar with and made little sprays of those. She took the leaves between her fingers and laughed as she identified them. Her face was growing damp in the drizzle.

'He makes the wind blow and the rain fall; for blessing and not for disaster; for life and not for death' he whispered. But she didn't know the language he said it in.

'Come in,' he said, and they crouched down to get in through the opening. They sat on the bare ground and at that point she was glad she had brought her old coat. The top of the shelter was almost open, the branches were sparse and loosely woven.

'You have to be able to see the stars in a *sukkah*,' he said. 'Jenny, shall we stay here to see the stars this evening?'

She shook her head. But she was no longer feeling that sullen, stubborn resistance she had experienced in the kitchen at home.

'We can come back this evening,' she said. 'If it's a clear night we can come and look at the stars for a little while before I have to go to the engine sheds.'

They sat quietly in the scent of leaves, already with a slight hint of decay, a moistly mouldering smell that was not unpleasant. He tried to tell her about his old grandfather and it was like being there at the feast, the leaves were rustling in the breeze of another time. He told her about the delicate cups he had held so carefully as a little boy, the flowers and fruit in the *sukkah* and the delicious little cakes.

How could he explain the festival to her? People were supposed to go out into the country and live in special shelters as a commemoration of parting. That was the real intention. We must always remember that parting, Jenny. We must be prepared for it. There is not a single life so firmly established that no change can take place, internal or external. That is why we must listen, inwards and outwards.

'Do you understand?'

310

What is going to happen? I cannot live here all my life. The security I felt here was no more than a habit. We must move on. To a better life or a worse? To camps or to green valleys? What has been promised us?

She must understand that the Feast of the Tabernacles known as Sukkoth was outside everyday life, even outside normal duty. It brought spring, although it fell in the autumn.

He took her hand, in its glove. They sat still, feeling rather solemn. Outside was the autumnal forest with the little sounds of shy birds and water dripping from the trees. He took off her glove, a thin glove knitted from the poor-quality wartime yarn. Her hand was cold and damp. He warmed it as he spoke, softly. He didn't say prayers or try anything strange, as she'd been afraid he might when he went all serious like that. They sat still and he said soft words now and then, about departure and parting. She had been taught that a person was supposed to stay in her allotted place and perform her work there. Work while the day lasts, she remembered from school, and the words had their own special aura of cabbage soup and scrubbed floors. Would he end up tricking her into crying over her own life? He said: arise. Arise woman and walk. We shall celebrate our Feast of the Tabernacles. The time of departure is near.

She got up and followed him when he said it. But she could only stand half upright because the shelter was low and they had to bend down to get out of the doorway. While she was still crouching, he turned and kissed her on the forehead.

In the week that followed, they went to the tabernacle every evening. The procedure was that she would hear Ferenc coming downstairs first. Then she would look up and her knitting needles would stop clicking. She would hear the clash of coat hangers as he took down his lovely blue coat. Once the front door had closed, her needles would move cautiously in the yarn. She was knitting the seconds, amassing them in loops alongside each other. After two rows and four minutes she would say:

'Think I'll go out for a walk.'

She had never been out for walks.

Fredrik often had to work overtime and then she didn't need to say anything, or wait many minutes before getting to her feet. Ferenc would usually wait for her at Heavenside Gates, the gusty wind blowing in his hair. He didn't like wearing a hat. She wondered what would happen when winter came, whether he would freeze right through. They walked slowly beside each other in the darkness. They had three clear nights in a row and could see the stars through the leaves and branches.

When they got home she would be freezing and have to make herself a hot drink. Fredrik would be sitting bent over his bids and tenders. The papers bore the black imprints of factory thumbs. Sometimes he had Ann-Marie's father there, the rustle of the stiff blueprints with construction designs could be heard from the living room and the air was fuggy with the smoke of Johannesson's Matanzas.

Several evenings a week she had to get her uniform ready for the night. She was standing ironing her apron dry when she heard Ferenc come back. His footsteps disappeared up the stairs.

'He didn't come in,' said Fredrik from the living room.

'I suppose he didn't want to disturb us so late.'

She could hear Fredrik yawning and shuffling the stiff papers into a pile.

'Shall we get to bed? What time've you got to be up?'

'There's a train due at four, so I've got to be there at half past one.'

'Watch out! There's a spy about. See how easy it was to get that information out of you. Women!'

She took his provocative remarks with equanimity. They were in actual fact prickly caresses, but they didn't have much effect on her these days. When they were about to go to sleep, he took her hand and squeezed it. Then she lay listening involuntarily to his breathing and could tell he was finding it hard to sleep too. He was no doubt thinking about tenders. Whether their quotation had been too high, so they wouldn't get the order, or too low, so there'd be no profit in it for the works. No doubt he had stomach ache as well. Jenny used to suggest he tried some herb tea. That damned straw, he would say.

If I don't get these three hours' sleep I'll never manage to get up, she thought. But it wasn't true. You managed most things.

The autumn dark intensified, the leaves rotted in the rain. Ferenc didn't go out after dinner any more. She knew that meant the shelter had been wrecked by rot and gales. She was glad not to have to see it like that. Glad he didn't say anything.

Just once he did, though, in the kitchen; he stroked the back of her hand and said softly: 'Schalom...'

Other than that, he hadn't stroked her since that first time, out in the shelter. There was nothing special between them any longer, no friendship Fredrik couldn't be part of. Rather, they had reverted to the time when the two men talked to each other most. She would knit and keep quiet, aware of not knowing as much as they did, and in any case she was bored with the war. She was sick of the very words: bridge-head, mass attack, demarcation lines, carpet bombing. And who was Ribbentrop?

War made the wheels turn round, they said. Fredrik had to get ready. They'd worked overtime all week and some of them were going in today, even though it was Sunday. He got up at ten past six as usual.

Jenny would have preferred to stay in bed. It felt as if the war in all its grey tedium was standing right outside the window, pressing in on the bare hedge of raspberry canes. But she knew she should be grateful. At least she wasn't unemployed. You always had to be grateful for work, even when the war touched the little wheels and cogs of the alarm clock on a Sunday morning.

She was tired after a long week with four nights on duty by the railway. She'd scarcely seen Fredrik.

'No, you stay there,' he'd said when she moved. But she was already sitting up with her dressing gown in her hand. Her foot was feeling for a slipper on the cold cork matting.

Downstairs in the kitchen she started running water into the coffeepot for him, but he said gloomily that he wanted tea. Then she knew how bad his stomach must be. He ate without speaking, dabbed the tips of his fingers on the oilcloth to gather up the last crumbs and put them in his mouth.

'Will you light the boiler after I go?'

She nodded.

He went. His bicycle clattered out of the rack and she saw him mount it, straight and tall in his trenchcoat and beret. She stared at the long, steady back for as long as she could see him in the road and suddenly wanted to cry out after him, open the window and scream so everybody could hear. Good God - it's Sunday! That's something special, a red-letter day when we wear better clothes, eat different food. They can't do this to time!'

But what had she been looking forward to, really? She couldn't remember with any clarity what they usually did on Sundays. Yet ever since she was little it had been a time when even the air and light were different and everything was much quieter. She and Fredrik sometimes did some gardening, she supposed. Went for a bike ride somewhere. In winter they had a lie-in and read the paper for a couple of hours. She often dropped off again; Fredrik read a book. Was it so remarkable? So golden that she could barely suppress a scream because he was going off as if it were a normal weekday!

She couldn't summon the energy to light the boiler. She'd never just not bothered with it like that before. She'd forgotten a few times and been reminded by the chill coming up from the floor. But this time she just hadn't the energy. She went up the stairs with unnecessarily heavy steps as if to prove to someone that she was tired.

She sat in front of the mirror hating herself for a while. Her synthetic satin nightgown was grubby. The smell of factory oil and tobacco forced its way right into their bedroom. It was cold in the room. Fredrik's clothes were lying on a chair. He never hung anything up when he took it off, or put anything in the laundry basket. It would be no relaxation to snuggle down between the sheets again; she'd just lie there thinking about what she ought to be doing: picking up Fredrik's clothes and putting them in the wash with her nightdress, changing the sheets and lighting the boiler.

When she heard sounds from the bathroom, she shut her eyes. It was Ferenc. He was peeing, in a great stream. She went to the door and listened without shame. He was holding his penis of course;

maybe it was swollen since it was first thing in the morning. She could hear the gushing. She could even imagine the smell.

What am I doing standing here? I'm disgusting. If he knew I was standing here listening to him, when he's so fastidious. But she didn't move. There was a rustle of stiff, brown toilet paper. Ah, he wipes it. If only she could have taught Fredrik to! But she wouldn't dare bring up a subject like that. Fredrik had his own fastidious habits.

Why am I like this? They weren't like that at home. Where have I got it from?

She dropped the hairbrush she was holding and it fell into the lacquered metal waste paper bin with a loud crash. What was he doing now? It had all gone quiet. He wasn't cleaning his teeth, he wasn't having a wash. What was he doing in there?

Then she realised he must be standing listening, too. But why would he do that? There wasn't anything to listen to, was there? He was standing quite still, listening from inside the closed bathroom door. It had a little ventilation grille at the bottom. The bedroom door was crooked, it didn't close properly. It didn't matter. After all, she and Fredrik didn't do anything that made noises which could carry very far.

Suddenly she stretched out her foot towards the door. She regarded her foot in its pale blue slipper which was soiled at the front from going down to the boiler room. She noticed the white rabbit-fur pompom was hanging crooked and about to come off. Then she kicked open the bedroom door. The door handle smashed back against the wall outside.

Oh, she'd made a hole in the wallpaper with the handle. He hadn't put in a doorstop, hadn't found the time. Since he let the works take up all his time, he'd only himself to blame.

The door was wide open and Ferenc stood in the bathroom in

complete silence.

Then he opened the door. He was much shorter than she was. He had striped pyjama trousers, the cord was tied carelessly and hung down over the opening. He wasn't wearing his pyjama jacket and his chest was covered in black hair, peppered with grey. Though he's so young, Jenny thought. Thirty-five. He must have been five centimetres shorter than her and ten years younger and she was thinking about those things when she noticed the curliness of his chest hair, which she didn't like at all. It nauseated her. But she stood her ground, hands clenched in her dressing gown pockets.

He had opened the door quite cautiously, but now came straight up to her, gripped her by the tops of the arms and propelled her into the room and over to the unmade bed. She felt chill and anxiety descend on her.

'Not here,' she mumbled.

But he felled her by forcing his knee and short, powerful thigh between her legs and putting his arms round her at the same time. His breath smelt bad this early in the morning and she wrenched her head away. He was heavy, but then he raised his top half, trapped her legs with his and opened her dressing gown. He only got it half off her. It was still hanging on the arm she had caught under her.

'Stop,' she said. 'Let me.'

She didn't look at him as she got up, let the dressing gown slide to the floor and took off her nightdress. Then she lay down naked across the bed as she had never done before, legs wide apart. Is this me? she wondered.

His face was stony. it looked like a mask, lips drawn back. He half stood over her, supported himself on one hand as he pushed himself into her, looking only long enough to find the right place. Then he shut his eyes tight, squeezing them shut until white lines appeared in the skin at the corners, and fell over her heavily. He raised and lowered his trunk a couple of times, but couldn't get out of her far enough to thrust properly. He grimaced and fell on her breasts with his whole weight. It hurt, but she couldn't change position and suddenly she realised it was all over.

When she tried to adjust him a little, he rolled off her and lay on his back. His face still had the same look. The lips were drawn back, his teeth were bared as if he were dead. His feet looked dead, too.

The bedroom door stood open wide and the house was totally silent. She found herself thinking about the radiators that were usually humming and ticking.

'I've got to light the boiler,' she mumbled, which made him take her hand and squeeze it. He let go of it at once when she made to get up. She looked for her dressing gown and something to stuff between her legs, But she knew it was already too late.

Well, she was going to change the sheets anyway, so it didn't matter. She would put on some coffee, try to get something into him to warm him up. So he came to life again. She would drink a little coffee herself, and most importantly she would comb her hair. She saw herself in the mirror and pushed her hair out of her eyes.

Yes, this is me. It really is. I'm in the middle of everything. This is me. She felt as clear-headed as if she had just awoken from sleep. But he must be feeling something else. He turned his head away.

'I'm sorry,' he mumbled. 'Sorry sorry sorry.'

On Saturday the 10th of June 1944, they arranged to have a little war. Compared with operations like Overlord and Barbarossa, it was a modest affair. It was nonetheless the most large-scale venture undertaken in this town where they had recruited 500 home guardsmen under the national flag and thirty-five WDV's at the Osby boilers. Over 3,000 people were involved, all told.

The Supreme Command of this war comprised the commander of area defence, who was a general called Magnell, a Captain Bernadotte who also happened to be a prince, and a Captain Löwenkopf who was on the area defence staff. General Magnell was very pleased with the local arrangements. Before first light and the sounding of the alarm, he inspected the preparations of the civil defence forces. In front of the fountain in the town park, on the front steps of the City Hotel and where the ridge sloped down to the gymnasium of the Co-Educational Intermediate School, the injured lay stretched out. They all had bleeding marked with red dye on their protective clothing and printed signs with instructions for the civilian health service personnel. These stated whether the individual in question had been hit in the legs or the head. The gas victims, with labels on their backs, were positioned outside the railway station and a wrecked car had been rolled down the embankment by Highway Bridge. Flat on his face in front of the car lay an injured man whose stomach wound was indicated by highly characteristic vomiting.

The air raid warning was sounded at 0300 hours and rapidly led to intensive exchanges of fire. Hardly a soul got any more sleep in the town that night, certainly not in the central districts.

The defending forces, designated A, had helmets; the attacking forces were called B or Foe and wore forage caps. Foe had landed airborne troops in the outlying villages of Vallmsta, the Ridge and Vanstorp, and at Pigs' Heath. All morning there were bombers, fighter aircraft and transport planes flying over the province of Sörmland with its bright, June grass, its pockets of mist, its lakes where black-throated divers and curlew called unheard through the roaring onslaught.

General Magnell's inspection had revealed the defence arrangements to be in excellent order and the organisation of the manpower present to be exemplary. Support points had been provided at Highway Bridge, Heavenside Gates, the Swedish Engineering works and the cemetery. He visited every post, wishing the last of them good luck five minutes before the alarm sounded.

Total silence initially reigned in the streets after the quick succession of hoarse alarm signals had sounded. What was happening was that about forty saboteurs were infiltrating the town to detonate bombs at specific targets, including the water and electricity systems. The watertower was blown sky high almost immediately and a notice was affixed to announce that this was the case. The power station went up too, and a head count showed that thirty saboteurs had got though unscathed and uncaptured. Twenty-one of them had carried out their missions.

Two women on air raid duty behaved like Amazons and took two men captive. These later turned out to belong to the A-forces although they had temporarily removed their helmets. The Amazons, however, did not accept their explanation but locked them in a potato cellar. General Magnell later declared that they

321

had acted correctly and he emphasised the importance of keeping one's helmet or forage cap on.

By six in the morning, the fiercest battles were raging at Highway Bridge, where the commanders of the exercise had gathered. Rapid rounds were heard from the bridge-abutments for over an hour. Smoke bombs were set off and at times the prince, very tall with spectacles reflecting the sunrise, was the only person visible up on the bridge. Yet he didn't get shot. Hand grenades and satchel charges were indicated by squibs and an acrid pall of smoke lay over the streets in the immediate area.

The men of the home guard were very keen to fight and had not realised that a decisive act of sabotage had now taken place at the railway station and Foe had invaded the Town Hall and installed radio transmitters in the municipal finance office. They blazed away, all guns firing, and engaged willingly in hand-to-hand combat, sometimes so enthusiastically the adjudicators had to call a halt to the clashes. The adjudicators had blue and yellow stripes round their middles for identification, but still were not always recognised.

At half past seven in the morning, a trumpeter sounded the cease fire from Highway Bridge. After that they all marched to the engine sheds. General Magnell gave a short speech and then the manoeuvres were analysed. The WDV's served hotchpotch with bread and butter, and it was such a fine, warm June morning that they were able to sit on the grassy slope in front of the railway workers' houses to eat. They spontaneously took up a royal anthem. Even the prince put aside his bread and billycan, got to his feet and joined in. Their mood gradually became more lighthearted and most of them agreed it had been a very nice little exercise, although it remained unclear whether the town had been taken by Foe or could still be considered free.

It took several more minutes for the news of how the exercise had ended for 23-year-old conscript Karl-Evert Palm to filter down to the slope by the engine sheds.

Palm had set out from 200 metres south of position r at Pigs' Heath, where a parachute drop was assumed to have landed him. On his way in towards town, he passed the house of the district doctor. He turned and sneaked back. It had struck him that the district doctor would presumably be taking part in the exercise and that this presented him with an opportunity to get into the closely-guarded town unseen. The car boot had been left unlocked. He climbed in, covered himself with a couple of rugs and closed the boot carefully without letting the lid quite engage.

At 0325 hours, the district doctor arrived at the makeshift medical centre in a vegetable warehouse opposite the Swedish Engineering works. Palm peeped out once he was sure the doctor had left his car and recognised where he was. He went swiftly over to the other side of the street and threw a bundle of dynamite at the huge factory building, or rather set off a squib, as the rules demanded, to indicate an explosion.

Naturally there were a number of guards posted at the works, but none of them had observed the saboteur. Now there was a great hue and cry as they pursued him up the road to the square. There were several helmeted home guards on his tail but he managed to get away by slipping up the hill and hiding behind the cut-price store while they rushed out into the square. They soon discovered they had lost him, and after hunting in doorways for a few minutes they gave up and returned to their posts.

The defender who finally captured Karl-Evert Palm was called Sven-Bertil Franzon. He was sixteen and in the lower sixth of the grammar school in Norrköping. He was a member of the junior home guard and had asked the headmaster's permission to stay in his home town this Saturday to take part in the war exercise. He got good marks at school and had been awarded Frans G. Bengtsson's *The Long Ships* as a prize when he passed his lower secondary school certificate.

From his sentry post at the bus station, he saw Palm in the act of placing an explosive charge under the steps. He raced across the road alone, rifle at the ready. Palm was quickly on his feet, disappearing in the direction of the goods shed, and Franzon ran after him. He fired all his rounds but the saboteur obviously didn't consider himself hit, and there was no adjudicator on hand. He lost sight of him but could hear his footsteps echoing on the loading platform.

Then he too sped up onto the platform, which ran the length of the goods shed. All the loading hatches were barred, so he knew his enemy could not have escaped into the shed. He couldn't think where he could have gone. There was complete silence all around him as he stood immobile on the platform with his rifle cocked. Suddenly remembering he was out of ammunition, he was nonplussed. Then he heard a slight sound from beneath him, but didn't realise straight away that he had his enemy right under his feet, crouching under the loading platform. When he did, he was scared.

He was holding his rifle with both hands round the barrel, and struck Palm in the mouth with the butt as he emerged. He dropped the rifle when he saw his face and screamed several times. Palm was still conscious, lying on his back and trying to shuffle back under the platform.

Franzon's screams turned to sobs and he ran back to the bus station and called the sentries, but so incoherently that no one could work out what had happened. Sven-Bertil Franzon disappeared at a run and no one saw him again that morning.

The wounded saboteur was discovered not by the railway employees but by a fishmonger coming to fetch some herring from the bus station. He drove him to the hospital. It was a wholly civilian procedure. The fishmonger drove home and threw up. The hospital staff operated on Palm, who had had both his upper and lower front teeth smashed and his upper jawbone shattered. At about eight in the morning, the chief nursing sister sent word to the engine sheds.

Gerda Franzon didn't get home until ten in the morning, when the last of the canteens had been washed up. She was pleasantly surprised to find Bertil at home. Strangely enough, he was still in his dressing gown. She told him how the civil defence exercise had gone and about the appalling accident.

'They say it was a young boy,' Gerda said. 'He was seen at the bus station.'

'Ssh, Gerda,' said her husband.

His black hair was tousled; he was standing at the far end of the room with his hand on the grand piano.

'What is it?' said Gerda sharply.

'He's here. We're going to the police.'

He held out a hand to her but she didn't move.

In his room, Sven-Bertil Franzon sat on the chair at his desk, where his school books lay along with the orthoceratite he used as a paperweight. He was looking at the door, listening to their voices.

A long, bare tendril of Virginia creeper had unhooked itself from the wall and was slapping against the window pane in the sleety rain. It was as if everything wanted to get in and the creeper was trying to announce the fact. The grey house sparrows were growing bigger and greyer in the hedge. Soon, the cold dusk would swallow them up, as the rain, sluggish with snow, ran down the angels' faces up under the eaves.

There were many dusks like this one, the Saturday before All Saints' Day. The kitchen lamp seemed awfully bright and blinding to the child, but still didn't shed enough light for Tora's eyes. She and the girl were sitting at the table, counting the market stall takings. There was newspaper spread out over the oilcloth, and on it were piles of coins. Tora counted the notes and silver, Ann-Marie the coppers.

'How much did the coppers come to?' asked Tora.

'Fourteen eighty', replied Ann-Marie promptly.

She had counted the piles of five, two and one öre coins four times, and really would have liked to do it once more. Tora wouldn't check it, she knew. That was why it was such a responsibility. Tora sucked her pencil and wrote the figure on her pad. Then she started adding up the total. She did it twice.

'Two hundred and sixteen,' she said. 'And ninety-two öre.'

'Have you deducted the money we keep in the cashbox?' asked Ann-Marie.

'Yes, I did that on the silver.'

'Well that was good, then!'

'Yes, good takings this time.'

'But just wait till Christmas Eve,' said Ann-Marie. 'That'll really be something!'

Tora got up and went over to the drawer where she kept her bank book, cash book and pension agreement. She limped, because one of her hips was worn out.

She took the money that was to be paid into the bank and put it in brown bags which she fastened shut with paper clips. She put some money in her big purse and Ann-Marie counted the cashbox money and put it back.

'That's that, then,' said Tora. 'We'll have a hot drink in a while. I'm just going to have a little rest first.'

And the dusk took the grey sparrows and rubbed them out in the dry-twigged hedge; it enfolded the sheds and little outbuildings in something even greyer than their own wood and made the windows blind. High on her bed lay Tora, eyelids unmoving and tinged with yellow. She let her mouth fall open.

'Don't do that,' said Ann-Marie sharply.

'No no, I'm just having a little rest. You play.'

The next time she looked up from her torpor, the girl had emptied out the contents of the button box and was arranging the buttons in rows. They glittered in the lamplight, black jet buttons from a dress for a funeral. Every single one had had to be fastened through a loop. Who did me up at the back when I was left alone? Imagine me not remembering that, though I remember the hymn we sang. Oh God our brother Abel's blood. What notions that good-for-nothing parson had. They don't sing things like that any more.

'Can you put the ring on? I'll heat up some milk in a minute.'

'Wait.'

Ann-Marie was busy arranging the little ivory-coloured china buttons in a circle. They were painted gold and violet and had metal rings on the backs for sewing them onto the fabric.

'Those ones looked smart on a blouse,' said Tora. 'I had them for an outing, I recall. Mm, it was very smart, that blouse with a mauve suit.'

'You had these on your clothes?'

'Yes, of course. I had them on my dresses and blouses.'

The girl had put all the most fabulous buttons, those that looked like flowers or had gold on them, in the centre of the circle. She looked at Tora as if she didn't believe her.

'A mauve suit,' she said.

'Certainly. And a hat with a bird.'

'Go on! What sort of bird?'

'Well, I don't really know. Something foreign, I think. Tiny.'

'Oh.'

She sounded disappointed, as if she'd been expecting it to have been a sea-eagle on the hat. The next time Tora looked up, all the stocking buttons of yellow bone, all the white shirt buttons and underwear buttons made of linen pressed onto a lead backing so they could be put through the mangle, all the black and brown trouser buttons, hundreds of dull, lustreless buttons were lined up into armies round the circle of jet flowers and the white china ones with their finely traced designs.

'Well I never,' she said. 'I must have dropped off. You didn't put the ring on, I hope?'

She hadn't.

'I saw you'd gone to sleep.'

Tora tried to muster her body and her will in preparation for getting up.

'I'll get up now,' she said to Ann-Marie, and to her body she said: you've got to.

But it had a heavy burden to bear, even when it was lying down. It needed persuading, joint by joint and sinew by sinew. The child beside her bore her own death without knowing it. She had so much stamina to spare that she was now tipping the buttons back into a heap and starting all over again. But this time she was doing it on the cork floor so you could hear the sound of the buttons rolling into place. She made them rattle as noisily as she could.

'Don't go back to sleep,' she told Tora. 'I want my milk now.'

And Tora got up.

It was the first year she hadn't managed to take a wreath up to the grave on Christmas Eve. She was too tired after her day in the market square. Fredrik could have taken it for her, of course, but she was too ashamed to admit she hadn't found time to get up there the week before Christmas either. Making the sweets had sapped her energy.

On Christmas morning she got up early and brought in the wreath, which she'd put out on the balcony. It had snowed during the night and nothing was itself when she looked out. Getting anywhere on foot was going to be hard work.

They'd started ploughing at any rate; she passed horses with snowploughs and chains that rattled as they turned. When she got up to the cemetery she had to trudge through deep snow, but she was sensibly dressed in boots and woollen stockings and woollen combinations that came down to her knees under her skirt. No, the worst thing was that she couldn't find her way amongst the graves. In fact she couldn't see any graves at all. It was as if a totally different landscape had spread itself over the old, familiar one. The new one was smooth and white and the dead had been buried anew, their memorials obliterated by the snow. The whole cemetery was on a higher level, the trees seemed shorter and their crowns were loaded with snow. Only the tallest gravestones were protruding, like mysterious bumps offering her no fixed points in all the whiteness. Everything was gone and she couldn't find the grave.

Growing anxious, she looked at the trees. They ought to show her the way. But she had obviously never looked at them carefully enough before. They told her nothing of where he lay. She didn't know what to do with the wreath.

She ought really to go home and put it back on the balcony until they'd cleared the cemetery so you could see the paths between the areas of graves. But she was suddenly worried there wouldn't be time.

Then she thought of Ann-Marie. She and her father lived quite near the cemetery. She soon made up her mind it was the place to go.

When she went in, the girl was sitting at the kitchen table drawing on an opened-out cardboard cake box.

'Are you all on your own?' asked Tora.

'No, Dad's asleep.'

The door to the study was open, there were sticky rings on the table and the air was heavy and smelt of tobacco smoke.

'Have you had anything to eat?'

'I made some cocoa with water,' she said.

'You can have some proper cocoa at my place but you've got to help me with something first.'

She hadn't really meant to let the girl see her anxiety, had planned to say casually as they passed the cemetery: let's see if we can find Otter's grave. But she found herself telling the whole story of what it had been like up there, and Ann-Marie put on her coat and a pair of non-matching gloves and the woolly hat Tora had knitted her.

They set off, and it was still just as hard going when they got up there. Ann-Marie went in front, her legs vanishing into holes in the snow.

'Your legs are getting wet,' Tora said. We'll have to hang your

330

stockings up to dry when we get home.

'This is it, I can tell by the trees,' said Ann-Marie. 'Put the wreath here.'

'Are you sure?'

She didn't bother to reply and when Tora placed the wreath of pine sprigs on the loose white snow, it sank in a little.

'Wonder where it'll end up when the snow melts,' said Ann-Marie, and Tora took her by the hand to hurry her away. That anxiety was gripping her again.

'We'll take one day at a time,' she said. 'Now let's go home and make that cocoa.'

They had often gone to the cemetery together. They would go and water the grape hyacinths and narcissus in the spring, and when it was lovely and light and all the gardens were in bloom they would always put sweet peas in the metal vase on Cis's grave. She had a shiny stone with a white dove on it. It had been paid for by her son who was a railway engineer in Stockholm and the dove had been what she wanted.

Doves were just pigeons and Tora could think of no filthier creature. She always shooed them off her windowsill. But she thought Cis's headstone was beautiful.

'That's different,' she said to Anne-Marie.

And it was certainly true, for this dove left neither feathers nor droppings.

Cis died like a bird. She gave a few terrified blinks and then her heart stopped. In death she was as delicate as in everything else; she had hardly needed washing.

In the six months that followed, Tora grew more and more tired. There was nothing that could really cheer her up, though sometimes she had to pretend to be happy. She thought it was a phase that would pass.

Hillevi had died one spring day. The ice had just started melting away from the shore and the flocks of wild geese were calling in the bitter air down at Little Heavenside. She and Tora had walked down that way many times and collected bulrushes and stems of willow for their vases.

When summer came, and more recently when autumn arrived with its lovely, fruit-fragranced darkness, she had thought her fatigue and malaise would be gone. She would be herself again.

But Tora gradually came to realise she would never be happy again. Her membranes were dry and brittle, her tendons creaked as she extended them. Internally, too, she had lost flexibility and mental agility. But there were still many acts - though not that many events - which were satisfying and made her feel warm inside.

She went hand-in-hand with the girl through streets crunchy with snow, thinking that really she was too big to need her hand held. She would soon be ten. But March came and the streets were wet and it was just as well to keep hold of her hand in case she jumped in puddles and splashed herself.

They went to the confectionery wholesaler and placed orders, because people didn't want home-made sweets any longer. They wanted sour bilberry and lingonberry drops that were all the same size and factory-made jelly babies, loaves of marzipan with ribbons round their middles and brightly coloured lollipops. Ann-Marie had such lively fantasies about the wholesaler's house she thought even the fruit in his garden was made of sugar and the icicles hanging from his woodshed roof tasted of mint. He had Jesus on his office wall, looking as white as marzipan on a chocolate cross. He talked about this Jesus a great deal and wanted Ann-Marie to come to know him. He asked her whether she already did, but that made her button her lips in embarrassment. At length she realised she would never be offered anything unless she said she knew him.

One day, when Tora was already on her way out of the big confectionery cellar under his house, he took a box of chewy mice from a shelf in the storeroom. They were lying closely packed and were fresh and velvety to the touch. He held the box right in front of her and asked again if she knew Jesus. With a glance at the cellar steps where Tora's legs were just disappearing, she whispered fervently:

'Yes! Yes!'

Then he sighed and stroked her head as if he didn't really believe her, but he let her have some chewy mice all the same. She made a grab and took eight in one fistful.

'Dear me,' said the wholesaler. But he didn't make her give any back.

They went to visit Ebba Julin too, and at first Ann-Marie was intimidated by her loud, hoarse voice. Sometimes Ebba was all done up to the nines with an agate necklace and a watered silk blouse. That meant she was off to Norrköping to a dinner at a restaurant with people she knew in the brewing trade. She never got Tora to go with her, although she sometimes tried to talk her into it. Sometimes Ebba wasn't done up to the nines at all, but sat trimming her corns over a newspaper.

Ann-Marie would go into the garden and pick handfuls of currants from the bushes. She had permission to pick them. But she was only allowed to take strawberries if they were offered to her. She went and stood outside the window of a room Ebba always closed the door of, climbed up on the water barrel and balanced with one foot on each side of the rim, held on to the window frame and looked into the room. There on his bed sat old brewer Julin, white as porcelain and wearing a clean, starched shirt. He rocked backwards and forwards making sounds like a little child or a calf. That's how you end up if you get too old, Tora said. You have to be grateful if it doesn't happen to you, and I want you to remember me saying that, she added.

He was so old now they celebrated all his birthdays with a write-up in the paper. Then Ebba would take him out into the garden so they could take his picture. But he couldn't always keep his white eyelids open in the sun, and he tried to touch people, just like a child or a puppy who wants to see what everybody feels like.

'What's it like when you die?' asked Ann-Marie, and Tora said it was just like falling asleep. But you never woke up again.

'But what about heaven, isn't that where you go?'

'No one really knows,' said Tora. 'You just have to be glad you've had a life.'

When Ann-Marie asked what dying was like, Tora turned away so she couldn't see her eyes.

'Are you scared?' she asked.

'Me? Oh no,' said Tora.

You couldn't tell a child about that particular terror, it was impossible and it would have been too cruel. Anyway, it wasn't so very dreadful once you'd let it in. It spent most of its time asleep in a corner, with bad breath, occasionally moaning a little in its sleep. But it was an intimate acquaintance, very intimate.

Tora and Ebba spread the newspaper on the table in the arbour to read the deaths column and work out what age people had reached. So young, they said, if it was someone who only got to fifty-five. But if it was somebody really old who had died, they simply sighed and said:

'So he's gone now. A blessing, really.'

The name of a building contractor they knew made Tora say that the devil always takes his own in the end.

334

'You're right there,' said Ebba grimly and cut out the notice and put it in a drawer. They read the little verses and looked up the hymns quoted and read the names of children, sons and daughters-in-law and grandchildren, telling each other what they knew of these new people, who were all younger than they were and busy serving in shops or driving buses so they met them everywhere. It seemed as though all the people they knew really well were now sitting idly at their kitchen tables. If they hadn't got so old they couldn't cope on their own. Then they would have moved up to Fir Ridge, which looked like a castle.

Though Tora was sixty-nine now and had her illness, she didn't dream of death or of seeing her own death notice in the paper, as it was rumoured Cis had done, a week before her heart gave out.

Tora sometimes dreamt she was having babies, although she was so old. But the babies were so tiny she put them in her chest of drawers or a little box where she used to keep hat feathers and collar lace. When she wanted to look at them or attend to their needs in the terrible hurry it always was in the dream, they were hard to find. She ran round in tears, looking for them. A child so small it could live in a box was far too delicate to survive without help. She knew its life depended on her finding it again and taking care of it. She hunted for those tiny children everywhere, running in anguish through all the stations of the dream. She dared not tell anyone about it and so didn't find out that old women's dreams generally do smell of milk. Tiny children whimper in chests of drawers and sewing baskets where they have hidden them; there are infant tears everywhere when old women sleep, and anxious little footsteps across the floor.

She went with the girl's hand in hers to those who had gardens and was given dill and potatoes, or a panful of broad beans, nestled in fluffy white down in their pods. They were invited to choose apples from the trees: the most translucent of the pale green, white-fleshed apples; the hard Åkerö apples that were a winter fruit; and the rosy, yellow-streaked Säfstaholms that went white and floury as soon as they were properly ripe. In his garden, Attil Glas grew the noble Gravensteins and Greve Moltkes as well as espalier-trained dessert pears, which he wrapped individually in tissue paper as he picked them.

There were lots of gardens with gravel paths that were raked into broad stripes on a Saturday afternoon, edged with shells or white pebbles and with currant bushes in their own little enclosed beds. There on the grass grew the old apple trees with grey-black trunks, supported by long poles in the fruit season to stop the branches breaking. They blossomed in May, a world of silken petals and buzzing bumble bees. Sluggish bees crawled about, their pollen baskets laden with yellow nectar, while deep in the foliage sat beady-eyed little birds of exactly the same hue as the leaves and dun-coloured twigs, birds spotted only by the girl as she lay on the grass listening to the chink of coffee cups from verandahs and arbours.

She wasn't allowed to eat the apples she found lying on the ground until they had been washed, otherwise she would be struck down by polio. It was lurking there among the snails in the grass; it came from the ground itself, they told her. It was the same with the bergamots, the little yellow pears, they had polio on them too. Such masses of them were shaken down from the fertile stock in the great crown that they could be neither weighed nor counted, not even by Attil Glas, who otherwise kept a record of every box, bunch, measure and sack he brought in from his garden.

Attil and Julia's garden was the most beautiful and productive of them all. He had his job at the power station but his heart swelled inside the little heads of lettuce as they formed and in the hope that the walnut tree would bear fruit once in his lifetime. Whenever Julia and Attil felt a rawness in the air they would climb up a ladder and drape curtains over the male catkins on the tree and the little upright female flowers you had to be so careful not to break. In early summer they would often stand on the steps of the verandah and test the air for the evening chill that can be a sign of night frost to come.

Attil took such delight in his garden that it didn't seem quite right to him it should be so. That was why he worried so dispropor-tionately about what was going on in it. When the fruit trees were in fullest, most luxuriant blossom, raising a dome of wings and song and scent of almonds over his life, which ought to be like other people's, he complained about the danger of frost, and when the tiny, embryonic apples began to swell in their thousands he would say there was no point expecting too much. 'We haven't had the June drop yet',' he would say.

That was his way of warning himself and Julia against hubris, and Julia would shake her head, for they were always of one mind in both troubles and joys.

They grew crown imperial and tiger lilies in their borders, and they always left two asparagus crowns to grow up into clouds of green fern as shade for the burnet roses and columbine. On warm summer evenings, when the heavy peonies had long since dropped their petals in little drifts on the grass and the honeysuckle had finished flowering on the shed wall and shrivelled into dead butterflies between the leaves, they would sit on the glass-sided verandah with the lamp lit, playing each other at five hundred. Sometimes Tora and Ann-Marie went home so late the moon had already risen and the clusters of currants on the bushes by the garden path looked like solid silver.

337

Most of the gardens were behind the houses; they backed onto each other and touched one another with the branches of their apple trees and the bright blue armies of scilla which cunningly found their way through the hedges. There were holes in the rows of bushes for hedgehogs and cats, while a flock of magpies could hold sway over ten gardens, keeping watch over the leftovers in all the dogs' bowls in anticipation of some canine owner dozing off by the sunny wall where lazy flies crawled. On the street side they showed nothing more than their pathways and the brown gravel where nothing grew. All growing things were shovelled onto the compost heap to await their next incarnation.

The gardens nearer the middle of town backed onto each other too; and these gardens with their long, crooked outbuildings, their overgrown gravel paths and secret shortcuts between the rows of privies, with knotty trees and hedges of raspberry canes, did not mark the same seasons as the streets. When the snow in the streets had been driven over and trampled into dirty slush, it could still be lying untouched in there, the loveliest blossoms of airy snow balanced on every bough. Along the streets scurried the people in charge and those they were in charge of. It was January, when the income tax forms arrived and returns were due. But inside the gardens, the white hellebores were still flowering, as fragile as the snow you pushed aside from their petals.

It was public taxation month, and the assessment board sat from early morning, bent in the lamplight over property registers, income registers and appeal board rulings. This was the time for the gardens to be visited by birds from the forest with breasts like red bloodstains in the snow. They ate seeds, rejecting the crumbs the sparrows lived on. The sun began to warm things. The tar-papered roofs dripped; towards evening the drips slowed and solidified in the cold and hung suspended, and icicles grew under the woodshed roof. The children knocked them off and sucked them, and went crawling up onto the rough roofs, now free from snow.

Those who had been given extensions on their tax returns hurried across the street on the last blustery evening in March, as the debris of winter swirled up behind the buildings and the glass of the verandahs rattled. The town councillors emerged with smoke-impregnated garments from sittings of many hours and their galoshes walked the night-time streets in the pale glow of the streetlamps.

Tax assessment was completed and the parish meeting was held as the lilac hedge came into leaf in that place where concerns were of a different kind. In there, people gave the squirrel rusks and put out a saucer of milk for the hedgehog; the brown earth formed mounds round the first asparagus crowns. The rope of the children's swing that had rotted in the winter damp was replaced, the swing started flying up into the spring sky and the fine drizzle could be heard as a light pattering and fingering in the gardens early in the mornings.

But out on the streets that were guarded by the facades of the buildings, the sound of the rain did not penetrate to those who made the decisions, who sold the houses and gardens and surveyed and numbered them on their maps. And yet, despite several changes of ownership, the same tracks ran between the sheds and the same holes in the hedge led from garden to garden for children and cats, with slightly bigger holes for people who needed to go and borrow some cream for their coffee.

Even in the houses that had torturers in them, the children could take flight over the tar-papered roofs in the garden, escaping with a crawl and a jump to the next and then the next. Above their heads stretched the forest of cowls and chimneys, while beneath them were the festooning clothes lines, the curses and the hubbub outside the little workshops that hammered their heartbeat into the neighbourhood.

In the hottest part of the summer, the time that was supposed to be set aside for tax adjustments, updating of the electoral register and the calculation of the proposed budgets of the child welfare, poor relief, pension and temperance boards, the ice man would come up to eight times with cold blocks of Vallmar ice in his tongs. He had a leather apron to protect his stomach from the cold, and swore at all the children who clustered round him in the hope he might catch the block on a stone step, chipping off some slivers of ice for them to lick and hold in their hot, summer hands.

It grew darker and darker; the darkness came from the very bodies of the trees and from the many outbuildings with black roofs. Lamps shone down on those who were selling, buying and managing, and on the papers they had in front of them. They had only papers in their hands and all they knew of the worlds they were exchanging was their ground area and where the pipes were connected to the water main.

Tora Otter too, who had carried out her business in public for over forty years, selling sweets in a market square, paying taxes and health insurance, needed to take a child by the hand to be able to see the town that looked inwards, the town where the thuds as the apples landed came so loud and so close together that you found yourself looking out of the window to see what funny creature might be hopping by.

In May they toasted the coming of peace in apple wine and Ferenc was very solemn as he raised his glass to Tora, Jenny and Fredrik. Then they joked that when those apples were growing and ripening, Hitler had still been alive. It was all good fun, until the newspapers started appearing, the ones Tora hid so Ann-Marie wouldn't see them. She put them in the woodshed, where she didn't often go now she had radiators and an electric stove. Even at Fredrik and Jenny's she collected up as many as she could see. They were newspapers with accounts of the concentration camps liberated by the Allies, where there were still people alive when they arrived. She even met some of them herself and got to know a couple of them. It was curious, in fact it affected her quite deeply, to discover that they had had a life before the war and the forced labour. They had played the piano and ordered new, fur-trimmed winter outfits; such facts emerged as she talked to them with Ferenc as interpreter. They had had fathers and gone to the dentist, and when you saw them knitting sweaters from a very difficult pattern you realised it was true that they'd had a life before the war. Until then she hadn't thought of them as anything but people in camps, with shaven heads and dark sockets with eyes deep inside, wretches who had come to them and thought they were in heaven when they saw the clean sheets in the school where they were accommodated.

Though now she was well aware they had seen sheets before. The parson read: 'These are they which came out of great tribulation, and have washed their robes, and made them white in the blood of the Lamb.' So they were apparently saints, the lot of them. The devil they were. One might well ask how Lili had earned her daily bread, and the one they called Elka was a spoilt little lady and no mistake. Not that you really knew, and you didn't want to either.

She happened to go into the woodshed one day that autumn. There was a rustling over in the far corner, under the window. Ann-Marie sprang up, dropping the newspaper she'd been sitting there reading. Her face revealed nothing, but she was afraid of Tora.

She tried to slip past her and get to the door. Tora grasped her arm. She found only a coat sleeve in her hand, the girl wriggled out of her grip like a little animal. She tried to get to the door again but then Tora smacked her in the face, a blow that really hit home. Tora felt a cheekbone under the palm of her hand. She pulled back her two hands and held them to her chest. She had palpitations and they were awful. Her heart felt fit to burst.

She and the girl looked into each other's eyes until Tora gave a sob. Ann-Marie took the opportunity to slip out through the half-open door and Tora could hear her footsteps on the gravel. Then it all went quiet.

She ran out to look. There wasn't a sound, nor were there any signs of movement in the row of raspberry canes where there was an opening through to the next garden. But one of that year's new canes was dangling broken, as if someone had just passed through in great haste.

She called her name several times, but all that happened was that the pigeons fell silent. She went back into the shed and began gathering up the papers. I'll have to burn the lot, she thought. She could see words and bits of sentences, advertisements for apples and pigs and pictures of human beings with shaven heads. They were looking out of a train window and some were trying to hide their heads under veils or headscarves. There was the chairman of the town council in an oval frame. Piles of corpses still crawling with maggots, the text beside him said. She kicked at the heap of papers and tried to get it under the shelf where she kept the paraffin can. But it wouldn't fit.

Had she read it all? Had she understood what she was reading? Surely a child couldn't understand all those words? The newsprint had aged rapidly in the damp. It was starting to disintegrate and had turned yellowish-brown, like the paper in the smutty magazines you sometimes came across in the woods. The pages before her were so familiar. 'Showboat' at the Park and the glasshouse at Gärdebro vandalised by children. Those ghastly bits she'd never read properly. She'd looked through one of them; it was about the children they beat to death hour after hour, day after day in front of the gas chambers. It was at the very end, just before the camps were liberated. What should she say if Ann-Marie asked: why did they do this? What should she answer when she didn't know?

How could she find her now and where was she running off to? The stench of corpses, it said. She wouldn't know what that was, at any rate, a youngster who'd never smelt even a hint of the stench of corpses.

But she was sure she would never need to give an answer, because the girl would never ask. She would keep quiet, as if weighed down by some great shame.

Yes, I'll have to burn them, with paraffin if they're too damp to light any other way. Why hadn't she burnt them long ago? Youngsters forget so easily, they say. Lord yes, surely she'll forget all this. But it had made her sick when the boys crucified a rat on the woodshed wall, she had to stay off school. I'll have to burn the lot of them.

She could still feel the smarting of the blow in her palm. How had it come to this? How could she explain? If only she could find her. First she would gather up every last newspaper and put them all in the wood basket. Hadn't there been more than this? Then she unlocked the shed where she stored her sweets; it was quiet and clean, with boxes stacked on the shelves Fredrik had made for her. She put the wood basket in there and locked the door. I'll buy a can of paraffin, she said to herself, and then burn them, out by the dustbin. It's nobody else's business. But before all that she must find the girl.

She did her coat up right to the neck against the raw air. The house where she still lived, the bare lilac arbour and the sheds and outbuildings had drawn closer together as the darkness sifted down though the cold air.

There was no point walking the streets looking for her. She'd never find her out there. She would have to take the route through the raspberry canes and across the gardens.

She found walking difficult. Her worn-out hip was hurting. She was sure she'd find her in the end. She had to, she had no choice.

Winter, and Jenny pushed her kick-sled in front of her up Heavenside Hill. She crossed District Road and pushed on, past the darkened school. Then a couple of kicks were enough to carry her down towards Hovlunda Road. But outside the library housed in the old Co-Ed School, the runners began to screech and scrape. Ferenc could never work out why she bothered to push this seat on runners ahead of her. It was because it was winter and because she didn't want to feel so alone.

She knew very well he was standing under the trees on the other side of Store Street. But it was so dark she couldn't see him. The whole idea was for him not to be seen. She left the kick-sled on the plot next to the laundry, where a building had burned down, then went round the corner and unlocked the door. She looked about her first as if she were a criminal, which indeed she was.

One evening she had suggested they go up to the WDV headquarters. She had forgotten to hand in the keys to her group leader. Ferenc had asked if he could keep them the next day, and cut copies at the works.

She waited in silence, just inside the door, until he crossed the street. Then she let him in. She didn't doubt for a moment that he too had looked about him before coming in.

The first time she saw Ferenc, she had thought him ridiculous. He was so short compared to Fredrik and he tilted his head on one side whenever he got excited. She'd found his politeness ingratiating. Occasionally, waiting there at the crack in the door for him to cross the street, she felt that first impression returning. But most of the time he seemed a completely different person.

He came in his thick blue overcoat from Budapest, bare-headed however cold the weather. He had the undeniable look of a foreigner. A foreigner who had cut copies of the keys to the WDV headquarters and was stealing up the creaky wooden stairs with her, fumbling for her, kissing her lips and cheeks with his cold mouth.

They moved swiftly through the meeting room and into the little cloakroom. He held the door open for her. They shifted the pile of extra chairs and put the flagpole with the flag rolled round it diagonally across the space. This was to clear the door to the scouts' meeting room. Jenny had discovered it by chance. It had an ordinary lock any room key would fit, with the key taken out on the scouts' side. Ferenc worked away at the chairs in silence. He knew the routine now.

They had to meet in town. After that very first time, it was an unspoken agreement between them. At home, they just couldn't. The house was Fredrik's, the chairs, the table, the beds and the boiler were his. So nothing unfit for his eyes happened there any more.

The light fell in through the little windows, set low up here at attic level. It was the pale light of the streetlamps, reminiscent of moonlight. They lay on a reindeer hide in front of the fireplace and Jenny looked up at branches arranged to look as if they were still growing, at pictures of scout camps and drawings of forest animals. They would have liked to light a fire in the hearth, but didn't dare. The glow might be seen from outside. He was eager to caress her frozen skin into warmth and thaw the stiffness of her body. She was often on the verge of feeling ludicrous and embarrassed. He wanted her to be as earnest and perhaps as eager as he always was.

But it was never like that first time for her again. That first time of which he was so ashamed and for which he was so keen to make amends.

She didn't feel guilty. It all seemed so unreal. It wasn't going to last long. The normal rules were suspended.

After all, Ferenc had no intention of staying, she knew that. He was only learning the language because he detested the feelings of inferiority and indignity which arise from ridiculous pronunciation and no vocabulary. He would be off. Not now. Not for a long time.

And she knew, after all, that what they were up to was going on all over town. People weren't content with the security and respect they had worked so tirelessly to accumulate. They wanted stronger sensations than the ones pickled gherkins and radio symphonies could provide. Plenty of people were surreptitiously out and about in the evenings. She'd heard the talk. Now she was one of them. That sort. That sort who. She hurried through the empty streets while everyone else sat listening to gramophone music.

But no. That wasn't actually quite how it was. This wasn't really about her and Fredrik. It wasn't about Ferenc either, as he sat with them round the smoking table in the evenings. And they were at home most evenings. The two men sat chatting, each in a sagging armchair, and she got out her knitting.

She read Dagmar Edqvist's story 'A Heart Seeks Refuge', which was also about a refugee and a married woman. She kept the magazine hidden for several weeks afterwards. But there was no need, because Fredrik would never think of opening *Housewives' Weekly*.

All three of them listened to gramophone records on the radio after they'd eaten in the evenings, and later the news. The men talked about the news, but of course it was Fredrik who always had the upper hand in any discussion. Ferenc's language was so soft and slippery, he dissolved hard sounds and had so many sudden ideas that he could never bring a discussion to its logical conclusion. Fredrik was logical - except on one point. If they were occupied and he found German guards on duty at Swedish Engineering one morning, he knew what he would do. He would go up and spit at the German's feet!

He had said this many times during the war, but in latter months Jenny had noticed Ferenc going quiet when he said it. He made no protest at all.

She sometimes wondered what they thought of each other. What did Fredrik think of this Hungarian who had fled his country? What did Ferenc think of Fredrik when he talked like that? For her part, she had known from the start that he would never really do what he claimed. Yet it wasn't just empty bravado, either. He genuinely did feel that way. But he would never actually carry it through. If things weren't as they are, if it weren't for you and the fact that we've got Ann-Marie here now Henning's at the clinic drying out, if we really had been occupied and I were the person I truly am, then I'd spit in the German's face. Or at his feet.

She felt as if she were living through the longest time of her life, the longest and most real. It was easy to live through the evenings, even when the neighbour's circular saw was whining outside and she could see the lamp he had hung up swinging in the gusts of wind. The knitting and the war talk were easy to live through. She knew she would soon be closing the door on herself in another room, beneath the branches and the scout camps.

Ferenc had crumpled a handful of paper and was lighting it in the open hearth. Maybe it was foolhardy. If they had to get out because someone was coming, they'd leave a smell of burning paper behind.

Still, the little jumping flames were pretty while they lasted. There was something written on the paper which very quickly went brown. Then the whole lot turned black and fell into nothing.

'A bit more,' she begged, against her better judgement. 'Just a little bit more.'

He bent over her and there was a smell of charred paper. Black flakes floated down over them. Then feet started climbing the stairs of the WDV offices. She sat up with a jolt and her first thought was: if somebody comes up the scouts' side too, then what do we do? He pushed her back down onto the reindeer hide and they listened together.

More than one person was coming upstairs. Loud, high voices. A door opened and she could hear quite plainly it was Hilda Kjellén and Ada Gustafsson. There were a few others too, voices she didn't immediately recognise. The sound of chairs and tables being moved about. God, they seemed to be shifting everything! If Fredrik had been here he would have made some comment about their shrill voices. But Ferenc said nothing, he lay heavily over her and there were flakes of charred paper in his hair which she carefully removed in the light from the street lamp.

She thought the volunteers must have just popped in to fetch something, until it dawned on her. Committee meeting. They'd changed the time.

She relaxed, their voices melted into the scent of his shirt collar against her mouth and his belly naked against hers. There was still a sound of wood creaking somewhere. At that moment she knew shame and regret are just inventions, contracts that can be declared null and void. Skin against animal hide, skin against wood and against the warm skin of another can never be deleted or declared null and void. This, now, was just as real as the chimney cowl shaking on the roof in the gale. Ada Gustafsson's voice was real and her hard little permed curls that would be bobbing in there as she spoke. But her agitation was simply something she had decided with herself. She would be even more agitated if she knew what was going on in here, on the other side of the cloakroom where they kept the flag the King had given them. It would make her voice go even higher, but the agitation would be no more real for that. The only reality was the weight, the sweetness inside her, the hard floor beneath her back and knowing this was life and would never be more intensely life than now.

Afterwards it went back to being like before. As she went to retrieve her kick-sled, she ought to have felt every brick she happened to touch in the wall, rough and granular under her fingers, and sensed the street's compacted layer of ice and mud like skin beneath her feet. But she didn't. It was over. She walked among alien objects and buildings.

When summer came, she took her bicycle to meet him far away. Once again, and without any help from shame this time, she found her sensations heightened. A summer evening with water like glass and the scent of meadowsweet and valerian was at once every summer evening she'd ever experienced, half-sunken and capsized in her memory, with sounds of water and beaches and the indescribably merciful silkiness of the air. All those summer evenings were a room to enter, and its door had blown open for her.

'I'm not from here, at all,' she told him. 'I grew up outside the town in a village called the Ridge. This isn't my town and never has been. If you knew Swedish properly you'd be able to hear I don't even sound like they do here.'

Because out at the Ridge, everything was different. Even the thrushes warbled in another dialect. There, the air was often damp and warm and tasted like fruit. Everything in the place, from lilacs, horses, grass and birch leaves to her mother's own rye bread dough and clean washing, smelt so intensely.

'Everybody walked much more slowly there than they do here,' she said. 'Except me, I flew along. I was nearly always running.'

Sometimes it would be quiet, and I mean really quiet. You don't find that sort of quiet here. It was as quiet as quiet can be. Only the stove would be mumbling. Outside were the wind and the people, the crooked old woman with fourteen cats, the cobbler who was like *that*.

'Like what?'

'Oh, you know, with men.'

And there was the grocer's and the dragoons who used to come every so often, the midwife and the waitresses at the restaurant by the bathing place and the whole population of this little world. But indoors it was always quiet.

'It sounds a remarkable village,' he said with a smile.

'Yes!'

The cows were so fat their backs gleamed like butter, and so lazy! Summer was all they knew. But in the sharp shadow over at the corner of the barn, winter was waiting, sure of himself.

'Brr!'

Well, he could come and see for himself. They cycled ten kilometres and she showed him the village from up on the stony ridge, where they sat themselves down among the sparse pines. She sat holding his hand as they watched the people down below, moving between the houses. It was so quiet they could hear the telephone ringing in the district nurse's house. Yet it all seemed so far away. They sat feeling the steam of summer rise from the cauldron of the valley, a brew of dung, green grass and honey that would soon boil away, leaving the brown whey-cheese of autumn in the bottom.

The war was over. Everyone was meant to be happy. Ann-Marie's school had been turned into a hospital for those coming with the Bernadotte contingent from the camps in Germany.

They were thin beings with dark eyes. To begin with, they never went out. But when the summer sun grew stronger and shone on the plastered walls of the school and the wide gravelled yards, some of them went out and sat on the benches. There were men whose shaved hair was growing back, though it still looked ragged and cropped, and women with their heads closely wrapped in headscarves and shawls.

Some of them had never had their heads shaved. There were women who asked for hairslides and curlers. They made clothes using material the WDV's had collected. They painstakingly altered old coats and made dresses to hide where the number had been branded into their body. Some of them did nothing. When people looked in at them from the street, they looked back with intent but expressionless faces.

One afternoon, when Jenny arrived to deliver a box of donated jigsaws and playing cards, she saw Ferenc sitting by the sunny south wall of the school. He was conversing with two women. Her heart began to race and her underarms and palms went sweaty. She couldn't understand why, but thought it might be because he had left work during the day again. That usually made her feel edgy.

He was talking to two Polish women and it wasn't long before he came and asked whether he could invite them home. They hadn't been in anyone's home for years. They had come from Ravensbrück but had only spent a few weeks there. Before that, one of them had worked in a forced-labour factory making uniforms. She was small, though not emaciated; in fact, her body and face were bloated. She had a long Polish name but Ferenc called her Elka because that was her name too. The other one was called Lili.

They sat opposite Jenny on the sofa under the picture of the swans, eating her sponge cake but unable to communicate with her. Ferenc couldn't speak Polish either. Lili had learnt a little German but Elka said nothing. You could see she understood everything, even so. Whenever he said something to her in German, all the expression drained from her face and she averted her eyes. One day when they were alone up at the school, sitting motionless and silent with their faces turned up to the sun, he suddenly said:

'Can I talk *mama-loschen*?'

Then she leant her head against the wall and tears began flowing from her closed eyes. He put his hand over hers in alarm. A succession of eager conversations followed. Jenny couldn't understand a word.

Lili had made herself a dress out of sheeting fabric. It was cut in the latest fashion, such as she perceived it from her schoolyard. She embroidered flowers on the pockets and round the hem of the skirt. When she started putting her hair up and applying lipstick, you had some idea what she must have looked like before the war. She never spoke of what she had been doing before she came to Ravensbrück. But she seemed to have emerged fairly unscathed. Jenny began to be suspicious and would have liked to warn Ferenc.

But how could she warn him against the inevitable?

When autumn came, he was hardly ever at home in the evenings. Yet he still treated her very tenderly and he sometimes brought the two women home with him. In October he announced he wouldn't be needing his room any more. He didn't say anything to her but went straight to Fredrik.

After the initial shock she was furious with him for being too much of a coward to dare tell her to her face. Her resentment gave her the strength to stand there looking on as he packed his things.

It took less than an hour. In a suitcase he put his shirts, then his socks and underwear. On top he put his heavy suit and she could have told him it would crease his shirts. But she refrained.

He put the candlesticks she'd given him for Christmas in a cardboard box, along with his alarm clock and lots of other bits and pieces he might just as well have thrown out. He wrapped his slippers and shoes in paper bags before he put them in. He stood and looked round the room, breathing heavily. For a moment she thought he was going to have an asthma attack and she would have to look after him. But he seemed to get over it. He emptied the ashtray straight out of the window, then took the heavy winter overcoat from Budapest over his arm.

'I've got to move on, Jenny,' he said. 'That's how I am. I can't stay long in one place.'

She nodded, without looking at him.

'But I'll come and visit you!'

She helped him downstairs with the cardboard box, despising and hating him for his cowardice. But her resentment only lasted that one day.

354

Ann-Marie was doing her homework at the kitchen table. She was reading something out loud, with no pauses at the full stops.

'Can you read that in your head please,' said Jenny, who was sitting opposite her, working on a lampshade.

'Why?'

'It's such a silly story.'

She was covering the lampshade in some silk from a blouse of pre-war quality. Ann-Marie watched her for some time, but Jenny didn't look up. Then Ann-Marie went on.

'*And left the inconsolable queen grieving at the bier.*'

'Quiet, for God's sake!'

She flung down the lampshade, frame and all. It rolled across the floor with a fluttering tail of silk. Ann-Marie stared at the shade and then at Jenny, who was on her feet, staring straight ahead with unseeing eyes.

The pain was tied up with queasiness, headaches and breathing difficulties. It wasn't attractive. People say: I'm so miserable I can't bear it. They ought to say: I'm so miserable it's giving me constipation. When I have to get up in the mornings, my whole body feels like lead and there's a nasty taste in my mouth. As soon as I get out I want to close my eyes because the light's too strong. I eat too much, too often, but I have no appetite at mealtimes. If I go and sit down after the meal, I stay there. The washing-up water goes cold. The food, which tastes of nothing, makes me feel sick afterwards. I can't stand noise and this morning I started crying when I heard the circular saw.

Before, when she saw people around town who were rumoured to be as unhappy as she was now, she had sometimes felt repelled. She couldn't explain why. Maybe she was now in a condition that gave certain people who saw her the urge to cast her out like a sick animal. She was at the mercy of whatever faces noticed hers.

She didn't believe there was any gossip, but thought what she was going through must show in her face. Some of the people she encountered round town looked evil, some indifferent. In some faces she thought she saw a hunger for events they could chew over in their boredom. But she saw no faces of mercy. Tired and out of sorts, she mostly kept to the house.

Then she did something she hadn't ever thought she would. It was a Saturday afternoon and she'd been sitting at her sewing. She'd planned to sit there until it was time to go and look out of the window for Fredrik and put the coffee on. Instead, she left the lampshade on the kitchen floor and went out into the hall to fetch her coat.

'I'm going out on my bike for a bit,' she said.

She took the bike from the rack and momentarily glimpsed Ann-Marie's face at the window. The expression was attentive and serious, but she didn't look afraid.

Without looking at anyone she passed, she cycled to the house where she knew Ferenc was living. She felt herself in the grip of some kind of intoxication, or panic. When she got there she didn't hesitate for a moment but went into the entrance hall and knocked on the door with his card pinned up next to the nameplates. Not caring what the landlady thought, she asked which was his room and saw from the woman's eyes which way she had to go. It was a strange house and there were strange smells around her. A canary perched stock-still in its cage, regarding her with one blinking eye.

She opened the door. Inside sat Ferenc in a basket chair at a low table, having tea with the woman he called Elka. She was no longer so bloated. Jenny could see from their faces that she had been mistaken. It had never been about Lili after all. But in other respects she had made no mistake.

She was too agitated to pretend she had just looked in. The bird had set up a shrill, whistling song out in the kitchen and a rustling outside the door presumably meant the landlady was standing there listening. Jenny asked if she could speak to him and he got up and went out into the hall with her. But he looked hesitant, almost scared. She could hear all the sounds in the house very clearly, the clatter of saucepans in the flat next door, stove doors slamming shut and the shuffle of slippered feet. It was inconceivable that he lived among these sounds, these pot plants and the staring canary. She wanted to scream, but managed to control herself.

'I've got to see you,' she said.

'Well of course we can see each other, Jenny.'

'I've got to talk to you. It's important.'

'All right.'

And they agreed to meet at one of the places out on the Vanstorp road where they used to cycle. Then she ran out, leaving him there.

When they met, she didn't know what to say. It was a Sunday morning and cold out, almost too cold to cycle. All the puddles were iced over and the trees had lost their leaves. She wasn't aware of having a plan as they rode down to the lake, catching glimpses of the water between the trees.

It was a long, narrow lake and at one end, the end where they had stopped, there was a tiny island with a summer cottage on it. It had been built by Assar Ek, Ingrid Johansson's foster-father. Jenny didn't know if they used it any more. The boat was still there, at

357

any rate. It lay upturned with the oars underneath.

'I know the people whose cottage it is,' she said. 'They won't mind us going in there. They usually keep the key under a roof tile.'

She felt she absolutely must be indoors with him and he made no protest. But as they set to work to right the boat, she felt a sense of shame.

The ice along the shoreline was thin, it splintered as they set the rowing boat in the water. Further out, the water was dark and open. It took only a few oarstrokes to get them over to the island; the lake was so shallow and reedy they could almost have waded. She knew the island was so infested with ants in summer it was almost unbearable. Nothing grew out there but alders and they were bare now.

Ferenc looked quizzical as they approached the little cottage with its tar-paper roof and a metal pipe for a chimney. A few months before, they would have thought it an adventure to come out here, she thought. They would have laughed at her crazy idea. As it was, he was merely polite, letting her enter first once she had opened the door.

The cottage consisted of a single room with a peculiar smell of mouldy fabric. Jenny was embarrassed when she saw they had been hoarding things in there and hadn't taken away the sacks of peas and boxes of flour and sugar. They had accumulated more than they could eat, presumably, and now their stocks were fair game for vermin. The long-tailed field mice had gnawed their way into the sacks. The candlesticks on the embroidered tablecloth, their stumps of wax eaten right down to the wood, were ringed with black mouse droppings.

They ought to try to light the stove, but Ferenc didn't look as if he wanted to touch it and she didn't dare. She'd been there with

Arne and Ingrid once and it had started to smoke. In the end, Arne had gone up on the roof and poked a scaffolding pole down the metal pipe, and a bird had come out at the bottom, a bird with a long neck that had died a pitiful death.

Ferenc took hold of the damper with his gloved hand and a mass of soot came down. He took a step back.

'Don't bother with it,' she said. 'I'm absolutely freezing.'

He went over to her and held her, in silence. It was so terribly chilly that she simply had to cling tightly to him. He ought to realise. After a while he let go of her and lay down on the bed. He lay there with his eyes shut. She didn't know what to do next.

'What's wrong?' she asked.

He reached out for her. Although she knew it was utter madness in this damp and cold, she huddled up next to him on the striped mattress that stank of mould. They warmed one another as they lay clinging together, but after a while she was aware that her back was getting freezing cold. She grew colder and colder. It was as if years of chill and damp had been stored in the old wadding mattress. When he undid his trousers and pulled them down a bit, she could feel his buttocks were ice-cold and covered in goose pimples. The trousers restricted his leg movements, but he couldn't take them off; it was too cold. She helped him pull them up again and he pulled his penis out through his flies. She found she was losing interest. It felt so strange not to be saying anything to each other, and the cold made her fearful. But she didn't know what else to do.

Her face started to feel odd. It felt taut and painful round her mouth. She tried to hurry him up a bit without letting it show. She tried to be passionate herself, too, to hide her impatience and make him forget this misery of cold and haste and the smell of the mattress. He mustn't notice anything, she thought. He mustn't remember this wretched encounter. It's never been as sordid as this. Not even that first time. She knew he thought that had been sordid. Maybe he wouldn't forget that, either.

He finally came, pulling out of her at the last moment. She felt relieved yet hurt by his carefulness. Herself, she didn't believe she could ever have a baby. He must be afraid of messing everything up now, she thought. He's so careful, so careful. She realised she despised him for it.

His semen ended up on her thigh and turned instantly ice-cold on her flesh. Then it really came home to her how cold it must be and she pushed him away.

'I've got to get my things on,' she mumbled.

He kissed her and it took an eternity. When she had buttoned up her coat and was smoothing down her hair in front of the mirror, she saw she was all swollen round the mouth. Big lumps had come up round her lips, a reaction to the cold. It looked so ghastly she covered her face with her hands. It was grotesque.

So this is how he'll remember me, she thought. Because there won't be another time. I'm sure of it.

With cold-numbed, aching hands she started plumping up the pillows on the bed without looking at him.

'Jenny,' he said. 'Look out of the window. But carefully.'

She went and stood by the curtain and saw there was a man over by where the boat had been, looking out to the island. It wasn't anybody she recognised. He walked slowly along the shore, looking at the cottage the whole time.

'I expect he lives round here,' she said. 'He probably thinks it's odd for anybody to come out here this time of year.'

She was surprised by her own lack of concern about the man. Ferenc was the one who seemed more scared.

'He's going now,' he said. 'But he's walking slowly. What if he waits up there for us?'

360

'I think he'll go.'

She thought about what would happen if it got out that they'd been here together. And reached Fredrik's ears. Then she would have to live with double condemnation: the town's and his. People would pick over her misfortune like monkeys and leave it tattered, scattered and soiled, robbed of all meaning. And Fredrik? She didn't really know how he would take it. But it would undoubtedly be something particularly grandiose involving lifelong misery, something really Old Icelandic.

She gave a short laugh in the cold room. But it just sounded like a dry cough. Fredrik was too proud even to gossip about people who did this sort of thing. He dismissed them with an oath. And now she was one of the worst. She didn't really care much. Strangely enough. Why should she have Fredrik's respect, after all? Why should she run round trying to muddle through everything she'd neglected, everything she did halfheartedly, feeling guilty she wasn't doing it faster and better, run as if she were in a dream smelling of dirty washing and burnt potatoes, when her real life was determined by Fredrik's respect?

It would be better in fact if Fredrik dismantled the walls that surrounded her, those walls of silence and esteem, to leave her sitting there with him in the greenish chill of winter. But he didn't want to venture out there himself. And why should she really care whether Ferenc remembered her? He was welcome to forget her. Why should she live a wandering pseudo-life in someone's memory or respect, when she herself sat at home on the bed, daydreaming to the roar of the vacuum cleaner because she'd forgotten to switch it off?

'We must go,' said Ferenc.

'All right.'

'You're freezing. It's dangerous to stay here.'

He passed her the gloves she had dropped on the floor.

'You know, don't you Jenny, we can't meet like this again?'

'No, of course we can't,' she said. 'You've got other considerations.'

He didn't seem to like her saying that at all. She felt an urge to be nasty, really nasty and ugly with swollen lumps on her face.

'Have you been to bed with her yet?'

'No,' he said, looking very tense. 'Not yet. She's been injured.'

'The two of you will go away,' Jenny said. She had sat back down on the bed and her whole body had gone so limp she could no longer feel the cold. But her hands and face ached.

'One day you'll be gone. You won't say anything. It's simplest that way. Just notify the police for their records. You're so organised. I'm sure she is too. You're alike, you know.'

She was sitting with her back to him, looking at the strip of rose-patterned wallpaper Assar Ek had used to line the set of shelves made out of sugar crates painted white.

'I've been feeling so grey and dowdy these last weeks. I haven't read any books, and I can't speak any languages. I haven't been in a camp, either.'

'Jenny!'

She knew more or less what he wanted to say. She was sickening. She was talking about things she didn't understand and never would understand. But his language let him down when it came to expressing it. That was always the way when he got upset.

'I'm going now,' was all he said. 'Adieu, Jenny.'

And he actually did pick up his hat from where he had left it on the sugar crate, and Assar's rickety door slammed shut behind him. She didn't even bother to listen to his receding footsteps. Once again she felt a desire to laugh, but this time it didn't even come out as a cough. She just gave a snort. He thought he could just go striding off, did he, thought the street was just outside, *Erzebet körút* with its trams and cafés.

It wasn't many minutes before he was back. Turning round, she suddenly saw him as she had the very first time they met. In spite of the hideous cold, he had removed his hat on coming indoors and was holding it to his chest. It looked ludicrous.

'Come on Jenny,' he said. 'I didn't think about the boat. We'll have to go together. Otherwise you won't get back.'

'Just go,' she replied. 'It doesn't matter.'

He took a small step towards her as she sat on the bed. He still had his hat pressed to his chest and his head slightly on one side. Jenny got up and looked round to check she hadn't left anything behind.

'You didn't think I was going to sit here until Fredrik raised the alarm and sent out a search party, did you? You think I couldn't get across by myself?'

'Swimming?'

He sounded ironic.

'So what if I did?' she said. 'And you're very keen to bundle me home to Fredrik all of a sudden.'

'He's a good man.'

She began to laugh.

'Well I never,' she said. 'Well I never did!'

When she got home, everything was normal. They listened to the radio and played casino with Ann-Marie. Once the child had gone to bed, Fredrik thought they ought to have a bite to eat, so they sat at the kitchen table and had brawn and beetroot on crispbread. They shared a bottle of beer. Then he sat flicking through the newspaper. She supposed he was waiting for her to clear the table. But she stayed where she was. She saw him.

Yes, she saw him.

He was a tall, powerful man with a well-shaped, slightly hooked nose and light blue eyes. Behind her current view of him there was always the memory of the young Fredrik she had once got to know. He had had thick, pale yellow hair and clear eyes and a sort of fervour she would never forget.

What she saw now was that he was tired, that his hair wasn't really blonde any more but the same indeterminate colour her own was at the roots. It was less thick than it used to be and receding noticeably at the temples, leaving a bare expanse of forehead. The finely-sculpted nose looked like her own, which was a bit pointed. It struck her that they were alike. They had both been very blonde when they were young and now they would in all probability grow more and more alike, perhaps ending up resembling a pair of old foxes with pointed muzzles and screwed-up eyes.

Things had run themselves for Jenny for a period of years. She had reached thirty, thirty-five and still kept her looks. She had had her own bike for the first time and new wellingtons. She hadn't known then that she would never have children. And Fredrik surely wouldn't have to work overtime forever!

'You have to get somewhere in life,' he had said when he was still relatively young. And in those days it had sounded right: you had to get somewhere.

'Where exactly?'

'Well, quite apart from *that*,' Fredrik had said, 'you have to make progress.'

Quite apart from that, she thought. But *that* had started to take root inside her. She hadn't noticed it at first. Yet it was there. She stared at her face in the mirror; she looked tired round the eyes. All her teeth had fillings now.

The war had ended, as everyone had known it eventually would. She wasn't a kitchen volunteer in the engine sheds at nights any more. She would make straw stars and hand-dipped candles for tombolas and bazaars. There didn't seem much she could do about it.

What did he want, the man on the other side of the checked oilcloth and beetroot-stained plates? He was disillusioned and growing old and she hadn't noticed until now. Did he know?

She would never find out, that was for sure. He was sitting with his head resting in his hand; the newspaper lay folded in front of him. No, he didn't look happy and it was quite something for him to let his feelings show.

'Why don't we invite a few people round?' he said.

'Yes, why not?'

She started clearing the table and he went down to the cellar to stoke the boiler.

When she had put the plates in the sink and wiped the oilcloth, she went into the living room to turn out the lights. The light fitting on the ceiling with its five imitation candles under silk shades was glaringly bright. Her knitting lay on one of the armchairs. They had had coffee, the cups were still there on the table. No one even mentioned tea anymore. The war was over.

She saw everything very clearly, precisely as she'd seen Fredrik just now. You can't always feel things intensely but you can be keenly observant.

Her life was here, in this room with the pedestal table where they sat when they had guests, her entire life from the distant nineteen-twenties. Time had sifted down to fall as dust on fabrics and carpets. She remembered how pleased she'd been when they bought the furniture. It was when they got married, and they'd had to borrow money from Tora. The dog wasn't allowed on the sofa but he'd taken to lying there all the same and the fabric was covered in stains left by his infected penis.

She would never be able to get the dust out of the fabrics and carpets in here. It was dreadful seeing everything as clearly as this. She didn't know what to do with all this clear-sightedness.

What was she to do on this dumping ground called middle age? The worst of it was that she was ravenous for life, like a strong, black-backed gull among the waste.

Frida's sleep was so thin now it could flow like transparent water over the memories lying beneath. She could no longer distinguish between experience and dream. Her hand often groped for something solid to feel, the arm of the chair and the rug with its blanket-stitched edge. But that wasn't quite what she was looking for either. It was in wakefulness all the voices were, and she hadn't the energy to stay there long these days. I keep losing track, she thought. It isn't the arm of the chair. It's a stair rail. I've got to go up the stairs in this building although they're swaying, because I've got to collect David's things. They're going to pull it down, the landlord says, and if I don't go and get his things now, they'll be lost in the rubble.

Her wakefulness always had a duality to it; the voices of memory were blended with those who had the more demanding tone of the waking day.

'Are you awake now Frida? Wake up!'

But they should know she hadn't time. She had to get upstairs before the staircase collapsed and she had to collect David's things. What luck the stair rail was still there. She held tight. Then came a voice, saying:

'She's dropped off again. Let her sit there a bit longer. We can make the bed in the meantime.'

A current of cold air passed over her face, but it didn't smell of anything.

She was in the house at the corner of Main Street and Industrial Road, opposite the Co-operative Stores. The doors had been smashed and she found herself walking in drifts of broken glass. Boys had been in here. They'd pulled long strips of wallpaper off the walls and written rude words and drawn the bits of the body you didn't want to see. The iron stoves gaped open and they'd hurled the rings across the floor to join old shoes and rusty nails.

Here was David's room, his stove and wardrobe. There were strings strung across the wardrobe; he'd used them to hang his clothes on. But there were no clothes in there except for a pair of trousers on the floor, and they seemed far too big to be his. It was his room, wasn't it? Who could she ask? And who had stuck up pictures from *Home Weekly* of Ingrid Bergman's face and unfamiliar, laughing girls on the inside of the wardrobe door?

'Don't you worry now, Frida,' said the voice behind her and she heard the sound of sheets being pulled taut with a crack.

'But you're not going to make up a bed in here?' she said.

'Yes Frida, we're making your bed.'

Was she going to have to sleep in this room with the broken glass and a stove without rings? Had David slept here? A place like this for someone who'd had an operation for TB? She started crying because it was so dreadful. They carried on making the bed behind her with cheerful voices and didn't seem to care how terrible it was that David had disappeared. Was he living rough? It must be dangerous for a person who's had tuberculosis to sleep in barns and brickworks where it's icy cold one minute and hot the next.

'He's dead,' said that man. 'And since you're his mother, you'll have to take his things.'

But it wasn't true! Because that's the most awful thing of all, when children die before their mothers. That hadn't happened to David. He'd just disappeared and nobody knew where he'd gone.

'Do you hear!' she tried to shout, then someone put a hand on her shoulder and said:

'Don't upset yourself, Frida. It's such a lovely morning, the sun's shining today. Look Frida, Britty's picked some colt's-foot daisies.'

What silly nonsense they got up to, these young girls who didn't realise how urgent it was. On the shelf in the wardrobe there was a shoe box with papers in it. There were papers strewn over the floor too, among the other debris. The boys must have been there and started throwing things that didn't interest them. They were promissory notes. Ugh, was David caught up in that sort of thing? Two hundred kronor. No further reminder will be sent.

She gathered up everything she found and put it in the shoe box, even a bottle with a label that said: KEEP YOUR CHIN UP when you feel low. Many TB sufferers have regained their health with ALMENTA. There was a letter which started: It's awful of me not to have written before. Looking at the end, she saw it said: I can't do so much these days and I had to lie down all day Saturday. After the final greeting it said Your Mother. Once more she was ashamed of having written David letters like that. Another one said he ought to go to the welfare officer in good time so he got some help for Christmas. You need bedclothes. I've thrown out the old ones, they stank. They're so old. But I've talked to the welfare officer so it'll be all right.

There was nothing else she could take but these letters and promissory notes, plus a pair of metal toe taps for tap dancing that were in the bottom of the box. Old newspapers weren't worth keeping and the medicine bottle was empty. He'd had cups and saucers of course, but the boys had smashed them. They'd sat on the mattress, drinking from a bottle they'd left lying there and reading smutty magazines. It had been empty here for so long, and they'd gone in and out, of course. But where had David been all that time the room had stood chilled and deserted? And where had she sent her letters? It was very odd. When he was living rough there wouldn't have been an address to write to. And surely David couldn't have travelled to some other place?

'I can't have written this letter!' she cried.

'No, Frida, it's all right. Look at the daisies.'

It said: 'How long will you be in Jail?'

'But David's never been in jail,' she said, and started to cry.

'No, no, of course he hasn't.'

But she saw the look that passed between them as they went back to their bedmaking. It wasn't the ordinary sheets making that cracking sound but the rubber one they had in between.

'Should I take these letters with me?' she asked. They seemed to know what was what, although they were so young. They knew everything.

'No, don't worry about it,' they said.

Then she remembered the letter about jail had been signed 'Father.' At that, she almost laughed. You see, Ericsson had died when David was just a little boy - no, David had never been in jail! It was somebody else.

She felt more cheerful for a little while but then began to wonder whether there really was anything of David's in that box. Perhaps there was nothing of his left. What was she to do then, there in that draughty block they were about to pull down?

'I haven't anything left to remember David by,' she cried, now entirely aware he was dead and she was at Fir Ridge. The girls had just finished making her bed and they felt her hands to see if they'd got cold with the window open.

'I've got to go and fetch David's things,' she said. 'Lucky I had that dream. I'd have forgotten otherwise.'

'Oh, I don't suppose there's any hurry,' said the big girl. She had a stain on the bib of her white apron. It looked like coffee. Just think if Miss Olga saw it. Her name was Britt but they called her Britty. Sometimes Frida thought they were talking about a kitten. They called the matron Olga when she wasn't listening. But that was just their girlish nonsense. What did it matter to her?

'It's urgent, they're going to pull the whole block down,' she said. 'The one opposite the Co-op.'

That made them laugh.

'They pulled that place down long ago,' said the big one. 'Don't you remember, Frida? Nobody's lived there since the thirties!'

Centuries ago, their clear young voices implied.

'Oh, yes, I forget so much,' she said.

She felt tired and wanted to sleep but it was impossible to immerse herself in that thin stream, that transparency which was now her sleep. Not properly, like she used to, and never for long. She only slept for a few minutes at a time, and in her sleep was always looking in two directions. She looked down into her memory where the big things had sunk, sprinkled over as they were year after year by a settling sediment of the little things. She looked out to where they were busy with rubber sheets, containers and trays and where the light was so feeble she could never really see what they were doing if they took a few steps away from her.

But they weren't far away. She awoke and the sun shone onto her hands from the window. It made her reach out to feel something in front of her. There was a big yellow patch in the light and it was soft to the touch. She felt with her fingers to get hold of it lower down, but was worried because she didn't know what it was she was holding in her hand. It was a big, wet mass shaped like a wrist. Yes, something fleshy and fibrous that was falling to pieces and down onto the rug over her knees.

'Frida, what are you doing?' they cried.

'We'll have to change the rug. It's all wet.'

371

They were quite cross with her and it made her cry. Britty gathered up the daisies on her lap and arranged them back into a fat little bunch.

'If you're going to do that, Frida, we won't be able to have any more flowers in here. You'll just have to stay in bed,' threatened the bigger of them.

But when that made her cry even more, the thin wailing which could be switched off and continue as silent tears, they were sorry and told her to cheer up.

'We're going to wheel your chair out into the corridor now,' they said. 'The visitors will be here soon.'

She was sitting at the far end of the corridor when Ingrid and Konrad got there and they had a long walk from the kick-plated double doors. They watched her all the way along and saw the auxiliary adjusting her wheelchair and smoothing the rug over her knees. The floor was shiny, reflecting Frida and her chair. Her feet were protruding from under the rug. They were clad in felt slippers, very clean. You could see the soles had never touched the ground. Konrad thought her feet looked like inanimate objects on the footrest. Her head looked almost bald, but once they could see her from the front there was still a little white cloud of hair covering her scalp.

'She's so pale,' said Ingrid under her breath.

But Konrad didn't think she looked any paler than usual. It was just more noticeable when you came in from outside where all the people you saw walked round in the sun all day.

When they reached Frida they took a hand each and Konrad asked:

'How are you, Mum?'

'Oh, fine,' said the auxiliary. 'She's just had a little sleep, so I expect she's feeling lively enough for a chat now. Aren't you, Frida?'

'I just sleep and sleep,' said Frida. 'I'm so tired these days.'

'Well, nothing wrong with a nice sleep,' said Ingrid. You could tell from her voice she didn't really know what to say.

The auxiliary left them and they sat down on the two high-backed chairs by the window. You could rest your hands on their arms and

Ingrid did so, staring at her own hands. Konrad was conscious that it made her uneasy coming with him to visit their old mother. But he didn't think she'd ever got on well with Mum, even when she was quite small.

Between the chairs there was a brown table covered in a white cloth with narrow red stripes. The initials of the old people's home were embroidered in one corner. On the table there was a pot of dry brown soil containing an amaryllis that was nothing but leaves. There were no pictures on the corridor walls. You could see doors and hear a distant clatter from the kitchens.

'Well, we've been up to the cemetery,' said Ingrid, 'and dug up the old flowers and put new ones on the grave.'

Then she shut her mouth and lowered her eyes. Konrad supposed she was embarrassed by having spoken about the cemetery.

'You are kind, both of you,' said Frida.

'Do they give you good coffee Mum?' Konrad said.

He thought a bit of banter might bring a glint into her eye. But she didn't seem to hear.

'Just think, I haven't got anything to remember David by,' she said. 'But he was never in jail, you know.'

They sat in silence for a while.

'No,' said Konrad eventually. 'Of course not.'

'It was Dad's grave we were at,' said Ingrid.

'Oh, Eriksson's,' was Frida's response.

Then Ingrid began to cry though she pretended she wasn't, blowing her nose as if she just had a cold. She might as well not bother coming, thought Konrad. He usually brought the children. It made things easier.

His mother was sitting with her eyes closed, and after a little while he asked her if she was asleep. There was no answer. They sat quietly for a while, then he and Ingrid started chatting to each other in low voices and he was conscious that neither of them really wanted to wake her. They talked about Ulf, who had got himself a summer job.

'He's going to be a delivery boy at the grocer's,' said Ingrid. She kept her eyes on Frida's face with its thin white eyelids.

'She's asleep,' she said. 'But why's she always talking about David? Maybe she doesn't even know it's you and me sitting here.'

'Oh, I think she does. But things have turned out all right for us, there's not so much to wonder about.'

Ingrid sat lacing her fingers together and looking down at them.

'Take you, you'll soon be a union official' said Konrad teasingly, to liven her up.

'I will not. I only keep the statistics at the factory. I keep a record of the hours and piecework rates. Somebody has to do it. We need all that when it comes to negotiations. Otherwise it'd be easy for them to rig everything in their own favour, you can be sure of that.'

'Yes, you've always been good at arithmetic,' said Konrad. 'But I didn't think you went to union meetings.'

'That was before, when I was younger. God knows what we had in our heads then. And I remember that time you conned me into taking that poem or whatever it was. About the joy of labour. I didn't think I'd ever dare show my face again. God, I was so embarrassed! I actually took it and read it at a meeting.'

They both laughed but Frida only stirred. Her eyelids quivered and her hands plucked at the edge of the rug, her fingers feeling along the blanket stitch of the border.

'Are you all Social Democrats in your section?' asked Konrad.

'Yes, but I think you're the only person left who doesn't say Soshies,' she laughed, forgetting to keep her eyes on her mother's face. 'The others all got voted out during the war, you know how the voting went then. But I knew you weren't really dangerous.'

375

She knew how to engage his interest; he had to smile.

'Dreamers, mostly,' she said.

'The hell we were!'

It was most unusual for him to swear. She set her finger to her lips. It was as if his words had carried right out to the office although he had spoken in a perfectly ordinary tone of voice, because there was a swishing behind the kick-plated double doors and Miss Olga came out. She came towards them and looked at Frida's face. Then she said, rather severely:

'She's getting tired. You'd better go now.'

'We'll be quiet,' said Konrad. 'We'll sit here with her very quietly for a little while.'

But he was thinking he'd come back on his own and sit quietly with his mother. Ingrid was so restless and the matron didn't like them talking over the old woman's head. She was right, no doubt. Frida might be able to hear, even in her sleep. Sometimes he noticed her crying in her sleep and he could never know for sure what was making her sad.

Ingrid found it offputting when tears started pouring down those dry, white cheeks without any warning. Her foster-mother Ingeborg Ek said it was just a reflex action and Assar said:

'Why do you and Konrad go there? She's so fossilised she can't feel a thing any more. She probably doesn't even recognise Ingrid.'

But they were wrong. Konrad knew that much about the old woman was brittle and fragile and would not stay intact for long. A great deal had already fallen apart. The dividing walls between memory, dream and waking were so thin. Her consciousness sometimes seemed clouded by things she had seen before, or by sleep. For she was very tired. But nothing seemed to have been lost. There were elements she couldn't retrieve and it made her cry sometimes when she was unable to find her way round the frail chambers of her mind, where so many of the walls had crumbled into her dreams.

I want to sit here. It's such a wonder you exist, he wanted to tell her.

When they were on their own, she liked him to read her hymns. Ten years before, he would have felt terribly embarrassed doing any such thing. Perhaps that fact was not lost on her; she never asked him to read when anybody else was there. He thought: there's a lot she understands.

He had read her endless hymns but she never seemed really satisfied. She was chasing him through the hymn book in search of something she so dearly wanted to hear again. But she didn't know the number of the hymn and couldn't remember any of the words either. He read on, finding some of them truly dreadful. Some were meek and pious and he thought she would like those. But she was as impatient as ever. Not that one, nor that one either! Some were great and beautiful poetry and Konrad got so caught up in them that his recitations in the corridor brought Miss Olga to stare at them. It echoed in there under the high ceiling. He was sorry he had never learnt to sing the hymns; he remembered nothing of his school years.

When he finally found the one she had been wanting to hear for so long, he was surprised. As he began, 'Ye mortal children, time is short,' he had no idea he was on the right track; she kept her eyes closed and gave no indication of hearing anything. The words were by Wallin, and Konrad thought the first verse must have been written for some huge, extravagant New Year festivity at the Bishop's Palace; they had doubtless washed it down with champagne. As he read the fourth verse, Frida started to smile in spite of only just having woken up and said:

'That's it.'

And he read:

'I am the tree upon thy land, Which sparèd was to be, And tended by thy loving hand, To fruit abundantly.'

'Yes,' she said. 'That's the one. I want you to read it slowly.' And he did.

He looked it up in the Bible for her, too, and it was Luke, chapter thirteen. But that didn't matter so much to her. It was the hymn she wanted to hear. He realised Frida thought of herself as one of the chosen and was amazed. He told Ingrid as they were coming away from the old people's home on one occasion.

'She thinks she's one of the chosen,' he said.

'Chosen?'

'Yes, chosen by God.'

'Oh really? Chosen for her sheer bloody-mindedness, then,' Ingrid said.

'We don't know anything about that,' he replied.

Thou say'st we must root out the tree. Cut down its drying wood. But may it one more summer see! He always said it silently to himself as he left her. He could still feel her cheek against his lips. It was like brushing them against brittle paper.

Outside, it was spring. The air was cold but full of birds calling. In the sparse fir forest behind the home, the ground was speckled brown. The snow was transforming itself into dirty drifts of beads, shrinking and subsiding at ever increasing speed. On the gravelled areas round the old castle that was now a geriatric home, the melted snow ran in all directions. There were birdcalls and bubbling water all around and the air, chilly and full of scents, was easy to breathe.

'I think the matron must have heard you swearing through the wall,' said Ingrid when they'd come a little way.

'She must have good ears in that case,' he laughed, 'I didn't shout that loud. But you didn't have to call me a dreamer.'

'A dreamer's not a bad thing.'

'The way you mean it, it's worse. A laughing stock.'

The road back to town from Fir Ridge ran between two fields. The meltwater running off them covered large parts of the road and Konrad, who had no galoshes, had to keep jumping. When Ingrid turned round and laughed at him, he thought she looked comical. She had on her stylish blue spring coat, which she'd bought with her employee discount at Curre's, and a brown beret. It had a little stalk sticking up in the middle.

'Is it warm enough for you all in the Ice Palace nowadays?' he said, trying to provoke her.

'No, but Arne keeps me warm,' she retorted in the same tone, and his face darkened because he didn't like her saying that.

The puddles of melted snow in the potholes in the street had been brown when they came the other way. Now they could see them from a distance, reflecting the spring skies. The streets were empty.

'Why is it so deserted?' he said. 'What's everybody doing?'

'Eating, of course. They're sitting round their kitchen tables having loin of pork stuffed with prunes, with cream sauce and gherkins.'

'I wouldn't be so sure,' said Konrad.

'Well they're out at meetings then,' said Ingrid, jumping over the puddles like a little child.

'Do you know what?' said Konrad, taking her by the arm. 'I think there's a different way to live!'

She glanced quickly at his face. But he was looking straight ahead and didn't seem to be making fun of her at all.

'Yes, I think there's a different way and some of them are already living it, here in these houses.'

'Oh,' she said, not entirely serious. 'It seems to me most of them only care about themselves and their own affairs.'

'Well, maybe,' said Konrad. 'Though sometimes I think: if they drop an atom bomb on everything, it would be nice if all this just happened to be spared.'

'All this?'

He had in fact gestured towards the tight huddle of houses in front of them, with their warped and peeling outbuildings and messy bird tables, racks for beating carpets and knotted clothes lines. The gardens were utterly silent and there wasn't a single person to be seen.

'It's only because it's what you've got used to and sort of grown fond of, you know,' said Ingrid. 'It's not as if you've been particularly happy here.'

Konrad thought she sounded rather dismissive. He didn't bother trying to persuade her he had meant something else. He had realised that even here there were people who had defended a way of life he thought precious, and done it quite cunningly, in virtual secrecy. It had been given neither praise nor name as yet, and she was unlikely to understand it.

'There's a pattern under the pattern,' was all he said.

'Well, maybe.'

'A town under this town. Or inside it.'

Water splashed up from the puddles as she walked. She was clearly irritated.

'Are you going home?' he asked when they got to Highway Bridge.

'No, I'm going to Tora Otter's to water her plants.'

'Doesn't Jenny do that?'

'Yes, when Tora goes to the Radiology Clinic. But she's having her operation tomorrow and Jenny's gone with her.'

She stood poking around in the gravel on the pavement with the toe of her boot.

'I really don't want to go,' she said.

He decided for her that they'd go to Anker's and have a cup of coffee first.

It was quite busy in Anker's that Sunday afternoon. The sun was shining in through the French windows that led out to the garden, and the air was thick with smoke and the smell of coffee and sweet with the scents of the plates of cakes. They found a table by a wall the sun could not reach and Konrad's round face looked rosy in the glow of the bracket lamps on the walls.

'Take your pick, my treat,' he said and Ingrid had to smile, because it was just like when she was a schoolgirl and used to sneak off from Eks' to see him. And just as he always did then, he got out his wallet and looked to see how much he had in it. He was oblivious to the fact that the waitress was standing beside him watching his every move.

Ingrid ordered a cream horn. She wasn't so keen on them any more, but she didn't want to disappoint him.

'But I drink coffee these days,' she said.

People spoke in such low voices; the clatter of the cups on their saucers was muted too. It was thick catering china with gold rims that had almost worn off. The sounds from the kitchen were more shrill. But that was another world, and when the waitresses emerged with their shiny blouses they spoke as quietly as the customers at the tables.

'Why don't you want to go to Tora's?'

'I don't know,' she said.

But she had a sudden inclination to stay at Anker's all afternoon, sitting under the ornamental wall clock and the picture of a town in some southern country, reading the much-thumbed magazines. It was so cold up in Tora's kitchen and even colder in her sitting room. Tora had turned down the radiators before she left. She had put all the pot plants together on the kitchen table for ease of watering and to keep them out of the sun. But there weren't many. She must have got rid of some.

'I was there yesterday,' she said.

'Well you don't need to go in again today, then.'

'Believe it or not, I forgot to water the plants, though that was the whole point of going.'

Everything had been so tidy up there. Ingrid had looked in the wardrobe and opened a few cupboards. In a kitchen drawer she found Tora's bank book, tied up in a bundle with her cashbook and the pension entitlement letter from Swedish Railways. It had seemed to her that things were missing. It was hard to say exactly what had gone. But everything that was left was in good condition and very clean. She had always had a big vase of dried winter cherry beside the big mirror from her old café. That, too, had gone.

'I don't think she'll be coming back,' said Ingrid.

Konrad made no reply. Their coffee had been poured for them but they let it stand. He took her hand in his. They sat like that for a time and Ingrid noticed the family at the next table looking at them. She didn't care.

A mirror hung on the opposite wall and in it she could see the picture above their heads. It looked different in the mirror. It was done in muddy colours, predominantly dirty yellow, and you could see it was meant to be a town on a slope, somewhere in southern Europe. There wasn't a soul to be seen on the streets and she started thinking about what Konrad had said earlier. So typical of him to see a town inside the actual town and a pattern under the pattern. She herself could see only empty streets and deserted districts. Perhaps society didn't exist?

When they finally did drink their coffee they were quite brisk about it, then Konrad asked the waitress for the bill. When she was younger Ingrid had always found this ritual embarrassing, because Konrad never left a tip. He put the exact amount on the tabletop, which had been shiny when she was a girl but was now dull and scratched. He wasn't stingy, but he disapproved of this system of arbitrary payment, as he called it. Instead, he thanked the waitress and, if he knew her, shook her hand. Ingrid could still feel herself cringing with embarrassment as he did it. But at the same time she was proud of him for daring to.

They walked slowly along the road to the block where Tora's flat was, because he'd promised to walk her there. It looked strange with her sitting room window empty.

'She's put all the plants on the kitchen table,' said Ingrid.

He took his leave of her outside the building, patting her hand in its damp glove between both of his. She went slowly into the courtyard and across the gravel without looking up at the empty windows.

When she was a little girl, she'd often looked up at the angels under the eaves. Konrad had said they flew into the house at night.

'But not in winter,' she said, 'because all the windows are closed then, aren't they?'

'Oh, they don't need windows to get in!'

'That might scare people, though,' she said

But Konrad had said people don't usually notice when the angels fly in. She didn't know whether she herself would have been scared or pleased if it had happened at the railway workers' houses where she lived with the Eks. The worst thing had been never getting the chance to find out.

That night, the angels detached themselves from their stone figures and flew into the house. But they could not see Tora.

She had taken off her Loneliness that was knitted from grey wool, folded it up and put it on the kitchen settle. Then she had stepped out of her black shoes whose names were Plucky and Capable and placed them on the floor underneath.

But she wasn't lying in her bed as usual. The angels thought she must have gone into the mirror.

Here is Gerda Franzon, née Åkerlund, standing before the hall table. She's about to put on her gloves. She's beautifully dressed. Next to her skin she has undergarments of silk charmeuse and a made-to-measure Spirella corset. It completely smooths her out. You can't even tell that Gerda has two halves to her backside like other human beings. She's wearing a pale blue, tailor-made suit trimmed with marten fur. No other forty-five-year-old in town has a pale blue suit. She had it made especially for this occasion. She'll wear it for many years of course; Gerda is no spendthrift. She has long kept an eye on Bertil's accounts. A fair degree of the prudence that helps counterbalance his liking for business gambles comes from her. She was the one who persuaded him to switch from paper investments to property, at just the right time.

She's wearing an asymmetric, blue velvet toque with a little feather and grey shoes with high, spindly, leather heels, not really suitable for walking outside. But Gerda's intending to stay on the pavement or indoors today.

The four-bedroom flat around her is very light. The walls are not papered but plastered and painted. Dean Åkerlund's pictures look dark against them, his finely-knotted Persian carpet is glowing on the new oak parquet flooring of the lounge. This room is entered through glazed sliding doors, behind which there is a glimpse of a fireplace. The kitchen has every conceivable labour-saving device, which the papers will be writing about tomorrow. It's small in comparison with the one she's just left. They had been living in a detached house on the northern edge of town. But that's in the past now. Gerda has made up her mind not to long for the darkness outside the windows curtained in Virginia creeper. They are going to live in the centre of town now. The fact is, it's good publicity.

There are a number of other apartments around her, bed-sitting rooms and two-bedroom flats. But this is the only one with four bedrooms. The stairways are cool and smell of fresh plaster. Underfoot is green Kolmården marble. The rubbish chutes are still almost pristine. Up at attic level there's an ironing room, and a drying room with a hot-air fan. Humming away up there too is the central heating unit, which also extracts used air from the rooms. There are fresh-air intakes under the windows.

Gerda mustn't forget to show the journalists the attic. But just now she has come to a stop and looks rather preoccupied. She's about to put on her gloves.

The whole building around her with its whirring fans and its humming motors in cinema and restaurant is being officially opened today. It's called the Grand and it cost a million.

Representatives of the bank, town dignitaries and the press have been invited and Gerda has enjoyed speculating about what the newspaper reporters will write. Undoubtedly there are a number of things she could tell them and be certain they would note them down on their pads. The reporters on *The Correspondent* and the regional paper are good-natured and grateful for ideas. Gerda thinks, for example, that they could say the big plate-glass windows release a flood of light to compete with the neon signs' interplay of vibrant colour. She also thinks they could describe the functionalist-inspired complex on the corner of Store Street and Industrial Road, on the drawing board since 1938, as a stimulating and refreshing addition to the urban panorama.

She's about to put on her gloves and go down to receive them.

They are to assemble in the foyer of the cinema, where everything's brand new and the pale green walls smell of expensive new fabric. Bertil has decided sherry will be served. The walls are covered in something that looks like quilted satin, and hung with heavy frames displaying Ingrid Bergman, Tyrone Power, Errol Flynn, Ava Gardner and Lassie. With any luck, Konrad Eriksson has set up the projector to show a short film, in colour, called *Sheila: The She-Wolf*. After they have watched it from their luxurious green plush seats and the light has come up from dull apricot to bright, goldenish artificial sunshine, they will stroll out onto the pavement and visit all the shops: the jewellers; the exclusive perfumery, with a proprietress whose black hair is encased in a silver net at the back; Stella's Fruit with confectionery in boxes lined with rustling paper, brightly coloured sweets, heavy purple grapes, coffee sending its aroma right out into the street, chocolate and a glass container of peanuts. The girl in Elisif's stockings has such a refined accent Gerda couldn't understand her at first when they were discussing the arrangements for cleaning the steps. There's to be a short fashion show in Almén's Ladies' Wear, for which Hertha's Modes will supply the hats. Brief visits will then be made to the laboratory of the Photographic Shop and to the ladies' hairdresser's, the only one in town with a male coiffeur. The final stop will be for coffee in the first-floor restaurant, and Bertil has hired a pianist. The piano is white with gold trimmings. It is brand new and was specially ordered for the occasion. All the tables in the restaurant have flower arrangements with cards offering congratulations and good luck wishes to Bertil and her in their new enterprise. They will be running the cinema and restaurant themselves and renting out the other premises.

Gerda will be going now, as soon as she's put on her gloves. She's standing quite still, her right hand on her grey suede gloves on the hall table. Ever since Sven-Bertil smashed the teeth and jawbone of a conscript from Järna, she's had these moments. She finds herself hesitating. A hand she has extended suddenly starts to tremble and she has to pull it back. It's most unlike her. Gerda is very much aware of standing naked inside her clothes and it's a strange feeling. She knows quite well she's fully dressed. Even the building and the town are part of her attire.

As she moves about the town, she is no silver-fish scurrying through its passages and gaps. She moves and the town moves with her, as if she were wearing it. It would be virtually impossible to remove it.

She's going to put on her gloves and go now. If she's forever going to be hesitating on the brink of whatever she's about to be involved in, people will call her neurotic. That makes her want to burst out laughing, because she knows she's a very robust person. But she's seen it in Bertil's eyes, along with the tenderness. That phase just after the accident is behind them now. She shouldn't still be hesitating.

The time has not yet come.